all my love

TWISTED SISTERS

BOOK 1

DAISY JANE

Before reading, please consider the content advisories for the best experience.

This book contains vivid imagery of a child in danger.

Move forward responsibly.

Thank you for reading.

warning

You might DNF because of a toothbrush.

one

OLDER AND THREE TIMES MY SIZE.

Dahlia

Age 15. Five Years Ago.

"You can't just sit in bed and stare at a photo all day!" My sister's slender fingers curl into the magazine, crumpling it as she swipes it away. She jerks back, holding it out of reach as I scramble off the bed to my feet, jumping for it.

"Give it back!" I demand, my volume spiking, pulse hammering, my entire body brimming with panicked, frantic energy. "I *need* it!" I shout, leaping for the magazine again as Juniper rocks to her toes, making it harder to reach.

"Dolly," she says calmly, always a wall of calm against my chaos. "Take the paint set you got for Christmas, go out front, and paint something."

"No!" I scream as my *other* sister Ivy appears in my

bedroom doorway, her jet-black box-dyed hair in two twisted knots atop her head. Eyes lined in black, she blinks at me, arms folded over her torn-up Blondie t-shirt.

"Dahlia, there's only a few days left of break. I'm all for your quirkiness, seriously, I am. But," she says, coming into my room finally, flopping down on the edge of my bed. Juniper is still holding my *People* magazine out of reach, so I sit next to Ivy, glaring up at my oldest sister.

Ivy rests her hand on my thigh, smiling at me, her black lipstick cracking. "You need some fresh air. Everyone does."

I look up at the nearly destroyed magazine in Juni's grip. "Henry Cavill will still be there," Ivy offers, smiling softly as I slowly nod. It's two against one, and in our house, we respect the numbers. It's how we've managed to live parent-free for eight years. That, and of course, our incredibly deep bond with one another.

"Fine," I huff, getting to my feet and grabbing the stupid paint set and canvas from my desk. "I don't even like painting," I groan, slipping into my cardigan, forgoing shoes. I've always loved the way the grass feels on the soles of my feet, the way mud curls between my toes. "I hate art," I add without care that I sound bratty.

So what if I want to stare at the photo of the love of my life in my bedroom all day, every day and envision our lives together? Is there something *wrong* with knowing what you want? I don't think so. In fact, I think it's smart.

I think knowing exactly what I want from life and *who* I want to share that life with, at my age, is brilliant. I don't have to waste time searching, all I need is an executable plan.

Juni and Ivy have come to understand the depths of my

love. I know they think I won't ever find a way to *meet* Henry Cavill, much less make him see that we're meant to be.

And as the youngest, I think it's normal to be underestimated.

"What about the old oak? Between our place and the one next door," Juni suggests, trailing after me down the hall, toward the front, still holding my magazine.

"Bob Ross that shit right now, Dol," Ivy adds, passing me one of her favorite sketching pencils. She's an aspiring artist, but I know for a fact this is her favorite piece of graphite. They nudge me out, and though I don't admit it, the gentle sting of crisp air against my bare calves and feet does feel good. The screen door closes behind me, and as I head toward the oak tree, my anger seems to lift, little by little.

Maybe I'll like painting. I mean, maybe not, but I'm out here and I know Juni and Ivy won't let me back in until this canvas is covered. Smirking, I place the canvas against an upturned watering pot, and take a seat cross-legged in front of it. They recommended the oak as a subject, but as I survey the palette of color options, I know I have everything I need to paint *him.*

I begin mixing cadmium red with yellow ochre and some titanium white, recalling a photo of Henry at Cannes, standing against a vibrant blue sea backdrop, his skin sunkissed perfection. Adding a touch of burnt umber, my smile shifts from smirk to grin as the shade progresses nicely.

Tipping my head back, I close my eyes, inhaling the scent of lavender and fresh grass, pretending he's here, standing over me, just returned from his trip. "It's going to be great," invisible Henry assures me, his voice smooth and sexy, as always. I open my eyes, surveying the paint shade.

After deciding it's perfect, I bring Ivy's sketch pencil to the canvas. The first line is drawn when the screen door opens in the near distance. I glance back.

With her hands cupped to her mouth, Juniper shouts, "And don't paint Henry Cavill!" She lowers her hands, head tipped empathetically to the side as she smiles at me from afar, adding less loudly, "No Henry Cavill for the next *hour.*"

Turning back to my singular line, I consider how I can turn what was supposed to be Henry Cavill's square jaw into a trunk. Juni and Ivy support my passionate personality—not because they're my sisters and they have to but because we're equally passionate. In our own ways. I've come to learn that real love is both tough and tender, and they've taught me that.

After adding some more umber, I mix the paint and lift one hand to shield my eyes from the sun that pours through the oak. It's our favorite tree on the ranch. I climbed it when I was young, my bare feet scraped on the rough bark, leaving cuts and aches. But as I sat atop that tree with my copy of *The Lightning Thief* and dreamt of adventuring the world with my love, Percy Jackson, I didn't have a care in the world.

I grew out of Percy but never grew out of loving the tree. Same with my sisters. The funny part is that it's technically not on our property, instead belonging to the ranchette next door. No one has lived next door for so long, we consider the tree ours.

I get to work on the trunk, stopping a few times to mix underlight and highlight tones for detailing. Pushing a strand of hair off my face with the back of my wrist, I glance up, past my canvas.

There's a truck in the distance, one tearing down the private dirt road. I blink curiously, since there are just two homes spread across this large piece of land and like I said, one's been vacant since forever. The truck grows louder as it nears, and I almost drop my brush when it takes the fork in the road *toward our house.*

What the?

Juni and Ivy come outside—that's how rare it is that someone drives down our road. Ivy's got black boots on, her legs covered in black fishnet stockings, her long t-shirt a dress of sorts. Juni is in overalls, barefoot like me, her long golden hair down, stick straight as always. Her green eyes grow dark when she's protective, and as the truck comes straight toward our property, she narrows her darkening gaze as she moves past the oak tree to stand in protection of everyone and thing behind her.

The truck parks at the empty house next door. I glance over at Ivy. "I didn't know it was for sale," I say quietly, my heart racing.

Neighbors?

We've never had neighbors. Like my dad always said, the Ellington sisters need their space. I didn't know what that meant back then but as I've grown, I've come to understand that three extremely passionate women can be... *frightening*, if you're not prepared.

I was even a little nervous two years back when Juni showed up with a man in the back of our truck, tied up, a kitchen apron rolled up and shoved into his mouth. She explained that he cut her off then flipped her the bird in town after church. I understood why she'd brought him back; he needed to apologize kindly and learn his lesson. *If you don't touch fire, you don't learn,* Juni is always humming. The next day she told us as soon as she sat him down and talked some sense into him, he apologized. He even walked back three miles into town to get home, because he wanted to clear his head for his newly learned perspective, she said.

"Someone had to own it. It didn't just belong to Earth, Dolly. Of course it was eventually going to be sold," Ivy says, stepping closer to me as the driver's door on the truck opens. Parked with his bumper toward the house, I can't see anything but rich sienna cowboy boots hit the ground as the door slams closed, rattling the trunk.

The paint brush topples from my hand, skidding down my white linen dress. My *favorite* dress forever stained by a Cannes-Henry umber and ochre. Yet I'm on my feet and slowly drifting toward the man who is coming around the front of the truck.

His hair is longish on top, wavy like maybe his dad had curly hair or something or maybe he runs his fingers through it a ton. He's *massive.* He's got to be over six feet something, and his shoulders are hulking. Wearing a black t-shirt, his chest muscles ripple through the loved fabric. And Christ almighty, he is wearing the hell out of those blue jeans. Worn and dirty around the thighs and knees, the jeans tell the story of a very hard-working man. And his body confirms this. My eyes finally make it to his face.

"*Oh my god…*" I breathe quietly, Ivy now at my side.

Because I'm not looking at her, I only *feel* Ivy's sharp eyes against my profile.

And I'm not looking at him. I'm *staring* at him.

Discreetly, I inhale through my nose, trying desperately to steal his scent. Does he smell like he's been working all day? Or like aftershave and beer? Bedsheets and whispered desires? I don't know.

But I am going to find out.

I need to know his smell. I need to memorize his taste. I want to see him stripped bare of clothes and carve it into my brain forever. I want to hear his private noises and have them to replay in my mind forever. I want to drape myself at his feet to absorb whatever he has to give. I hope it's everything.

"It's been less than thirty seconds, bitch," Ivy hisses, her sarcastic tone fused with fear. "Do not look at that man like that. He's massive. He's, like, *three times your size.* And... he's, like... *old*, anyway."

Just then, Juni turns around. "Ivy, Dahlia, come meet our new neighbor, Hudson Gray."

"Our *neighbor*," Ivy says without moving her lips, keeping her voice private. We loop arms and walk toward him, and I ignore her warning.

I don't care if he's older, if he's our neighbor, or that *he's three times my size..*

I don't care that I've only known of his existence for thirty fucking seconds or not. It irritates me that she would mention that because love and passion care nothing about trivial things like *time.*

Everyone knows, time is just a construct.

I mentally push Ivy aside as electricity scorches through my veins, searing my soul, awakening every limp and lifeless synapse, nerve ending, and pleasure receptor in my brain and body. I'm warm and wet beneath my cotton panties, and I know without a doubt, *without a question at all...*

I am in love with this man.

And *he is mine.*

"Hi, Ivy," he greets, slipping his hand into hers after Juni nods her way. Jealousy spikes inside me when they touch, my cheeks simmering and my ears burning. After too long, his hand finally slides into mine. Our gazes collide in silence, and he graces me with his focus.

My stomach flips and my lips tingle. A vision flashes before me, one of me reaching up to press my mouth to his then licking along his lips after taking a leisurely, hot kiss. *God*, I want to suck on his bottom lip and trace his teeth with my tongue. *I want his spit in my mouth, sliding down my throat..*

"Hi, Dahlia." He smiles, and *I am a new woman.* I have a new, overwhelming ache coming from deep inside me. Deeper than with Henry. This thing I feel, it's bone-deep. Like he is the missing piece of my soul, returning to make me complete.

"That's a pretty name," he says, smiling at me as the sun breaks free from the oak overhead, illuminating him. *My handsome Hudson.*

"Everyone calls me Dolly," I tell him as he takes his hand away. His eyes fall to the smear of paint on my white dress. He twists to see where I abandoned my canvas and supplies.

"I love paintings," he comments, smiling down at me. God, this man is a tower. A towering wall of a man. "You're the artist?"

I nod reluctantly.

"That's incredible. I love that," he says.

Smiling, I reply, "Thanks."

He returns his focus to Juni, where they exchange phone numbers as neighbors apparently do. Another wave—his monstrous hand hovering in the air making me ache for a spanking. Then he's gone, and Juni and Ivy are blinking at me, sharing a knowing look.

I turn to them, and hide nothing. *"I have to have him."*

That night, I take down all of my Henry Cavill posters and magazine pages. I print out a photo of a big, black truck, just like Hudson Gray's, and pin it on the wall next to my pillow.

My future husband's truck.

two

SOMEONE LIKE HER.

Hudson

Present Day.

My stomach howls. I've been out running errands all morning and I'm starving. I'm not a guy who's nice when he's hungry. Last night, Bear had a nightmare. I didn't want to wake him this morning by making myself breakfast, so I didn't eat. And I slept terribly, since he ended up coming into my bed around half past one, after the nightmare returned.

He pressed his little foot into my kidneys for most of the night, but he slept as sound as ever.

I catch a stray yawn with my gloved hand as I turn to leave the Feed 'n' Seed, peering out at the back of my pickup truck weighed down by chicken feed.

I never wanted chickens. But five years ago, newly married with a baby on the way, *we* wanted a ranchette. *She* wanted animals.

She's been gone for four years and now I have chickens, an entire small dairy farm worth of cows, and two horses.

"Hope to see you again soon, Hudson," Jade calls, leaning over the counter a little extra as my eyes float back to her. It may've been years since I've acted on *it*, but I still recognize *it*. I pinch the top of my hat and slightly tip it, without lifting, and step into the fresh air.

Jade is the daughter of the Feed 'n' Seed owner, Winston, and never misses a farmers market out on my property.

Another thing that started as a *we* and do as just *me*. The farmers market. We started one for the entire town, which is small as all get-out. We have more than enough room on our ranchette and our neighbors even wanted to contribute and help bring our dream to vision. It was a success, unlike my marriage, and it's since been Bluebell's weekly tradition.

Saturday farmers market out at Gray Farms.

We sell our fresh milk there, me and Bear. Ev works there since she's at my house most of the time anyway, helping me. Speaking of the devil, my sister Everly calls, and I answer my cell as I slam the driver's side door closed.

"Hey, Ev," I say as I twist the key in the ignition a few times, appreciating when it finally starts up on the third try. I flick on my blinker, and scrunch down in the cab to peer out the side mirror, checking for traffic. Truck or not, not too many places are comfortable for you when you're 6'4".

"'Bout wrapped up?" she asks, the clatter of lunch dishes in the kitchen sounding off in the back.

"Yeah, it took longer than I'd hoped. Jade didn't want to stop talking." I pull out into the street and lean back, fingering through my hair. My hat sits on the passenger seat, because it has to—I'm too tall for this pickup with it on.

Ev snorts. "I'm sure she didn't."

"Yeah, yeah," I sigh, not wanting to hear it from my sister again. She's always telling me how Jade is practically throwing her panties at me with her eyes when we go to the Feed 'n' Seed, and while I know it's true, talking about it makes me... *uncomfortable.* I've never been one to enjoy the attention I get from women.

All that noise is almost... a turn-off. Someone wanting me is good, but going so far as to behave like an animal in heat over a bag of chicken feed? *Could not be less interested if I tried.*

"How's Bear?" I ask about my four-year-old son.

"Rowdy as ever. Keeps harassing me about going to the creek to skip stones." Back at the house, she calls to my son, and his wild footsteps bring a curl to my lips. "Tell your daddy what you've been doing since he left," she says playfully.

My son takes the phone. "Daddy, when you get back, can you take me to skip stones? Aunt Ev is mean. She won't take me."

I smirk. My boy and I started skipping stones across the creek over the summer. Tessa and I always planned to give Bear the life I had growing up—open land, a taste of the earth, a country upbringing full of rewarding chores and hard work. That's what we wanted. So that's what I've been giving him.

And he loves skipping stones.

I love that he loves it.

Only problem is, my boy gets hooked on things. Obsessed, passionate—however you'd describe an all-consuming fixation—that's what he's got. Since I've always played an active part in helping work my own ranch, despite the five-man crew that helps, I don't have as much time to skip stones, but I always try.

Ev takes him when she can, but Ev is also planning her wedding, which understandably takes precedence.

"I'll take you when I get back," I promise, knowing that the chickens need to be fed, the coop needs a repair, there's a fence pole down on the east side of the property, and I need to call someone to come out and assess the fungus on the old oak out front. I love that tree, I don't want to lose it. But the soil in the last few years has evolved, becoming not just less fruitful but somewhat degrading to the trees and some bushes. I guess I'll see what the guy says when he comes out.

Either way, I have time to skip stones on the water with Bear today. "I'll be home soon, okay?"

"Yeah!" he cheers, running off, leaving my sister to collect the phone and return to me.

"You there?"

I laugh. "Yeah. I'm here. Thanks again for today," I tell Ev, navigating my truck onto the dirt road that leads to our place. We're not far from the center of town, yet another reason why my property is perfect for the farmers market.

"Sure–" she pauses, "oh, there you are. All right, we'll see you in a few."

"Okay," I say, readying my thumb to end the call, but

Ev's voice calls out again, so I press the receiver to my ear one more time.

"Dolly's out there painting so... careful not to kick up dirt if you park near the oak."

I end the call, and narrow my gaze to the base of the massive oak, spotting a tiny, huddled-over figure. The closer I get to the house, the clearer she becomes.

Dolly, the twenty-year-old girl that lives next door. She is an artist. A painter, to be more specific. She makes greeting cards for her business—*Designed by Dolly*—but in her hobby time, she paints full canvases of nature. She's out here all the time from what it seems, because every time I come out, she's there. Painting.

Parking as far away from her as I can, as not to disrupt, I step out of my truck and click the door closed, also not wanting to startle her. But no matter how quiet I try to be, it seems like whenever my eyes go to hers, she's already found me.

"Hey, Dolly," I greet, lifting my filthy hand in the air as I glance over at her place. She lives there with her two sisters. Her older sister Juniper has been raising her for years, since their father passed early. I never grew up around a house like that, and though all three of them are vastly different, they're all good seeds. I think if Ev and I would've lost our Mom and Dad any earlier, it would've wrecked us. But Juniper has clearly kept herself and her sisters on track. "What are you working on?" I ask, moseying over for a minute, waving at Ev who's standing in the kitchen, smiling out the bay window.

Wide blue eyes pinned on me, the way they always do, I have half a mind to tell Juni one day how impressed I am with the manners her sisters have. She never fails to make eye contact with me when we speak, and she's always so damn thoughtful.

Smiling, she turns her canvas to show me. The entire thing is a mix of blues and grays, with white sponged over the top to create what looks like gauzy clouds. "A sky on the cusp of rain," she says finally after I analyze it quietly for a moment.

My gaze flicks to hers, and I smile. "It's beautiful. You've got talent. Have you ever thought of selling these alongside your cards? I'm sure the folks in town would love them."

Her eyebrows lift as if I've jostled something free in her brain, and she reaches into her apron pocket, digging around a minute. Moments later, she extends her hand to me, a tiny two inch by three inch canvas in her hand. I peer down at it, a twitch in my gut as I realize what it is.

"The creek," I say, smiling at the painting that looks exactly like Bear's favorite place. I flip it in my palm, seeing black paint on the back. *TO BEAR, FROM DOLLY.*

"It's for Bear," she says quietly, my eyes holding hers.

"He will love this," I tell her just as Ev opens the screen door.

"We're gonna paint one together, soon. But for now, this should make him happy," Dolly says. Bear's head pops up on the horizon, the air suddenly full of echoed laughter.

"Daddy!" Bear shouts, racing toward me full speed, his pockets filled to the brim with his skipping stones. "You ready? *You ready?*"

"Hi, Dolly," Ev calls to our neighbor from the porch. "Hey, does Juniper have any of her clementine jam?" Ev wrings her hands in a dish towel that hangs from the pocket of her jeans. "I'd like to take some to the bakery this week, for a filling possibility."

Dolly collects her things and makes her way toward Everly, and the two of them chat about wedding cakes and what flavors would work well with clementines. I slip the little painting in my pocket, and take Bear by the hand, heading for the creek.

Halfway there, Bear gets tired of holding all the stones, and attempts to offload them into some of my pockets. I take out the tiny painting Dolly did for Bear so it doesn't get ruined.

She's so thoughtful when it comes to us.

Looking at the graphite-colored river rock in my palm, I say a little wish, because skipping stones and blowing dandelions are one in the same when you live in the country.

I'm not actively doing anything to make this wish come true but I hope one day, I meet someone who cares about my son as much as I do, someone to share skipping stones and sunsets with. For him, but for me, too.

The stone skitters over the surface, leaving a trail of beautiful rippling water in its wake. Next to me, my son jumps and claps. I pocket the painting.

"Your turn, buddy."

three

MY FAVORITE BREAKFAST.

Dolly

My eyes flick open to my phone erupting in music next to my bed, my alarm set to a playlist.

Stretching my arms above me, I instinctually sing the tune, each lyric etched into the spongy parts of my brain from repetition. A lot of my life is repetitive, especially Friday.

And I like it that way.

Ivy, from the next room over, throws her fist against the wall. "Turn it off, Dolly!"

I reach over and turn off the Lana Del Rey song that speaks to me like nothing else. All of her music does. Lana understands passion and imperfection better than anyone.

Though I feel certain that if Hudson knew my passion, he'd understand it.

Soulmates always understand each other.

Stretching, I finally climb out of bed, knowing I have four minutes to get to the window. I toe into my fuzzy slippers and wrap up in my matching robe, then position myself behind the curtain in my room, binoculars in hand.

I can see just fine.

But *details*. I'm a *details* girl.

The cool metal binoculars touch the bridge of my nose with comfortable familiarity, and I suck in a sniper's breath, holding myself steady as I peer and wait.

Like clockwork, the worn black lacquer door with a rusted knocker and offset peephole opens. I can only see the side of the front porch from where my room is in the house, but it's more than I saw out of the window that faced the lawn five years ago.

The first day I met Hudson, I forced Ivy to switch rooms with me. She knew why and made no effort to thwart my plans. After all, I needed a front-row seat while biding my time until I was old enough for Hudson Gray to love me back.

The last two years have been very fucking aggravating.

There has seemingly been an endless stream of things in our way. Like his soon-to-be brother-in-law hanging around all the time now that he's officially engaged to Ev, the fire on the property two days after my eighteenth which had Hud knee deep in labor then paperwork for months.

My tactics have been put on hold or cast aside for too long.

I'm getting serious about it now.

I turned twenty a couple of weeks ago. I'd hoped to be married to Hudson by now, to be growing one of his beautiful babies in my belly too. Instead, we aren't even dating. He doesn't even look at me like a woman.

Not *yet*.

Finally, after the door stands wide open for its normal fifteen seconds, Bear sails out, and I find myself grinning. I love how fast he's gotten, and how sometimes, his legs go faster than the rest of him and he burns out, giggling the entire time. When Hudson asks me to watch him, we have so much fun.

He's obsessed with skipping stones now, but before that, we ran. And told jokes. Most of them fart related.

Everly and Deuce follow, his hand on her hip, toe to heel, whispering things into her ear. Hudson follows them, stepping out in dark blue jeans, a fitted white t-shirt and his sepia and sun-worn boots, his hair still damp from the shower.

Arousal rushes out of me, soaking my panties, and I reach down, still holding the binoculars with one hand, and reach under my satin pajama shorts. I'm slick and warm, throbbing at just the sight of him.

I bet if I dragged my tongue up the side of his throat he'd taste like shaving cream. My hand works faster as I swallow, following them as they make their way to the truck.

This is their weekly stock-up trip. They get everything they need to host the farmers market. Groceries, change, all that stuff. It is routine.

For all of us.

I get my first orgasm of the day when I watch him usher everyone out, taking care of the people he loves. God, that's hot. Not to mention his nipples are always poking through his t-shirt when he's freshly showered, and I love imagining them grazing my chest, rubbing against mine.

Once they're gone, I make my thorough weekly pass of his place. Ivy sketches on the porch while I do it, as my lookout. But I don't wake her up to do it until right before it's time. Even then, I still bribe her with coffee.

Everyone else gets in the truck, but my focus stays on him once he leaves the house. I can't look at anyone or think about anyone but him when I have my fingers spearing through my pussy, teasing my achy clit in his honor.

He twists to put his seat belt on once he's in the truck, and I rub faster, picking up the pace as I imagine riding bitch, bobbing in his lap, sucking warm semen from his cock, making him feel things that only *my* mouth can make him feel.

My cunt clamps down around my fingers as my orgasm explodes in my groin, sending a rush of cum onto my hand and into my panties.

I *always* gush for Hudson.

I lift my sticky fingers beneath my top and pluck at one of my hardened nipples, imagining it's him. My abs clench as my orgasm continues tearing through me. When the engine starts, I open my eyes and watch him toss his muscular arm over the seats and twist his gaze to back out. A soft humming twitches between my thighs. If I watched him for another few minutes, I *could* come again.

I'm always so hungry for him in the morning.

When the taillights are tiny, I replace the binoculars and use the restroom, swapping my soaked panties for fresh ones, washing my hands then face, and brushing my teeth.

After running a brush through my hair, I pull overalls over a tiny white cropped tee, slide into my sneakers, and carefully tap on Ivy's door.

"Five minutes," I tell her before heading to the kitchen to start her coffee. While it brews, I return to my bedroom, where I pull open my largest desk drawer, the bottom one. The tracks squeal quietly as I tug it open, exposing its contents. Reaching in, I take a newly packaged red toothbrush out. Now there are 78 red toothbrushes in that drawer.

I slide it into my pocket and make my way to the kitchen, where Ivy is sharpening a pencil through a yawn. We don't say a word as I mix her protein powder with her lactose-free milk, then pour steaming caffeine over the top. Shuffling along behind me, still yawning, we head to the front porch where I hold her cup as she settles into her chair, resting her sketch pad on her thighs while she pulls her hair off her face.

After a ponytail is secure, she reaches for her mug. "Okay, have fun," she says, looking down at the drawing which is, so far, a photorealistic sketch of a knife with something dripping from the pointed tip.

I pause and take it in. "That's pretty," I say, twisting my neck to see it upright. She sips her coffee and beams.

"Thank you."

I wrinkle my nose. "Still thinking about Rhett?"

Her blue eyes roll to high heaven. "What gave it away?"

I smirk, tapping her paper. "The bloody knife."

Freeze—I know what you're thinking. But no, Ivy didn't murder Rhett. We may be passionate, but we're not killers.

She just wants to kill him and sometimes wishes she

would have. Because he was a horrible boyfriend who thought the world of himself and in doing so, managed to minimize everyone and everything around him, including Ivy.

I hate him, too. But the next guy she meets will be totally different. I mean, how many ego-driven, self-involved, *really a five but think they're a ten*, narcissistic pricks can there be in a super small town? One feels right.

"You don't know for sure it's blood until I add color," Ivy says, taking another sip from her coffee. I trot down the porch stairs and lift my hand over my head, waving back to her as I head to Hudson's.

"It's blood, we both know it."

As I pull open the door, my senses awaken at the scent and temperature of Hudson's home rushing against my face. Crackling, comfortable warmth hits my nose along with smells of coffee and aftershave, and a trace of pepper hanging in the air—maybe left over from last night's blackened cod. I twist the deadbolt after clicking the door closed, and slide out of my sneakers. Stepping out of them, I get to work, making my way through the kitchen first.

His mug sits dead center in the white porcelain sink basin, an inch of unfinished coffee left behind inside. My chest squeezes. He hasn't left a dish in the sink in a few weeks. Carefully, I lift the mug from the sink, running my thumb over the block letters reading WORLD'S GREATEST DAD. Turning it over in my hands carefully, so as not to spill the remainder, I search for an indication as to where he drank from. But without a single drip in sight, I play it safe, and drag my tongue along the entire rim, my veins going hot at all the unseen things I'm collecting.

Traces of his lips. Maybe even saliva.

Tipping it back, I drink the rest of the cold, bitter coffee. I don't drink coffee unless it's his. There's a fork in the sink that I notice as I replace the mug, but because Bear eats pancakes almost every day, I'm willing to bet it's his.

Lifting a stack of mail from the countertop, I see the water bill, electric bill and a bill from... "The Feed 'n' Seed sends statements?" I question aloud. Hudson always pays for the chicken feed with three crisp hundred-dollar bills. There's always four dollars and thirty six cents change. *Always.*

Carefully, I slide my nail beneath the seal, popping it open. After unfolding the paper stuffed inside, I find that I was right. Feed 'n' Seed did *not* send a statement. Without hesitation, my blood goes fiery, anger thrashing in my veins.

The paper is a letter from Jade, inviting herself over to Gray Farms before the market on Saturday.

I'm good here at the store, which means I'd be pretty darn good at your place too. If you ever need help setting up, just give me a call.

xo

Jade

632-5524

You dumb little bitch. Thank God I come here and do this. Hudson doesn't want to be hit on by some crazy Feed 'n' Seed skank like Jade.

Sliding the letter into the envelope, I move back to the sink and run it beneath the tap. I keep it there, the scalding water singeing my skin while also freeing the ink, both printed and written. After wrapping it in a paper towel, I stuff it in the trash under the sink, and make my way into the living room.

Bear's blanket dangles from a chair, and his pajamas are inside out, strewn across the coffee table. Getting out of the door this morning was probably a hectic rush. It's great that Everly helps but Hudson needs *more*, it's clear. I would wake early, make him coffee, fix Bear his food, help Bear get dressed, and get everyone out the door happy and on time. Everly is so wrapped up in Deuce lately and honestly, I think the universe brought Deuce to Everly so that I could finally have my time, step in, and show Hudson that his soulmate has been under his nose for the last five years.

Everly and Deuce were benefactors to the universe's shift, and while it was meant to stir chaos in Hud's life in order for him to see *me* as more, it brought them together, too. I know that sounds crazy, claiming someone else's love as my fate. But fate is complicated and weaves a web often hard to follow.

Good thing I'm very smart.

My fingertips burn as I walk past Bear's mess, leaving it despite the fact that my body aches to tend to it. Because *I belong here.* Hudson in his white t-shirt flashes through my mind as I make my way down the hall, toward his bedroom.

Sometimes I go into Bear's room, mostly to imagine the

three of us in there together, a bedtime story in Hudson's arms, me in his lap, Bear in mine. So perfect.

Today, though, is not one of those days.

Hudson leaves his door open, and there's something so sexy about a man with nothing to hide. And yet I can't wait to live here, and give him a reason to keep the door closed.

Before making my closet and bed rounds, I head into the adjoined bathroom, and flip on the lights.

Hudson remodeled this bathroom for *her* years ago. My teeth grind as my jaw clenches at the thought of that sorry excuse for a wife.

The first year he lived next door was agonizing because she was still here. She came the day after I met him, and let's just say, had she not been Bear's birth mother, she'd have had to go... for other reasons. Luckily, she showed herself out of Bluebell permanently.

What a foolish, ungrateful woman his ex-wife was.

He bought land, animals, remodeled a house, moved his sister—he did everything to give *her* the life she wanted, and still, the ungrateful whore trampled his heart and took off. "Fucking cunt," I breathe, taking in the gorgeous wainscotting and the immaculately painted walls, the claw-foot tub and wide, open-air shower, plush navy towels and cerulean tinting the overhead light. The attention to detail in every inch makes me so needy and wet.

He stepped into this shitty old bathroom and thought of every single thing she liked, and with his bare hands, brought it to life. And what did she do? Sucked his best friend's cock and ran off.

I would appreciate it. I *do* appreciate it, even though it's not for me.

Lifting the lid off the wicker hamper, I collect Hudson's morning towel. When I live here, I'll nudge him to hang them out before hampering them. But because they never smell like mildew, I know the man is good at laundry.

And that's hot, too.

I press the damp terry to my nose, sucking in the scent of cedar and patchouli. I love that he buys a masculine soap. I don't like thinking of anyone else smelling him, but still, I love the way he smells. I wish I could bathe in it, bottle it, drink it, roll the fuck around in it. It's so good.

Pressing it to my cheek, I rub the damp fabric along my skin, imagining Hudson wiping cum off my lips and nose after a facial. My body warms at the fantasy. *Hot sprays over my face, feral, deep-rooted grunts in the air, followed by his utter attention and care as he cleans me afterward—so perfect.*

One day.

One day soon.

Dropping it into the basket, I replace the lid and face the sink, where my eyes go easily to the red toothbrush that rests idly in the silver cup. Reaching into my pocket, I produce the brand-new red toothbrush, or item number B0124AZG8Y as I know it. After removing it from the package, I shove the plastic wrappings and strip of cardboard into my pocket and switch the new one with his. My mouth waters now that the sleek plastic is pinched in my palm. I clutch the counter's edge as I bring the toothbrush to my mouth, sucking in a steady breath before I plunge it inside.

"*Ohhh,*" my soft moan wraps the brush as the tough bristles sink into my gums and teeth. The taste of his cavity-protection toothpaste floods my tongue, and below my waist, everything goes a little haywire. The brush is still damp from use, and still carries lingering traces of him on it. I suck it, minty liquid running onto my tongue from the bristles, and any traces of him left behind... I swallow. I keep the brush pinched in between my molars as I slowly get undressed.

With my shoes by the back door, all I need to do is ditch my overalls. Unclipping each strap, I look at my pink toenails as denim pools on the floor around me. A few more steps and I'm tugging back the haphazard covers on Hud's bed, exposing the sheet where he slept.

I smooth my hand over the wrinkled fitted sheet, sad that it no longer holds warmth from his body. I close my eyes, still chewing on his toothbrush as I envision tangling my legs with his, reaching into his boxers before he's awake and pleasuring him until he's conscious. I can't wait to press my lips into the soft, private spot on the side of his throat *that every other woman can see when he's dressed* and know that *only I get access to it intimately.*

Carefully, I slide under the covers, not having to protect the sensual shudder that racks my shoulders at the feel of being in his bed. I also don't have to mask my moans, because I'm alone, and so as I pull my baby t-shirt up, letting his top sheet rub against my hardened nipples, *I moan.*

I turn onto my side, rubbing my cheek on the pillow as I hold his bedsheet in my hand, bringing it to my body. With another swallow, still somewhat minty, I pull his brush from my mouth and fall onto my back, in the center of his bed.

I can't smell his soap and cologne here, which makes me happy. If his bed held his fresh, clean scent boldly, that would mean he's getting into bed wearing cologne. Which means he wouldn't be alone.

I don't want him to be lonely, but I'd rather him be alone than with anyone that isn't me. We're soulmates. And I'm going to make him see that.

There's a buzz roaming around my hips, dipping into my pussy, my uterus and ovaries heavy with need. An aching need I'm very, very familiar with.

One I thought I satiated this morning when I saw Hud in his fitted tee.

Knowing that coming to the fantasy of my man can be messy, I refrain, instead running the tips of my fingers along my clit, over my panties. A gentle tease isn't enough, but with his mouth inside of mine, my toes curling into his sheets, the ceiling he sees when he wakes every morning right above me—it's enough for now.

After a moment of bliss, I slide out of bed and redress, keeping Hud's toothbrush in my mouth. I'll be sucking on it all day, as I always do the first day I have it. It's still fresh *with him.*

Moving into his closet, I flick on the light, ignoring the small ring box that has sat on top of his dresser for as long as I can remember. I opened it once, only once. I think everything else in this house I've discovered time and time again, but I only needed to open that box once to know it has no place in my story. Our story.

Why he kept it after she left, I don't know. Maybe he's saving it to give to Bear someday. I don't know. All I know is, good fucking riddance. Letting my fingers graze the sleeves of his work shirts, I stop on my favorite one. It's nothing special. Long-sleeved, button-up, blue denim. It may even be a chambray. There's a tiny hole worn into the breast pocket, and the top button is completely gone. The shoulders have been lightened from all the time under the sun, and there's a small stain on the collar from a shaving knick that bled. When Hudson wears it, he looks so handsome. He was wearing that shirt the first day I met him, and whenever I see him in it, I remember that first time. The sureness I had in my bones, the promises I made to myself—it all comes rushing back, reminding me that he came here for me, whether he knows it or not.

I bet he'll be wearing that shirt when he discovers I'm right about it all.

I pluck it from the hanger, and slide one arm in at a time, catching the ends of the sleeves in my palms. Bringing my hands beneath my nose, I eat up his scent, my nipples going hard to the note of fabric softener. With my toes, I push the door closed, enjoying the temporary darkness and privacy of his closet.

Looking around, I take in my favorite elements. The way he folds and hangs his jeans, the different bottles of cologne atop the dresser, the way his boots are lined up in a neat and perfect row, how his belts stay rolled tight and organized in a drawer. The space is tidy and masculine, no frills and all function, and it makes me dizzy as I turn circles in the space, basking in this sliver of him.

He's naked when he comes in here, and that's the singular thought that always has me opening the door and leaving. If I focus on it for too long, I'll make a mess.

It happened one other time before and I lost all of my valuable *indoor* time to cleaning.

With a small spritz of his cologne to my wrist, I shrug off

the shirt and rehang it, stepping out of the closet with my pussy pulsing and my heart racing. With his toothbrush tucked comfortably into my cheek, I move through the house, memorizing the small things that are different this time.

There's a *Field & Stream* magazine on the counter, and to my knowledge, Hudson's never been a subscriber. When I pop open the fridge, I notice Bear's yogurt is cherry this week, when it's usually strawberry. The hand soap at the sink smells different, too.

One last survey of my favorite place and my future home, and I'm stepping outside quietly, closing the door behind me. Traipsing back to our house, Ivy looks up from her sketch pad.

With the toothbrush still in my mouth, I pull it out and smile at her as I take the porch steps. "Thank you."

She picks up her mug, tipping it all the way back to finish her coffee. "How was *indoor* time today?" she asks, collecting her things as she gets to her feet. I hold the screen door open for her as she filters past me inside, tapping the end of the toothbrush.

"Good," I reply.

"Cool. I'm going out later if you wanna ride with. I think Juni is coming too. We're on the hunt for test ink." Ivy, who is vying for a tattoo apprenticeship at Deuce's next ink parlor, is finally ready to try out her gun but first has to procure the perfect ink.

Ivy wants to tattoo in mostly white ink, which I think is so cool. So many people base their body art on colors, or having them all be in black and white. But Ivy's hoping to make her specialty demonic women in white ink.

I love it.

"No thanks," I reply, heading to the kitchen to grab a bottle of water. "I'm going to be in the barn most of the day."

Ivy smiles as Juni appears, a towel wrapped around her wet hair on her head, a bathrobe tied at her waist. "Painting today?" she asks, overhearing part of our convo. With the bottle of water under one arm, I move for the back door, which leads to the barn.

"Yeah, I'll be in there all day." I wiggle my fingers at my sisters. "Have fun. I'll be back inside at five." Read: *don't come in.*

I head into the barn, a new canvas waiting for me. I sit down, knowing that before I paint, I have an itch to scratch.

And I use the handle of the toothbrush to scratch that itch, moaning Hudson's name the entire time.

And then, I paint.

I WANT AND NEED SOMEONE.

Hudson

"C'mon, please!" Bear begs, both of his hands tucked into my back pocket as he tugs on me, hoping to pull me all the way to the creek. From my position bent at the waist, the leg of one of my canopies in my hands, I get to my feet, the white-topped tent toppling onto its side.

"Bear, buddy, we gotta set up for the farmers market tomorrow. Gray Farms is the host. We're good hosts, too," I say, smiling down at my little spitting image. His dark hair is messy, despite the fact I held him between my legs and combed it as he ate pancakes this morning. "You wanna be a good host, don't you?"

He kicks, his boot sailing through a small clump of dirt. "I guess so."

I smooth my fingers through his hair, pushing it off his face. Crouching, I meet his eyes and take his hand in mine. "We'll get to the creek, okay? But I don't have a lot of time today. Tomorrow, after the market?"

"Tomorrow?!" he whines, his eyes wide as if I told him Santa isn't real.

"Buddy," I start, maintaining patience. "I gotta tag the cattle after I'm done here." I stroke my hand along my forehead, beneath the felt rim of my hat. "There won't be much sunlight left when I'm all done. It's better for tomorrow."

He moves dirt around with the toe of his boot, hiding his tears. They plunk heavily into the dirt. "Okay."

Fuck. I haven't cried in four years and six months but his tears of disappointment threaten to break my streak.

Making a spur-of-the-moment choice, I hook my hands beneath his arms, hoisting him to my chest. He loops his legs around my waist and I keep my hand firmly planted in the center of his back. "Okay, buddy, let's skip some stones."

I know I don't have time. In fact, I have even less time than normal, which is usually pretty limited as it is. Ever since my sister got engaged, she's... busier.

And that's good. She should not exist to take care of her brother and nephew. I'm happy for her.

On Friday, Everly and I normally set up for the market together, then I go on to do my chores, leaving Bear to hang out with her for the rest of the afternoon. We convene at dinner, and I spend the evening with him, even though by that point in the day we're both exhausted.

Today, though, Ev has to leave before we even set up, and the worst part? I forgot.

She told me a month in advance, I know she did. But

with the fence coming down on the east side of my property and one of the farmhands getting injured two weeks ago, I've been preoccupied. My best-laid plans have been lost to the chaos of every day.

I carry Bear down to the creek, mostly to make the most of the moment. With little boys, they don't let you carry them and snuggle them often, and I know as he nears age five, his independence is coming.

He wagers how far his stones will go as we walk on our way down. Feeling his heartbeat against mine, I'm over-whelmed with love. I want to do right by him in every way, and raising him without his mama is something I hate. A boy needs his mama.

But since she left, I'm all of the following: I'm the tough disciplinarian, and I'm also the one who holds him tightly as we walk to the creek, talking about our days.

I'll be the best of both for him, because he deserves it.

We skip stones so long that the sun shifts positions in the sky, and by the time we're back to the house, Ev is on the porch, anxiously tapping her foot.

"Good Lord, Hudson, why don't you try answering your phone?" she breathes out, clutching the deck railing as Deuce approaches from behind, glancing at his watch.

"Baby, we gotta go." His hand comes to her hip as he looks up, spotting me and Bear. "Creek?"

I nod. "Yep. You..." I scratch my forehead beneath my hat. "Checking out a venue?"

I leave it vague, because *venue* works for wedding loca-tions as well as tattoo shop locations, and I can't quite remember what they're doing today.

Ev smooths her hand over the side of her head, pushing

back a flyaway. She's wearing lipstick but hasn't ditched the boots and jeans, so it's safe to assume today is a tattoo shop hunt.

"Shop possibility in town." He reaches into his back pocket, his long hair curtaining his face as he torques. My sister reaches up and smooths it back behind his ear. He doesn't acknowledge it, and neither does she, and it's a small thing. But it's all the shit I miss about *belonging to someone.*

Those little things. The ways you can touch each other. The subtle ways you help one another or show affection to each other all day. All the subtle caresses, lingering looks across a crowded room, the shared expressions, the smirks that hold private meanings, the hand on the lower back or palm between pecs... all of that shit. That's what I miss.

To be fair, I don't know how to miss *love.*

Looking back, I don't know if I was in love with Tessa or if I was in love with the idea of a wife. Having someone who wants to live and grow with me, to raise human beings together, to clink mugs and champagne flutes with as we journey through life with one another.

If I did love her, all of it is gone. I fell so hard and fast for Bear that I never allowed my heart to feel the loss. Or maybe I only ever felt it on his behalf. Either way, I don't miss love because when it comes to a woman, I've never had it.

I miss closeness. Companionship.

Intimacy.

At that word, for whatever reason, Dolly's face appears in my mind. It's just a flash, a mention of her broad smile, a glimpse of her shining eyes, a subtle remembrance of her night-blooming jasmine and lavender scent. But it's enough to have guilt pouring through me.

Tugging off my hat, I pin my eyes on Deuce and put the young woman next door out of my mind.

"Oh yeah? Where about?" I ask Deuce as Everly comes off the porch, heading toward her fiancé's truck. She takes a seat in the passenger side as Deuce follows, stopping to chat.

"Across from Goode's Diner."

I rack my brain, trying to imagine what's across from the one and only diner in town. "The video rental place?"

Deuce nods. "Yep. Turns out Bluebell doesn't watch much VHS."

I snort. "No one does."

"Anyway," he says, cupping his hand on my shoulder. "I'm taking Ev out for dinner, upstate a ways. We won't be back tonight."

I peer past him, to the house, where Bear is on the floor coloring near the sliding door.

"I know you got to tag cattle today, and I'm sorry about that–"

I stop my future brother-in-law. "No, it's okay. You two have a good day out." I lift my hand and wave to Ev, who waves back at me through the rolled-up window. "And good luck with the spot."

Deuce says goodbye, and after they've pulled off the property and are heading down the road, I turn back toward the house. Bear has a coloring picture of Bluey pressed to the glass of the sliding door.

I wave him out and he comes running, discolored Bluey

in hand. "Hey, you wouldn't mind spending time with Dolly, would you?"

His eyes widen. "Dolly!" he squeals, taking off like a bullet toward their place. My long strides with adult legs means I catch up to him before he rings the bell. I ruffle his hair as he smooths out his coloring. "Let me ask her, okay?"

I rap my knuckles against the screen, forcing myself to think about the way the doorbell has been hanging by a wire for the last two years.

"Hiya, Hudson," Juniper greets as she pulls open the door, catching it with her hip before it closes. She wrings her hands out on the apron tied at her waist, a smear of purple on her forehead. "Hi there, Bear." She crouches, pinching his drawing to lift it up. "That's great," she says, her Australian accent rusty, but much better than mine.

"Daddy wants to know if Dolly can hang out with me," he says, using the words we practiced together. In the past, "Daddy needs you" didn't feel right, so I taught him something a bit... better.

"Is Dahlia around, Juniper? Everly and Deuce are out viewing properties with their real estate agent, but I have to tag today and I can't take Bear out there with me." I nervously tug at my cowboy hat, but wouldn't you know it, it's perfectly in place. "It's too dangerous."

She smiles, all white teeth framed with thin pink lips. Juniper and Dolly look alike, with Juni wearing ten more years of life on her shoulders. She's taller than Dolly, the tallest of the three, actually, and runs her own company making jam.

I like living next to the Ellington sisters, and they've

been nothing but sweet and helpful. They get along with Ev and Bear, too, which makes life... nice.

"She's here," Juniper replies before turning her head, hollering into the house. "Dolly, Hudson and Bear are here."

Heat stalks up my spine, though I've been in this spot many times without feeling anything. In fact, I've stood on this porch and asked these women for help quite a bit in the last four years and never felt anything but guilt.

I stroke my hand up the back of my neck, finding it unusually damp. I don't know why I'm feeling anything. Her face popped into my mind when I thought about intimacy. But there wasn't more to it than that.

"Hey," Dolly's soft voice comes around the open door before she does, a genuine smile on her face as she crouches to greet my son. "Hey, Bear. Oh, is that Bluey? And it's for me?" She clutches the coloring book page to her chest, grinning. "I love it!" Her eyes stay on him as he smiles and giggles in response, reaching out to smooth a rough edge of the paper.

"Wanna make art together today?" she asks, studying the coloring book page one more time before rumpling her brow. "I love this but... I really like painting with you."

"Paint!" he squeals, because at this stage in his life, paint is far more enthralling than anything else. I know I can only ride that out for a few more years before it's something rowdier.

I place my palm on his head as Dolly gets to her feet. "I'm so sorry, Dolly, but I forgot Ev and Deuce have plans for the rest of the day. I have to tag cattle till late afternoon." I lift my brows, fighting against the heavy guilt weighing them down. I wish I could be here for my son, but when you own a ranch, you work a ton. It's why having a strong family dynamic at home is important.

Something I foolishly thought Tessa understood.

I swallow. "I'll pay you double what I normally pay and–"

Dolly's face falls into serious territory, and my stomach twists into knots. If she already has plans–

"You will not pay me," she breathes, keeping her voice calm while her eyes grow stormy. Feet bare, she steps closer toward me as Bear clings to her leg now instead of mine. "We love hanging out. Your money's no good here."

Canvases and paint. I'll repay her in canvases and paint, and that thick cardstock she buys online to make her cards from. Whatever it is, I'll find a way to repay her for her generous heart.

"Thank you," I reply, surprised at how soft the words come out. I clear my throat. "We already went to the creek," I tell her, more so Bear can hear it as much as Dolly knows it. "So no more creek today."

She raises her palms, smiling innocently, her golden hair falling in natural waves around her face. Bear's always loved Dolly. I take in the smattering of freckles that journey along the apples of her cheeks and down the bridge of her nose, and her wide eyes and the soft dip in her voice when she shows him affection. I get it. Dolly is gorgeous, seemingly from the inside out.

And she's an artist. Kids love art.

I do, too. But as a rancher, it's not often I have time to take in art and its beauty. Thankfully, I find beauty all around me. In the crisp, vastness of a cloudless sky, in the unending green that kisses the horizon as the sun rises, and the gentle rasp of Dolly's voice when she says my name.

"What's that?" I ask, finding myself playing conversation catch-up as I simultaneously process that I find Dolly's voice to be beautiful.

She reaches up, and it's then I consider just how much smaller she is, too. When you're six feet four inches tall, built to play professional football or be a rancher, dwarfing people is a given. Something I don't even consider anymore.

But standing over Dolly, the top of her head coming to mid-chest, the difference between us radiates through me, warm and electric. I can only imagine how gentle she needs it...

"Did he already eat, is all I asked," she says again, smiling, a touch of pink on her cheeks.

"Uh, no, no he hasn't had lunch." I shove my hands in my jeans to divert the sudden rush of blood to my groin. "Sorry, I was just trying to remember what Ev told me, but uh, no, I don't recall lunch."

"I'm hungry!" Bear champions from between us. He reaches up, wiggling his fingers toward... her.

She lifts him easily despite the fact he's more than half her size. Their gazes come together. "No creek, but lots of paint, and how about peanut butter and marionberry jam?"

Bear wiggles out of her grip, tearing into their house with comfort and familiarity. That brings me peace, knowing I'm leaving my boy next door, at a place he feels safe. It's second best to him being home.

"Bye, Bear, be good for Dolly," I call after him, but he's gone, and I'm suddenly acutely aware that I'm alone with Dolly on the porch, the midday sun dripping over half of her face, making her impossibly more beautiful. "Thanks again," I say, balling my hands into fists in my pockets. *Baseball. Horseshoeing. People who wave you on at a four-way stop when it's their turn.* "I'll be back around dinner," I tell her, holding a tight, controlled smile.

"Great," she replies, her long lashes fluttering. "Have a good day out there, Hudson."

On my boot, I turn and take the stairs, the distance between our houses feeling nonexistent as I head back with a foggy mind.

Once I'm out on the land for a few minutes, the electricity I'd felt earlier around Dolly all but disappears. Cow shit will do that to you.

It's been a long time since I was intimate with a woman. Too long. I never planned for it to be this long. I never planned this version of my life, in fact. And maybe that untended urge is all that has me looking at Dolly differently.

I need to get laid.

And more than that, I need to find someone else who can watch Bear now that Ev and Deuce are on the cusp of starting their own lives together. Everly is not going to want to be around with her first child, at my house, watching my son. Deuce won't want that for her once she's his wife, either.

I do need someone. More than that, I'm realizing just how much I want someone. Not just for Bear, though for him too. For me.

The thought of trusting anyone as much as I trust Dolly, though, is hard to fathom. I trust her with my son, therefore, my life.

five

I'M CLOSER TO HAVING HIM THAN EVER BEFORE.

Dolly

"How was the creek today?" I ask Bear as he balances atop a barstool at the kitchen counter, his little smock already tied on. I've learned in the few years I've been watching Bear that as soon as you are in possession of a little kid, you need to protect their clothing.

Eating, coloring, running outside, taking a nap—somehow, all of that is a messy sport to a kid. Wrapping him in a smock the moment the front door closed was a must.

Plus, I take pride in returning Bear to Hudson in his best form. To show him what a good mother I am. Or, *will be.*

"Good. Daddy's stones went super far," he says, reaching

for a half-full jar of jam, which Juni swipes before he can reach.

"Not this one," she says, her tone stern at first, but soft as she adds, "but this one is yours to play with."

While I set up our easels, mix paint, and plan today's art project, Juni lets Bear play with food.

I know, *don't play with your food* is a huge thing growing up. But she also teaches Bear that breaking the rules is okay sometimes, too, so playing with it under her supervision is just fine.

He plunks his little fist into the open canning jar, coating his fingers in the violet-colored jam. "Smells yummy," he says as he fans his fingers out, chunks of fruit falling onto the wax-paper-coated countertop. Juni always thinks ahead.

"It's a trial recipe," Juni says, pulling the pencil from her bun as she jots down extract amounts on the spiral notebook next to her. "But yours to play with for now."

"Bear, do you want to eat before or after we paint?" I ask, coming behind the stool to swoop him off while tickling his sides. He squeals just as Ivy enters the room, yawning.

"Heya, Grizzly," Ivy greets, ruffling his hair the way everyone must do. It's hard not to; Bear's sporting a thick head of silken, chocolatey waves that shine in the sun, fluffy and beautiful. Not unlike his daddy's hair.

I bring my focus back to Bear, unwilling to *think* about Hudson that way in his son's presence. And yes, I know all I've done is draw a comparison between Bear's hair and his daddy's but it doesn't take much to put me in a moany, achy place where I need to be alone to think about Hud.

I don't want to be in that headspace right now. All

squirmy in my seat while I paint with Bear, sweating, trying to regain focus and composure all the while the only thing I want to do is toss the canvas and fuck myself while screaming his daddy's name.

No.

Bear deserves better than an absent-minded horndog.

Bear deserves the world. Just like his daddy but... different.

"Painting today?" she asks him as I finish dropping his paints into his tray. I keep a plastic tray handy for when he comes over, and the rule is, anything in the tray is yours to use on your project. I hand him said tray and he clutches it to his chest like a pirate with his treasure.

"Yeah," he answers, "then we're eating lunch."

"Peanut butter and marionberry," I tell Ivy, who nods in support.

"Wow, that sounds fun. Maybe I'll come peek at your art later," she says, winking.

He twists his torso, blinking up at me with his wide, innocent eyes. "But we're paintin' a surprise, right, Dolly?"

I volley my head. "Kind of. More like, it's a puzzle we're making. And it won't make sense until all the pieces come together."

I rest my hand on his shoulder and guide him toward the back door, his little boots clunking against the hardwood. "I can't wait," he breathes, fishing around in his tray to assess what we're working with today.

Once we're in the barn and I have him set up next to me, I tell him today's paint project theme. Every time we paint together, I choose a theme, and when his piece is finished and long dried out, I add his piece of art to the greater piece I'm working on.

"Today is going to be chartreuse with moss glued over the top." I pluck a piece of crafting moss from the tray, and lift it up, holding it under my nostril. Bear giggles and swipes the moss from my hands.

"Chartoose?" he says, mimicking me by holding the moss under his nose, too.

"Chartreuse," I say, overly annunciating. He repeats it back.

"Chartreuse."

I smile. "That's right. And it's kind of a yellowy green," I explain, pointing to the place on my palette where I've begun mixing yellow ochre with toxic green, a new color I picked up at the supply store that Ivy frequents in the next town over.

He dips his brush into the mixed color we share, and smears it along his canvas carefully. "Looks like the tree by the creek."

"The weeping birch," I offer, guiding his hand slightly as he nears the canvas edge. With his small hand in mine, our connection burns through me. I'm meant to be in Bear's life, I can feel it in the way his breaths come easy around me, the syncope in our crooked grins, how in tune I am with his needs. I'm meant to be in his life, and that sureness I feel in my bones only strengthens my belief that I am meant to be Hudson's girl. *Without a doubt.*

If we weren't meant to be, he would not have moved next door. He would not ask me to babysit. His son would not like me. The universe is just not that fucked up. I refuse to believe it. Things may be complicated, but as I mentioned, I'm smart. I can sift through it. But asking me to believe that they're just people that moved next door and that everything that has and does happen between us is just a fluke? No fucking way.

After Bear finishes his piece, he asks for more paper, and I oblige, passing him at least four full sheets of thick cardstock. Though he's crazy in his designs today, lots of shooting stars and gray blobs that look like portholes to hell, I believe his attempt was to paint a creek with skipping stones. Knowing the intentions of his heart, I stash his paintings away before washing him up for lunch.

"Maybe we skip some stones before we eat?" he asks, blinking up at me with eyes I am not good at saying no to. For a moment I imagine Hudson asking me for anything, using his dark and seductive gaze as a weapon. I'd give him things I didn't even have, like bank account information, drop spots and launch codes. That's how intoxicating and penetrating his eyes are.

And his son's are not far off, though their effect on me is platonic. Still, I smirk.

"Fine, we can skip stones for an hour—it'll be our secret —but then we have to get back." I glance at the green numbers on the oven. "Shoot, by the time I feed you lunch, it'll be dinner."

He shrugs. "Aunt Ev is out tonight. That means Dad's cooking." He wrinkles his nose and drops his voice to a conspiratorial whisper. "Probably better that I'm full."

I press the back of my wrist to the underside of my nose, capturing a snort that breaks free. "Hu—" I stop myself, knowing that just his name will rile me up. "Your daddy isn't a good cook, huh?"

Bear pinches his nose in an over-the-top plug. "Stinks."

Laughing, I nod my head toward the basket lined up against the shed. "Grab the basket. We'll collect stones on the walk out there."

I've never seen the kid move so fast. He's back at my side with the empty basket dangling from his chartreuse-stained hand. "Ready?"

I nod, pulling my hair up into a messy bun on the top of my head. I knew Everly and Deuce were heading into town for a real estate appointment and dinner date today. I saw it on Hudson's calendar every week for the last month.

He forgot.

But I didn't.

It's why I'm skipping stones at the creek in one of my favorite sundresses. A dress with a slit up the right thigh, ties at the top of each shoulder, a smocked bodice to accentuate my slight curves, and in a sky blue color that would make any complexion look dreamy.

Bear and I skip stones for a solid hour before his arm and shoulder get tuckered out, and we make the walk back to my house as the sun crests in the sky. When the barn comes into sight, I see Juniper setting pillows out on a blanket underneath my favorite oak. I lift my hand to wave hello, and she does the same.

Once we're closer, Bear says quietly, "Having a sister is pretty cool, huh?"

We stop in our tracks, and I crouch to meet his eyes. In a few more years from now, he'll be taller than me. Most kids are, considering I'm just a hair taller than five feet. "Yeah, I like having sisters. Juniper and Ivy are my best friends." Half of my lips lift in a smile. "Are you thinking about wanting a brother or a sister?"

He shrugs. "Don't matter. I don't have a mama."

At that moment, Juni's bare feet appear, and I blink up at her with tears in my eyes. Poor Bear. Poor, sweet, innocent Bear.

He needs me.

I hold his hands with mine. "You have a wonderful daddy, a great aunt and a pretty darn cool guy who's gonna be your uncle." I look at my sister who quickly catches on to the tone of our talk.

"And you have Dolly, sure, but you also have me and Ivy, too." She extends her hand to Bear, and he slides his tiny one in the most mismatched handshake ever. "All you have to do is love jam. Do you love jam, Bear?"

His sadness quickly morphs into a smile. I love that about kids. How easy they can be to please. "Yes!"

She waves her arm over the picnic blanket, two sandwiches and two tall glasses of lemonade out for us. "Time to eat." She passes me a damp cloth, and I take each of Bear's hands in mine, wiping them clean as Juni presses on. "How was skipping stones?"

"I'm getting good," he starts, before taking a big bite of sandwich as he crumples to the ground, immediately comfortable on the blanket. Another large bite and he adds, "Dolly's real good, too."

I arch my eyebrow at my sister who is walking backward toward the house. "Stay and eat. You set this whole thing up," I tell her, but she waves her hand down.

"Jam is on. Enjoy." She taps her watch while looking at just me. "Soon, just so you know."

I nod.

Hudson will be over here to collect Bear soon, which means one bad thing and one good thing.

Bear will be back home, and the fun, carefree time we spent together will be over.

Bad.

Hudson will be here after a long day in the sun, grateful and exhausted—when he looks his best.

Good.

"Did you have fun today?" I ask him as he tears through the second half of his sandwich, albeit moving a bit slower. He sips from the sweating glass of lemonade.

"I had so much fun, Dolly," he says, wiping his upper lip with the back of his hand, leaving dirt there instead of lemonade. I collect the hem of my dress in my hand, leaning over the picnic to swipe at it.

"Better," I say, once I've wiped the brown away.

"Now you gotta let me pay you," Hudson says, surprising me, suddenly behind us, his deep voice ricocheting through my pussy, warmth immediately spilling out of me, seeping into my panties. Bringing my fingertips to my collarbone, I steal a deep breath before turning my hungry eyes on my favorite thing on the planet: him.

Oh god.

He looks far sexier than usual and let me tell you, when this man gets done on the ranch for the day, there isn't a sight sexier. The thick strip of dark, sweat-drenched fabric on his back makes my clit throb, and the sheen of dirt coating his rough, Herculean hands and his stubble-laden jawline... my ovaries ache, my nipples burn, and another rush of liquid has my panties completely soaked.

He raises his arm, pinching the hat from his head, gracing my eyes with a tousled, sweaty heap of soft, thick hair. He strokes a hand through it, smiling. "You know, because of your dress." He motions to his upper lip. "I saw you cleanin' up Bear."

My heart is fucking racing. His tone is low and rumbly because it's the end of the day. He always sounds sexiest in the late afternoon. I know this.

But tonight, for some reason or other, I swear on Joe Goldberg himself, Hudson seems to be slightly... flirty with me.

I shift on the ground, my saturated panties making the bottoms of my ass cheeks cool from the continual wetness. I wiggle into the blanket a little, knowing if he pulls any gentleman moves and asks to help me up that he'll see the effect he has on me... or think I peed myself.

My mind goes swimmy and hot from the sheer proximity of him. Not to mention, I've been taking care of his son all day, faintly smelling traces of Hud off and on the entire afternoon, clenching and unclenching to both torture *and* quench myself as I dreamt of being railed and bred by him. I blink up at him, realizing I'm hornier than I've ever been. I'm literally one wink away from humping the fucking picnic blanket.

His Adam's apple bobs. "Thanks again. I wish you'd let me pay you."

I swallow, recovering as quickly as possible so he doesn't realize I was staring, dreaming of his dick, pulsing and throbbing, ejaculating deep inside me without protection.

I want his babies.

I want him forever.

I love him so much.

"Nah," I wave off. "I like you enough, you don't have to pay," I tease playfully as I dunk my brush into more paint, staying seated. If I appear to still be painting, he won't ask me to stand.

See, I'm smart on my toes.

Hudson turns, and my mind gets to work. I swallow, jotting it all down mentally.

I'll give him about two minutes before I make my way around the side of his house, to the yard where the garden is tucked. It's also at a perfect location to see in a window near the laundry room, giving a peek of the hallway and ultimately the main living space.

I'll go there first.

I'll wait there for an hour if need be, and watch.

But the mental list destructs, erupting into a million pieces as he faces me again, apparently no longer leaving. God, I want him to stay. I want him to crawl over me, unzip those filthy fucking jeans and slide that fat, thick cock of his so deep inside me that my toes curl and my eyes roll to heaven. I want to see God when he fucks me, and I know I will.

Bear, who has been running sluggish circles in the yard adjacent, getting out his "daddy's home" wiggles, comes crashing into Hudson's leg.

"Thank you for watching me," he says, making Hud's eyebrows rise. Of course he is saying thank you, he's polite and well mannered, just like his daddy.

"You taught him well," I say, keeping my voice soft, just a bit huskier than I'd use in the bedroom. If he wants to hear that voice, he needs to take me there. "Thanks for painting with me," I smile, ruffling Bear's hair a little.

"It's a secret," he tells Hudson quite seriously, making my heart skip a tiny beat. He's so adorable, and the thing with kids is that... their emotions are out there for anyone to see. They haven't learned the curse of masking quite yet.

I *know* he enjoys his time with me, I can see he's genuine.

I hope his daddy sees that same bare truth in me.

Hudson smiles at his son, and my ribs grow tight at their connection. My breasts ache for his hands, hands that I'm currently staring at like a starved woman as he connects with his son after being gone all day.

After a moment, my eyes find his. "Thank you again."

I smile easily. "You're so welcome."

They turn and leave, and I sit on the ground for ten minutes, clinging to my composure. We had a *moment*.

Fuck that.

We had a *series* of moments. I won't gaslight myself out of them. There's a tiny, itty-bitty spark there.

I see it. I feel it.

It's tiny but burning intensely between my thighs, and I can't wait for him to drop the match, to explode, to turn into something so big and grand it fills the darkest night sky, forcing onyx to vibrant embers.

That's how it feels when I come for him.

After collecting everything from the ground, I head to the barn and wash my brushes out with the hose, then put all of my supplies away accordingly. Carefully, I slide the rolling wall away from the back of the barn, exposing the piece Bear has been unknowingly working on. With steady hands, I place today's small canvas against the wood and drive three long nails through it. Replacing the dummy wall, I leave the barn and head inside for a shower and dinner.

Juniper made beef stew, and while it tasted slightly different than usual, I think it was the full bottle of port wine she dumped in instead of her usual half bottle. I don't think you can get drunk from wine in beef stew, but conversation with my sisters over a warm meal after a long day with Bear and so much engagement with Hudson—I feel a little drunk. My cheeks are sore from how much I've smiled, and in my belly, a hopeful happiness is blooming.

I'm closer to having him than ever before.

After Ivy and I assembly line the dishes, I head to my room just a few minutes before Bear's bedtime. I call Hudson's house, using *67 to block my phone number. He answers, saying hello three times before hanging up. His frustrated exhale between hello number two and hello number three have me touching myself for the third time today.

Holding my breath, I dial him again, holding my orgasm until he answers. As soon as he lets loose an aggravated hello, I shatter into a million pieces, squealing into my hand, gushing around my fingers buried deep between my legs.

He hangs up, and I fall asleep almost as soon as my head hits the pillow.

Because my dreams are finally starting to come true.

I can feel it.

six

HARD-ON BEGONE.

Hudson

It's one of my favorite sights.

I always thought it would be, and then for a while the sight made me curl in on myself and gasp on panic and anxiety. Once that stage passed, with time of course, I started to like it again.

And now, years later, as I said, the sea of white canopies spread over my property is one of my favorite sights.

I built this with my own two hands as a way to get to know the people in town, as a way to build a familiar community for my child, and to have something that we can do together as a community, for ourselves and one another.

With my hands on my hips, my hat firmly planted on my head, I take in the landscape of my creation. So many townspeople are vendors now that most of the town is likely here today. I know for a darn fact that the Feed 'n' Seed and Goode's Diner both close for the farmers market.

Familiar faces with a variety of goods, it's a mix I like. There's a stand with pickled peppers and flavored vinegars and oils, Juniper's stand for Juni's Jams, open jars of flavorful spreads waiting to be tasted, sliced baguettes and fresh fruits for dipping. With her long hair swept into a neat bun, she waves and I wave back.

Next to her is a woman who sells crocheted pot holders and trivets made from alpaca yarn from her alpaca farm. There are tables with keychains that double as emergency window breaking tools, gourmet chocolates filled with fancy booze and fruit, an entire station dedicated to fudge and its many, many variants. There are face painting stations, booths that sell potatoes on sticks, churros, turkey legs, handsewn women's clothing, used books, and so much goddamn more.

All of these people have come here to share their Saturdays, spending hard-earned money, trying new things, laughing, chatting, getting a pulse on their people, sampling new items and enjoying themselves. I don't take that lightly.

I created this space, and I take pride in being the epicenter of their happiness for one day a week.

It fulfills me, but I don't know if it makes me happy. Not in the way I'm starting to think that I need.

Snagging my phone from my back pocket, I swipe open the camera just as Bear comes tearing through two stands, the canopies rattling as he leaps out on the path. Orange and black painted onto one cheek, the other cheek coated in red paint. He pounces, beaming up at me, a little bit of sampled fudge in the corner of his mouth.

"What'ya get this week?" I ask with a grin on my face as Bear proudly tilts his head side to side, pausing to let me snap a photo.

"Tiger," he says, of the glittery cartoon tiger on his right cheek. "And a heart."

I laugh at that, stroking my thumb along the edge of the heart to see what I'm up against later when I have to scrub this mess off. He's never gotten any face painting with red before. I lick my thumb and swipe again, making Bear wince away a little.

"Sorry," I tell him, not wanting to be too uncool. With just one parent, it's important I try very hard to be the best of everything. Because that's what Bear deserves. It's not his fault Tessa left. "Well, you know the drill. Aunt Ev and I are setting up at the very end. Come and sit with us once you're done checking out the booths."

Bear keeps me up to date on what vendors change from week to week, and though I never thought I'd be curious, I've grown to enjoy his updates. I actually look forward to them. He runs off, and my brows pinch as he passes the "make your own bottle of colored sand" station run by the librarian, and sails right on by the "build your own smoothie" stand, too.

I scratch under my hat, my head suddenly hot and itchy as I wait to see what is better or more important than a milkshake very thinly veiled as a smoothie and a bottle of layered sand with a face glued on.

That's when I see her.

Dolly.

It was hard to see her before, crouched down next to her canopied booth, arms open, waiting for my son.

There's that shimmy of guilt running down my spine again.

I should turn away but I can't take my eyes off the details of the situation. She doesn't just hold him in a hug and pat his back. Her fingertips are *sunk* into him, her eyes are closed as they embrace, and when they part, both of them are beaming.

She's a beautiful girl, inside and out. She's sweet and kind, creative and funny, and she loves Bluebell and Bear, and comes from a good family. I drag my closed fist up my sternum, trying to alleviate some of the sudden tightness. But it doesn't help, because it's then I realize the tightness isn't in my chest.

I pull my hat down, clearing my throat, trying to recenter myself so I don't look like I *really* love this farmers market. But before I can panic, Ev appears at my side, the crook of my elbow in her hand.

Hard-on, begone.

"There you are," she comments sweetly in that voice she uses on the phone or for people at the checkout. I blink at her, my eyes burning to flick back to the moment between Bear and Dolly, but I don't.

"Why are you using that voice?" I question, looking down at where she tenderly grasps me. "Why are you…" My question trails off as another woman appears at my sister's side, one I've never met. She's wearing a nervous smile. Come to think of it, so is Everly.

Goddamn it. I have never, ever asked to be set up. In fact, I've asked *not* to be set up.

I look around, feeling like the entire farmers market is

aware of the impending awkwardness, but the only eyes I catch are Deuce's. He winces, his broad shoulders rising and falling in a *sorry, man* type of shrug.

When he's officially my brother-in-law, I expect more loyalty than this. Also, I'm definitely holding this against him for at least six months.

My eyes come back to Everly, then to the smiling brunette at her side. She extends a hand to me, her smile unusually large.

"Hudson Gray, in the flesh," she says, shaking my hand like she's got something to prove.

I chuckle awkwardly because I do not like weird introductions. You say your name, I'll say mine, that's how it goes. "That's me," I say, my lips twitching in an effort to hold my phony smile. I also don't like being around people that I have to be phony around. I'm learning that this second as the sun beats against my back and the brunette is now blocking my view of Dolly and Bear.

"I'm Tiffani," she finally says, "I went to college with Everly. I just left my law firm in the city and decided I'd start my life over out here in the country." She's still shaking my hand as she tells me things I did not ask to know, "I had no idea Everly and her *very handsome* older brother lived in Bluebell." Finally, she releases my hand and looks around the farmers market at the near hundreds of canopies. Her hand comes to her collarbone, where the tips of her long, pink fingernails clack against her beaded necklace. "This must cost a ton of money to put on. There are so many vendors and accouterments here." She says that sentence like she's talking about a slow-cooked brisket, and I don't like that. "Looks like you're the king of this place."

I don't know what it is about the way she puts those words together, but I don't like it. She smiles up at me, fanning herself with a linen accordion fan, one she bought from Mabel Beacon, an older lady who loves Gray Farms.

"Oh, I won't go so far as to say that," I say, stepping back slightly, trying to find an exit. I look for Deuce, but he's moved from where he was.

Thankfully, Everly loops her arm through Tiffani's, patting her hand where they link. "I'm going to go show her around but she just had to meet the man who hosts the Bluebell every week."

"It was nice meeting you, Tiffani," I say, tipping my head with my hat pinched in my hand.

"The pleasure was most certainly mine," she dotes, blinking too much.

They stroll off, and when I look over at Dolly's booth, she's peering down at one of her birthday cards with one of the seniors in the community, smiling as she points to the little red balloon painted on the back, above her logo. The old woman smiles, nodding, and I watch as she slips the card into a paper sack, handing it to the woman.

Bear is inside Dolly's booth, sitting at a table in the back, his little legs swinging like wild beneath. His tongue is curled over his top lip, brow furrowed as he focuses on the tiny canvas in front of him. Near his elbow is a palette of paint, and in his fist is a brush.

Something about him always trying new things with her, being so comfortable with her, and the way she glances back to check on him every few minutes, despite the fact she's inundated with customers, it's *nice*.

"You know," Everly says, popping up again out of

nowhere like a goddamn jack-in-the-box. "You could've been nicer to Tiffani."

"I need to put a bell on you. That way I can hear you coming."

After rolling her eyes, she folds her arms over her chest. "Why weren't you more friendly?"

I press a hand to my chest. "I was friendly. What was I gonna do? Hug her goodbye?" Goddamn, I can't stop looking up at Dolly, and I don't know why. Everly snaps, collecting my attention offensively.

"Ask her out, Hudson. She likes you. She's new to town. She could use... *a friend.*" And when I tell you that my stomach actually goes upside down as my baby sister wiggles her eyebrows at me, implying that I should not just take Tiffani out but have sex with her, I am not lying.

"Don't be vulgar, it's gross," I tell her, towing the line of *what happens in a bedroom, stays in a bedroom.* I want to teach my son that talking about what you do with your partner is tacky and small, therefore, I give the same lesson to Ev.

She's never given a shit about my lessons, though. From the time she was four, and I told her taking her training wheels off her bike too soon would result in an accident that made her too scared to try again.

She still doesn't ride a bike.

"Hud, I'm just saying, it's been four years since..."

Since my wife fucked my best friend and ran off with him, leaving me with our infant son, undeveloped property, and a dream I only partially shared. "I *know* how long it's been," I respond gruffly.

Ignoring sexual urges and needs, at first, was a challenge. But I'm a professional now, ignoring the achy hardness I wake with, denying the weighty steel that begs for me in the evening when the world is quiet. I'm not saying I'm a saint or a priest, but as a whole, I've learned to live without love and orgasms.

"I'm fine and I don't need to be hooked up," I tell her, meeting and holding her gaze to impart the *'do not fucking do that ever again'* sentiment.

"Just... think about it. For me?" She touches my arm again and I shake it.

"Don't get all *Little House on the Prairie* just because you reconnected with some college friend," I warn her, suddenly very grouchy.

The fact that Ev continues to smirk at me is also annoying. "I'll play the card if I have to."

I narrow my gaze on her. "Don't."

Her smirk widens to a full-on grin. "I help you with Bear so much, the least you could do for me is take Tiffani out once or twice."

She's warned me teasingly in the past that her helping me with Bear is only because she wants to have a card to play against me later in life. She loves Bear like he's her own, but right now, I'm wishing that I could rip that card to shreds.

"First it's take her out, now it's once or twice?" I shake my head, scratching at the back of my neck as uneasiness swims through me. I don't typically feel uneasy, either. "I don't know, Ev. She really didn't seem like... *my type.*"

Her hands go to her hips, and I know I'm in trouble. "Oh really?" Her tone is biting. Yep, I'm in trouble. "And how would you know anything about her and whether or not she's *the great Hudson Gray's type?* Hmm?" She pushes her finger into my chest, scolding me, and my eyes veer off, hunting for Deuce, but that shithead is eating fudge with a WWII veteran.

"Deuce agrees," she says, clearly reading my mind. "He thinks you need a woman."

"I don't care if Deuce agrees," I tell her, though in truth, Ev and Deuce are my family. I do care what they think, even if I say I don't. I don't want them living their lives with good old Hudson needing help all the time because he was too brokenhearted to move on.

That isn't even true.

My heart healed a long time ago.

But I'm a father. And a ranch owner. A business owner. I have commitments that matter, and come first, and there's not a lot of room to find love in that equation.

But that's bullshit too because I would make time for it. If I had it.

"Go out with her," she says, slapping a piece of paper into my palm. I look down to see Tiffani's name scrawled across a torn piece of paper, along with her phone number and two hearts. I look up at my sister.

"She drew hearts next to her number." I frown. "That's stupid."

My sister wastes no time in responding. "You're stupid. Who cares if she drew hearts. So she likes hearts. You have something against heart doodles?" The veins in her temples pulse. I fight a smirk. Even at my age, riling up my sister just... it makes me a little happy. *Can't help it.*

"I may have something against heart doodles, yeah," I reply cooly, shoving the number into my pocket so I don't have to look at it. Heart doodles are stupid.

"Hudson," she starts, all the frustration and contention in her voice gone, leaving behind a softness full of guilt. For me, though, not her. "I want us to live our lives side by side. I want more for you than this."

I grow prickly from her words. The truth makes me grouchy when I'm not looking to hear it. "I'm happy."

Her hand on my forearm gives me pause. We aren't touchy-feely. Everly isn't even touchy-feely with Bear. It's just not her style. Wasn't our mom's style either.

It was Tessa's style. I always loved that about her the most. How warm and loving she was with small kids. I thought it was a sure sign she'd make a great mom.

But you gotta *stay* to be a good mama.

"You're happy with what you know. But the unknown holds so much more for you, Hud." She lets go of my arm and steps away, turning to go meet up with Deuce. "Go out with her for me, okay?"

I glare at her, keeping my sight pinned to the back of her head as she trots to her fiancé, who is at the Gray Farms booth. I don't want to go out with Tiffani, but I can't deny what Ev is saying. And I don't want her getting married, starting her new life, all the while worrying about me.

I'm the older brother. She shouldn't worry about me. She's done so much to help me in the last four years, she deserves her time.

I know then I'll call the woman who likes heart doodles.

I'll do it because I love my family, and I want them to be happy.

I just told Ev *I'm* happy. I'm not really.

I'm glad to have the market, and I'm glad to have the loyal people in this town. But that doesn't mean I'm happy.

Bear comes crashing into me, his little hands damp, smelling like mint and rubbing alcohol. He holds up a tiny canvas, waving it in front of me. "Daddy! Look!"

I take the piece from him, holding it with both hands, the brim of my hat casting shade over it. Though it's abstract due to the artist being four, I know just what it is. And I realize the guidance it took to get this painting to look like what it is. I look up, smiling at my son before my eyes go to Designed by Dolly, her hand-painted greeting card booth. But she's not there.

"Dolly helped me! It's the creek. Can you tell?" Bear asks, stepping onto my feet to gain a few inches, his hands gripping my forearm to steady himself. I sift my hand through his soft hair, sun-warmed to the touch.

"I love it. Did you tell Dolly thank you?" I ask, my eyes veering back to her booth. She's still not there, but there are people around, sifting through cards in plastic sleeves, chatting with smiles on their faces. Up pops a head of jet-black hair, and a moment later, Ivy's blue eyes are on mine. She smiles, then returns her focus to the customers.

Maybe Dolly popped out to get something to eat. I know she loves funnel cakes.

Why am I looking for a twenty-year-old girl right now?

"Daddy?" Bear calls from below. "Give it here," he begs, reaching for the canvas.

I hand it to him. "Take that inside. Put it in your room. It's too special to be out here."

Bear sighs, staring dreamily at the painting. "Yeah, it's too special." He turns, headed toward the house with his creek painting.

I'd love to tell Dolly thank you, and I'd love to thank her

again for taking Bear at such short notice the other day. But as I glance back to her booth, feeling like a goddamn creep for checking in on a girl that, *in theory*, could be my daughter, I see that it's still just Ivy.

I walk around the market for the next few hours, checking in with folks, catching up on people's lives, tasting the food, and have a few beers. Eventually, I make it back to the Gray Farms booth, selling the last few bottles of flavored milk.

As the market wraps up, I shake hands with most of the town, waving them off as they head up the road. Still, I'm hyperaware that Dolly never came back today.

And even though I shouldn't, I wonder where she went... *and why.*

seven

I'LL MAKE SURE OF IT.

Dolly

As soon as I saw the way the woman sidled up to Ev and Hudson, I knew why she was there. I'd never seen her before today's farmers market, and that was my first uneasy feeling.

Not a lot of people visit our town, and none that do visit come organically. They either have family or a friend, or some other reason, to come to Bluebell.

And it's one thing to come into my small town and visit my farmers market like you're one of us, but it's quite another to visit and ask out the town's most prominent dairy farmer.

Under the guise of wanting to try Gray Farms's new butterscotch-flavored milk, I snuck out of my booth and visited Deuce, asking him about the woman with his fiancé.

Tiffani Ledbetter. She went to college with Everly up in Northern California six or so years ago, and moved here randomly for a change of scenery after getting burnt out on corporate law and the city.

Sounded pretty fucking convenient to me.

I texted Ivy from behind the booth, begging her to come work Designed by Dolly for the rest of the afternoon. Shaking, cold sweat sheeting my back, I promised to owe her, and once she came and tagged in, I went straight up the drive, past Hudson's, to our place, and locked myself away in my room.

After burying my face into a pillow and screaming until my head hurt, taking a baseball bat to my unfinished canvases out in the barn, then glaring at Tiffani through the blinds in our kitchen, I returned to my room with a cup of tea and resolve to cut the emotion, and get to work.

And now, with my laptop on my thighs, my nostrils flaring, anger and impatience creeping through my veins like a slow drip narcotic, I'm learning all there is to know about the woman who *dares* to challenge my claim on Hudson as my soulmate.

I saw him stuff the paper into his pocket.

He took her number.

But I don't blame him. His sister does so much for them and she was clearly pushing him. My man likely felt pressured. But that's why *he has me*. As soon as he lets me in, I'll make sure everyone else stays out.

Opening four new tabs, I start my research.

I did this to Tessa, too, when they first moved in and I

realized some pregnant woman married my soulmate. I researched every detail about her but it was all for naught, since she took off anyway.

But this Tiffani Ledbetter person.

I saw the way she ogled my Hudson. I recognize that horny, *fuck me and come on my face and into my open mouth* gaze.

That's *my* fucking gaze.

It's proprietary.

Quickly, in the first tab, I type her name into the People Pages, a generalized phone book listing that kicks back most home addresses for the name you give, unless the civilian has paid to protect that information. Almost no one does that, so after typing in Tiffani Ledbetter Bluebell CA, I spend a handful of minutes sifting through the results until I find *the* Tiffani who also lived in Northern California. I save all four of her former address listings, then look each of them up on Google Maps.

The first one is an apartment, and the building is run-down, and up north, and likely where she lived as a student. My ignited nerves settle a little as I move to the next street view. The second location is also an apartment, this one not any better, despite the fact the years listed were post-graduation.

Maybe she's a saver.

Though her Tory Burch sandals in dusty gravel at a farmers market don't exactly scream *coupon clipper*.

The next location is a home, but the listing shows various inhabitants, and is located in a small, desert town in Nevada. When I look at the street view photos, there's something about the home that looks *strange*. Additions have been made, with an entire extra wing added haphazardly to the side of the home, eating up most of the driveway. On the street out front are bumper-to-bumper cars, as if this photo was taken during a party. But when I enhance the photo, there's a visible layer of dust on some of the windshields. As if they've been stagnant there for some time.

The final location is actually in the town she said she left, and I don't know why that surprises me but I have to admit, I thought it was a lie. Something about this woman that comes into a close-knit community in a small town and thinks she can just swoop in and date the best, handsomest, sexiest, sweetest, most devoted man? I don't like her, and I don't like her angle.

Though the last home is small and part of a duplex, it is neat and cute, with blue shutters and a large ficus on the covered porch. It's cute and nice.

Why couldn't she stay there?

I replay the small bit of information acquired from Deuce, and in the next open tab, I type in the name of the college she attended with Everly.

I know what year Everly graduated, and so, if she and Tiffani went to school together, I should be able to find Tiffani within a four-year range on the alumni listings.

It takes just ten minutes to search for her name or potentially misspelled variants of her name. I throw her a bone and search through not four years but *eight* years of alumni listings. I found Everly but there is no record of Tiffani Ledbetter graduating from this college.

Interesting.

Then again, Deuce didn't say they graduated together,

only that they attended. I keep the fact that she didn't graduate in my back pocket as I move on to the next open tab.

Quickly, I type in "Tiffani Ledbetter" followed by all major social media platforms. I roll my eyes when I discover her Instagram account, the profile picture one of her laughing, veneers on display, mouth open, head tipped back. No one gets their photo taken organically while they're laughing, but to be cracking up by yourself and then take a photo? No fucking way. Not to mention, hysterical laughter isn't pretty. And this is a gorgeous photo.

I take my anger out on my keyboard, slamming my fingers against the keys as I move to the tab with her Facebook page open.

The profile picture is the same, but the background image is of a law firm, a proudly displayed banner of her thriving, impressive career as a lawyer.

You can't get into law school with an undergraduate degree, though, so I'm immediately skeptical. Opening another tab on Google, I type in the law firm, and when the page loads, I click the Meet Us tab. Scrolling through, I don't find Tiffani, but then again, maybe they're quick to draw on updating their website?

One more open tab and I'm typing in the Wayback Machine, entering in the law firm website. I wait for the results to generate, and when it does, the site gives me a variety of snapshots throughout the last few years. I click one from the middle of last year, when she likely would've been working there. According to her employment history on her LinkedIn, which I pulled up while the WayBackMachine was loading, she didn't leave that firm until a few months back, so in theory, she should be on the site.

When the snapshot from last year finally loads, I click the same tab, and wait as the old listing of lawyers populates.

There is no Tiffani Ledbetter.

Backing out, I end up spending a full hour going through every single snapshot of the legal firm site over the last year, and there isn't one single time that I find her name.

So she's lied about graduating college maybe, and she's definitely lied about where she worked.

How could she possibly be telling the truth about coming here? I don't believe her and I don't trust her.

Back on her Instagram, I sift through her photos, finding that two years ago she was in a relationship with a man named Mark Leary, a businessman with very deep pockets and a ton of connections.

I think the deep pockets is what she's after.

Slowly, the pieces fall into place.

Her sights are on Gray for his money. I cannot be convinced otherwise.

From her Facebook account, I save photos she's posted of her office from an album titled "Where A Law Firm Partner Works". Her office is huge, the entire back wall made of floor-to-ceiling windows and a grand desk with a massive, tufted leather chair tucked into it.

Squinting, I analyze the four photos posted of the office space but find no personal identifiers. There's no nameplate on her desk. No family photos. No ugly orchid in a stupid pot sitting in the window. Nothing that makes the office personal.

Opening up TinEye, I put the first general image of the

office into the uploader, and hit submit. A moment later, the generation is complete.

A smile twists my lips as I read.

Over 538 results! Searched over 65.7 billion images in 3.0 seconds.

Scrolling down, I find that Tiffani Ledbetter's office is actually a staged office, used by marketing companies, stock photo sites, and phonies just like Tiffani all across the world.

Where a law firm partner works, my ass.

Hudson is a good man through and through. He'll figure out that Tiffani is... *not for him.*

He has to. He will not fall for some lying money-grubbing phony over his soulmate. No way.

I'll make sure of it.

I CAN'T PERV ON THE BABYSITTER. I'M NOT THAT GUY.

Hudson

I had no plans on spending my Friday night anywhere but on the couch, my boy in my arms, the newest Disney movie on the TV, cocoa in mugs, popcorn all over as we relax. I'd sink into the couch, letting my aching body rest after a long week of work, and Bear would melt into me, the only time he truly lets me cuddle him.

As a thirty-eight-year-old man, I don't think much of cuddling. Fucking? Yeah, that crosses my mind, but cuddling? Never.

Unless it's with my boy.

A mother would cuddle their son. A loving, warm mother would, at least. And because Tessa left, it's my privilege to cuddle him. Show him the softness and warmth that children usually find in their mothers. Not saying men can't be soft and tender—they can. That's fine. Deuce has that side in him.

It's harder for me. But I've grown comfortable in sharing that side of myself with my son. For my son.

But tonight, there will be no slowed evening, comfortable cuddles, and scattered snacks.

My fingers twist the top button on my shirt, but it leaves me feeling strangled, so I unbutton it. Taking a step back, I peer uncomfortably at my reflection.

Dark jeans, a nice white button-up that I haven't worn since I went to Deuce and Ev's engagement party last year, and my nice black boots. Ones that haven't trekked through cow patties and horseshit. Freshly shaved, I pull my hand down my face, igniting the scent of the aftershave smeared into my skin. I wear aftershave every day, but I usually shave in the morning. Smelling it at night just feels... *weird*.

I'm a creature of habit, and I realize finding someone to share mine and Bear's life with requires breaking the habit, but I don't want to. Not right now. Not yet.

And yet.. I do want someone. I do want to break the habit. Just not with Tiffani.

But I promised Ev. And she deserves her life. Hell, Deuce too.

"You look great," my sister says, stepping into my bedroom since the door is always open. Another great thing about ignoring all of your primal male needs is that you never get caught doing anything unsavory by your little sister who is at your house as much as you are.

"I don't want to go," I say again, angry at myself for not

being able to hold it in. "Sorry," I add, wincing. We turned it into a double date to take the pressure off, and I'm glad. I don't want to have a meal with Tiffani Ledbetter, but it makes it slightly less terrible if Ev and Deuce are there.

"Just… keep an open mind, okay?" She smiles, smoothing her hands down my shoulders, taking a small wrinkle from my shirt with her. "Tiffani's nice."

"You went to State with her?" I ask, trying to remember the connection again. "I don't remember meeting her when I'd visit." I visited my sister in college several times, conveniently when she needed help moving, putting something together or repairing something she broke. I was always glad to do it and show up for her the way our dad would've had he still been around.

"Yeah," she says, tucking hair behind her ear. "We had different majors, but we were in the same graduating class. We even had a few classes together."

I nod. "Okay."

My sister folds her arms over her chest, narrowing her eyes at me. I shake my head. "I don't know why I'm in trouble," I admit, buckling my belt. "But quit giving me that look."

Ev flops down on the edge of my bed, exasperated. "You didn't ask me a single question about her!"

My brows pull together. "I just did. I asked if you went to college with her."

She smacks the mattress. "You already knew that! You didn't ask anything new! Like… What did she do after graduation? What does she do for a living? What's she like?"

I turn away from the mirror, smoothing my hands through the sides of my hair. I need a haircut. What Ev has previously noted as the *"Henry Cavill coif"* is now moving into unacceptable territory for a man my age.

Ev rattles a list of things to ask Tiffani at dinner, as if I've never been around other human beings, and I let her go while my mind drifts to my last haircut.

I pulled my hat off in the barn one day, sifting my hand through my long, sweat-laden hair. Dolly had been playing hide-and-seek with Bear, and she popped out from behind a bale of hay, her finger pressed to the center of her lips. My heart raced, and though I never admitted it to myself, I don't think it was because she startled me.

The way her eyes raked over me that day, it was unlike any way I'd ever been looked at before. It was like she was taking me in and saving me off as a file in her brain to revisit later. And before I could feel guilty about liking it, she whispered, "After hide-and-seek, I can give you a trim." Her tongue slid along her bottom lip as she added, "You know, if you want it off your neck."

I don't know why but right then, with nineteen-year-old Dolly crouched behind a bale of hay in overalls, a long blue ribbon in her ponytail, I envisioned her hand curling the back of my neck, bringing our faces together.

I let her cut my hair. And that was also the last time I gave in to my urges, spilling weeks down the shower drain.

All from the soft fluttering of her fingertips against my neck, the gentle grazing along my scalp, and the tender way she stroked my skin to cast off the trimmings.

"Are you listening?" Ev asks, getting to her feet. If we were in a movie, I think my chest would be full of smoking holes from her laser glare.

I push Dolly from my mind, because I *should not* be

thinking of her. She's so young. But more so, I'm about to see her because she agreed to watch Bear tonight.

"I'm listening." I lift my hands in innocence. "I'll ask her questions, okay?"

Ev sighs as Deuce and Bear come into my room, Bear on his shoulders, ducking to enter. "We ready to roll or what, my people?" Deuce offers as Bear tugs at his long hair to hold on.

"Ready," I say, lifting my son from his shoulders. "I'll take him over."

Ev hooks a thumb toward the open bedroom door, where the hallway leads to the living room. "She's here. I asked her to watch him here tonight, since he'll need to go to sleep. Figured that would be better."

Sweat forms beneath my arms, and the back of my neck grows hot. I was just thinking about Dolly, and now I feel guilty knowing she's just a few feet away.

And strangely, my cock thickens a little at the mention of her name.

"Fine, that's fine," I say as I clear my throat. I hold my son's hand as we filter out of my room, finding a smiling Dolly standing in the center of the living room with her hands behind her back.

"Hello again, Grizzly," she beams, looking directly at my son, like greeting him is the most important thing. And I like that. But I can't deny that I suddenly find myself liking her eyes on me, when they do come.

"Have fun on your date tonight." She smiles as she says it, but it doesn't reach her eyes. What's that about, I wonder. Maybe she had plans tonight and felt guilty turning me down?

"I'm sorry if you had plans tonight—" I start, but am cut off by her response, which stops my heart for a moment.

"There is nowhere I'd rather be on a Friday night than in this house, with this little boy." She smiles at Bear who rushes through the room, crashing into her with an open-armed hug. Whispering, he looks up, asking, "Can we skip stones tonight?'

I don't know what she answers, because my brain goes into a temporary state of suspension.

There is nowhere I'd rather be on a Friday night than in this house, with this little boy.

Truth held her voice steady and solid, and the way she always embraces my son only speaks to the authenticity of her words. Adjusting my collar, I stroke my pulse in my throat, finding it chaotic and quick. I watch Dolly, whose golden hair is down around her shoulders, damp and drying. She just showered before she came here.

I turn away, shoving my wallet into my back pocket as I internally chastise myself for thinking of her in the shower.

What in the world has gotten into me?

Fuck.

Ev is right, though as my sister she's not gonna want to hear what exactly she's right about. I don't know about needing a relationship, but I do need to start *seeing* women.

All these things I'm thinking about Dolly are a direct result of not being laid in a long time. And all the ignoring I've been doing of those needs... It's catching up to me. *Clearly.*

Because I know I have no business eyeing a girl like Dolly. Hell, when I got my driver's license and took my horse

Dixon out for a ride, she was an *infant* just gurgling and crying.

I need to get laid.

I need to reroute my brain so that I don't end up mentally defiling the gorgeous young babysitter from next door.

"Ready," I tell Ev and Deuce, who are whispering and hugging, something they've been doing more and more as the wedding date approaches. "All right, love birds, are we gonna go?"

Ev giggles, turning to face Dolly. "Thanks so much for coming here, and for doing bedtime."

Dolly smiles as she opens a bag of goodies at the kitchen table, Bear's hands dunking inside immediately. "Of course. You know you can always rely on me," she says, speaking to Ev while her eyes come to mine. "Always."

Needful, heavy, all-consuming heat wraps my spine, and I pull open the door to take advantage of the cool air. "Thanks, Dolly," I call, having to put effort into my tone sounding even keel.

Ev and Deuce follow me out, and fifteen minutes later, the four of us are parked in a booth at the diner, Tiffani sitting next to my sister but directly across from me. I wish she would've sat next to me because I'd much rather watch Deuce deep throat his chili dog than stare at a woman I don't know while she envisions what my cock looks like as she tries to impress me with shit I couldn't give a fuck less about.

When we arrived, she was standing near the hostess station. Tight blue jeans and tall leather boots eating up her calves, a fitted turtleneck giving away her shape and cup size, Tiffani's hair shone beneath the bright diner lights. She smiled and we exchanged a hug, I told her she looked nice, and then we sat down.

I've managed to ask all of the questions that Ev prompted me with, and in my mind, when I envisioned this date, I thought as I asked the questions, I'd slowly become more interested. I figured by the end of the night, I'd have laughed more than I thought, spoken more than I planned, and had a better time than I ever imagined. I envisioned my sister punching my bicep, saying, "I told you."

Except, the more Tiffani talks, the more I find my mind drifting to Dolly.

I wonder what she and Bear are doing right now. I think she brought her paints, and I remember the painting of the creek last Saturday. I love that she knows what matters to him and helps him create art around it. It's thoughtful and sweet, but that's her.

"And that's when I realized, marital law is just... *not for me*," Tiffani says, slicing her hand through the air to show her absolution on the matter. "And I know, years of law school down the drain is crazy but... I don't want to be jaded," she says to Ev and Deuce as her eyes lift to mine. "I don't want to not believe in love."

I have never wanted to roll my eyes so hard.

If I've mislabeled Tiffani Ledbetter and she actually is just a single woman looking to revamp her life and add love? Fine. I'm wrong.

But everything about her screams insincere, from her overly white veneers to her too clean boots.

I don't miss the way her eyes linger on my lips when I speak, either. She wants me to notice, too, and I don't like that. I've never been attracted to women who are desperate for my attention. Tessa was that way when we met. And that didn't end so well.

The opportunity that she's looking for, though, despite her corny ramblings on love, is pretty obvious.

She wants to fuck me.

No matter how long it's been, I know the look. I know what the subtle bite of her bottom lip means, I know that adjusting the heart on her sterling silver necklace is meant to draw my eyes to her breasts, and I know the slide of her boot up my calf isn't an accident, either.

I've never been a man who enjoys a casual fuck. I've done it, sure, but it doesn't offer much fulfillment to me. But it has been a long time.

Dolly flashes through my mind again, causing my spine to jolt slightly, because when I see her smile, my balls tingle a little. I reach into my pocket and slide out my phone, looking to the table. "I'm gonna see if Bear's all good."

But when I slip my hand in my jacket pocket, I find my phone and a small piece of paper. I pull it out and Ev, who is watching me, snatches the paper before I can see.

"Aww," she chides, pressing her hand to her chest. "How cute is this."

I take the paper back and find a small drawing, done by Bear, with the help of Dolly. They're painting together, and below are the scribbled words, "Have fun. We miss you, Daddy."

My chest tightens at the sight, and I blink away the immediate heat that forms behind my eyes.

Deuce leans over, peering at the drawing. "Ahh, *the kids did it.* Cute."

Kids. He means Bear and Dolly, because he views Dolly as a kid. I know she's legally an adult but the fact that my family views her as youthful and childlike makes my gut churn with self-loathing and disgust for thinking about her the last few days.

I shove the phone and art back into my pocket. "I'll check on them later," I say, smiling at Tiffani.

I don't love Tiffani.

But I need to have sex.

I can't perv on the babysitter. I'm not that guy.

nine

Dolly

The credits roll as Bear hides his yawn in a couch pillow. "What next?" He bounces on the cushions, onto his knees, eyes wide with excitement despite the sleepiness that hangs in light bags beneath.

Bear gets up early. I know this because I have taken note of their daily routine for the last five years. Ever since he turned one, his bedroom light comes on around 5:30 in the morning every day. He's an early riser, but likely because his daddy needs to be out on the land before the sun is up.

Ranch families are early to bed because of how early they are to rise, so even though Bear is still plucky, I know he must actually be tired. Tonight he's in cowboy pajamas, a hundred little cowboys in various stages of bull riding printed all over on top of the deep blue flannel. They're adorable, and as I take a bit of his sleeve in my fingers, tugging gently, desperation washes over me.

I want to fold those little cowboy pajamas. I want to be the one whose fulfillment comes from carefully washing, folding and putting away Bear's laundry, so that when he gets out of his bath each night, everything he needs is carefully put just where it belongs.

I want to be the one to read him a bedtime story, like I will tonight. But I want it as a constant, not as a task as a babysitter. I catch up to his conversation, replying, "No, buddy. It's dark, you're clean and in your jammies." I pinch my hoodie and yoga pants, "And so I am."

Bear pushes out his bottom lip in an adorable little pout. It would work on me if I didn't love this little boy so much. The creek at night is risky, and he's far too precious. "It's too dark out there. It's not safe."

He folds his arms over his chest, not hiding the yawn that comes.

"How about two bedtime stories?" I nudge him, smirking. "I brought the Wimpy Kid book we started last month. It's in my bag."

His beautiful eyes widen. "I'll get it! I gotta get my blankie from Daddy's room, too." He slides off the couch, his bare feet slapping the floor as he hustles down the hall, into Hudson's room. I watch him disappear, and keep my eyes trained on the open doorway.

I'm jealous of Bear at this moment. How easily and

freely he runs into Hudon's room, touching his things, breathing his air. I want that kind of access to Hudson.

"I can't find my blankie!" Bear shouts, frustration rattling his little voice.

I don't get up to help.

I've been in his bedroom hundreds of times. No one has been in the house while I have, and I won't start now.

I love Bear. And that love and respect I have for him is completely separate from how I feel about his daddy. I won't ever use Bear to get close to Hudson. I don't and won't need to. I will show Hudson that I am his, and the fact that I love Bear will only complement *our* bond.

And when that happens, I'll be able to go into his room and enjoy the way my cunt clenches at just the sight of his shower, the way my tits ache when I look at his tousled sheets and imagine him and I there, on our sides, Hudson sliding his cock into me over and over from behind, his hand planted on my pregnant belly.

"That's it, Mama," he'd croon, dragging his tongue up the back of my bare neck, making me moan. "Ride it out, let that pussy quiver all around my cock. I wanna feel you come, *sweet thing*."

Bear runs back out, breaking the spell of my fantasy. But I have to stop thinking of it as fantasy. It's reality, in the future, I just don't know how far.

Because Hudson will be mine. And I know how that sounds. It sounds crazy. It sounds like I should have a dart board in my room with Tessa's and Tiffani's faces on it, that I should be in my car wearing a black hoodie with my binoculars pressed to the window as I watch Goode's Diner. It sounds like I am going to one day be in a prison interview explaining my childhood.

But I am secure with who I am. And my sisters are my support system.

I am not crazy. I am passionate. There's a *clear* difference.

I realize that going into Hudson's house when he isn't home every single week for four years is... strange, to the outside perspective. But that's without context. Once you know I'm only entering his property so that I can better understand him, it's the same as googling someone. Seriously. It's not that big of a deal.

I do plan to come clean, though. Because when Hudson is officially my man, there will be nothing between us. Not the past, not lies, not unspoken truths, not a condom, *nothing*.

And he will accept me. Because soulmates accept each other, no matter what.

And he *is* my soulmate.

Without question.

"Wanna read them here, in front of the fire, or do you wanna get comfortable in bed first?"

He considers my question, but I make an executive decision as he yawns again. "Okay, bedroom, c'mon."

I follow after him, and take a seat on the edge of his bed, leaning against the wall as he snuggles down into his cowboy boot sheets. I crack the book but before I start reading, Bear twists in the sheets, looking up at me with sleepy eyes.

"Are you coming to Aunt Ev and Uncle Deuce's wedding?"

"The whole town is coming," I reply with a smile, and why it only just now occurred to me that Hudson may bring a date to the wedding, I don't know. But my stomach twists into a thousand intricate knots, the taste of sick burning at the back of my tongue. "Of course I'll be there," I say, maintaining my smiling disposition as I sift my fingers through the pages, finding where we left off.

"Good," he sighs contentedly, snuggling back down into his bed, clutching his teddy bear. "'Cause I want to dance with you."

I pull my hair up into a ponytail, finger combing the bumps as he watches me with tired eyes. "Well, I wanna dance with you, too."

He yawns as I crack the book back open, moving my finger beneath the words to find our spot. "You gonna dance with my daddy?" he asks, surprising me before I can even start. Though the way his eyes sag, I don't think I'll be reading too much.

"Maybe," I consider aloud, wondering if by the time the wedding comes around, I'll be... further along in my mission. "Why'd you ask?"

Bear yawns again. "My Auntie Ev says Daddy needs a girlfriend, and sometimes dancing with someone makes you feel special about 'em." He flicks the ear on his teddy a few times. "I'd like it if Daddy felt special about you."

My heart thumps and my eyes warm. "Why's that?"

His voice is growing soft and distant as he says, "You make me happy. And if you can make me happy, maybe you can make Daddy happy, too." Another yawn, then immediate silence.

His words render me incapacitated, making the book

slip nervously from my lap to the floor. Bear doesn't notice because he's already drifted off. After retrieving the book, I press my lips to his head, and whisper, "Good night."

I stand in the hallway, clutching the book to my chest, my heart racing. I could use this. I could make Hudson see how bonded Bear and I have become, and I can dangle that bond in front of him. He loves seeing Bear happy, and I've picked up enough conversations between Ev and Deuce over the years to know that raising Bear alone is tough on Hudson. Not because he lacks help but because a single father was not what he wanted for his son.

I won't do it. Not that way. Because it devalues what I've built with that little boy sleeping soundly in that room. And he does not deserve that.

Anyway, Hudson will realize how right I am about us on his own terms. Because that's how I see it in my mind. That's how it's going to happen.

I head down the hall into the kitchen, and put the book back in my bag. I glance at the clock over the oven and see they've been gone for two hours now. It's totally unlike Hudson to even go out in the first place, and he did not sound enthused to go, from what I *accidentally* overheard. I can't imagine he'll be gone too much longer.

Which means my time is limited.

And I'm about to break my streak.

All this thinking about Hudson and how fated we are to one another, I can't help myself. I lose control, *just a little.*

Standing in the doorway of his bedroom, I move my bare foot past the threshold, just a little. I stare down, analyzing my pink toenail polish against the cherrywood of the floor.

I've never gone in here when Bear's home. I've only ever gone in when I've let myself into the home, all alone.

His cologne hangs in the air, and my jaw clenches. I love that smell, but I don't like knowing that turd Tiffani is the one that gets to smell it. Walking through his room, I enter his closet, keeping the light off. I know where everything is from memory. I pick up his cologne bottle and bring it to my nose, inhaling deeply without spraying.

A shudder racks my body, and my skin grows warm and bumpy, my nipples hard and aching. God, I love his scent. Just smelling his cologne has me imagining being at his feet, my face tipped back as he paints my lips and mouth in his cum.

God, I want his cum so bad. I want to know what he sounds like when he orgasms, if he comes a lot or a little, does he shoot? Does he dribble? Does he grunt? Does Hudson Gray have a dirty mouth? Has he ever tasted his own cum? Has he tasted his cum out of a lover's used-up pussy? I don't know. But I want to know. I need to know.

I need him.

I make a reactive choice, the heady scent of warm amber and patchouli making me foolishly high on Hudson. I strip from my yoga pants and hoodie, and make my way to his bed. After slowly turning down the covers, I slip into the cool sheets, wasting no time.

I roll and thrash in his bed as I bury my fingers inside myself, moaning and cursing as I envision him here with me.

It's our Friday night. The kids just went down.

And now he's going down on me.

After which, I'll beg him to fuck me in my pussy, then

fuck me again in my ass, then watch all his cum drip from my holes as I crawl to the floor and get on my knees, waiting for him to lower his balls into my mouth so I can suck them to say thank you for all the cum he's given me.

The spool of orgasm unwinds in my groin as I imagine us together, in this room, feasting on one another with passion and fervor. He's groaning how much he loves me, how he's so glad to have me, and I'm praising him for his goodness, reminding him how he doesn't just mean a lot to me, but that he's my everything. He owns all of me.

When my vision returns and the last of my orgasm has torn through me, I force myself out of Hudson's bed, knowing they must be on their way soon. After using his bathroom to wipe away the arousal post-orgasm, I wash my hands and quickly redress, flicking on the bedroom light. There's a dark spot in the center, where my pussy oozed its appreciation for Hudson and all the delicious, sinful, private things we will do together.

Because we will.

I believe that.

I smile at the dark spot, wondering if it will dry before he's home. Wondering if he sleeps naked, and if he does, will his bare cock touch that spot? Will traces of my cum smear against his naked balls? Will he unwillingly wear my scent all night?

I remake the bed, my cunt still pulsing, despite the fact I've just come.

After taking a step back to make sure the room has been righted, I flick off the light and tiptoe down the hall, checking on Bear. His night-light has flicked off, so I slip inside and turn it back on, as well as his sound machine.

White noise floods the space, and the gentle rise and fall of Bear's chest brings a fullness in my chest that I always feel around him.

I kiss his head and lie down on the floor, using a stuffed dinosaur from his basket of toys as a pillow. And then, as I listen to Bear's soft little breaths, my eyes flutter closed, peacefulness lulling me into sleep.

ten

I WANTED TO THINK ABOUT TIFFANI, BUT I ONLY THOUGHT OF DOLLY.

Hudson

Quietly, I close the back door, twisting the deadbolt before adding the security chain. My house is dark and quiet, and while I know Bear is asleep, I wonder where Dolly is. I drop my keys and hat on the counter, and fish my wallet and phone out, leaving them there, too.

Heading toward the hall, I stop halfway across the living room, a violent floral scent hitting me. I lift my collar to my nose and inhale.

Fuck. This shirt smells like Tiffani. She hugged me three times as we said goodbye, and I'm fairly certain she meant to rub her smell on me. I'm not some hydrant that needs to be marked, and anyway, the scent does nothing for me.

Quickly, I unbutton the shirt, peel it off, and hit the laundry room in the hall, shoving it in the open, empty washer. In my boots, jeans, and white t-shirt, I slip into my son's room, stopping in the doorway at what I find.

Bear is tucked neatly into his bed, his teddy clutched to his chest. The night-light casts a tangerine halo around him, and there is not a single time that I don't look at my son and see the beautiful gift that he is.

I'm so lucky.

But my eyes tumble to the tiny blonde on the floor, her small frame nearly curled in half, a stuffed dinosaur under her head. Sweet Dolly. A lump jumps up my throat as I process my own thoughts.

Sweet Dolly?

I pull at the back of my neck, feeling guilty and ashamed for the semi I feel while looking at her. She's so tiny but so sweet and fierce, creative and... beautiful. I don't think I've ever met anyone like her.

I don't need to be thinking about her, though, so I slip out of Bear's room and find my phone on the kitchen counter. Quickly, I send Tiffani a text.

> I'd like to take you out this week. Name the time and place.

I hit send and lock the phone, not waiting for a response. She's gonna say yes, I know, and that's all I need. A few dates, some casual sex. That's it. Then maybe I can stop drooling over a girl who had braces and a learner's permit when I first met her.

I stand in the doorway of Bear's bedroom, staring at the two of them as a funny tingling spreads through my chest, into my limbs, making my fingers curl and my throat dry. I don't know how long I stand there just looking... watching... I don't know. Finally, though, I crouch down next to her, noticing the light freckles on her cheekbones, the Cupid's bow of her perfectly plump upper lip, and all that honey hair pulled into a ponytail. I don't know why I never considered or saw it before but, Dahlia Ellington is gorgeous. Breathtaking. I even stop and take her in another second before finally cupping her slender shoulder with my hand, giving her a gentle shake. Her body is warm, and feels so slight against my large hand. "Dolly," I whisper, sending a rush of heat to my legs.

I've never whispered her name, but that's how it would sound if I was waking her up with my fingers, or cock. She blinks a few times, coming to as she smiles up at me. Goddamn it, I know what I'll be doing later.

"You're back."

Nodding, I extend a hand to her. "Let me walk you home."

Dolly smiles, clambering quietly to her feet. She stretches, and my eyes ignore the inch of bare skin that appears between her pants and hoodie as she does.

"It's just next door. I'll be okay."

I clear my throat, guiding us both from Bear's room, out into the hall. Pulling his door closed as we exit the space, I tell her the truth. "I wouldn't be."

We share a smile, and though I've been hip to hip with Dolly hundreds of times over the years, I'm suddenly acutely aware that it's dark and quiet, and there are only two feet of space between us.

Standing in the dark hallway, I make the move to usher

her through the house, to the front. I need to get her home. I need to shake these thoughts and urges and get laid with a woman my own damn age.

When we get to the foyer, I pull open the door, letting my hand barely graze the small of her back as I usher her out. We start the small walk to her house next door, less than thirty feet away.

"Thanks again for watching him tonight," I say, my voice a little raw. My cheeks flush and I'm grateful for the darkness, so she can't see that I'm embarrassed that my tone matches my thoughts.

She bumps her arm into mine. "Oh stop. You don't have to thank me. You know I love Bear."

Though I know it's true, for whatever reason, hearing her say that as plain as day does something to me. Something that will require my hand in about ten minutes.

Fuck. I'm glad I already texted Tiffani. I need to get laid. All this time of pretending I could *go without* is catching up with me, and I don't want to creep out a genuinely sweet girl who loves my boy.

"Still," I hedge, my steps drifting away from her a little, because it feels like I may need physical distance. "I appreciate it." *You*, I think. *I appreciate you.*

"So, how was your date?" she asks quietly. This time her eyes stay on her toes as we take the last steps up to her porch. The light, a motion detector, flicks on as she steps up to the door. I stay on the ground, forgoing the steps. This isn't a date, so down here is just fine.

I rake a hand up the back of my head, my eyes falling to my cognac boots. There's nothing wrong with Tiffani. She's just... *not my type*. Still, I understand that getting back into the swing of things is important, and I'm gonna date a lot of fillers until I find the one worthy of being with us.

Finally, I look up, and our eyes idle together in the moonlight. "Okay, I guess."

"Are you going to see her again?" she asks on the heels of my response. I can't tell if she's just trying to be nice or genuinely curious.

"Yeah, this week I think."

She smiles, but it takes her a second, like she isn't sure if she likes my answer. "I hope she knows how special Bear is," she adds softly, reminding me that whoever I choose to date, is also going to be in Bear's life. Not that it hadn't occurred to me before but nothing about Tiffani says peanut butter and jelly, stone skipping and living room forts.

But I don't tell Dolly that I'm only seeing Tiffani again because it is my belief she only wants sex and I'm looking for the same. Not because it makes me look bad or because it's inappropriate, though both are true. I don't tell her because, in a quiet voice, she adds, *"Or I'll have to kill her."*

Her face is impassive for a second before a smile breaks out, and we both laugh quietly. "Kidding," she adds, with a sexy little smirk that sets off big feelings inside me. I've always loved a dark and twisted sense of humor.

"Thanks again, Dolly." I step back as she moves inside the house, closing the door all but a crack.

"Good night, Hudson. Sweet dreams." Her full lips come together in a smirk, and then the door is closed, followed by the reassuring sound of her twisting all the locks.

When I get back to my house and strip down to my boxers, I crawl into bed, exhausted from a long week of work but in truth, more fatigued from my brain than anything.

As I roll in the sheets, I swear to God, I think I smell Dolly.

Fuck. of course I don't. I found her sleeping on Bear's floor. She's never been in here, much less in this bed. I'm now so hard up to get laid that I'm hallucinating perfume on my linens.

I roll onto my back, closing my eyes, reaching down to grab my cock. I'm already a hard, leaking mess as I begin to stroke, willing myself to think about Tiffani in this bed.

But as I paint myself in cum, my stifled groans lodged in my throat, guilt chokes me.

I wanted to think about Tiffani, but I only thought of Dolly.

eleven

STAY THE COURSE.

Dolly

"I'm making valuable progress," I tell my sisters as we pile into Juni's small SUV, the three of us on a journey into town. Ivy, who has been practicing her line art, is picking up her new tattoo gun and demo supplies.

Deuce found a shop a few days ago, and as soon as the ink on the lease was dry, a sign was up in the window. "TATTOO PARLOR COMING. ARTISTS APPLY INSIDE."

Before she applies, she has a handful of techniques she wants to practice, including floating her needle, line work, and her arm position. I love her art, and always have, and can't wait until she's hired. She'll be great at tattooing, and I'm so proud of her for chasing her dreams.

"Yeah?" Ivy asks, clipping the seat belt at her hip, pulling her black hair from where it's trapped. "That's great. So, babysitting the other night went well?"

Juni casts her eyes in the rearview, eyeing me. "But you were just babysitting so... you didn't spend time with Hudson, did you?"

I shake my head. "No, but when he got home, he woke me up and walked me home and... I don't know." I peer out the window at the world whipping by. "It felt different."

Juni does a little squeal of happiness on my behalf. "Ooh," she coos, "that sounds promising."

I love that my sisters are aware of and support me in all my endeavors. And I to them. But when it comes to Hudson... I know I'm passionate. I know I can lose my temper and do things that can be misunderstood, from the outside looking in. I appreciate that they don't see me for my flaws but for my strengths. And that they're on board with my mission.

"Yeah," I breathe, "except... I was babysitting because he went on a date."

Ivy peers around the passenger seat at me, one eyebrow arched to heaven. "So that's why those canvases were obliterated and burned behind the barn."

I give her my beauty queen smile. "Yes, ma'am."

The three of us giggle. "Anyway," I say, "the date was set up, a friend of Everly's from college."

Juni pulls onto the main street, and Ivy points at the post office, where an open parking spot rests. "There. I'll run in and grab it."

Juni nods, turning into the spot. She unclips her seat belt, swiveling to face me. "Wanna get some pancakes? To go?" She tips her head toward the diner.

I shrug. "Okay."

The three of us exit the car, Juni and I linking arms as we push through the double doors of the diner, Ivy heading into the post office.

"You don't seem concerned," she says quietly as we drift past empty tables, finally finding the one we like best. We sit at the same table every time. She smirks. "Except for the canvases."

"I don't want him to date," I admit in reference to the destruction I'd done when Tiffani showed up. "But I know I'm his soulmate, Juniper. I know it. I know it without a doubt."

She flips open the laminated menu, eyeing me despite the fact her face is tipped down to the table. "I believe you."

That. That right there is everything in the whole world and why I will stick by my sisters until the end.

Someone else might've tried to tell me I'm silly, that I can't love a man I don't know, that I'm too young, that what I'm doing is weird.

But Juni and Ivy don't invalidate me. They don't make me believe I don't understand my own inner workings. They trust that I understand myself, and I do.

And anyway, at this point, Hudson Gray is no stranger.

He just doesn't know how well I really know him. But once he finds out, he'll understand why I've done all that I've done. He'll see that I've done everything from a place of love and desire.

He will see me and my efforts the same way my sisters do, I just know it. Because a true soulmate loves and accepts you no matter what.

I'm just about to launch into everything I discovered

about Tiffani when long, dark hair shines in my periphery. Juni and I turn our heads and immediately, my nostrils flare and my skin grows hot.

"Oh no," Juni breathes, immediately understanding the situation. I slide out of the booth and get to my feet, Juni already at my side looping her arm through mine.

A moment later, we're at their table, smiling.

"Hi, Hudson," I beam, and I swear to God, whether he's on a second date with this bitch or not, something flashes behind his eyes when he sees me. Surprise mixed with lust, maybe? A rush of needy warmth slips out of me as I take in his stubbled jaw and confusing reaction.

"Hi there, Dahlia." He twists his gaze to my sister. "Hello. Juniper."

Slowly, my eyes go to her. Tiffani. I catch her sizing us up, but when she sees me looking at her, she smiles off the judgment, outstretching a hand to me over her plate of mixed fruit.

Mixed fucking fruit. C'mon. He's a goddamn dairy farmer. I look at his plate, finding it piled high with eggs, bacon, biscuits and gravy. A real plate of food for a man who works with his hands all day. My nipples harden, imagining all that it takes to power a man so large and powerful.

Tiffani with her plate of cantaloupe can't handle a man like Hudson.

"Hi, I'm Tiffani, I just moved here," she says, her words nice but not overly so. It's almost like she doesn't want us to interrupt her date. A man dressed in work boots and an old Carhartt hoodie passes by, saying hello to Hudson with a clap on the shoulder.

I love how much this town loves him and how much we need him here.

Tiffani with her social media profiles and phony degree and ulterior motives is the piece that doesn't belong.

He'll see that. He has to.

And yet, he's on *another* date.

Juni shakes Tiffani's hand, and then I do, too, but I feel Hudson's eyes on me, and I know... despite the fact he's on another date, I know I'm getting closer.

I can feel him finally drifting toward me.

I just need to stay the course.

"It was nice meeting you, Tiffani," I add, splitting a smile between her and Hudson. "But Ivy's just picking up her fake skin from the post office, then we're headed back home."

Tiffani's nose wrinkles, but her Botoxed forehead stays unoffended as she says, "Fake skin?"

Juniper points out the diner window, to the leased but empty shop across the street. Hudson and Tiffani both follow her finger, looking at the window as she uses her other hand to swipe Hudson's fork from the table, sliding it up her sleeve.

I love my sister. She's kind of a criminal, but I love her anyway. And if minor theft is her worst offense, that's not so bad.

"See over there? That's where Hudson's soon-to-be brother-in-law is opening a tattoo shop. Our sister Ivy is vying for an apprenticeship." She smiles at Tiffani as if we aren't both staring intensely at her. "And yeah, you can order fake skin online. I mean, unless you know of a place where she can find a person whose skin she can borrow?"

Juni holds her sunshine smile, silent discomfort oozing from Tiffani.

Breaking the tension, Hudson slips from the booth, dwarfing us as he gets to his feet. Juni is the oldest and tallest, standing at five feet and nine inches. But hulking Hudson still makes her look small. *God* the way this man could own my body, bend me like a pretzel and slam me into the mattress without so much as breaking a sweat is such an incredible turn on.

"Men's room." He smiles, slipping past us, leaving his cologne to tickle my nose and cunt. Juniper takes his place, likely to passively intimidate Tiffani. Have I said I love my sisters lately?

"I'm gonna catch the ladies' room before we head out, too," I tell Juni, making a beeline through the diner as inconspicuous as possible. Hudson is stopped short right before the hallway that leads to the restrooms, but that's exactly what I'd hoped.

The town's wealthiest, sweetest man can hardly move through the crowded diner without a barrage of greetings. While he talks to another farmer, I slip into the hall and duck into a private phone booth. With my back to the fogged glass, I wait.

Two minutes and thirteen seconds later, Hudson passes by, his shirt visible through the murky privacy stall.

Slipping into the hall, I peer around the corner to make sure no one else is headed this way. When the coast is clear, I gently press my ear to the door, and nudge it open just a sliver. The tiniest of slivers.

The sound of him tugging down his fly has me losing my fucking mind, I swear, so I cup my hand to my mouth to hold in the drool and moans.. I've never heard him touch the zipper on his jeans until today. The zipper that keeps his cock tucked away. The infamous zipper that gatekeeps everything I want inside me.

Then it happens.

His stream starts, and my entire body incinerates. I'm not into piss, or at least, I never have been before. And certainly, I've never been turned on by my or anyone else's body's ability to produce and eliminate waste.

But listening to Hudson piss is a cathartic, holy moment. The stream is powerful and heavy, causing me to drop my hand from my mouth to my stomach, applying pressure to satiate the immediate wanton ache the noise puts inside me.

He grunts a little, the heels of his boots clicking the tile as he shakes himself into his jeans, the zipper immediately coming back up. The urinal flushes, and the sink sounds off. I slip back into the restaurant crowd a handful of paces ahead of him, my clit pulsing in the privacy of my panties. His stream was so big. I swallow hard as I return to my sister.

Juni, back on her foot, smiles as I come to her side. A moment later, Hudson returns to his breakfast, though he's so large it looks tiny in comparison. Like he could lift the plate from the table and dump the entire thing in his mouth, like some sort of roaming, starved and wild cartoon giant.

God it's hot.

"Well," Juni says as I approach. "We better go get Ivy. It was nice meeting you."

Hudson's eyes are on me as I smile, waving goodbye to him and his date. Juni starts toward the door but before I follow her, our eyes idle as I say, "I hope you two have a nice date."

His lips part, like he wants to argue, maybe, or say something, but then he glances at Tiffani, then me, and nods. "Thanks, Dolly."

Outside, on the sidewalk, Juni slips me the fork, which I slide onto my tongue immediately, everything between my legs incinerating as I do. I can't taste anything, but he ate with this, and God does it make me horny to know my mouth is somewhere he was.

"Thanks," I say around the fork, though neither of us acknowledge it as the topic.

"Sure," she says, walking backward toward the post office, facing me. "I'm gonna see if Ivy needs help."

I hold up my hand. "Toss me the keys, I'll wait in the car after I'm done."

The *after* goes without explanation, because Juniper is very aware of what I'm about to do.

She nods, rifles through her purse, then tosses me the loaded key ring.

I catch them, then dig out my phone, opening the file that I'd compiled after the farmers market a few weeks ago.

I see her car is a blue sedan, a Toyota. Quickly I stuff my phone in my pocket and eye the busy main street for a blue sedan. I find it easily.

Once the traffic slows, I step out into the street, completely natural, because some things are best done in plain sight. Like slashing a tire.

Crouching by the car, I rear my arm back, imagining Tiffani with Hudson at the table, and my arm drives forward of its own accord. She really thinks she's going to lie about everything and come here and take the best man in town? My man? Fuck that.

The old metal fork pierces the tire, sticking out of it like a knife in someone's back. Rising, I bask in the slow whirr of air rushing out as I walk back to Juni's car, getting in and waiting for my sisters as I promised.

"I'm fine," I say aloud, trying to steady the rattle in my chest. I didn't expect him to date her again but it's okay. *I'm fine.*

Everything is just fucking fine.

twelve

BUT THERE'S NO SPARK.

Hudson

"You like the space then?" I ask Deuce, walking my fifth circle around the space. The floors are fake hardwood, but that's probably best for a tattoo shop. Something easy to clean. The walls are painted black, the crown molding the same dark onyx.

Deuce nods. "And yeah, I do. It works nice for a parlor."

I stop in the middle, glancing up at the pave and crystal chandelier centering the space. "Remind me," I say, blinking at the shiny, ornate light. "What was in this location before?"

He pulls the toothpick from his lips, rocking forward slightly in his motorcycle boots. Deuce loves Ev, who is a country girl to the core, but nothing about him has remotely turned country. He's still a tatted-up rocker through and through.

"A palm reading place." Returning the toothpick to his lips, he shoves a hand through his shoulder-length hair, letting out a sigh. "Location is prime. Place needs some paint–"

"And a new light," I add, pointing to the monstrosity above. He chuckles.

"Yeah, but otherwise, I should be ready to open in a month, and it's in much better shape than the last place, the old movie rental store." He sinks into one of the two folding chairs in the corner, stacking one boot on top of the other as he brings his hands behind his head, relaxed. "Already ordered the stations and gear. Now I just need to find one more apprentice."

I hook my thumb toward the front of the store, which is all glass windows. Every location on Main Street is glass windowed. It gives downtown a true small town feel I love. Large pieces of kraft paper are taped up to the windows with blue painter's tape, keeping the inside private. And kind of dark.

"You know Ivy wants to apprentice, don't you?" And though I'm mentioning Ivy, a vision of Dolly curled up on Bear's floor flashes behind my eyes.

His lips twist as his nostrils flare, giving me the biggest *no shit* look I've seen. "She's in—" He stops himself, widening his eyes. "—but don't tell her. I don't want her to know yet."

I let out a little chuckle. Ivy has been on Deuce's ass to

hire her as an apprentice ever since she learned of his businesses out of town. He owns several other shops, but only seriously began plans to grow his chain to Bluebell when Everly told him she would not, in fact, be moving anywhere after they married.

"All right," I say, lifting my hands to promise my complicitness, "I won't say a word."

"She's gonna fucking freak when she finds out who I hired, though," he says, his lips turning up into a sinister grin. His silver nose ring shines as he leans forward, dropping his elbows to his knees as he gets serious. "Her favorite artist ever, Trace Calhoun." He shoves his hair from his face again before smoothing his hands down the lapels of his leather jacket. I think Deuce is just as excited, but I don't say it. "God, I can't even believe he agreed to come *here*."

"Why did he, you know, if he's the best?" I ask, having some semblance of the name somewhere in my mind. I've heard Deuce talk about artists to Ev a ton over the years, and this is one that sticks out. He did some of the pieces on Deuce, too, if I remember correctly. And all of his ink is fucking incredible.

"Well," Deuce says, getting to his feet as he opens the front door after a light lap. A man in a blue jumpsuit steps inside, and Deuce takes him back to the water heater, which is getting repaired. Returning to the conversation, he adds, "I think he needed to duck out of the limelight in Los Angeles for a while... and just lay low. Focus on his art."

Sounds a lot to me like he has a trail of scorched earth behind him, and I don't know if that's the type of person that belongs in Bluebell , but I trust Deuce to know what he's doing. And if he doesn't, I trust him equally to be a quick learner with even quicker reactions.

"So," he says, smirking. "How was that second date? Better without me and your sister there, huh?"

Deuce came into the diner to pick up an order, shortly after Juni and Dolly had left. He spotted Tiffani and I together, came to say hello. After I paid for a plate of fruit and one *actual* breakfast, I walked Tiffani to her car and waited with her while the Uber came, eager to be done. Came to the shop after watching Deuce cross the street and enter.

I didn't *want* to go out again.

I do, however, recognize the need to reenter the relationship world is more prevalent than ever, and Ev wants her mind at ease as she starts her new life.

But it wasn't until Dolly and Juniper came into the cafe that I realized I really did not want to be out with Tiffani. I really do not like her—not in any capacity that would lead to what I want, love, marriage, intimacy.

Tiffani is beautiful, and from all of her statistics she's so carefully listed to me, she has all the trademarks of a good catch.

But there's no spark.

"There's no spark," I say to Deuce, at the risk of sounding stupid. I meet his eyes.

He shakes his head. "No spark isn't good but... what about just to get back in the game? Someone to just... grease the gears a little?" He shrugs, knocking his fist against the counter. "Could be good."

I sigh, shoving my hand through my hair beneath my

hat. "That's... not me. I don't want to sleep with a woman if I don't see a future with her."

He blinks. "You *can* see a future. A future of sleeping together until you meet someone better."

"That's... not right."

Deuce crosses the space, resting his hands on my shoulders. With his ink and piercings, long hair and leather, I laugh at him. "You're the devil on my shoulder."

He grins. "Damn right I am. And as your personal devil, I'm telling you, there's nothing wrong with getting back in the swing of things with someone *temporary*." His dark eyes hold mine uncomfortably. "And yes, your sister is worried but you gotta get your feet wet, so to speak."

I rake a hand up the back of my head as he moves to sign the paper held out to him by the water heater technician. Once the man is gone, I tell Deuce, "That sounds a lot like *using* her."

Deuce smiles. "That's called *dating*."

After waving Bear and Ev off, I slide my boots and vest on, adding my hat as I step out the back door. She's taking him in town to look at wedding stuff with her so I can bale hay today, something I cannot do with Bear under my feet. Way too fucking dangerous. The bales are extremely heavy.

Tugging my right glove on, eyes set on the barn, I stop in my tracks, a shiver winding through me, leaving my spine straight at the sound of a piercing feminine scream.

What was that? Quickly I turn around, jogging back through my house, out the front door, my breath already coming fast. Ev's SUV isn't out front—so it's not like she drove back here in a second with a massive, screaming emergency.

That's not her style anyway.

I stand ten paces out of my drive, front door open, one glove on, heart racing as the piercing cry comes back, louder, more violent, echoing through the vast ranch land.

I turn to face the Ellington household. When I'd taken Bear out to Ev's SUV and buckled him in, giving him a kiss goodbye, I'd seen Juni and Ivy loading the back of Juni's car. I overheard Juni telling my sister they were going up north for a few hours to procure some of the tattooing supplies that didn't come in Ivy's shipment.

I didn't notice that Dolly was there.

The scream echoes through the sky one more time, and my boots are tearing through the gravel before I realize it, headed straight for their front door. I slam my fist against the aged, flaking wood.

Juni raised herself and her two sisters after their father passed, and she did a damn good job. The women that we moved next door to have been nothing but helpful, sweet and kind. The way they embraced me using my property to have a farmers market, which would undoubtedly press on them due to their house location, was incredible.

But raising good people while trying to pay the bills has

clearly and rightfully been the pressing responsibilities. The Ellington house could use some work.

No one answers my knock, and just as my pulse sinks into a normal cadence, there's another chest-rattling scream, raw and painful. Urgency and fear have me racing around the back of the house, to the glass sliding door. I cup my hands to the door and peer inside, but the house is undisturbed.

Cautiously, I bring my fist to the glass, knocking gently so as not to break the door. I could, though. My panic and strength could easily get the better of me. The scream sounds off again, and bumps rise up along the length of my arms.

I see Dolly again, curled up next to Bear, and again at the farmers market in her booth, glancing back at him as she greeted folks.

I try the door but it's locked, and I'm one second away from breaking a window when she appears.

Dolly steps out from the back hallway, her honey hair a tangled, damp mess around her face. She calmly tucks it behind her ears as she comes toward the sliding door, a blue-and-white gingham sundress clinging to her youthful curves.

But all I see is blood.

Streaking her forearms, splattered across one of her thighs, smeared along her forehead and another drop above her top lip. She walks slowly through the living room and I find myself pressing both palms to the glass impatiently, watching her walk to me, my heart pumping as fast as it did the day Bear was born. Different kind of adrenaline.

As soon as the click of the lock sounds and she slides the door back on the track, I'm inside the Ellington house, Dolly in my arms as I carry her into the kitchen. "What's wrong? What happened? Are you okay? Is someone in the house?" I pepper her with panicked questions.

Lowering her to the counter, I study her face and head, using my hands to manipulate her body, lifting arms, moving hair, *searching*. Searching for an injury, a bruise, a cut, a gash—something to explain the horrendous screams and all the blood.

After my breathing and panic steadies just some, I rest my hands on the counter on either side of her slender legs. "Dahlia," I breathe, unable to find a cut of any kind. "What's hurt? Where are you hurt?"

"No one is in the house," she finally says. "And... it's here," she answers quietly, outstretching her leg. She takes my hands, bringing them to the top of her thigh, her wide blue eyes holding mine captive as she wraps my grip on her soft, private skin. Her blue dress is all bunched up at her waist, and I know my hands should not be this high.

"Where?" I ask, focusing on my hands banding her upper thigh.

"Down," she urges, her voice calm and kind of detached, a little eerie after all the screaming.

I pull my hands down her leg and when I get to her knee, my cock thickening from the velvet feel of her bare skin, I ask, "Where, Dolly?" I find my worry compounding.

"Keep going," she says softly, swiping her tongue along her top lip, licking away the drop of blood left there. I keep moving my hands down until I'm holding her foot in my hand, her leg lifted an inch off the counter. I move my thumb along her arch, and discover a large gash, about three inches long.

I press around it, seeing if it's still going to bleed. It does, so I grab a dish towel from nearby, and wrap it around her foot. Holding her small foot tight in my hand, I use my other hand to free my belt from my jeans. She gasps as I tug it free, and the little breathy noise she makes does terrible things to my already aching halfie.

I should not be getting erect as I take care of Dahlia. Jesus, what is wrong with me?

"You need stitches, Dolly," I tell her, my eyes coming to hers, the crimson in my periphery making me nervous. Creating a tourniquet using my belt, I wrap her foot and lower her leg down. Moving to the sink, I wet another dish towel beneath the tap, returning to her. "Let's clean you up and I'll take you in, okay?"

I smooth the towel down her temple, watching as the red turns pink, then wipes clear. "What happened?" If she cut her foot, why is there so much blood everywhere else? I move the towel down her arms, taking a break to rinse it beneath the tap again.

Never once has she rambled or cried. She answered the door and calmly sat atop the counter watching me move around the space and tend to her.

"I saw a spider and... overreacted," she says, finally smiling. I press my hand to my chest, kneading the unease that's been there since I heard her scream.

"Jesus, Dol, I thought... I don't know." That's the truth. I don't know what I thought. "I was concerned," I admit instead.

Then, answering my question, she lifts her hand. "I

started screaming more when I pulled the glass from my foot and it went into my hand."

I bring the towel to her hand and press it there, meeting her eyes. "What's the glass from?"

She wastes no time answering, and though maybe most women may be embarrassed by her big reaction, Dolly doesn't seem the least bit fazed. "A vase. When I saw the spider, I got so angry at it for invading my space. It was crawling all over my favorite painting," she says, her eyes focused on the cut slicing her palm as I blot the towel against it repeatedly. "I got irrationally overheated. I don't like creatures coming into my space, trying to claim my things, you know?"

Our gazes idle as I blot her palm, the house quiet around us, my mind a mess. Confused by her explanation, concern worms through me. I clear my throat. "It's... just a spider, Dolly."

"I *hate* spiders."

Chuckling, I help her off the counter, into my arms. Her hands link around my neck, and my chest squeezes at the way she relies on me, the safety she finds in me.

"Well, as much as you hate spiders, I'm not sure it's worth stitches and all this," I say, stopping in the doorway, peering down at her. "You need anything from in here? You're going to the hospital—no ifs, ands or buts."

"My bag," she says, pointing directly behind me to the small purse dangling from the hook. I step close enough for her to grab it with her good hand, then kick the front door closed behind me. Thank God for living in the country and leaving our vehicles unlocked. Opening the passenger side, I slide her in, gripping the top of the truck as I take in her tiny frame crumpled in the seat.

I got some of the blood off, but a lot still marks her skin. Glancing into the back, I make sure I have a spare shirt. I drive my truck all around the ranch and because angry steer and loose fence posts are my biggest enemies, I always carry a spare shirt with me. Once we're at the hospital, I'll get her to change so that she doesn't have to sit in bloody clothes.

On the drive to the hospital, I ask Dolly how her foot is feeling, and how the cut on her hand is. Keeping the makeshift tourniquet on, she tells me she's feeling great, and if it wasn't for the spider, she'd be having a pretty good day.

I like that she's so positive. I like that for Bear.

"Funny seeing you at the diner this morning," she hedges as I turn down the long road to the small hospital. I glance across the cab at her, looking nearly Bear's size in the big truck seat. Holding her against my chest felt like nothing.

"Yeah?" I ask. "Why's that? I go there too much."

"Well, when I watched Bear the other night, you didn't seem like you were too keen on that woman." She shrugs, twirling a piece of blonde, bloody hair around her finger like it's nothing. That hair wrapping her finger has me thinking about that hair wrapping my knuckles as I guide that sweet mouth down my shaft.

"Getting back in the saddle," I practically spit out, panicking that she can read my foul thoughts. Deuce is right. I need to grease the gears, date, whatever the fuck he called it. These fantasies of the babysitter are out of control. She's coated in blood with two gashes that need medical attention and this isn't the first time I've gotten kinda hard around her in the last ten minutes.

I'm sick.

"She's not my soulmate, Dolly, but I gotta start dating." I drum the steering wheel as I wait for the light to change to green. "Ev and Deuce are right."

There's silence in the cab for a second, but as soon as I crank the wheel into the hospital parking lot, Dolly asks me a question that takes me off guard.

"Are you lonely?"

I put the truck into park and level my gaze at her. "You're young and beautiful," I say, the admission making me flush a little. "Do you mean to tell me you really want to know if your old neighbor is lonely?"

"Yes," she answers quickly, stealing the oxygen from my lungs. "I don't want you to be lonely, Hudson." She licks her lips in a way that makes it clear—Dolly Ellington may be younger, she may watch my son, she may be tiny and sweet —but she is in fact *a woman.*

Not a girl, the way I always think of her. But a bona fide woman, with needs and wants. And right now, as I collect her from my truck, I'm starting to wonder if all the blood loss is getting to her. Because her heated, hungry gaze licks at my profile as I walk her inside, lowering her to a chair in the waiting area.

"All right, you wait here and worry about my loneliness and I'll go get you checked in," I say, attempting to bring a bit of lightness to what felt like a heavily charged moment out there.

It's probably all in my head because Ev and Deuce are right and I'm now thinking every woman is sexualizing everything because of how hard up I am for another person in my life. Either way, she smiles, and everything seems to feel normal again, leaving me to believe maybe it *is* all in my head.

By the time I'm at the nurses' station, I've thoroughly convinced myself Dolly was not flirting with me, nor has she ever. It's all me. I need to date. I need to fuck. I need to be a man outside of my home and land, and meet needs I've long been ignoring.

"Hi there," I greet the nurse with long dark hair. "My neighbor is here, she needs sutures. She's got a gash in her foot and one in her hand, about three inches long. Could have debris in them still. I haven't let her walk on the foot or use the hand but she definitely needs sutures."

The nurse eyes me as she slides a clipboard full of papers to me. "Have her fill this out. And there's a co-pay."

I nod. "Okay."

She smiles. "Pay when you come back. It'll be one hundred dollars."

I return to Dolly, who is using her good hand to text message. "Juniper and Ivy are two hours away," she says as I sit next to her in the tiny chair made of old wood and vinyl upholstery.

"It's all right," I tell her, "I'll drive you back." I click the pen open, realizing her right hand is the injured one. "I gotta get this filled out for you, then turn it in and you'll get seen."

She rifles around in her purse, handing me her debit card. "For the co-pay, Hud. I heard her mention it."

Hud.

Damn, I like the shortened version of my name on her lips.

I shrug. "All right, when's your birthday, Dolly?

I learn a lot I didn't know about Dahlia as I fill out her paperwork, enjoying the little crumbs of detail she offers up with each answer.

My birthday is March 8th. When I was born, you were celebrating your 18th birthday. That made me feel old as fuck.

You know my address. You know, the day you and Tessa showed up next door, I hadn't realized the house was for sale. I guess I thought it'd sit empty forever. Though now I'm sure glad it didn't.

Yes, I've had the chickenpox vaccine. I had them once, though, after that. It was mild. I had one near my belly button and I couldn't leave it alone.

After ten minutes, I know about the time she got six stitches above her eye from slipping on stones near the creek as a little girl, everything she's allergic to and that she doesn't like doctors. She presses the card into my hand and I carry her papers and payment up, passing them to the nurse.

She takes the clipboard easily, swiping the card next. "Debit or credit?"

I turn and look at Dolly, whose gaze is already all over me. My skin grows hot. "Debit, you said?"

She nods.

"What's your PIN?" I ask, not wanting her to get up despite the fact we're just ten paces apart. I'm concerned about glass still being in her foot. The gash was so big.

That must've been a terrifying spider.

"Zero," she mouths, "eight," she adds, rubbing her lips together in the middle, making my brain short-circuit in ways I completely fucking ignore. "Eight, five."

I nod, and face the nurse. She swipes the card for me and right as that PIN code settles into my brain, the screen asks me for the numbers. My thumb presses the zero then the eight, the eight again and then the five. I hit enter, earning me a green check mark on the payment screen.

The nurse hands me a receipt, and tells me that Dolly will go back next in just a few minutes. I return to her, passing her back the debit card. "Your PIN is my birthday," I muse aloud.

She zips the top of her purse. "I know."

Her blue eyes idle on mine, her small hand drifting over the armrest, fingers tangling with mine just as a man calls, "DAHLIA ELLINGTON."

Startling to my feet, I grab a vacant wheelchair from nearby. The male nurse stuffs her folder under his arm, coming to help me get her into the chair.

Her PIN code is my birthday... She said she knew. She must have meant she knew that was my birthday, but not that she knew it was my birthday when she made it her code. I almost laugh at myself when I think of it that way. *Dolly did not make her bank card PIN the birthday of the old guy next door.*

"You'll have to wait here," the male nurse says as he pushes a wheelchair-confined Dahlia into the private hall leading to the waiting rooms.

Twisting in the seat, her pink fingernails wrapped around the chair catch my eyes before I find her face. Cheeks pink, dried blood in her hair, she smiles and says, "Thank you, *Hud.*"

I fall back into the waiting room seat and pull my phone from my pocket, dialing Deuce. He answers right away, and

I'm glad that Ev is out with Bear because I don't feel like sharing this with her. Right now, I don't really even know why I'm calling.

"Hey," I reply to his hello. Around me there are two groups of people and I suddenly feel like I'm screaming. "Hang on a sec, let me step outside," I tell him.

"Step outside? Ain't you stackin' grass?" Deuce asks. Despite the fact he's basically lived on the ranch for the last eight years, he still uses the wrong terms for everything. Doesn't bother me. *I speak Deuce.*

The doors seal closed, leaving me outside in the sunshine, no one but a security guard roaming about. "I'm actually at the hospital."

"Fuck—what's going on? Ev there? Bear okay?" His voice is immediately rattled, and I know he's the right man for my baby sister because she was the first person he thought to ask about. But I already knew Deuce was solid before now.

"No, no, I'm okay, Ev and Bear are out doing wedding stuff." I walk the length of the sidewalk, watching my boots as I say, "Dolly had an accident. I heard her screaming and went over there." I swallow, remembering the blood on her arms, the deep gash in her hand. "She said she threw a vase to kill a spider, then she stepped on the broken glass and when she tried to pull it out of her foot, she cut her hand, too."

"Holy shit—is she okay?" he asks, the bell on the shop door dinging. Sounds like he slipped outside for privacy, too.

"She's getting stitched up but, yeah, she's okay," I report. "I brought her and I'm driving her back. Juniper and Ivy are out hunting supplies."

"Damn," Deuce breathes out. "Little thing surely hates spiders, huh?"

"Yeah," I say, dragging out every last letter as I attempt to phrase my thoughts.

"What's up?" he questions.

"Well... I don't know. I wanna tell you something because I wanna know what you think but you can't tell Everly, all right? Because... I don't know. I just... I want it to stay between us."

"You got it, brother," Deuce says earnestly.

"I think I was processing this earlier when I saw you but..." I pull my hand down my jaw, then waste no more time. "This morning after breakfast, I walked Tiffani out to her car and... someone had... punctured it," I tell him, remembering the pancaked rubber on the front left wheel. No weapon was around, only one of the old metal forks from the diner, likely snuck out by a kid who dropped it in order to avoid getting caught. I stayed a few minutes while the tow truck came. I could've put her donut on, but she didn't have it.

"Really?" Deuce asks, his tone mirroring mine. "Bluebell has a tire slasher, huh?"

"I guess."

"Well, what's this got to do with Dolly being at the hospital?" he asks, and not for the first time, I wonder if I'm an egotistical maniac for taking these two random things and trying to make them share logic. Still, I'm committed. And I can count on Deuce to tell me the truth. He always does. He told me the first day we met years back when we shook hands that my sister is the most important thing in his life.

His actions have never, not even once, proved otherwise.

"So, okay," I say, catching him up. "I helped her fill out the intake forms, here at the hospital. And then she needed to pay her co-pay."

"All right…"

I stop walking, analyzing a rather serious crack in the foundation beneath me. "I took her card up, you know, because of her foot."

"Okay…"

"Her bank card PIN." I scratch at the side of my jaw, feeling pretty stupid now. But I'm already here, so… "It was my birthday."

Deuce says nothing. And the other end is silent for an amount of time that has me checking the screen to see if the call is still active.

"When you say her PIN code is your birthday… I mean… remind me," he replies. "You're a handful years older than Ev, and I know your birthday is in August because we're a week apart."

I turn back and glance at the hospital doors, feeling nervous. "My birthday is August 8, 1985. 08/08/85. Her PIN is 0885. And after I paid, I came back and handed her the bank card and I said, *Hey your PIN is my birthday*, and she said, *I know*."

Deuce snorts. "Yeah, of course she knows when your birthday is. Ev and Bear put Christmas lights up in summer every year and go apeshit on balloons. She lives next door. She sees that shit."

"I know," I tell him, because I've already thought of that. "But, I don't know. She gave me this… *look*."

A man goes by me, pushing a woman in a wheelchair, a

baby bundled to high heaven in her arms. I move out of the way, stepping onto the lawn under a tree. The shade cools me, still my palms are sweaty as I pass the phone from one hand to another.

"A look, huh? Well... all right, how about this," he says, the hum of traffic on mainstreet filling in the noise around him. "You give me the look back at the house, and I'll try and tell you what it means."

I tip my hat up and look at the sun through the oak leaves. "I am not doing that."

He sighs. "I thought you'd say that. Okay, well, if I can't see the look I'm going to go ahead and need to talk it out a little, to see what you're gettin' at."

"No," I stop him, " you're... there. Around people. Just–" I yank my hat off, sinking into a metal chair bolted to the concrete beneath the tree. I think this chair is for sick old ladies who need fresh air, but I think that's me now. "I don't know. She gave me this weird look when she came by the table and then the tire... now the PIN code..." I drift off, but Deuce picks up my wandering thoughts.

"Ahh," he laughs, "so you're thinking she's, like... crazy."

"No, I don't think she's crazy, I just... I don't know. Nothing ever happens here," I sigh, placing my hat snuggly back on my head, mostly to hide my face from this embarrassing phone call. I should've just kept it in like all good men do. "And then a few strange things happened in one day."

Deuce's laughter throws cold water down my back, making me shrivel in on myself. "I think Tiffani had unfortunate luck and I think Dahlia making her bank card PIN the same as your birthday is just... weird coincidence. Anyway, she's probably had that card as long as she's known you, or longer."

"Yeah," I say, "you're probably right. For a second, I don't know, something just felt... *off.*"

"Your lady receptors are messed up because you've been hanging out with a kid and your sister for the last five years," he says, adding, "no offense."

"None taken." He's not wrong.

"Ev's right. It's not just about wanting time alone when we're married either. She genuinely wants you to find someone."

"I'm starting to think she's right," I admit to Deuce, before qualifying my words. "Don't you dare tell her I said that."

"I promise but know if she holds sex over my head, your ass will be under the bus in a split second."

I snort at his honesty, and cringe at the idea that my sister has sex. I don't care how old she is—I don't need to know. In fact, when Tessa and I announced our pregnancy years ago, Ev's first reaction was to look at me, wrinkle her nose, and say, "*You have sex? Ugh, gross.*" We're basically still in that mindset.

"Don't tell her a single word about this call either." I get to my feet and make my way to the open entry doors and saunter through. "I feel stupid."

"That's because it's been so long." He pauses. "I know Tiffani isn't your soulmate.. But a couple of meals, maybe a movie, maybe a casual fling just so you both *get it out of your system?* Could do you good."

Nodding to acknowledge the young couple huddled by

the door, I take a seat in the waiting room. "I'm starting to unfortunately think you two are right," I tell Deuce.

After ending the call, I text Ev and let her know what's going on, all the while laughing at myself for ever thinking sweet young Dolly would've made her bank PIN my birthday.

I don't acknowledge the sliver of disappointment in my chest that comes when I think those numbers were just her PIN and nothing more.

thirteen

THE UNIVERSE MAY HAVE TO WORK HARDER.

Dolly

In the last week, I've become pretty decent at painting with my left hand. My sutures are coming out today, and hell am I excited. I can't seem to paint Hudson's sharp jaw quite as well with my left. There are at least ten crumpled versions of him in the trash as we speak.

I dip my brush into the chestnut color I've mixed for his hair, and begin creating those soft waves I love so much. My favorite is when he's fresh out of the shower but he's been outside once or twice, letting the elements give some body to his natural wave. His hair thickens, and when he lifts his arm to run his hand through, the sight of him makes me so wet.

I let the brush make generous strokes, closing my eyes as I paint my love from memory. In my mind I'm envisioning him on Christmas Eve, freshly showered and dressed up, waiting for Ev and Deuce to come by. He came out onto the porch with Bear on his shoulders. They were catching snowflakes. Without his signature cowboy hat, dressed to the nines in charcoal slacks that barely contain his monstrous thighs, and a fitted cream sweater—when I tell you I came six times in a row that night, I'm not even exaggerating.

"Hey," Ivy calls from the hall, her hands above her head as she braids her hair. "I'm going down to the creek to do some freehand nature sketches." She loops the elastic on her wrist around the end of the first braid, getting started on the second. "Wanna come with?"

"Nature?" I question as I work on the tiny fleck of emerald green that exists right next to Hudson's right pupil. It's tiny but it's there. From my desk drawer, I pull out *one* of his photos.

The first one I reach is of him rinsing his mug out over the kitchen sink. His Henley sleeves are shoved to his elbows, dark chest hair peeking from the top of the unbuttoned shirt. His face is heavy with sleep, his hair a total mess. But it's so hot. It's him when he first wakes up and has coffee. A private, intimate him that you get only when you're *his*.

Or if you have a EF 70-200mm F2.8L IS III USM optical telephoto zoom lens and live next door to him.

Ivy finishes her remaining braid. "Yeah, nature," she replies, peering over my shoulder at the photo of Hudson. "That's a good one of him."

"They're *all* good," I correct, because of all one hundred and twenty-seven photos of Hudson that are in this drawer, not a single one of them is anything less than fucking perfect. "But you hate nature," I remind her, confused. Plus, her area of expertise when it comes to art is violence, darkness, sexy badass women and skulls. A creek with stones? "That makes no sense."

She sighs, reaching into my drawer to grab another photo, this one of Hud with his back to the camera, far off in the field baling hay. Sweat soaks his shirt, clinging to the center of his back, his hat blocking the sun from the lens. It's a perfect photo. One that has given me countless orgasms.

"Well," she says, replacing the photo carefully, holding on to the edges so as not to get screamed at for smudging. "I don't know what Deuce wants. He won't tell me anything. So I'm just trying to be prepared. If he does hire me as an apprentice, I wanna be good at everything."

I drop my brush in the rinse cup and get to my feet, angling my easel to face the sunshine pouring in the open window. "Sure, I'll go. Let me get a fresh canvas and grab my bag from the barn."

Under the guise of painting the oak tree, I move around the ranches a lot when I paint. To be fair, I have painted that oak many times. But I also have painted *him* many times, too. After having a quick lunch to try Juniper's new Chelan cherry jam, Ivy and I head to the creek, surprised to find Bear there.

Alone.

When Hudson showed up at my door last week, eyes full of fear as he stared at the blood on me, I took it as a sign.

He said he heard me screaming, heard the shattering

glass and the distress and ran over. Still, he scooped me up and took care of me. He took off his belt to make a tourniquet, and he carried me to the truck... into the hospital... he's just.... The universe is definitely pushing us together. For two years I've been waiting for her to help, and now she is. And I'm ready.

I told him my PIN code. And when he said it was his birthday, I told him that I knew that. And the way he looked at me–*like he was seeing me*, in that split second, for the woman who loves him.

But by the time I'd been stitched and drugged, I'd been rolled back out to a new Hudson. Like that tiny bit of information about my bank card PIN had been rationalized as a fluke or weird coincidence, and that he'd already moved on.

That's fine.

The universe may have to work harder, and if she doesn't, *I will.*

"Is that Bear out here all alone?" Ivy says, shading her eyes from the sun with a hand over her forehead. I drop my bag of supplies and my canvas and slip out of my Birkenstocks, then launch into a full sprint toward the water's edge. Beneath my ribs, my heart hammers in a way I haven't felt in years.

Fear echoes through me, a list of what-ifs running like ticker tape behind my eyes. He's out here alone. If he slipped on a mossy stone and went into the water— "Bear!" I scream as I near the sandbank where he's playing. He twists, turning around completely when he realizes it's me.

"Dolly! Did you see? That one did three skips!" His eyes are shiny and bright, his accomplishment making him stand taller than usual.

I drop to my knee in front of him, taking his shoulders in my hands as I catch my breath. "Bear, who's watching you right now?"

"Aunt Everly," he says simply, unaware that he just gave me the scare of my life and that in a few minutes, when Ev realizes he snuck out, he's gonna give her a good scare, too.

"Did you sneak out?" I ask, searching his eyes. He's honest, always has been.

Once, I watched him dump out two of my most expensive paints and mix them up with a stick, in an attempt to make a "pretend cow patty" and when I questioned if he knew what happened to the paint, he fessed up. I don't expect lies from him, so when he tells me that Aunt Ev was on the phone and he got bored and decided to pick flowers, I believe him.

"But I got tired of picking wildflowers so then I walked to the creek," he explains, his little voice growing wobbly as he realizes the problem. "Aunt Ev's gonna be mad, huh?" he asks, tears filling his eyes.

With my hands still on his shoulders, I take a steadying breath and try to explain to him what the problem is. "Yes, Aunt Everly will be upset because she loves you and when she realizes you're gone and she doesn't know where you are, she will be scared. And there are scary things out here, Griz, and us grown-ups know that. So we ask you to wait for us to go exploring because we don't want you to get hurt or lost or both."

He nods, and I wipe the gentle stream of tears from his soft cheeks as Ivy finally catches up, carrying all of our stuff.

"Thanks," I say, looking up at her. She narrows her gaze on Bear.

"I had to carry all this stuff because of you, my dude," she says, "so you owe me a special lemonade today when you get home."

He grins at my sister. He loves making lemonade and selling it out on the dirt road. Except, no one lives out here but the Ellingtons and Grays. But because a little adorable boy with lemonade tugs at the heartstrings of three women, my sisters and I make multiple trips a day to be his best customers.

At one point, Hud didn't like any of us up on that road, so to make everyone happy, he moved Bear's stand in front of the house... but built him a tiny booth, like a miniature version of the farmers market booths. He now delivers straight to our front door.

"I will." He glances back at the trail where we came from. "Should I go back?"

Ivy and I share a glance. "I'll take him back," I tell my sister. "See you in a few." She nods, ruffling Bear's hair as she says goodbye. But about three minutes into our trek back to the ranch, Everly appears, hair wild, eyes wide, cheeks stained with tears.

"Bear!" she screams, her voice so frightened and sharp that it echoes through the fields. She collapses to her knees in the field, ten feet back from us, shaking her head that she holds in her hands. "Oh, thank God."

I nudge Bear. "See?" I whisper. "She was worried. That's why you can't sneak off. And you can't go to the creek alone, either, okay? It's too dangerous."

He nods. I place my hand on the small of his back and give him a nudge. "Go apologize. And I'll see you later today, okay?"

I stay rooted to my spot as Bear and his aunt share a hug, her hand clamped onto the back of his head, relief lifting her from her collapsed position on the ground.

She lifts her head off his shoulder, looking at me through the tall grass. "Thank you," she breathes, still holding tight to her nephew.

"Ivy and I came out here to work and he was out here, skipping stones." I smile at Bear, and realize he's carefully taking in every word of this. I like Everly, and she likes me. But I hate this moment because she *is* at fault. And had we not come out here, who knows. Maybe Bear would have been fine.

Maybe not.

"I'm glad we came out and explained to him why adventuring alone isn't okay, and why it's dangerous." My lips twitch with the unused rant hovering on my tongue. Everyone makes mistakes, and *Everly will be my family very soon.* I can't dislike her. I don't even want to. Still. "Bear, your safety is of the utmost importance to everyone around, so make sure you don't sneak off again."

I pass a glance back to my sister. There are years between the three of us, but I swear to God we share that twin bond. Ivy and Juni know what I'm thinking as soon as I think it, and vice versa. Ivy rests one hand on the weeping willow as she stands amidst our art supplies. She smiles at Ev. "Thank God we were here, huh?

Ev blinks a few times. "Yes," she says, "thank God."

She thanks us again and they head back up to the house. I haven't spoken to Hudson since he came by the morning after the hospital, asking how I was feeling.

When he brought a bag of spider killing supplies.

Ever masturbated to a man bringing you spider killing spray? I have.

But after this mini incident, I wonder if I'll hear from him today. I hope I do. Deuce's bachelor party is this weekend, and he's taking his boys to Las Vegas to celebrate. Hudson is leaving Bear with Everly, and they'd invited us over for a sleepover the first night. Juniper has plans, and Ivy has zero interest in hanging out with Everly now that Deuce is going to be her boss, so only I said yes.

Between the incident of Bear sneaking out and the upcoming weekend away, he'll surely come talk to me today.

After I'm done working on my greeting cards for this weekend's farmers market, I plan to go home and prepare for his visit.

He will come see me.

I just know it.

fourteen

LET ME LIVE IN DELUSION, DAMN IT.

Hudson

"I don't expect you to cook all weekend, either," I tell Everly as she tugs a t-shirt over Bear's head. I'm gonna take him to the creek for a few hours before I leave for the weekend, to store up quality time with my favorite person doing his favorite thing. "That's why I just ordered three pizzas and a salad." I tug open the fridge, my eyes gravitating to the large tupperware on the middle shelf. "Tiffani brought food by, too."

Everly, who has been Tiffani's personal damn cheerleader thus far, stills, her fingers still lost in Bear's hair as she styles it. "She did?"

I hide the smirk threatening to coil my lips. She doesn't like that Tiffani did that, and yet she's the one pushing me toward her like a magnet. "What?" I question, feigning innocence.

Bear grips the chair handles as she continues styling his hair, a furrow in her brow. "Well, I mean, it's not like Bear is staying home alone all weekend."

I bring a can of Coke to my lips straight from the fridge, letting the carbonation wash away the chuckle in my throat. "Well, hang on a second now," I start, crossing the house to stand in front of them. "Has she tasted your biscuits and gravy?"

Bear brings his hands to his face, cupping his mouth as he giggles. Everly elbows me. "I'm choosing not to be offended by the casserole but instead view it as her trying to impress you."

I finish the Coke with a second drink. "Casserole doesn't impress anyone."

Bear laughs again, and this time, Ev and I do, too. "Well," she adds, walking to the sink to wash product from her hands while Bear runs off to grab his rock bucket. Bear made a habit of collecting stones on the way to the creek, so last summer, I bought him a bucket and asked Dolly to paint his name on it. He's got hundreds of dollars of stuffed animals and toys, and that rock bucket is his favorite damn thing.

Once he's out of earshot, Ev continues. "I know she isn't your dream girl, Hudson. But she's trying. And you need to try too."

"We had breakfast," I reply, even though I already told her that. "And we're meeting up again next week."

"Really?" Her eyes widen with excitement at the mention of another date between me and Tiffani, and it's that moment I realize just how much my sister worries about my life long term.

"Yep." I'll go out with Tiffani. I gotta do it for Ev. She's been living for me and my son for the last four years. It's time she had her life back.

"That's good, Hud," she says, her relieved smile blanketing me in guilt. "Just have fun for a while. Don't over-think it."

I salute her. "Will do."

It's that moment that Dolly strolls through the front door, looking a tiny bit startled when her eyes land on mine. Taking her in, I almost want to laugh.

Not at how she looks because, Christ on a cracker, she looks way too good for a man my age to be making a comment. She strolls across the living space, tiny jeans so tight that I wonder if she poured herself into them. A baby t-shirt covers her top half, leaving just an inch of exposed belly for my eyes to roam over. Her feet are bare, and her honey hair is wavy today, lips painted cherry red. She smells like jam and perfume, and the tiny smudge of paint on her elbow makes my chest tight.

What had me nearly laughing is thinking that she made her bank card PIN my birthday... *on purpose.* And that Dahlia Ellington, who probably has every single man in town in a puddle at her feet when she rolls through, punctured the tire of a woman I went to breakfast with because *she likes me.*

You are fucking delusion, Hudson, I think as I watch her plop down on my kitchen floor alongside my sister, trying on a pair of heels Ev is thinking about wearing with her rehearsal dinner dress. Dolly has the same size foot, so Ev likes her to try them on and walk around to get an idea of how she'd look.

Seems like a lot but then again, I own three pairs of shoes and have only ever owned three pairs of shoes my whole life. And when I got married? I wore one of those pairs. Women are cut from a different cloth.

"Now imagine a long gown covering the top," Ev says to Dolly as she turns, studying the profile of the strappy glittery thing in the floor-to-ceiling mirror by the door. Everly snaps her fingers. "You know what, I have the rehearsal gown. It'll be too big on you because you're tiny, but wanna pop it on? Give the full effect?"

Dolly laughs. "If that's what you want, I'll do it." She smiles, her eyes veering to me. "Hey, Hudson," she says, acknowledging me formally for the first time since being in my house. Had Tiffani waited so long to say hello I would have been irked. But I like that Dolly is comfortable in my home and comfortable with me.

"Hey, Dol. I hear you're sleeping over this weekend?" I muse, knowing the plans inside and out but unsure what else to say. My recent unsavory thoughts about Dolly have me feeling awkward. Heat flares up my neck at the memory of me calling Deuce to get his thoughts.

At that moment, he strolls through the door, a stack of pizza boxes in his hand. He hooks a thumb over his shoulder. "I intercepted," he says, handing the boxes to Ev who rushes over to take them.

Dolly appears in the hallway, wearing Ev's rehearsal gown. I guess I assumed she'd put it on over her clothes, but nope. In both hands she delicately holds extra fabric, keeping the hem from sweeping the floor as she walks toward us.

I know it's not a wedding dress.

It's a rehearsal something or other.

But it's white.

It's silk.

And her tiny little curves are on full display.

And I tell myself it's just that petite frame with those sweet hips and full breasts that has my breath gaining speed, my chest feeling tight, and sweat beading on my upper lip. I bring my hands together, my fingers circling the empty place where my wedding ring used to be.

Dropping my hands to my sides right away when I realize what I'm doing as I watch Dolly and Ev discuss things. Deuce knocks open the box of pizza, plating up a slice for Bear, who runs out when he smells pepperoni. With him eating and the women now back in the bathroom together, Deuce casts knowing eyes on me.

"Don't say it," I grumble, tucking into a slice of pizza as I tug another Coke from the fridge. If I'm going to Las Vegas with Deuce and a bunch of younger guys from his tattoo chains, I'm gonna need caffeine. Old dads aren't used to Vegas life. I'm not sure I'll enjoy it, but I'll do it for Deuce.

He smirks, tipping Bear's stone bucket up. "Gonna skip stones after pizza?" he asks my son.

"Yup," Bear says around a mouthful.

Deuce looks at me, still smirking. "And how about you? Think she'll let you go skip stones or is she too obsessed to let you out of her sight?" He catches his explosive grin in a closed fist, chuckling.

"I *am* sorry I called you," I admit, shaking my head as my

pulse rockets. I peer around the corner to the hallway, noticing a swish of denim. Dolly is getting dressed in my house. Dolly is in my house with her pants off.

Stop it, Hudson.

"And don't... say anything. Just... forget I brought it up," I breathe.

"Whatcha talking 'bout?" Bear asks, reaching for another slice.

"Your dad thinks a very, very pretty lady likes him," Deuce says, harassing me so passively that I'm one comment away from bailing on this trip.

"Deuce," I start, but Everly and Dolly come into the kitchen, sitting on stools opposite Bear.

"What are we talking about?" Ev questions, digging into the conversation.

"The pretty lady who likes Daddy," Bear supplies easily, swiping his sauce-coated fingers over his *The Amazing Spider-Man* t-shirt.

I cast murderous eyes at Deuce, who needs to remember that we're going to be related forever and my memory is long. He snaps, breaking the spell of the conversation.

"I got you a shirt for the trip! I almost forgot!" he says, jogging around the island to the foyer, disappearing outside.

"You ready to go to the creek?" Bear asks as I take a bite of pizza.

"Yeah, buddy, let me finish my pizza and we'll be skipping stones in no time, all right?" I rifle my hand through his hair as Deuce runs in, a black t-shirt balled up in his fist. He throws it at me, and I catch it with one hand, shaking it out to display the front.

Ev squints, reading it aloud slowly. "*Blow me for good luck.*"

My hands jerk down to cover Bear's ears. "Dude."

Ev snarls at her fiancé. "Deuce," she scolds.

"What?" He laughs. "It's not like he knows what getting blown means."

My eyes find their way to a very quiet Dolly. She's leaning toward Bear, willfully distracting him from the conversation by doodling a little stone on his paper napkin. That makes something at the back of my brain tingle a little.

"All right," I say, folding up the shirt and dropping it on the counter. "I'll bring it."

"You'll wear it," Deuce says. "And who knows, maybe you'll get your groove back in Vegas."

I narrow my eyes at him, shaking my head. I'm too old to feel embarrassed and yet right now, I wish Dolly wasn't witnessing the pathetic attempt of my sister's fiancé trying to get me laid.

"I never lost my..." I'm not saying *groove*. "Never mind."

"Oh," Dolly says, her light voice breaking the tension in my chest. "Bear, I forgot. I brought you something." She reaches into the small bag by her feet, one I didn't even notice she brought in. Maybe that's because my old pervy eyes were all over her hot little body.

Jesus Christ, Hudson. Get your thoughts under control before you get a hard-on in front of your kid and your sister.

She rifles around until there's a heavy plunk on the counter. Bear's hands tear into the brown package, immediately revealing a small, desk-sized easel, his own paint palette, and a bundle of brushes with a red ribbon tied around them.

His eyes fill. "Is this for me to keep?"

She nods, and I notice her eyes are wet, too. "Yep. Your very own. You can be an artist at home like me," she says excitedly, adding to Bear's already untapped excitement. He hugs her so tightly she grunts a little, and Deuce nudges me.

In a private voice he says, "God, look how obsessed with you she is."

I eye him. "*Shut up.*"

I've given Bear a thousand hugs and kisses, but it still doesn't feel like enough. He's four years old but I've never spent a night away from him. Not a single one.

I tug my flannel up over my nose, looking for his scent as I wait in the passenger seat. Deuce has been making out with my sister on the front porch for way too fucking long, and I'm a moment away from honking the horn to break up the damn tonsil hockey when a car appears at the top of the drive.

A *familiar* car.

"Fuck," I groan into the cab, peering back up at the house.

Deuce is right.

I was wrong, off and just plain hopeful if I thought Dolly was sending off any certain… vibe. But still, I find myself glancing between Tiffani's approaching car and the house, hoping that Ev will go back inside and distract Dolly.

It's ridiculous but something in my gut still flares at the idea of Dolly... It's irrational and senseless, but I find myself reactively ducking beneath the doorframe, sliding my big ass out of Deuce's truck. I meet Tiffani at her door as she's putting her car in park. She came by yesterday night to drop off the casserole. I didn't want to see her then. I stifle a sigh.

"Looks like I made it just in time," she says, stepping out of her car in... pink high heels.

I know some guys have a thing for heels. They like them over their shoulder, more so. But fancy shit doesn't do much for me. I blink down at her shiny, pointy shoes, and find myself widening my stance to accommodate my stiffening cock as I remember *Dolly's bare feet*.

She's a salt of the earth kind of woman, and that's what I like. Someone who wants to feel the ranch beneath her and live on the land that keeps her fed.

"Guess you did," I reply, forcing a small smile. "We were just about to go."

I glance over at Deuce, who is now peppering kisses onto Everly's hand while she giggles. *Jesus Christ*. If they'd cut this *no, you hang up first* bullshit, I could've avoided whatever this is going to be.

"Look at that," she says quietly, though even when she's keeping her voice low, the pitch is still somehow.... *grating*. "They love each other so much it's hard for them to spend a weekend apart." She pokes my belly, and I don't care for it. "Don't you wonder what that feels like?"

"No," I answer quickly. "I know what it's like." I hook a

thumb to the truck behind me in the drive. "I was trying to smell Bear on my shirt because I miss him already."

Her face falls, because even though my response was honest, it's clear she was trying to flirt and thinks I missed the cue.

I didn't miss the cue.

I don't wanna pretend that I'd ever stand on my front porch and be kissing Tiffani's hand because I don't want to say goodbye.

I'm all for getting back in the dating game and slowly introducing Bear to a woman who becomes important to me, but I'm having a hard time believing that Tiffani could ever be more.

"That's sweet," she says, her face suspended in an unnatural smile. "Well, I thought I'd come to tell you good luck." She leans in, grabbing my shirt to tug me down to her. "Just don't get too lucky." She winks as Deuce approaches, slapping Tiffani on the back, causing her to jolt.

"Hey, Tiffani."

"Uh, hey, Deuce," she says, straightening a little from his brazen greeting. "I just came to say bye to Hudson and to tell him good luck. But... don't get too lucky."

Deuce steps onto the side of his pickup, talking to Tiffani over the hood. "No such thing as too lucky." He looks past her to Ev, who is still on the porch, holding the door closed. "Bye, baby. I'm gonna miss you and your sweet lips and that soft little—"

"I will come around this truck and beat you senseless if you finish that sentence," I deadpan sternly. I already told him, I'll go on this bachelor trip as long as no one says a goddamn word about my sister. As far as I know, she's still a virgin.

Let me live in delusion, damn it.

Deuce buckles up, laughing, and as he pulls out of the driveway, I catch an eyeful from the side mirror.

Dolly on the porch, feet still bare, her eyes set on the back of Tiffani's head in the driveway, waving us off like we're going to war. Her eyes are narrowed, and I swear to fuck, her lips are pulled into a scowl. But then Bear appears, and her expression morphs to softness and adoration.

I sit a little straighter in the seat, nodding along with Deuce's plans to double down on roulette to win big.

All the while I keep thinking... *Am* I right about Dolly?

fifteen

FAIR IS FAIR.

Dolly

This *isn't* the plan. This is veering very far off course and while I pride myself on always being able to see the bigger picture, I'm having a very hard time understanding why *Tiffani* is at Hudson's house while he's on his trip to Las Vegas.

"Maybe Everly invited her?" Juniper offers, her hair in an elegant bun on top of her head, a silver pin through the center. She's making more cherry jam today, and if I didn't know it, I'd wonder who she killed because there are thick streaks of red all over her forearms and apron.

"Or maybe she just stopped by? Remember, she popped in *before* Hudson left for Vegas," Ivy offers, coming to stand on the opposite side as Juni. The three of us stand in our living room, curtains pulled, sights set on the shitty teal car in front of Hudson's.

"I don't want her bonding with Bear and rekindling her friendship with Everly." *Don't play family with my family, you cunt.* "She's a lying, money-grubbing whore," I breathe, my anger spinning up at the speed of light.

"I can go over there and pretend to need sugar or something?" Juni offers softly, stroking her hands down my hair to soothe the storm she clearly knows is twisting around inside me. "Find out why she's there?"

"Wait," Ivy says, sliding her hand in mine.

A few years ago, the three of us saw a therapist together. It's not like I don't know that obsessing over a man isn't *completely* normal. And Ivy and Juni, well, they have their things too.

Turns out, we're happier having our things and protecting each other than being boringly normal. But in therapy, we did learn that a hand hold and a hand squeeze from someone you love and trust can sometimes help to break up the budding cyclone of anger.

It works a little. But the longer I stare at Tiffani's car, the more ineffective the hand hold technique becomes.

"What is she lying about?" Ivy questions, turning to face me in an effort to get me to break my laser gaze on the car.

"Everything," I breathe, facing Ivy only when my eyes go fuzzy from staring so hard. "I looked her up," I admit, motioning for them to follow me as I head down the hall to my room. Bypassing the *toothbrush drawer* and the *photo drawer*, I open my *research drawer* and pluck out the file titled *HER*.

I hand it to Ivy, who sifts through it with Juni over her shoulder.

"But she went to school with Ev," Ivy says, confusion rippling her forehead, a strand of dark hair falling over her face as she brings the paper nearer.

"You're understanding just fine," I say, watching her try to make the words change on the paper. "They did go to college together. But Tiffani lied about graduating. And she lied about her high-powered job, too."

Juni shrugs. "Maybe she's just embarrassed and those lies are, like, just for her, you know? The things she tells herself to feel better."

"She's lying to Hudson and Bear about who she is," I say, "and that's not right."

An awkward silence fills my bedroom, and I slide my foot over the drop of blood that didn't get cleaned. I keep it there because it reminds me of being rescued by Hud that day.

"You guys know that I'm going to tell him," I say to my sisters. "As soon as he realizes that he loves me back, I'm going to come clean." I slice my hand between us. "It's not the same thing. Tiffani is purposefully lying. I am protecting my love. *There's a difference.*"

"Definitely," Juniper agrees because no matter what, inside these walls, there is endless loyalty and under-standing.

"So, what're you gonna do? Because laundry listing her lies to Hud may not be received well. You'll look jealous and crazy," Ivy says simply.

I lift a photo of Hudson from my night table and look

into his soulful eyes. "I'm going to go over there and get to know her. And Ev's going to get to know her, too."

"Ev already knows her," Juni says, confused as we walk back into the kitchen. I leave the photo of Hud in my room.

"The real her," I clarify. "The Tiffani who looked up college classmates to see who she could use." I swipe my finger through a cooling pot of preserves. "I'll be back."

My sisters offer their luck, but I don't need it.

The universe is still on my side and Hudson is my soulmate. Tiffani is just a blip in the timeline, a blip *I'm going to get rid of.*

"Oh," I smile sweetly as I collect an excited Bear in my open arms. "Hi, Tiffani, I didn't know you stopped by to visit."

Because that's all you are, Tiffani. You're an unwanted visitor.

"Hi, Bear, you missing Daddy yet?" I hold Tiffani's eyes as I speak to him, nestled against my neck as he embraces me warmly. "I miss him."

Everly's eyes cut to mine. I've never made any comments about Hud around her, not even subtly. But the message is just for Tiffani, and something she needs to hear. Still, since Everly is eyeing me cautiously, I veil the statement as my eyes go to her. "After all, if he doesn't skip stones with you, I guess that means I have to..."

Ev's caution melts into a sweet smile. "We already went out this morning. How are you, Dolly?"

I get to my feet as Bear skitters off, promising to return with his new teddy bear and matching storybook. I don't recall him getting a teddy from Hudson or Everly recently.

I want to hold the question back and preserve every ounce of cool while Everly is here, but my veins heat and my mind starts spinning, my skin breaking out in a nagging, uncomfortable itch. Turning to Tiffani, I wear a sweet smile as I ask, "Did you buy Bear a gift?"

She returns the smile, though her eyes don't lift. *I see you, bitch.* "I did. Just so he doesn't get sad on his first weekend away from his daddy."

My hand flies to the kitchen island, palm slapping the cool tile as I grip it. I reach and grip so loudly that I startle Ev. "You okay?" she asks, pressing her palm to my forehead. I shrug her off.

"Fine." I smile at Tiffani, who *apparently* also knows that this is the first time Hudson has ever left Bear. I already knew that because I have seen Bear every single day of his life since he was born. *I* have been here, celebrating all of his birthdays, watching him develop through milestones, watching Hudson grow in fatherhood. And this bitch with her red lips and her *lies* thinks we're the same.

We are not the same.

"That's great." I take the teddy from Bear's hands when he appears. "Oh wow, how special. It's brown and fuzzy," I say excitedly to Bear as my eyes take a pulse check on Tiffani. "How *special.*" She wants to be called stepmom for getting a shitty teddy bear from the drug store on the way here? Fuck that.

I held Bear when he fell off his scooter and got a pebble lodged in his knee. He screamed and cried until Hudson rode in from the field and scooped him up. His blood and snot stained my white sundress. I *still* think about his painful cries when I put that dress on.

I stroked my hand through Bear's hair when he was an infant in a bassinet the day Hudson and *she who we do not mention* brought him home.

Me.

Not Tiffani.

I've been a collector of Hudson's details for the last five years.

Not Tiffani.

"Ev, I just came by to offer to stay with Bear while you run into town to get things from the market." I swipe my hand through his hair. "If you help me and my sisters set up the canopies, I'll skip stones with you at the creek for two hours on Sunday." I hold out my pinkie, offering him a promise.

Bear bounces. "*Please*. Can I stay with Dolly? Pretty please?"

I smile at Tiffani. "You can spend the morning with Everly getting ready for the farmers market. Hudson will be so grateful." Hudson won't give a shit that Tiffani rode shotgun while Everly did the work, collecting invoices, taking payments, gathering supplies, picking up ice and food. More than that? I want her away from me.

And I don't trust her setting up the farmers market. I don't want her lying, grubby hands on the canopies, on the tables– I don't even want her breathing the air on this property if I'm being honest. But I can't control where she goes and breathes, unfortunately, so the next best option is shoving her off on Everly.

I love Ev, but she made a mistake bringing this woman around. And today she will have to take her punishment with her as she runs errands.

Fair is fair.

Bear slips his hand in mine. "Wanna go now?"

I shoot him a wink. "Soon. I thought I'd grab a cup of coffee while I'm here." Typically, I'd be sneaking into this house ten minutes from now, licking my way through his dirty dishes in the sink on my way to the bathroom. But because he hasn't been here today and his toothbrush is with him, I'm here now.

I only drink coffee if it's been in his mouth, otherwise it's disgusting, but I'll take one for the team.

"Oh, I'll brew you a cup. I got that single-serve machine for Hudson last Christmas, remember?" Ev asks, shoving a stack of envelopes in her purse. The Feed 'n' Seed passes through my mind. "Oh," I snap my fingers, pretending a memory has returned, "I'm supposed to pass a message to Jade, from Hud. He said to tell her, I got the note and the answer is never."

Ev wrinkles her nose. "Never?"

I smile. "GMO feed. It's cheaper, apparently, and she was looking to unload some." I shrug.

"Got the note, never," Everly nods, repeating. "Okay, I'll tell her."

She slides a coffee pod into the machine and places a

mug beneath. I turn to Tiffani, who is tapping away on her phone screen. *Rude. You're with people, put your phone down.*

"So you and Everly met in college?" I say, mentally cracking my knuckles. But I need Everly to hear Tiffani's response. She'll lie, no doubt, but it's *how* she lies that Ev will catch on to. Everly is sharp, and she was the first person to notice something going on with Hudson's ex years back.

I sip my coffee when she passes it to me, quickly make sure the mug isn't a keepsake, and drop it, watching glass and coffee go everywhere.

"Oh my gosh!" I cry, leaping up. I hold my palms out, stopping Ev who is already armed with a roll of paper towels. "No, let me."

"You're okay? You didn't get burned?" she asks, bending to collect the glass. Unsurprisingly, Tiffani stays seated. Ev grabs a big bag, and together we pick up glass. She doesn't even seem annoyed.

I can't wait until she's officially my sister.

"So while we clean, Tiffani, tell me about college and meeting Everly," I say as I drop the broken handle into the bag.

Tiffani places her phone on the counter, her smile neatly in place. *For now, bitch, for now.* "Well, I transferred as a freshman after the first semester. We lived in the same apartment complex, that's how I met her."

I already knew that but I say, "Oh yeah? Did you two live together?"

"No," she laughs, "I always had to live alone. I *love* having my space."

My mind goes to the small house in Reno and the mass of cars parked there. "I get that." I drop a handful of collected shards into the bag, then get to work on the spilled coffee. Everly hands me the paper towels as she moves for the Lysol. From the other room, Bear shouts he's ready to go to the creek. Me too, buddy.

But I've got a job to do while Hudson is gone, and that job is to introduce doubt in Everly's mind. Shouldn't take too much; Ev is smart and Tiffani... *isn't.*

"So, what's your degree in?" I ask, knowing that the next few questions probably have very practiced answers, since she's likely been telling these lies for years.

"I'm a lawyer, Dolly, so my undergrad was pre-law." Her eyes dart to Everly, like she's going to pass her a silent joke about my ignorance, but Ev doesn't look.

"But that's not a degree." *I would know, I looked it up when I researched you.*

I thought she'd have an easy answer to this. Maybe this stupid answer of hers has worked everywhere else. But not here. I'm on a mission. *Hudson is mine.*

"So, what was your *actual* degree in?" I press.

I feel Everly's gaze lift from the mess. She laughs. "Gosh, Dolly," she says, tapping her chin with freshly washed hands. "I don't think I even know this." She faces Tiffani. "What *is* your undergraduate degree in?"

Tiffani's smile falters, but stays in place. "Business."

It's clear she does not remember what Everly's degree is in. Ev laughs. "I was a business major, I think I'd remember that!"

Stringing my fingers through my hair casually, I comment, "Maybe I should buy a lotto ticket. It's not every day you meet a lawyer with a bad memory." Everly laughs along with the playful jab, but Tiffani's glare is sharp.

Doesn't matter. I'm impenetrable when it comes to the person trying to take the love of my life away from me.

"So, what firm did you leave? I think I heard you got tired of law and came out here for some country livin', right?" I ask, moving my finger along the grout on the kitchen counter. I sat on this counter and touched myself while licking Hudson's plate clean. I have memories here and a past with him, whether he knows it or not.

"Right," she nods, "time for something new."

"But what firm was it?" I ask again, the names of the partners at the time she allegedly worked there pre-loaded on my lips. I'm not just making her uncomfortable, I'm poking holes in her bullshit and watching her boat slowly fill. And I want Ev to watch, too, because Hudson will undoubtedly turn to his sister for advice at some point. She has no reason *not* to be on my side, but the college cama-raderie bullshit that Tiffani is leaning into has to *go*.

"Dallas & Sons," she simply states.

I press a hand to my chest, feigning shock. "Chuck's office?" I look at Everly, eyes wide. "Chuck and Nancy's firm on West Elm Street?"

Tiffani's swallow is audible. "You've been to San Francisco?"

I tried three stories out on Ivy and Juni at home a few weeks ago, preparing for this very moment. I go with the one that got two of our three votes.

"After our dad died, my sisters and I needed to find a lawyer who could answer questions regarding the estate, and more." The *and more* is important since the law firm she lied about working at doesn't practice estate law. "My dad actually knew Chuck Dallas from way back," I explain, "so yeah, I know them well."

I shake my head, grinning like a madwoman, because I know that's exactly what I am. "You know what, I'm gonna call him this week and tell him he will never believe who's living here now."

Bear reappears, his arms crossed over his chest.

"I wanna set up the canopies. I've been waiting six minutes for you, Dolly." He sighs, and six minutes for a four year old is like two hours for adults.

"You did good," I tell him. "Thank you for waiting. I'm ready." I face a wide-eyed Tiffani, who doesn't even acknowledge Bear when Hudson isn't here. I hope Ev notices that, too. I slip my hand in his, and take the bag of tools off the countertop, ready to get to work on Hudson's behalf. "It was nice chatting. Have fun in town. Text me when you're back and I'll bring him in," I tell Ev.

Then I turn and leave, taking Bear with me.

He doesn't tell Tiffani goodbye on his way out, and I hold his hand a little tighter for it.

<h1 style="text-align:center">sixteen</h1>

MY MILK ON HER UPPER LIP THOUGH...

Hudson

I was given strict orders to make sure that Deuce doesn't misbehave on this trip but it's been Deuce who's been doing the babysitting. His close friend, world-renowned tattoo artist, is on this trip and I can say, without a doubt, I have no desire to take another trip with Trace Calhoun.

First of all, *the man can drink*. And I don't mean hold some shots and beers but finish a bottle and seem... relatively sober. On the first night, he didn't get sloppy until after the first bottle, and tonight, he's been sloppy for a while, despite the fact he's *only* had a handle of Crown. I think it's other substances, or, I don't know.

When he gets in a group of women who love ink and know who he is, he seems to get completely lost. His ability to function normally is all but gone and the Trace left to socialize is loud, boisterous, offensive, grabby and... *annoying.*

He's Deuce's friend, so I'm trying not to burn out. Though I can't help but think that Bluebell isn't the right fit for him.

Deuce and I sit at the end of the bar in a keno lounge, waiting for our next round of drinks before we hit the blackjack tables. Trace has been playing blackjack for two hours, and hit the ATM twice in that time.

"I mean, he's good, right?" I ask Deuce, who is eyeing his friend across the casino as he sips from the long neck.

Deuce shoves a hand through his hair, letting out a sigh. "No, he's not. But this is... his last hurrah."

I cock an eyebrow, confused but wanting clarification. A cocktail waitress in a blue sequin corset passes by, dragging her fingernails along the terrain of my shoulders. "Hi, guys," she offers, her voice throaty and strained against the diluted casino rumblings.

Deuce waggles his eyebrows at me after she passes by. I roll my eyes.

"No," I say before sipping my beer. "Not my style."

"Having some fun with a beautiful woman who you have no obligations to?" Deuce questions, nudging my arm with his. He sips his beer slowly, eyeing me. "You really don't got a one-night stand in you?"

I shrug, finishing the beer. "Tell me about Trace. Let's go back to that."

Deuce laughs. "All right. Fine. But your sister is set on you not being single."

"Trace," I say simply, finishing my beer. My head goes a

little flighty after I finish my fourth. I don't usually drink unless it's after a hard day on the ranch, when I feel like I've earned the vice. Being day-drunk just isn't a thing for me.

Until now, apparently.

I rub my temples as Deuce twists on the barstool, legs spread wide in dark jeans and combat boots. "He's coming to Bluebell to work at my new place, you know?"

I narrow my eyes. "Yes."

"Okay, so... he wants to come here and open this location and get it thriving. But he's also getting away from some... *bad PR* in Los Angeles."

"What did he do?" I ask, my skin prickling with unease as I glance over at the wealthy tattoo artist and TV star.

"He was engaged and it ended... publicly."

I tilt my head. "I think you answered that question without actually answering that question."

Deuce strokes his hand down the stubble growing. He's growing a beard, apparently, and when I asked why he'd do that right before his wedding, he told me "the wedding night" and I wanted to bore holes through my eardrums and set my brain on fire.

"He cheated on his fiancé with his assistant... on a live stream. And, yeah, he's... recovering." Deuce shrugs. "No one's perfect. I'm just helping a friend."

I peer over at Trace who is slamming his inked hands against the green felted table, whooping in delight. This guy is clearly a mess, or a piece of shit, or both, but I respect Deuce for wanting to help.

I clap a hand on his shoulder and squeeze. "You're a good man, Deuce."

He shrugs. "I never thought I was until Everly told me

she loved me." His face grows serious. "A woman like her would never love a loser. That's when I learned my value, when your sister said she wanted to be my girl."

That's an incredibly thoughtful answer, so we both face forward and clear our throats, staring down the long neck of our beers, analyzing the booze.

"I'm glad Ev found you, Deuce, I am," I finally say. The bartender slides us another, and I don't remember ordering it but I take a long drink from it anyway, enjoying the fuzzy calm settling into my veins.

"So I won't tell Ev but... what's the deal? You really *still* ain't into Tiffani at all, huh?" he asks, his words slurring together a little. Maybe blackjack isn't our best play after this.

I consider his words, and find it interesting that it takes a healthy amount of work to get Tiffani's face to appear in my mind. And she showed up as I was leaving. And before that, she dropped off a casserole. Still, imagining her face takes effort. And it's not the beer.

"I just... don't get a feeling from her, you know?" I realize that I'm drunk as I say those words, because I'm not the kind of man to talk about my feelings in ethereal, general-ized vagueness.

He nods. "When I laid eyes on Everly, I swear to God it was a movie moment. Like, the world around me jumbled into a slow, quiet blur and she was all I could see. And the first time we fu–"

"*No.*"

He drags his hand down his mouth. "Sorry, sometimes I forget you're her brother."

"Anyway, all I'm saying is... I get it."

I peer over at him. "Does Everly? Because... I don't want her to worry. And I want her to be free to live her life, I do. And I get that she can't help with Bear when you guys have your own brood but... I don't know." I play with the cardboard coaster beneath my drink, the casino logo wearing from the condensation left behind. "I don't like talking about this shit," I huff, tugging the label from the bottle.

When I'm in a relationship, what me and her do is for us. I don't wanna talk about what we do in the bedroom or how I feel for her or any of that shit— not with anyone but *her*.

I've always been that way. Relationships to me are private. But I know that isn't how everyone is, and I also know that Ev and Deuce are only trying to help. In their own way. "I don't wanna sleep with Tiffani when I know there's no future."

But I do want to stop feeling strange things for Dolly. That, even with the beers in my veins, I don't say. Instead, I offer, "It would be nice to have a relationship, though. I won't deny that."

Deuce catches a burp with his shirt sleeve. "Don't tell your sister I had terrible manners all weekend," he warns before stacking his boots on the barstool and leaning in. "You really aren't a one-night stand guy, huh?"

I shake my head. "I've had exactly zero one-night stands." I finish my drink, fully drunk now. "I don't want any, either."

"You haven't been laid since your ex?" He lets out a low whoop of shock, one that has no effect on me. I'm wearing my booze shield. "You must be close with your hand, eh," he laughs, shaking his head.

"We aren't talking about this," I breathe, pushing away

from the bar, glancing over to see Trace covered in doting women, a stack of chips up to his head in front of him. "Now, it's your last weekend free from Everly's clutches. Let's go make shitty choices and gamble."

Deuce gets to his feet, dropping his arm over my shoulders. "Let's fucking do it."

Jesus Christ. Is this hotel room on the surface of the fucking sun? My hands shoot up from beneath the sheets, getting tangled as I curse and groan in a hurried attempt to block the glaring light and heat from my face.

"*Motherfucking, cocksucking…*" I slur, stumbling violently out of bed. One of the grommets pops loose from the rod above as I fall into the blinds, yanking them closed, darkness enveloping me. I fall onto the other queen bed, still neatly made, and hold my head.

I don't hardly drink and I don't hardly curse and I almost never gamble.

Last night was… I think it was great. Though I can't be so sure because as of right now, the only thing I'm focused on is… "Water," I say aloud. *I need water.*

I stumble to the sink, taking the paper hat off one of the tiny glasses. Holding it beneath the faucet, I fill it and finish it at least ten times. Damn tiny playhouse-sized cup. As soon as I can get myself in the shower, I'm heading down-stairs for some more water followed by coffee.

Just then, my phone vibrates on the nightstand. *Shit.* Today is the farmers market. In my drunken stupor last night, though I'd checked in with Bear and Ev before things got too wild, I forgot to send a reminder text for final details.

Everly knows, so it's a moot point, but still, I feel like an asshole leaving her with my son and the market without so much as a good-luck and thank-you text this morning.

I stumble to the phone, getting to it right in time.

"Hello?" I couldn't see who was calling, but I know as soon as she speaks that it isn't Everly.

"Hey, Hudson," Dolly greets, and despite the egregious amount of beer still in my system and the fact I haven't taken a piss yet, my cock stirs at her soft, effusive tone. The good part about a dark hotel room in Las Vegas? The guilt doesn't seem to know where I am, because my cock gets fat as I fall back against the pillows, holding the phone to my ear.

"Hey, Dol, how's it going? You guys ready for the farmers market?" My voice is hoarse, stretched thin from talking over machines and Deuce all night. I sip from the tiny water cup I brought from the bathroom.

"Oh, yeah!" she says proudly, which makes me grin as I shift beneath the sheets, searching for a pocket of cool fabric. I take another drink of the water as she puts Bear on the phone.

"Hey, buddy," I greet my son. "Are you excited for today?"

"Yeah," he says, out of breath from running around like a crazy person, no doubt. Another smile hits me as I envision the farmers market on my property back home, all of the town out there, smiling and chatting. "I got to help Dolly, Ivy and Juni set up the boofs–"

"Booths," I correct softly.

"Yeah," he breathes, "those. And it was so much fun. And this morning before the market, me and Dolly did another painting together in her barn. And Dolly promised she'd take me to the creek for two full hours today after. Daddy, I'm so excited. I'm having so much fun with Dolly!"

I stroke my hands over the stubble coating my chin, finding I'm still smiling. "Where's Aunt Ev?" I knew Everly had wedding things to do, and that she was working those errands in with the market errands, but from Bear's perspective, Dolly's doing an awful lot of work.

"She's here," he says, answering nothing. "Anyway, love you, Daddy, I gotta go." He disappears from the line, and I envision Dolly's phone with a lit-up screen sitting in the midst of the dirt as he takes off, oblivious. Fortunately, that's not what happens, because Dolly's soft voice is back a moment later.

"Sorry–I wasn't sure if Ev called you and let you talk to him this morning and he just wanted to tell you how much fun he's having," she says. I look between my legs, finding the crisp white hotel sheet tented between my thighs.

"She..." I glance at my phone. Two missed calls. Shit. "She did, but I guess I slept through them," I admit. Wrapping my hand around the sheet, I take a breath and tug it down, exposing my wood to the cool, dark hotel room.

I close my eyes and sink into the covers, enjoying the melodic sweetness of her voice. "Oh, well, must've been a great night if you slept through your phone ringing! Well, I won't keep you. Just wanted to let you know that the market looks gorgeous. You'd be proud."

I see Dolly at her booth, her golden hair glowing as she holds out a greeting card with red balloons painted on the front. Her lips are painted the same fiery red as the balloons, and she's wearing that blue-and-white sundress that hugs her petite frame and full curves just perfectly. *I'd fucking wreck Dolly Ellington if I got my big, grubby, old hands on her.*

I crack an eye open, watching my erection bob, gaining girth at the sound of her voice. "Glad it's going smoothly. I hear I got you to thank for most of that, too."

"Hmm," she breathes, making this little noise in her throat that has me reaching for my cock, something I know is wrong. She's so young, and *still*, I stroke myself. I've never felt more free than I have in this hotel room right now. "Well, you know the market means a lot to my sisters and me, too."

"I appreciate that," I groan, knowing that I *should* feel guilty for touching myself while I'm talking to her but... my sexual needs have come roaring back to the forefront of my brain lately, and seemingly been focused on... *Dolly.*

"I'll send some pics after we hang up. Anyway, have fun and... hey, if you wear that shirt Deuce got you, send me a picture. It's too funny not to remember."

"Will do," I say, reaching under my shaft to give my hot, heavy balls a healthy tug.

"Bye, Hudson. See you tomorrow."

"Bye, Dol," I tell her, "Thank you again."

When I hang up, I'm about to finish what I'm starting but she sends three text messages right away.

The first one is a shot of all the canopies, everything set

up the way it always is. The next one is a photo of Gray Farms's milk stand, the bottles front-faced perfectly. The last one...

Dolly is holding a jar of Gray Farms's vitamin D milk in one hand. The jar is beaded in condensation, a flicker of the summer sun peeking into the tent from the corner, causing a stripe of orange to fall against her face. She's grinning, her perfect tits pushed up in that white sundress she wears, the one that's thin enough to make me hard but opaque enough to drive me mad. Fuck, that's the first time I've acknowledged that Dolly is usually a turn-on. I've always ignored it. It always felt so wrong.

But I'm still kind of drunk.

And her voice is so soft.

She'd curl up so nicely against me.

My eyes steer back to her face as I get to my feet, placing the phone on the edge of the mattress, in the covers. I grip my cock with one hand, using my free hand to zoom in on the image.

Rimming her full pink top lip is... milk. *My milk.* Fresh and creamy, it sits in a thick white arch, her tongue peeking out the corner of her mouth only slightly. The photo is... harmless. She's showing off Gray Farms, showing me the booth, smiling, proving I've got nothing to worry about here.

My milk on her upper lip, though...

My bicep flexes and torques as I begin furiously stroking. Sticky and clear, precum threads between my open, hungry slit and the screen of the phone, fogging Dolly's breasts.

I know it's wrong as the day is long but I can't help but see that strip of white above her lip as *my cum.*

I'd trace her beautiful face with one fingertip, and swipe through it as it drips from her chin. Those pink lips would part and I'd press my finger onto her warm, waiting tongue, and she'd close around it, sucking every drop off. She'd want it. She'd *really* fucking want it, in her mouth, on her skin, *inside of her.*

My arm works faster at the mere flash I get of myself swaying over Dolly's slender build, my legs engulfing her as I push my cock into her silk panties. *"Just a little,"* she'd breathe, my eyes fluttering, fist pumping as the fantasy consumes me. I see my large hand hooking a finger around the soaked satin, tugging the crotch aside to expose two perfect lips covered in blonde curls, arousal glistening. I use my finger to part her, stroking up and down, teasing before I push inside, taking my time so I don't hurt her.

What would sweet Dolly sound like with me fucking her? "Mmm," I groan, my eyes opening, fixating on Dolly's upper lip and her full breasts.

The last fantasy to cross my mind before I come is Dolly, wearing that dress, on her knees in front of me, palms on her thighs. *"Feed me,"* she whispers, her tone husky with desire, lashes fluttering, lips slowly parting.

"Fuuuuck," I grit out, choking my fist down to the wide crown of my cock. I watch with rapt attention as I coat the screen in streaks of cum, my desire for Dolly emptying everything. The bed around the phone is soaked, the screen is coated, and cum drips from my knuckles as I stand on wobbly legs over the bed.

Post-nut clarity doesn't know it's way to Las Vegas, either, apparently.

I grab a towel from the bathroom and clean up my

phone, taking one last look at the photo of Dolly before face-planting into the unused bed. I'm not quite ready to face what I just did... or this day.

I drift off, thoughts of Dolly's loyalty on my mind. If only she were older...

seventeen

ADRENALINE-CRASH SLUMBER.

Dolly

I am focusing on the good.

One, two, three—deep breath in. Hold—one, two, three—release. Though a vice of anger and hurt keeps my chest tight, I tilt my chin up and replay the good.

Hudson came to the house to see me the day he got back from Las Vegas. He thoughtfully brought a basket of goodies from my favorite vendors at the market. He'd gone to their respective stores and collected the items that same day. Even though it was also for Ivy and Juni—for all the hard work—*he came to see me.*

I know it.

I opened the door casually, smiling without giving away that I'd been tracking his flight, then Deuce's pickup the entire ride back. I love AirTags, they fit anywhere and never lose signal. Slipping one into Deuce's truck liner eased my anxiety. Knowing how close to home Hud was helped me.

When I opened the door, he never once asked where Ivy or Juni were. Even though he was there to thank all three of us.

His hand brushed mine when he passed me the basket, and after I watched him walk back to his place through the peephole, I ran my fingertips along my nipples and down my bare belly, hopelessly trying to scatter the traces of his touch along my skin.

There's a knock at my bedroom door but I can't move. My palms are sticky and damp, plastered to the glass, my heated breath fogging the window. "Dol?" Juni calls gently, walking on her proverbial tiptoes around the bomb ticking down to detonation.

Me.

Only, the closer I get to him, the nearer he is to realizing what's in front of him, the more I know *I have to* control my explosive behavior. He won't run over and rescue me from broken glass *again* and not have questions or concerns.

I'm not stupid.

"Come in," I reply as my sisters filter in regardless. That's what sisters do.

"I saw her car," Ivy says, mentioning *the thing* that caused me to destroy six canvases in my barn, one of which was going to be a wedding present for Everly and Deuce.

I got a little... *upset.*

I'd gone to Hud's place to see if Bear wanted to work on our painting project together. The guys were headed out to pasture to mend the downed fence from the storm.

Tiffani answered the door and said *she'd* be watching Bear today while Hud and the guys worked.

I don't know if I snapped as much as I *exploded*. Internally of course, like every good raging woman since the dawn of time.

I held a smile long enough to fool her, then walked casually back to my barn—though I don't know *how* I did it because I couldn't see a single thing. My vision was utter havoc; motion in explosive bursts of darkness and color, fragmenting my reality, leaving the world a distorted mess.

I always lose my vision when I'm hit with *passionate* rage. And I only ever get hit with this anger when it comes to *my soul mate*.

I destroyed things I loved, cut my forearms on the broken frames of canvases, shit all over my sacred workspace (metaphorically, of course), and ruined another sundress with blood and paint.

I stood there, chest heaving, tears streaking my face.

This isn't *just* about Hudson.

This is about Bear.

I love Bear. I have always loved Bear, and that love is separate from my crushing, consuming love and adoration for *his father*.

Bear loves me back. Hud's selection of *Tiffani* to watch Bear while he works instead of *me*, the person who has cared for and loved that little boy since his near-first breath—it *hurts*.

It hurts so fucking bad.

And I really hate being hurt.

"Why is he hurting me like this?" I press, my bottom lip breaking into a rare tremble. "He *loves* me," I tell them, my nostrils flaring, heart racing as I spit out the truth I *know* in my bones.

"He's in love with me and I'm his. I belong to him. I love Bear, I want Bear." Tears come fast and my stomach swirls, unease and pain causing a riptide of nausea to pull me under. "Why is he doing this?" I sob, crumbling to my bed, wrapping my arms around my torso, clinging to myself. Trying to take my own pain away. Juni and Ivy sit with me, rubbing my back tenderly, pushing hair from my tear-streaked face.

They talk about the situation as I cry, but because I know without a shadow of a doubt that the universe brought Hudson and I together because we're soulmates, my brain doesn't let me wallow for long. I take in their conversation, and mentally get back on my feet.

When you really love someone and *know* they love you back—whether they've arrived there or not—you can't let them push you away.

I know this.

I also know he doesn't mean it.

He doesn't *want* to hurt me.

He's... protecting himself.

"Maybe he fucked some chick in Vegas and now feels guilty since he's dated her a few times and…. He's having her over to ease his own guilt," Ivy offers. I sit up long enough to stab her with my trained, honed and pointed death glare.

"*My Hudson* doesn't have one-night stands." There is no possibility of this. I know my man. He wants love, or nothing. That's why I'm so fucked up over Tiffani being here to watch Bear.

I don't want that bitch in my house. I don't want her in

the house that *we* will bring *our* newborn baby home to. My memories are on the horizon in that house, *not hers*. She needs to get the fuck out.

Poor Hudson is just... confused.

Juniper massages my neck, my head cozy in Ivy's lap. "Maybe... I don't know. Maybe he's feeling guilty over how he's feeling about you and this is... to try to convince himself otherwise."

My pulse picks up.

"He didn't give a shit if we got that basket the other day," Ivy ruminates.

"And when you called him about the farmers market, did he ask to talk to Ev or Bear?" Juni inquires.

I shake my head, sitting up. "No. I put Bear on the line but he... he sounded tired. Maybe hungover." I twirl hair around my finger, taking a bite of my bottom lip. "He was happy to talk to me." *I'm sure of it.*

Ivy gets to her feet, outstretching a hand for Juni to take. "He's coming around, definitely. And Juniper's right. If he is starting to see you as a woman and not Dolly the babysitter next door, he could be feeling guilty."

I shake my head. "Why? Why feel guilty about wanting me?" *I want all of you, baby, and I want you to have all of me. Every ounce.* My body shudders at a hot flash of him.

Juni purses her lips, crossing her arms over her chest, her overall straps tugging. "Come on, Dolly. You're sickeningly smart. This is a small town. Hudson is thirty-eight and you're twenty. He probably feels like a perv liking a woman nearly half his age. He's likely concerned about what the town would think."

Fuck the town. "You think he likes me?" I sit on my

knees in the center of my bed, steepling my hands together beneath my chin like a little girl settling in for bedtime prayer. Excitement has my heart soaring. My knuckles ache from the abuse I put them through, and I briefly imagine the ruined art in the barn.

I shake it out of my head. "Okay so... he *is* starting to see that all he needs is next door. But he feels bad so... he asks Tiffani to watch Bear in an effort to convince himself to date someone his own age?"

Stringing it out like that, it makes sense. And Hudson *has* been more interested in me than normal. "Yeah," Ivy says, peering out the window at the movement outside. "Hey, Deuce is here, I gotta go."

"Good luck," Juniper says, pulling Ivy into a hug. With her jet-black hair styled into two buns atop her head, a studded purple kitten ear pinned to each, her eyeliner winged and her lips black, she looks ready to be a talented, badass tattoo artist. I really hope Deuce hires her for the apprentice role, and equally, I hope the men he hires to work there show respect to a female apprentice.

Deuce is a good guy, though, so I can't see him choosing anyone that isn't stellar.

"Good luck," I tell Ivy as I get to my feet and pull them into me.

She pushes us off, miming a gag. "Too much love. It's stifling my creative urge to draw knives and blood," she teases, scooping her bag from the floor before heading out.

Juni and I watch as she hops into Deuce's pickup. The two of them share witty banter across the cab—I can tell by the movement of Ivy's head, and by the raucous laughter that comes when Deuce tips his head back.

"She's definitely gonna get the job," I say, watching until he puts the truck into drive and leaves.

She turns to me. "I'm going into town for some more canning supplies. My order came in yesterday. Wanna ride with?"

I shake my head. The mess I made in the barn needs to be rectified, and with the new hope that Hudson only has Tiffani over in an effort to convince himself he doesn't want me, I feel invigorated and reenergized. I'd probably have spent the afternoon snooping through Tiffani's apartment in town had my sisters not helped me see I was being silly.

Of course Hudson didn't want to hurt me.

He was just trying to be a good guy.

And on that note, before I can go clean up my mess and start over on Everly and Deuce's wedding gift, I need a moment to celebrate my sweet Hudson, and how far he'll go to be a good man.

He'll date a woman he doesn't even like, because he thinks that's what his community and the world would rather have from him.

"I should stay here and clean up."

She arches a knowing brow. "I kind of thought you'd ask me to take you by Tiffani's while you know she's not home."

I smirk, pulling my blonde hair off my sweaty back to wrangle a ponytail. "I'm gonna clean up my arms, change my dress and get the barn back to normal."

"Wow," Juni says, stuffing her hands in her pockets as she leans her back against the doorframe. "That's growth."

Smiling at her, I speak honestly, "Hudson makes me a better person."

"I really do think he's just trying to do what everyone

wants him to do. Remember, it was Everly's deal hooking him up with someone." Juniper turns, waving me off as she moves through the house, collecting her empty milk crates used for transporting canning jars. A few minutes later, she's nothing but taillights, my arms are clean, my dress is changed, and I know I need to go right to the emotional devastation of the barn.

But all this talk about Hudson *wanting me* and not wanting to want me.... Finally, I'm getting close to the end of all of this. He's *almost* mine. My lips tingle and beneath my tongue, saliva fills as I think of *how close I am to having him.*

With my bedroom blinds closed, I reach into the drawer opposite the new toothbrushes and gather an old one. I like to believe Hudson still lingers deep in the bristles, despite the fact I've thoroughly sucked and swallowed as much of it as I could.

I take another toothbrush, and kick the drawer closed, my nipples already hard beneath my clean sundress. *The barn can wait.* Right now, I need to feel Hudson. *Badly.*

Using the bristles of one brush, I lower it over my clit, a feral moan tearing out of me. "*Oh god.*" I imagine Hudson dragging his teeth over my blooming clit, his body so large over mine that we sink into the bed. *God, he's so big.* His hand splayed over my belly would eat all of me up. And if his cock and balls match the size of his body, God, *I cannot wait* to be torn open. I would let him wreck me with a smile on my face because my pussy was made for his cock and my body exists for his use, so no matter how big he is, *we'll make it fit.*

Holding the head of the other toothbrush, I nudge the handle between my lips, swollen and wet. Just thinking about Hudson's body makes me so slick that I have to change panties. With my skirt around my hips and my thong trailing from one ankle, I move the handle in and out. It's too thin to pass for his perfect, veiny, thick cock, so I can't pretend *he's* fucking me. I can, however, pretend he's here, moving his tongue around between my legs, smiling up at me, making me burn and squirm.

I think about waking with his large frame wrapped around mine, his cock that feels like the size of my forearm pressing hungrily into my ass as morning spills through our bedroom window. I move the toothbrushes faster, fucking myself in frantic thrusts, still using the bristles to tease my achy clit. My arms burn from use.

His name echoes around my room, bouncing off the walls as I gasp and scream, coming in hot, long rushes, soaking my thighs and sheets. I sit up after my awareness returns, and I decide another outfit change is probably in store. This time I slip into an adorable little romper. The white fabric is thin and slightly transparent, and the light pink hearts scattered over it are soft and feminine. It's perfect for him.

The first time I wore it was the first time Hudson paused mid-compliment. I admit I'm a little... *unhinged.* But even so, when a man has to pause to take in your outfit, *that's a good thing.*

I hear his words in my mind as I pull the zipper up.

You, uh, you look really, really pretty.

My sweet Hudson.

My ponytail is sliding down my head after my brutal toothbrush session but since I'll be working in the barn most of the day, it doesn't really matter. Instead, I grab my water, a garbage bag, and head out to clean up my emotional roller coaster's head-on collision.

Three massive garbage bags full of *rage* are propped against the barn door, tied off and ready to go. After sweeping the ground, repositioning the drop cloths over my big project lining the walls, and realigning the dummy wall, I finally feel ready to paint.

I'd planned to paint a portrait of Everly and Deuce for their wedding gift, since I destroyed the original in my *fit.*

Once when I'd been in Hudson's house, I'd gotten startled, thinking the truck I'd heard out front was his, and that I was going to get caught. In my panic I grabbed what I could—a ton of photos.

To put it into perspective, at the time, I'd been developing his family tree. That obviously required me to *borrow* photos from his albums. I'd grabbed a ton of pictures and ran home. Once home, I discovered that the truck I'd heard had belonged to the mailman, and that I'd also swiped a photo of Ev and Deuce.

I never took the photo back, and now it serves as the inspiration for a gift.

Mixing ultramarine blue and burnt sienna, I work on the color I'll use for Deuce's ink while analyzing the photo. It takes several iterations of mixing, lots of trial and error, but around ten past two, with the barn warm from the midday sun, I think I've finally got the right hue

With my brush hovering, I'm ready to add detail to the fleshy blobs waiting on the canvas, when I freeze. The hairs along my neck and forearms stand tall, and my paint-loaded brush topples to the dusty ground, leaving a smudge of ink along the bare toes on my right foot.

My hand hovers in midair, empty, fingers still curled like the brush is between them. My heartbeat echoes through my ears, my breath hostage in my chest. I stand silent for a second... and wait.

There's an echo in the distance somewhere, a sharp noise muted by wind and time, and I bolt from the barn, running into the space between our house and Hudson's, listening.

My ears tingle as adrenaline builds behind my ribs. I hear it again, the same muffled but jarring muted noise, and this time I know *where* it's coming from.

I take off in a full sprint through the tall grass, toward the creek, my body reactively pulling toward the noise.

A piece of sharp stone tears through the bottom of my foot, and I glance down briefly. One of my feet is completely red, blood splashing up the side of my leg. The other is coated in creek mud and sand. The singeing ache of the tear sears up my leg, scorching my calf and knee. Grass whips against my calves as I leap over a huddle of stones stacked around a trimmed tree trunk. The half mile to the creek has never felt so long, and my lungs burn from the obligatory combination of urgency and speed.

It's when I'm on top of the hill above the creek that I

realize exactly what I'm running toward, what the noise that had me stopped in my tracks was.

It's Bear.

The top of his head bobs on the surface of the creek, which is likely freezing cold today, the waters made icy from the storm that just passed through. The kind of cold that steals your breath, filling you with panic and terror. I *know* that cold. I know that creek. And he's all alone, in the freezing water, thrashing and screaming. Aware of the fear he's feeling, jagged sobs tear from my lips as I intermittently scream his name, so loud that one of my eardrums bursts.

"Bear!" My hip pops as I charge downhill, but my legs are moving so quickly that my upper half can't keep up. Before I know it, my head is connecting with dead, grounded branches of a tree and small stones as I roll head over feet, coming to a stop at the bank of the creek. "Bear! *Bear!*" I scream, his name rattling through me, the rest of the world around me falling away. I only see Bear and the water around him, threatening to swallow him.

His lips part as his eyes open. Through the splashes and my horrid, piercing screams, he *tries* to call out but water spills into his mouth, and he disappears beneath the surface.

The urge to vomit hits me, but I swallow it down as I thrash through the creek, swimming in the places where my feet reach because it's faster. *"Bear!!"* I scream again, the sound of rushing water frustratingly stealing the bulk of my volume. Panic clenches my insides, and hot tears slide down my icy cheeks, the contrast leaving a trace of steam in the air as I search the freezing cold creek.

Dunking beneath the icy surface again, I reach out into

the darkness, closing my hands, searching for anything. My eyes open, but it's murky. The temperature burns me, but I keep them open. Bubbles filter from my nose and pursed lips as my breath gets harder and harder to hold.

Bear with his creek painting between his hands flashes through my mind, and a wild howl tears from my chest, causing me to breach the surface in a panicked scream.

"*Bear!*" I scream again, this time my entire body racked with fear and sickness. His head bobs to the surface, and I don't wait to see his face or see if he's breathing. I reach out, my legs thrashing, working hard to keep us afloat as I wrap my fist in his shirt and pull him to me. With him finally in my arms, I roll onto my back, spitting and choking on the water that attempts to sink us. The creek isn't choppy but I've run half a mile at top speed and dove headfirst into this rescue mission completely breathless. Fatigue is setting in, but I know I have a ways to go yet until he's safe.

My foot burns against the rock as I flail, kicking until I move us nearer the bank, where the struggle will decrease tenfold. When my feet finally reach the slippery bottom, I peer down at Bear, and choke out a frantic sob when I see his eyes are open.

"*Bear*, you're okay," I soothe, attempting to calm myself as much as him. "I have you, *I have you, I have you,*" I breathe, my chest full of fire, my body exhausted. Steadily, my legs manage to climb out of the sinking sandbank, my arms locked around Bear's body so tight that my shoulders burn.

Two steps onto solid shore and I collapse over him on the ground for a second.

Ivy went under the surface at the community pool once.

She puked when she came up, and I remember Dad saying that was a good thing. *Getting the water out of her belly and lungs was important.*

I loop my arm around Bear's waist, ignoring his whimpers and soft cries, and jerk him to his hands and knees. He gags, and attempts a cry, but nothing happens. The weight of water soaking my clothes and hair, paired with the rush of adrenaline has me on the brink of blacking out.

But I fight so hard to stay alert and awake.

I yank him again, and a rush of relief passes through me when he gags and burps, then finally vomits. I pat his back until he's done, and then I collect him in my arms, stand up, and begin walking back to the house. My heart is beating a million miles a minute, my foot is on fire from the gash I got on the way here, and my eardrum is blown.

But in my arms, Bear blinks up at me. He's shaken, thoroughly, and not speaking, but he's alive. I have him.

He's alive.

"You're going to be okay," I tell him, tears stinging my cheeks as I trek through the tall grass, anything and everything sticking to my damp body as I do. I don't care how hurt and filthy I am. I'm just so glad Bear is okay.

I don't know what I would've done.

I love this little boy with all of my heart.

That bond is inside me, and as soon as Hudson realizes who I am, I'll set it free, and Bear and I will finally have the title that we deserve.

I may not get to spend every night with him, comb his hair or help him with homework, but one day I will. One day I'll be there with finality, and because I've already devoted myself to him now, without that title, the idea that someone

could offer to watch him and then let him run into danger....
It makes me mad.

Very mad.

Irrationally mad. Like, *dig my nails into her face and tear her skin clean from her fucking skeleton* type of angry.

My breathing never evens out but Bear settles against me, his little hands curling around the straps of my sundress as my barn comes into view. "Oh, there's the barn where we work on our special art project," I remind him, knowing he's eager as ever to see it finished. I love that he smiles up at me at the mention of art. "Once we're there, we'll call Daddy and he'll make you feel all better. Okay? Everything's okay." I lick my lips, smiling down at him, grateful as ever to see his shining eyes.

"He's gonna be mad," Bear finally whispers, and I had no idea hearing his small voice would shatter me, but it does. The ranchettes come into view, and when I reach the oak tree between our properties, I drop to my knees, gently lowering Bear from my arms and to the ground.

"No," I say sternly. "Daddy will be happy that you're okay. Trust me," I tell him, my voice shaking with stifled anger.

"I wasn't supposed to go," he says, his tears coming fast now. I swipe my thumbs beneath his cheeks, glancing up to see Deuce, Everly and Tiffani springing from the porch steps, shouting and hollering.

"*You are four.* You need a grown-up to watch you. This is not your fault, Bear. Okay?" I kiss his forehead and stroke a knuckle down his cheek. "Stay right here and wait for Aunt Ev."

I get to my feet, my romper streaked with mud and

blood, my hair a tangle around my face as final bits of the creek drip from my elbows and chin.

My eyes find Tiffani.

And I run for her, feeling the air rush free from her lungs as I knock then pin her to the ground with my wrath. My fist comes down across her face once, and I keep my arm reared back, waiting for her reaction. She coughs and cries, her legs flailing beneath me as she attempts to get attention, to get help.

I reach down and put one hand over her mouth, using the other around her throat. Her eyes bug out as she thrashes, her hands flying to the place where I hold her pulse with my palm, drawing blood from my hand a few times with her nails.

Tiffani has a few bra sizes and inches in height on me, but right now, my love for Bear is giving me strength I don't normally possess. Beneath me she thrashes as a shadow falls over us, tall and slender. It's Deuce, but I don't give a shit who's there.

"Can't breathe? That's how he felt. *Scared*." I take delight in getting uncomfortably close to her face. "Fighting for breath." With my hands firmly on her mouth and throat, I apply more pressure, making the vein in my forehead pulse. Blood trickles from her nostril where I kissed her face with my fist, but *it's not good enough*.

"He's four! He's four! He could've died! He could've died, you stupid bitch! *He could've died!*" I scream, over and over, choking her. Suddenly, Deuce's arms hook beneath my armpits and he lifts me off, telling me things the whole time.

Bear's okay.

It was an accident.

You need to see a medic.

My legs thrash and kick, but with Deuce's large frame dwarfing my tiny one, I'm suspended over the ground.

"Put me down, Deuce!" I scream, eyeing Tiffani as she rolls off her back, holding her face, playing victim.

"You almost killed me!" she screams, crying as she touches her nose, looking at her hand, at the blood left behind. "You *broke* my nose! You're fucking crazy!"

I jab my elbow back, into Deuce's stomach, right as Ivy comes flying from the house, her feet bare, her hair down and wet, a towel wrapped around her.

"Deuce, *what the fuck?* Put her down!" she screams, the space between the two ranch homes looking like an episode of *Jerry Springer.*

Because of stupid, selfish, lying Tiffani.

From somewhere far down the dusty drive, ambulance sirens sound. I don't know how long Bear was gone, and for how long Tiffani failed to keep him safe, but it must've been long enough for her to panic and call Deuce and Ev back. Hudson, likely, too.

I thrash free from Deuce's grip and walk past Tiffani toward Bear. When I reach him, I lower to my knees where Everly is rocking him in her arms, crying.

"I'm so sorry," she whispers as I lean over, stroking my fingers through his hair, breaking the panicked spell she was in. "Oh my God, Dolly," she cries, reaching over Bear to loop her arms around my neck, hugging me with him between us. "Thank God for you, Dolly, thank God," she says, unable to move past the shock of the situation. I peer down at Bear.

"There's a van coming with doctor helpers inside. They wanna check you out. And they may take you to the hospital for tests, but if they do, it's okay. It's just to make sure there's no more water inside you," I tell him calmly. Everly is struggling right now.

Bear nods as the sight before his aunt finally registers my state. One of her hands comes to cup her mouth. "Dolly, oh my god, you need to see the paramedics. You're hurt," she breathes, slowly reaching for me, but I stand, stepping back.

"No," I tell her. "I'm fine. I just want Bear to be okay."

I look through the cluster of paramedics gathered around Deuce and Ivy, watching me. "They just got here. Let's let them check out Bear and... *her*," I nod toward Tiffani because I can't say her name. "I'm okay."

She starts to ask me if I'm sure, but the men in blue jumpsuits with red-and-white medical bags start toward Ev and Bear, so I split, running past Deuce and Ivy, up the porch stairs, into my house.

I fall across my bed, coated in dirt and sweat, dried blood and splashes of Bear's vomit, and I cry. I cry so hard that I don't hear the door open and though I can't fully make out who comes into my room, the hands stroking my spine tell me it's my sisters. They tell me things I need to hear.

You did good.

You saved him.

We're so honored to be your sister.

They stay with me for another ten minutes until the adrenaline drains, and the aches and pains start to set in. When my stomach is cramped from crying so hard, and my eyes are so swollen I can hardly move my face, I turn to my sisters and tell them exactly *why* I'm so upset.

"I would die if something happened to him." My body

trembles angrily against the mattress. "I love him as much as I love Hud. And the same way I know Hud is my future, *Bear is, too.*" I swallow thickly around the burning pain eating up my throat, raw from the screaming. So much damage was done in just a few pivotal minutes. I roll onto my side, tucking my hands beneath my cheek.

"He's okay because of you," Juni promises quietly.

"Rest," Ivy says, placing a wet towel over my face, sweeping some debris and blood away.

Hudson's truck rumbles loudly in the distance, and despite the usual stirring in my belly, I don't get to my feet.

I turn in my bed and face the wall, aches echoing through the gash in my foot, a painful pulse in my blown eardrum. "Good idea," I say, closing my eyes as I sink into an adrenaline-crash slumber.

eighteen

"TELL ME ABOUT DOLLY."

Hudson

The phone call I received when I was the farthest from my house was utterly terrifying.

Tiffani. Whose voice I hardly even recognized, screaming over and over, the words echoing in my mind as I sink my boot to the gas pedal, tearing through my land as fast as my truck will go.

Bear's gone. Bear's gone. Bear's gone.

I know my boy, and if he ran off, there's only one place he'd go. And it's the one place I never let him go *alone*.

My eyes try to blur but I blink away the heated moisture, summoning unfettered strength and calm for my boy. I'm tearing through the land between the cow barn and the hay bales when I spot a mass of people scattered on my property. Slamming the brakes, then shifting the truck into park, I jump out, not bothering with the door.

"*Bear!*" I hear my voice rattle through the open land, echoing up to heaven as I shout over and over, "*Bear! Bear!*" My eyes lock with Deuce's. "Where is he?" Deuce leaves the huddle of EMS workers, springing to my side. Taking my shoulders in his hands he forces my eyes to stay on him, our gazes idling.

His expression is serious and my stomach roils with unease because of it. "*Bear is okay.* He is *fine*, okay?" he starts, and even though he isn't a father, he's doing a good job of telling me the one thing I need to know to take me out of my frantic mental state.

I reach up and hook my hands on his wrists, holding him as he grips my shoulders. At some point in my efforts to get up to the house, I lost my hat, and I know it now as the sun pours over us in the lawn. Deuce continues. "He is okay. Okay? He's getting checked out by the EMS but they don't think he'll even need to go in." My hands fall away with the good news.

"He's okay," I repeat, needing to hear it again as my eyes slide from Deuce to the open ambulance. Bear is there, wrapped in a gray blanket, sitting in my sister's lap, her arms looped tightly around him. A man with a clipboard is writing while talking happily to Bear, and he's got a sucker in his mouth.

Seeing Bear snips the threads in my chest, releasing the suspended weight of doom that had filled my guts since my phone rang eight minutes ago.

Deuce leads me over, where I scoop Bear off Ev's lap and kiss his face everywhere I can. "I love you," I tell him a thousand times, soaking up the little giggles and squirms he gives back to me. "Love you, too, Daddy."

"You're all right?" I ask him, sizing him up and down with the paramedic standing idle, allowing us a moment.

He nods, twisting his gaze to Everly, who is still swiping at tears. "I'm so sorry, Hud," my sister says.

"It wasn't your fault." My focus slides to my son. "I'm gonna go talk to Uncle Deuce," I tell him, reaching behind me to clasp my hand around the back of Deuce's neck. "When we're done, I'm gonna meet you inside and we're gonna have a Daddy-Bear day, okay?"

"Them cows will get out if you don't fix the fence," Bear says, making my heart nearly explode. My boy is thinking of his daddy. I press another kiss to his head and put him back on my sister's lap.

"I'll get some guys out there. Don't you worry about *them cows*," I say, shooting him a wink. Outstretching a hand to the paramedic, we shake as I lead him a few steps away from the back of the emergency vehicle.

"He's okay. His lungs are clear. Vitals are good. Make sure he stays hydrated and for the cut on his calf, he'll need to keep it bandaged for a few days, just until it closes." The man scribbles something on his large metal clipboard and rips off a carbon copy, handing it to me. We shake hands again, and then Deuce pulls me into the tall grass under the oak, for privacy.

"He's okay," I say aloud just to hear it, to make sure that I know it's true. Once I've processed that, my eyes slide to Deuce just as my anger seeps in. I look him square in the eye. "What happened?"

I should never have left him with Tiffani. Never.

After I got home from my trip and thanked Dolly for everything, I was feeling supremely guilty for all the things I'd been feeling and thinking. I thought asking Tiffani to hang out with my boy for a few hours was a step in the more ethical direction, despite the fact my gut hated it.

I know it was the wrong choice. And this trying to date Tiffani bullshit? It's done now. *This fucking second.*

I'll find a way to assuage Ev's worries, but it is not gonna be with some woman who lets a four-year-old wander off to get into an open body of water alone.

"Tiffani says," he starts, and my spine lengthens, my shoulders going rigid. Deuce gently rests his palm on my chest, leveling his gaze on me. "Hey," he quietly grabs my focus as my gaze shifts to Tiffani, who is emerging from the house with an ice pack pressed to her nose. Her hair is shiny, and her strappy sandals are in place. The ice pack is the only visible disturbance.

I look back to Bear, who is soaked. Ev is dry except for where she clearly held my boy, and Deuce is dry too.

He watches me sorting things out and keeps me there, using that hand on my chest. "Listen now, okay?"

I give him my focus because in truth, I need a minute to pull it together. Seeing Ev emotional always fucks me up, and the way she's doting on him tells me she's still going through it.

Deuce's hair curtains his face as he leans in, his menacing ink a stark contrast to the lightness in his voice. "Bear asked Tiffani to take him to the creek to skip stones. She said no, but she got a phone call and went into your room and closed the door." My blood boils so much that my back and underarms sweat. "Bear said she was in your room for the entire *Trolls* movie, and so he thought she fell asleep."

I shake my head. "I'm so fucking mad at myself."

"Why?" he asks. Soon, after he and Ev have kids, he'll reflect back on this moment with full understanding.

"I knew she shouldn't watch him. What was the point?" I shout, my misguided anger flying everywhere but where it should.

"Don't do this, don't blame yourself," Deuce says, shaking his head. "You had to work. It was three hours. She had one job, she sucks, Bear is okay."

He nods until I nod along with him.

"Now, Bear snuck off and slipped on some stones on the bank. Then his foot got caught–"

My head falls between my shoulders as I choke on a singular breath. My sweet little boy was in trouble, and *I wasn't there*, and I was the one who put him in that trouble. Deuce's voice is smoky and calm when he quietly pulls me into him with a hug. "*He's okay.*" He slaps my back. "Thank God for Dolly."

"What?" My head snaps up too fast, breaking the comforting connection.

"Well," he says, "Dolly was in her barn working when she thought she heard something. She said she ran out near the oak, and kept listening. She thought it was coming from the creek, so she took off running that way, and when she hit the top of the hill, she saw him, out in the creek, just his head. Ended up getting in the water and going under and getting him. She swam back with him and then carried him in her arms the whole way back. Oh, and she stopped on the banks after she pulled him out and got him to puke, so the water wouldn't stay in his lungs, then she carried him back. Ev and I had just got here, we were running out when she was traipsing up."

I stand there blinking at Deuce like he's speaking another language. "She... *what?*"

He repeats it *all* again, and I find myself searching. "Where is she?"

"Home," he says, "I tried to get her to see the EMT but... she was... *in a state.*"

I shake my head, thoroughly and frustratingly confused. "What—why did she need an EMT? Why was she *in a state?*"

"Well," Deuce says, looking down at his combat boots as he strokes his ring-covered fingers through his hair. In the distance, a sports car pulls up next to my pickup. Deuce turns around, waving at the man. "Give me five."

The guy is the new artist for the shop. His custom plate reads TRACE69. Trace Calhoun waves, sinking against the sports car with his eyes on his phone.

"He was already on his way to meet me, I told him I had an emergency and dropped my location pin here," Deuce explains.

It's not that I don't care about Trace or the shop but right now, I have a singular focus. *"Tell me about Dolly."*

"Okay, well, she fell down the hill, she was running so fast. And on her way out to the creek she cut her foot really badly. Likely made it worse in the creek and on the walk back. Hell, if you retrace her steps they'll be bloody." He grimaces as he stares in the direction of the creek. "Her face was banged up a little, and her clothes were torn. Fuck, man, she was a mess."

"Dolly saved Bear's life," I say aloud, imagining her with

him in that cold water, both of them small, both terrified. She was so strong and brave for my boy.

"I should probably tell you about the *last* part," Deuce says, glancing over his shoulder at Tiffani, who is weaseling into the paramedics' space to get her nose looked at. I'm realizing now that—

"Why is Tiffani hurt if Dolly is the one that found him and brought him back?"

It doesn't make sense.

Deuce grimaces. "Dolly... she... *beat the shit out of her.*"

"*What?*" I swear the ground beneath me shifts with the weight of his words. "Dolly isn't more than five feet tall and a hundred pounds soaking wet. How in the hell did she beat up Tiffani?" I lick my lips, trying to understand what he's saying until Everly sidles up, slipping Bear's hand into Deuce's from hers.

"Go on inside with Uncle Deuce, show Trace your paintings, hmm? I wanna talk to Daddy for a minute," my sister says as I lift my boy from the ground, covering him in another sheen of smothering love in the form of hugs and kisses.

I lower him back down to skip along with Deuce and slide my focus to Ev, who is already shaking her head. "I'm so sorry, I should have been here. My stupid wedding can wait."

"Your wedding isn't stupid, for one, and for two, nothing's your fault, Ev. I'm the one who thought Tiffani could sit in a house for three hours." I press a hand to my chest but nothing can compete with the heaviness inside. "It's my fault." Those last three words have me feeling like the worst father.

I should've asked Dolly.

But I've been thinking such impure, terrible things about her lately. After the morning in the hotel room… asking her felt *wrong*. So I asked Tiffani, in an effort to open myself up to the possibility of more.

She shakes her head. "Damn woman was on the phone for over two hours! Poor Bear."

I clear my throat, and why I feel nervous about this, I don't know. But I need answers, so I ask, "Where's Dolly?"

Everly blinks at me. "Hudson Gray, that woman loves your son."

That woman.

Why am I relieved to hear my sister reference Dolly as a woman and not a girl? She's twenty years old. She's been an adult for two years. Still, hearing her referenced as an adult does something to my sore nerves.

"Deuce said she heard him, ran out and got him." I scratch my head as something behind my ribs flutters at the thought of Dolly saving my boy.

"Tiffani called me in a panic and we were already almost home. By the time we got here and ran through the house, Dolly had already got him and was carrying him up the bank. She was drenched, covered in dirt and blood. And she set him on the ground, waited until I had him, and then she…." My sister shakes her head, eyes drifting into the distance as she relives it clearly. "Something came over her, Hudson. I've never seen Dolly like that. She was screaming and yelling and crying. She kept saying *he's only four!* and *he could've died!* By the time Deuce got over there, she was… *choking* her. He had to pull her off of Tiffani. We tried to get her to stay to get checked out by the paramedics but… she was shaken up bad, Hud. She gave Bear another hug and kiss, then Ivy took her inside."

"Did Dolly tell you what happened?" I ask, trying to piece together how the details came to be.

She shakes her head. "No. Ivy came back out after she and Juniper got Dolly settled. She told me that Dolly doesn't want to go to the hospital, that she's fine, and she just needs to rest." She smiles sadly. "She said Dolly is more upset about Bear than her own injuries."

"I need to sit down."

Around me, the world whirls and whooshes, and Ev's hand pinches my elbow as she attempts to help me to the ground. I clutch my chest with one hand.

"I don't even know how it's possible that she got him out of the water and carried him," I tell Ev, trying to picture it.

"She was determined." Everly falls to her ass next to me in the grass and drops her head on my shoulder. *"I think she would have killed Tiffani."*

I swallow, waiting for the shock of her words to set in, waiting to feel uncomfortable.

But the feeling never comes.

I watch the sun sinking slowly into the horizon before glancing over, stealing a peek at Dolly's house. "How do you feel about her attacking Tiffani?" I ask, dipping a toe into reality.

She saved my boy. I recognize I'm gonna feel some type of way about her for doing that, and therefore, my silent celebration of her physical outburst toward Tiffani *must stay silent.* Being glad someone got the shit kicked out of them isn't a good thing.

"I think she loves fiercely, and that Bear should feel honored that he is on her roster, *that's* what I think."

I get to my feet, heading inside with my sister to go see my son. We stop outside the back door when I see Tiffani's car is still here, partially hidden by the sports car. "She's *still* here?" I question, my voice shaking with raw anger.

"She wanted to talk to you."

I stare at my house, my entire body aching with how bad I want to be in there with my family, appreciating what I have, being grateful for everything that was saved today.

"Send her out, please," I tell Everly as I extend my arm to the door. "Head on in, and send her out. She'll need her purse."

A moment later, Tiffani appears, the bruising beneath her eyes making my cock strain against my worn denim, a surprising reaction for my body to have under the circumstances. Stress and fear don't usually breed an erection. But the situation and her black eyes aren't what's doing it.

It's envisioning tiny Dolly, throwing her body over Tiffani's, punishing her while protecting my son—my entire world. *That's* what bricks me up.

She opens her mouth but I just don't care. Fool me once and shit.

"Go. Don't come back."

Like a fish dying on the bank, her mouth opens and closes fruitlessly. I stare at her until she turns to go, but she stops herself. "She's fucking crazy, you know?"

I know she's referring to Dolly now that I know everything that happened, and the idea that this woman thinks she can neglect my son and almost get him killed, then shit all over the woman who saved him is... *incredulous.*

"Stop talking."

She snorts, and having the audacity to do so considering the circumstances is quite... angering. "I could press charges against your little girlfriend, you know." With one step, she invades my space, pressing her finger into my chest as she snarls, "You should be ashamed of yourself. She's half your age."

I step back, watching her hand fall away from my chest. "Ashamed of what?" What am I supposed to have done wrong according to the brilliant Tiffani? Heat snakes up my spine, causing the angry truth to spill free. "Don't you dare lecture me about a damn thing! I'm not the one who endangered a child today."

She shakes her head, walking past me to her car. I follow her, because after what's transpired, I don't personally think she's got the right to shove away all indignant and shit.

Fuck that.

"Hey, answer me, what was that supposed to mean?" My shadow swallows her as I follow behind, causing me to drop my pace. I'm angry, but I don't want to scare her. "Tiffani—"

She spins, gravel spitting around her feet as she lunges forward, getting in my face. "Don't do that. Don't play *oh, oh, I'm just a good old handsome cowboy daddy who knows nothing of his looks and oh, my eyes don't work either,*" she snarls, mimicking me in a dry, loud voice. "Don't insult me. I see the way that girl sniffs around you." She steps into me, and I notice a tiny spot of dried blood she missed beneath her nose. "I'm sorry about your son. I made a mistake. A lapse in judgment." Her head falls and she shakes it pitifully before she lifts her face to mine, eyes wet. "I am very sorry, Hudson."

I don't know what to say, and her sudden shift from anger to guilt renders me quiet. Her sad smile is the last thing I see before I turn around and head to my house, eager to spend time with the people who mean something to me.

Or at least, *some* of them.

nineteen

THIS TIME IS DIFFERENT, FOR REAL.

Dolly

I wake up to the voice of a man whom I don't recognize. And in Bluebell, that rarely happens. *If ever.*

My body is stiff and sore, almost like I did a barrel roll down a bumpy hill. The cut on my foot aches enough for me to cling to the wall as I edge through the hall to eavesdrop. My blown ear makes my entire head throb.

Ivy is at the door, speaking to whoever is at our house.

"Dolly's here?" he asks, though it doesn't sound like a question as much as an assertion.

I can just imagine how twisted up Ivy's face is right now. She's sensitive to narcissistic assholes, and from the few things I've heard from whoever is on the porch... he's *triggering.*

"Seems like you know so… you tell me," she panders, her voice ripe with sarcasm.

It's quiet, and I'm about to peer around the corner, when the man says, "You're the chick that's gonna apprentice at Ink Time in town, aren't ya?"

"Ink Time?" Ivy repeats, deadpan.

"Yeah," he says. "Deuce's place." He pauses. "Should probably know that if you're gonna work there, don't you think?"

A smile lifts my lips. I'm happy Ivy gets to use her well-crafted death stare today. She stays quiet, and it makes the asshole on the porch a little nervous, I think, because he adds, "I mean, if you're her."

I love when Ivy puts an arrogant man in check. It's one of my favorite things. "I guess you'll just have to find out, won't you?"

"Eh," he says casually, his voice rough with ages of wear. He's got one of those voices that sounds fucked up from partying, not age. "I meet so many *girls*, you may have to remind me we've already met when I see you down there," the guy says, referring to the shop. "Anyway, Hudson sent me to extend Dolly an invite to come by tonight."

"You'll remember me, and by the way, I'm a woman, not a girl. And why couldn't Hudson come ask?" Ivy prods, and I don't care what the answer is because I heard the question. After what happened today, Hudson wants me to come over.

I step out from behind my hiding spot, and blink into the open doorframe at the man on the porch. He's tall and thin, not really muscular, just lean, and he's got on a Jack Daniel's t-shirt, shredded and worn, with an open blue-and-black flannel over the top. His faded black jeans are rolled at the ankles, and his feet are in Vans sneakers. Not what I thought the infamous Trace Calhoun would look like. I've seen his work in the books that Deuce brought for Ivy to peek through. He's clearly talented, but he's also an egotistical-ass clown, too.

I hate that Ivy is going to work with this asshole, but at the very least, hopefully she learns something about the trade from him. Deuce says he's the best.

"He's helping Deuce load his truck, firecracker. Can you just pass the message along?" he peers around her, only just now spotting me, a grin curling his lips as he takes in my blood- and mud-stained romper, my bandaged foot and filthy hair. "Holy shit, little mama, you fucking tumbled, huh?"

I pinch my gaze on him, ignoring the way he freely comments about my appearance. "Tell Hudson I'll come over."

Trace steps off the porch, eyeing us with a smirk that really irritates me. Before Ivy can swing the door shut, Trace digs his phone out, snapping a photo of the two of us before we realize. He smirks. "I love chicks who fight."

That warrants a door slam.

But enough about Trace. I turn to Ivy. "*Chicks who fight?*" I look down at myself, the memory of Bear's muffled scream causing me to jolt on my feet. "I didn't get like this because of a fight. I got like this trying to get to Bear," I breathe, wondering if the whole town is going to hear about me attacking Tiffani.

I don't want them to know, not because I am ashamed of what I did. To be clear, Tiffani deserved her karma, and because the universe is already working on my order for

Hudson and Bear Gray, I know she's busy. I took care of Tiffani for her.

Universe, you owe me.

I don't want people in town talking because I don't want Bear to know. His back was to us when it happened, thank God for Everly, but still, I don't want him to know the ugly, monstrous side that would do anything on his behalf.

Ivy pulls me into a hug, resting her chin on top of my head. "Don't worry—if Bear finds out what happened, you can explain that you made a mistake," she says, rolling her eyes, because knocking Tiffani's nose into her eyes was not a mistake, and if the situation presented itself in the same way, I'd do the same thing. But still, *violence is bad* is the line to tow with Bear, no doubt. I love how she knows me so well. I can't wait for Hudson to know me the way my sisters do.

I step back, processing Trace's message, heart racing, eyes wide. "Wait—what if he only invited me over to apologize to Tiffani?"

Ivy rolls her eyes. "That would be insanity, Dol. Seriously. You saved Bear. You saved his kid. I doubt he's thinking about Tiffani at all."

"He asked her to watch Bear, though."

Ivy smiles, her lips twitching with something good, I can tell.

"What?" I prod.

"She left about ten minutes after you fell asleep." She peers out the window. "Truck's all loaded—looks like Deuce and Everly are heading out, too."

Holy crap.

He's inviting me over and it's going to be *just the three of us.*

And after today, I'm sure Bear will be wiping out early.

I lick my lips, mind moving as I turn down the hall, headed back to my bedroom.

"Don't get your hopes up, Dol," Ivy calls down the hall after me. I know she's trying to help me keep my expectations reasonable, for my own good. I don't need to worry about getting my hopes up only to have them fall, though. This time is different. It's not like how it was when I foolishly showed up at Hud's to ask him on a date one week after Tessa left. Juni and Ivy told me it was a terrible plan, considering Hudson had a two-month-old, but I did it anyway.

I never even got to ask him out. I went over there with a congratulations card I painted for him, a bottle of champagne (that I had to ask Juni to buy for me), and at sixteen years old, I truly thought that would be that.

Instead, my knocking woke him up, and when he answered the door, a sleeping baby Bear was pressed to his chest beneath one of his large palms. He blinked at me and said, "Are you sellin' something for school?"

I knew right then that I had to stick to my original plan. That I had to wait until I was old enough for a respectable man like Hudson to even see me. Still, my hopes were so deflated, I drank the entire bottle of champagne and spent the rest of the night puke-crying while telling Ivy just how shiny his hair is.

We will not be repeating that tonight.

This time is different, for real.

I just know it.

The shower I take is the same shower every woman takes before going to hang out with a man whose face she wants to smother with her bare pussy and whose cock she wants to devour with all of her clean, hairless holes.

Everything is soaped, shaved, perfumed, and perfected within an hour. In my favorite pair of leggings and an off-the-shoulder Metallica t-shirt from Ivy, my hair blown out and all the creek picked free from my freshly painted pink nails, I've never been more ready to walk twenty-three and a half feet. My body is sore, my foot is throbbing and my ear canal is nothing but pressurized pain.

But I'm headed to him, so I choose to ignore those things. And as I wait on his porch, I think of the speech.

The one I've practiced many times.

When Hudson realizes that I'm eternally his, I'll need to come clean about everything I've done. It's the only way he can trust I truly love him, and I'm not just obsessed with him. I mean, I am obsessed with him because he's obviously the most incredible man in all of Bluebell, in the entire state of California, and even farther, maybe.

The speech rumbles around my mouth, most rehearsed yet some parts flimsy. I chew my bottom lip as I wonder if I should give him a few days before I come clean? I definitely have to do it before he finds himself thinking about putting a baby in me.

With a virile man like Hudson, it won't be long.

I feel it.

The door swings open, knocking the air from my lungs as a peer all the way up at the massive man stretched before me, his black t-shirt clinging to him. His hair is damp, and his jaw has a light beard now, which my pussy loves. I lick my lips as I blink up at him, smiling while thinking of being on my knees behind him, his big hands spread over the wall, my tongue deep in his ass.

God, I hope he lets me do stuff to his ass.

I want to do everything to *and* with him.

His patchouli and laundry scent rock me toward him and I find myself smiling shyly as I push past, moving inside.

"Come in," he rumbles. When I turn, I find him smiling. "Thank you for coming over." I run his tone through my database. He's sincere, but he's also tired, and that combination usually leads to a very honest Hudson. I learned this once or twice after babysitting for him that after an extremely long day on the farm, he speaks freely, doling out tokens of advice about life and other things.

He's using that same thoughtful tone now, and my insides rumble as heat cascades through my chest, my nipples hardening. *I love this tone.*

Looking down, I notice him in socks. This is only the third time he's been in socks around me. Third! It's crazy because I've watched Bear plenty, but Hud's a very private man. His walls are up. That's why it's taken me two years to get this far. Well, that and the universe. She has a part in this.

"Where's Bear?" I ask as I watch him flip the lock on the front door, despite the fact we never do that out here. He turns to me and chuckles. "Paranoia. Bear has never sleep-walked in his life but I lock the door all the time in case."

His paranoia will only be worse after today, that's for sure. My stomach twists with discomfort because I do not like the idea that Hudson will carry so much stress. His big, broad, muscled shoulders already carry so much weight—running the farm and the entire crew, being a single dad, hosting the farmers market, and being a family man. He doesn't need any extra weight.

I would take it away from him if I were his.

I would check the door for him every single night and report back to him. I'd slip into bed, tangle my bare legs with his, stroke my nails down his cock. I'd say, *Baby, the door is locked, now fuck me.* And eventually, after lots of time, he wouldn't worry about the door. He'd know he could trust me to lock the door.

"I get it," I tell him, smiling.

"And to answer your question," he sighs, walking past me to lead us into the living room, "he's finishing getting his pajamas on. He'll be out here in a minute."

"I can't wait to see him," I admit, sliding nervously into the couch as Hudson takes a seat in the chair across from me. A glass table divides us. My cunt aches against the soft fabric of my leggings, knowing I'm on *his* couch. He rests his elbows on his knees, leaning forward, and I want to steal a look at his cock but he takes a deep breath before tipping his head slightly, eyeing me.

"I'm sorry, Dolly," Hudson says, catching his forehead in his hand. "I can't make small talk." He gets to his feet and takes three steps around the table, coming to stand right in front of me. My eyes are level with his crotch, and my mouth fills with saliva. But he lowers his hand, palm up, and I instinctively slide mine into his.

With a small tug, I'm on my feet, mentally spinning as Hudson pulls me against him, smoothing his hand up and down my spine. His scent infiltrates my senses, making me dizzy and hot, my heart beating so fast I'm sure he can feel it. I can feel his beating against mine, after all, heavy and steady.

I wrap my arms around his waist, and the pain from my aches and bruises fall away as we hold each other, the fire rippling a few feet away.

He's so tall, his head hovers well above mine. He holds my head against his chest, rubbing my back, quietly saying, "Thank you, Dolly. Thank you so much."

Heat burns the backs of my eyes, and I blink, loving that I'm so pressed against him that my lashes graze his t-shirt. "You're welcome," I whisper, afraid to look up at him and break the spell. Afraid that if he sees the impact this moment has on me, he'll break it up and sit back down and start talking about the farmers market or something.

I have to leverage this vulnerable, raw moment into more.

Hudson gives me an in, pulling back from me, though still touching my lower back and my head when he asks, "You hungry?"

For your cum, yes. "Yes," I reply with a smile.

"Late dinner after Bear goes down?"

"Yes," I reply, swallowing down the mouthful of drool.

Tonight's the night.... I can feel it.

twenty

I CAN'T BE WITH SOMEONE WHO HAS SECRETS.

Hudson

I don't know how to describe it but when I opened the door and laid eyes on Dolly, covered in scrapes, cuts and bruises, something happened to me.

Though no part of me is ever going to be okay with what I did to her photo in Las Vegas, I no longer feel the invisible barrier between us. In fact, I wanted to hug her right there on the porch. I wanted to feel her petite frame melded to mine, to hold the woman who risked her life to save my son. The same woman who has been there for me and my son for years...

As she strode past me, into the house, I saw things. Christmases near the fireplace, with Bear in Dolly's lap, the two of them tearing through wrapping paper as they open gifts from Santa.

Dolly at the kitchen sink, bubbles up to her elbows, me by her side, catching her pinkie beneath the water as we wash dinner dishes.

Bear beneath a crisp white canopy, a little taller, a few more permanent teeth, and his hand in the hand of a smaller boy. *Another son.*

Hugging Dolly a few minutes ago felt better than it should have. Something in me that has been dormant for years was stirred to life. The thing that should've awoken in me with Tiffani was alive and kicking with Dolly in my arms.

I know had I hugged her a week ago and felt all that, I would've run. Hell, after I dumped a load all over her photo in Las Vegas, I was so ashamed that I'd asked Tiffani to sit with Bear for three hours.

Her age hasn't changed in a week, yet everything is different.

She risked her life for Bear, who is *my life.*

And now all of the things that I'd been trying to leave unnoticed are hard to ignore. Like the swell of her perky breasts as she bends over Bear, running the comb through his wet tangles. I have a perfect peek of her cleavage, and I turn to face the microwave in the kitchen, looking away from them as I get a flash of holding her tits together with my hands, and sliding my cock in between them, leaving proof of her unbelievable sexiness all over her chin and face.

Your son is thanking Dolly for helping him today, the way you coached him to do, so stop perving and fucking focus. After a quick tug at the crotch of my sweats, I collect the mugs of hot cocoa and meet them in the living room.

"Smells yummy," Bear says when I carefully hand him a mug. "Thanks, Daddy."

"You're very welcome," I tell him, passing Dolly a mug, with no marshmallows, the way I somehow know she likes. "I'm not sure how I know you don't like marshmallows," I admit, scratching at the back of my head as I sink into the large loveseat adjacent to them.

"You know me better than you realize. That's what five years of being close does," she says softly before leaning into Bear, whispering something in his ear.

He nods. "Yes! Can we tomorrow?"

Dolly smiles at him, and heat blooms behind my ribs. Seeing Everly with Bear is beautiful and I am so grateful to have such a wonderful sister. But seeing Dolly with Bear makes me remember why I wanted all the things I did back then.

Like a loving wife who is the best goddamn mom in the world, same as me and Everly had.

Someone who wants to be home with the kids, making bread and cooking meals, who can handle being married to a rancher and is okay with the demands of working the land, someone who doesn't mind living in a tiny town, in the country, no less.

A partner whom I trust with every ounce of myself, that's what I really want. To have a confidant, a best friend and a lover.

Walking into my own bedroom to find Tessa's mouth around my friend's cock, well, that wasn't the dream.

I decided right then and there that I'd never love again.

It simply isn't worth it and with a son in the equation, it's double the loss and pain if something doesn't work out.

But as Dolly walks Bear to his room, after he asked me if she could put him to bed while I finish making our dinner, the dreams I'd smothered, choked and forced down into darkness, have returned, more vibrant and beautiful than ever. And I want them as much as I did then.

I've never wanted them until Dolly.

Outside of Everly, I haven't trusted a woman again, until today.

After she returns to the living room, she stays on her feet near the couch, eyeing me in the kitchen. "Need help?"

Those little black leggings are hard to keep my eyes off of, but I manage. "You've helped quite a bit today, wouldn't you say?" I tease, casting her a wink.

"Fried steak is nothing after a creek rescue," she jokes back, coming to boldly sit on the kitchen counter. She swings her legs, and something about her comfort in my home is arousing.

I flip the steak and turn off the skillet, throwing the dish towel over my shoulder. "Drink?" I ask, pulling open the fridge.

"Just water," she smiles, and it's then I realize she isn't even old enough to drink. And while that should remind me that she's far too young, I can't stop looking at the gash above her eye, and the bruise on her elbow. She wasn't too young to be a hero, and after what she did today, I'm no longer sure age matters.

Or if it ever did.

Handing her a bottle of water, I plate our food as she drinks, the slow glug of her throat making my cock stiffen.

We take a few bites, and I'm overwhelmed with the need to know Dolly better. Truth be told, I've had questions before, but a man my age has previously had no business sniffing around a woman her age.

Previously.

"Have you always wanted to be a painter?" I ask, sipping from my beer.

She tucks hair behind one ear, exposing a tiny diamond stud in her lobe. I bought a pair just like that for Tessa years ago, and she almost never wore them. I've noticed that Dolly never takes those out and I wonder who gave them to her. Irrational jealousy snakes through my core when I envision some pimple-faced teenager handing her a box of jewelry that they bought with their parents' money.

"I like your earrings," I tell her as she chews, unable to answer my question about painting just yet because her mouth has been full.

When she swallows, her shiny eyes come to mine, and my chest tightens. "I know."

I arch a brow, pushing steak around my plate. She smiles. "I saw you looking at them," she clarifies. "So I assumed." Another bite of steak, then she adds, "And no, I didn't always want to be a painter. Some handsome guy once told me that he loved paintings, and was impressed by artists." I feel her wink in my balls. "I always wanted to do my own thing, though."

I nod, understanding that. I did always want to ranch, but I didn't always want to run a farmers market, or parent alone. Sometimes we get pieces of our dreams, and the world teaches us a lesson about being grateful. I wonder if the guy who told her he likes art realized he shaped her career? That's pretty fucking flattering, to have a bright, sexy woman like Dolly be so wrapped up in you that a comment guides her entire career. I'd be flattered, I think.

I clear my throat, focusing on the conversation. "What about greeting cards? Do you want to make greeting cards your forever career?" I wonder aloud, realizing that I've actually thought these questions time and time again, but I've never felt like I could or should ask.

Knowing more about her now doesn't seem like a choice but more so, something vital.

"Forever is a long time." She laughs softly, the gentle tone causing my nipples to harden beneath my t-shirt. Everything that Deuce tried to tell me about dating a little to get back into the swing of being comfortable comes rushing back, and part of me wonders if I was wrong to disagree. A one-night stand sounds awful, but as I peer across the dinner table at a beautiful, young, sweet Dolly, I get it.

Having a few rounds fired off, getting comfortable with all the equipment again—that probably wasn't awful advice.

It just goes against everything I want in life, to fuck someone I don't have an emotional connection with.

"Forever is a long time," I agree, laughing a little, too, as I bring my beer to my lips.

"There's one thing still up in the air right now, otherwise, I'd be able to tell you my full plan," she says, finishing her plate of food. "But yeah, I do want to make greeting cards and stay in Bluebell."

"Sounds like you got it pretty close to figured out," I reply, liking that she knows she wants to stay where her family is, where her family's land and legacies are, and that she wants to continue making greeting cards. "Everyone loves cards. I think it's a really cool thing you do, Dolly. Making cards— I've always loved that."

She smiles. "I love that you love it."

That comment has my mouth opening and closing, tangling my words. Why does she care what I think of her job? I run a hand up the back of my neck as I stare down at my empty plate. I suppose if she said she hates cattle ranchers that I'd... Well, hell, I think I'd be disappointed. As foolish as that sounds.

"You know, Dolly, I know I said thank you but I also know that it's not enough. That all the gratefulness I have in my heart for you is hardly even touched by a simple thank-you. I just... I want you to know that. That what you did today was something I will never forget."

Right as she reaches across the table, her smaller hand sliding toward my large one, there's a soft knock at the front.

Her gaze flicks to the door, then she digs her phone from her pocket. "No missed calls, so that's not Ivy or Juni," she tells me, taking her hand back from the center of the table.

"Could be Deuce. He may've left his shop keys here or something," I say, moving from the table through the house, toward the door.

But when I open it, I'm surprised and disappointed to see Tiffani.

Her face is makeup-free, and she's wearing sweats, her dark hair in a ponytail at the base of her neck. "Hi," she says, keeping her voice low, though she isn't aware that Dolly is here. I think the volume is out of respect for a sleeping Bear, which is ironic considering she completely dropped the ball today, when it actually mattered.

"Can I come in?" she asks.

I'm ready to tell her no, that it's a bad idea all around, but her eyes veer off to something behind me. "Why is that little psycho here?" she questions, having the audacity to chuckle a little as she eyes Dolly who is now behind me.

Something about Dolly providing emotional support with her presence gives me half a mind to tell Tiffani off.

Then I process what she's said and I'm ready to take up for Dolly and demand that Tiffani apologize. But I'm bumped aside as Dolly pushes past, stepping directly in front of me. She's a sprite compared to my six feet four inches, but warmth floods my chest at her squared-off shoulders and her hands on her hips.

"Psycho?" she calmly questions, keeping her voice low, and when she tries to be quiet for Bear, it's so much more genuine because I know she actually cares. "Funny, considering you're the one who lied about graduating, the law firm you worked at and the last place you lived." Dolly takes another tiny step toward Tiffani, who recesses back, her face pale. *"Liar, liar, pants on fire."*

"You... looked me up?" she asks, eyes wide. Tiffani keeps her focus strangely locked on Dolly, and I don't know if this is about what happened with Bear today, or if this is about *me.*

"The law firm has never heard of you, which makes no sense for someone who was a partner. And living at a *bunny ranch* is interesting, considering you told Ev and Hud that you've never had a roommate." She taps her chin before slipping into a mock, high-pitched impersonation. *"I love having my own space."*

Tiffani goes a little green under the porch lights, her eyes veering to me, looking for approval or maybe an escape, I'm not sure. "It was you," Tiffani breathes, shaking her head. "You fucked up my tire, you little psycho."

"I think it's best if you go," I say carefully. I know Tiffani is sorry about what happened, but she also made that clear earlier, so I'm not sure why she's here. And I don't like the energy brewing between Dolly and Tiffani.

"I just wanted you to know I'm sorry about today," she reiterates, and it's then I realize she came back thinking I'd forgive her. Not in the emotional sense but that I'd still see her.

Wrapping my hand around Dolly's hip, I give her a gentle tug back. "C'mon, Dol," I say softly, "come on in."

Tiffani turns and walks five paces to her car, gets in, and drives off without giving either of us a second glance. And when I close and lock the front door, the mood that existed just minutes ago is gone.

It's a reality check. One that I desperately needed. I push a hand through my hair, studying my socked feet.

"I'm sorry she came by," Dolly says, her voice soft and sweet.

I look up at her, tipping my head to the side, finding her even more beautiful amidst the injuries. But something nips at me. "How did you know all that stuff about Tiffani?"

Dolly swallows, pushing a hand through her hair, but I don't miss the split second of fear that flashes in her eyes. But I don't understand it, either. Why would she be nervous?

I close the distance between us, and our eyes idle together as I search for the hidden truth in all of this. "Did you puncture her tire?"

She doesn't speak, but she nods.

My heart free-falls. "Why?"

Her tongue sweeps along her lips thoughtfully as she reaches up, cupping my face in her hand. Her touch is soft, and stirs up things below my belt, things that feel wrong to acknowledge right now.

"She wanted you for your money. I just... knew it from the first moment I met her."

My... "My money?" I question, pressing my hand to my chest, peering around my humble ranch home.

She nods. "That's what she does. She looks for a man who can support her." Dolly makes a sad face. "She isn't even a lawyer."

I know what Dolly's done. She's gone out of her way to keep a person from me and Bear that she doesn't trust. She's all but telling me that tonight.

I don't let myself wonder why she cares so much because I can't stop hovering on the undeniable fact that *Dolly has secrets.* And I know we aren't more than people that live a house apart, but it's exactly what I need to know to pull me out of this insane headspace I've been in.

I think I was actually going to kiss Dolly tonight.

But I can't be with someone who has secrets.

The last woman who had secrets left me a single dad with a new mortgage and an entire business.

"I think we should call it a night, Dahlia," I say, my voice husky with a backbone I force but don't feel. "Thank you for everything today. I will never be able to repay you, but I want you to know," I tell her, taking her hand in mine, because this is separate from her looking up Tiffani. It doesn't change a thing with Bear.

"Hudson, I..." She blinks, her eyes shiny with what I believe are unshed tears. I can't see Dolly cry. I'm too... fucked up in my head right now.

"Why'd you puncture her tire, Dolly?" I don't even like Tiffani, but I hate secrets. I hate thinking I know someone, only to know they're a different person behind your back.

Been there, done that.

She doesn't answer, so I pull open the front door and usher her out. I watch her walk back to her place, ignoring the attempts at eye contact she makes as she looks over her shoulder several times.

I stack the dinner plates in the sink, and skip my time on the couch in front of the fire with a bourbon, because it smells like her. Instead, I say a prayer of thanks that Bear is safe, I sneak into his room and kiss his forehead, then slide into bed.

Everly and Deuce's wedding is next weekend.

That's what I should be focused on– my sister's big day.

I can't deny, when my eyes close, I see Dolly in the street, the sun shining over her as she pulls her arm back, stabbing Tiffani's tire while wearing a sexy, sinister grin.

I doze off, refusing to acknowledge the hard-on it gives me.

twenty-one

I WILL BE HIS HUMAN TOWEL.

Dolly

My alarm sounds, the lyrics of "Every Breath You Take" rousing my senses into the new day. Today is Friday, my day to explore Hudson's home, and also the eve of Ev and Deuce's wedding.

I haven't talked to Hudson much all week.

After Tiffani showed up and killed the most perfect, prime evening between Hudson and I, he's been very distant.

Learning that I slashed Tiffani's tire and looked her up seemed to disturb him.

I get it.

It's the exact reason why I have a *come-clean speech*. Why

I planned to tell him everything, sparing zero details. So that he wouldn't give me that disturbed, mistrusting look.

I know exactly what he's thinking. Because we are soulmates, of that, I'm sure.

He's thinking he *knew* me, that in the last five years, he's come to know and appreciate the Dolly next door. The one who skips stones in the creek and paints with his son, the one who sits barefoot under the oak with a paintbrush in her hand and a dream in her heart, the Dolly that helps her sisters pick berries for jam, the woman in overalls that always wants to help and who cherishes the farmers market as much as him.

The thing he's got wrong, though, is that I *am* her. I am also the Dolly that is currently watching him load the pickup truck while she touches herself, binoculars pressed to the window. I'm the Dolly that has been head over heels, utterly and completely in love with him for five years, and has worked tirelessly to learn the ins and outs of him and Bear, so that when they're ready, so am I.

That side, when not properly introduced, can be... *intense*.

Attempting to calm down, I reassure myself that when Hudson realizes there's an answer to every question, I'll be here. Waiting with answers. All of them.

After enjoying Friday morning Hudson in faded blue jeans, a long-sleeve light blue work shirt, his coffee-colored boots and matching belt, I wash my hands and head to the kitchen to make Ivy's coffee. She's already up and awake this morning, so no wall tapping needed.

Once I'm done at Hudson's, Juni, Ivy and I are going to pick up our dresses from the seamstress in town. We haven't been to a lot of weddings so we each selected a nice dress. Juni's had to have the hem let out because she's tall, Ivy needed the hip and waist area let out to make room for her voluptuous curves, and as the shortest of the three, I need my dress taken in some length, and let out some around the boobs. When Bear came by yesterday, he asked if we could paint today. I told him this afternoon, when I'm done with the fittings.

I'm looking forward to seeing him. It's been days since that night at Hudson's, when I combed his hair, put him to bed, and told him that pulling him from the creek will be, forever, the best thing I've ever done with my life. I miss him. And today he'll be painting the very last swatch for the project I've been working on for a *year*. Well, the project Bear and I have been working on.

"How ya doing this morning, Dol?" Juni asks, coming into the kitchen with her white apron tied over her clothes. Her hair is up in a neat bun, two roses speared through. With red lipstick on, and her usual overalls swapped for a floor-length dress, I wiggle my eyebrows.

"I'm okay... but wow, Juniper. You look gorgeous for making jam in your kitchen all day," I tease her while mixing Ivy's protein powder with milk, the slow drip of the coffee decanter calming my nervous belly. I run my hand along the back pocket of my jeans, where the new red toothbrush is stashed. Touching it, knowing it's there and that I'm on the cusp of a much-loved ritual seems to ease my frayed nerves a bit.

"Thanks," she smiles shyly. "After we pick up our dresses, I'm going on an early dinner date at the diner."

"*Bluebell Locals?*" I ask, naming the dating app centric to our small little town. Juni wants to be married, but she doesn't want to leave this town or our home. She only dates men in Bluebell because of that.

She nods. "Yeah, but he could be a total dud, so back to you. How are you doing? Been a long week, huh?" she asks, and my eyes flick to the tiny bandage on her forehead, where a piece of shattered glass ricocheted off the counter and slashed her.

I tap my forehead where her bandage is. "I'm sorry again about that."

She waves away my apology. "It was an accident. Don't even worry." She rests the brown spoon against the trivet, bracing her hands on the countertop as she glares at me. "How are you, Dolly?"

I slide into a barstool at the counter and check the coffee. It's almost done. "I'm okay. After I got it out of my system," I reply, sparing the details she's already aware of. When I went to Hudson's after saving Bear, I thought it was *our night*. The big night. What I've been working toward for the past five years, more active and solidly the last two years. I came home and destroyed the living room in a hazy rage, but once I'd purged those big reactions, I helped my sisters clean up my mess and reset my mind.

"I feel better. I mean, I understand why he's pulled away some. He thinks I have an entire side to me that he's unaware of, and that reminds him of Tessa." Ivy filters out with her sketchbook and favorite pencil, going straight for the coffee.

"You do have an entire side he's unaware of," she says through a strained yawn.

Juni fits her hands in heat-resistant gloves, using her

tongs to lower a canning jar into the pot on the stove. "But she's going to come clean all the way so, really, it's only temporary that she has secrets."

"Exactly," I agree as Ivy fills her mug. I leap off the barstool and grab the door, holding it open for Ivy as I call to Juniper that we'll be back soon.

From her comfortable spot on the front porch, cozy in her rocking chair, Ivy pulls her phone from her bathrobe pocket, just in case. "All right," she says, steam lifting off the surface of her coffee dreamily. "Go."

"Thanks, love you," I call, skipping across the dirt until I'm at Hudson's back door.

Goddamn, the house smells so good today. Coffee, aftershave, Bear's hair detangler, fresh muffins, and clean floors. My eyes fill with excited tears knowing that one day, *this* will be where I wake up and live my dream life. This is the home I'll enter when my arms are full of a bundled newborn baby, this is the kitchen where I will bake Bear's 5th birthday cake and every cake thereafter.

Empowered, my veins buzzing with adrenaline and need, I make my way to the sink for my first taste of Hudson.

I stare into the empty basin for a second, saddened by the fact he loaded his mug into the dishwasher today. There are no plates or forks, either. My mouth waters, anticipating the cold sips of his coffee, but my brain is already rerouting, eyes wandering around the counters.

Collecting the stack of mail, I sift through, happy to discover no more notes from Jade. *He'll be feeding me his seed, thank you very much, Jade.* The living space is quiet and still, everything in its place without even so much as a drink coaster astray. In fact, as I walk down the hall and poke my head into Bear's room, then the hall bathroom, and the laundry room, I realize the entire house is cleaner than usual.

He tidied up, but then again, the wedding is tomorrow, so maybe he wanted the place looking nice for friends or family to come back to afterward.

The ceremony and reception are where we have the farmers market, and there will be restrooms set up along the dirt drive so there shouldn't be a need for anyone to go into his house.

As I enter Hudson's bedroom, a very intrusive thought comes into my mind. Is the house picked up so he can bring his date home after the wedding?

Tiffani.

Did he reconcile with her?

In the middle of Hudson's room, my head spins and my breathing intensifies. Heat stalks up my neck, leaving my skin damp and my thoughts frantic. I clutch my head in my hands, trying to shake free the idea that *he's going to be with her.* That he'd take her to the wedding after everything that happened, and then bring her back here and give her every perfect inch of his hot dad dick?

No. No way.

Burying my face in my knees, I wrap my arms around my legs and rock back and forth for a few minutes, trying to quiet my brain so I can at least enjoy my weekly visit. I wait all week for this, really. It's *my time* in *my house.*

I can't let this anxious fear of rejection get to me.

I have to be stronger and remember the truth: *he is mine.*

The chaos in my chest dies some as I repeat the truth aloud several times, finally steadying the panic attack that overwhelmed me a moment ago. When I get to my feet, I wipe the sweat from my upper lip and head for his attached bathroom.

But the back door handle rattles.

My eyes go wide, and my hand flies to my chest, sinking against my heart to find it beating frantically. Only now, it's not an internalized panic attack but the threat of being caught.

Frantic, I reach into my pocket and dig out my phone which immediately begins rattling in my palm. Six missed calls with one currently going—*Ivy*.

A text pops up.

IVY

HIDE

The back door swings open, the doorstop thudding, the blinds on the window rattling. Surveying the space quickly, I slide under his bed, deciding it would be the last place for a grown man to look while running into his house. He could go in the closet if he forgot his vest or jacket, and he could use the restroom. And since I'm limited to *his room*, under the bed it is.

I don't recall seeing his wallet or phone on the counter, and he definitely had his keys since he made it into town and back.

What has him coming home, alone, in the midst of his errands? He's never done this before.

His boots appear in the doorway and when he lifts one leg, my brows furrow in confusion until—*SLAM*. He kicks the door closed. Something plunks onto the bed above me, and the sound of a belt being yanked open and a zipper being jerked down makes my skin hot.

Oh my god.

No way.

No. Fucking. Way.

Maybe the universe is trying to repay me for taking so long, or maybe she's throwing me a proverbial bone after Hudson pulled back some. Either way, Hudson Gray came home to masturbate, and I'm going to get a front-row seat.

He grunts and bumps scatter reactively along my entire body, my nipples hardening against the floor. Both hands are splayed out, gripping the ground as my hips grind down, searching for friction to go with the show.

He moves through the room, entering the bathroom for a split second before returning. He does something on the surface of the bed, which sounds a lot like throwing a towel down, and the idea that he is putting something down to *catch all of his hot cum* makes me literally shake. I cup a hand over my mouth and my body gently writhes, my pussy dripping into my panties, making my thighs sticky.

The slick glide of his wide palm over what must be the thickest, veiniest, heaviest, most perfect cock in existence has me biting into my bottom lip so hard I draw blood.

"*God,*" he groans.

He grunts and my eyes flutter closed, imagining myself on top of the bed, not under it. To be laid out for him, to be his canvas, his cum the paint that turns me into *his personal masterpiece.*

Opening my eyes, I hear the zipper and the metallic clank of his belt buckle as he widens his stance. More grunts, another long groan that comes from somewhere deep inside him, so prodigious and weighty that my toes curl and the pressure between my legs comes to a head.

My cunt pulses in rhythmic, hungry waves as I soak my panties, my orgasm crashing down, leaving me in hot, wet, rushes.

"Oh fuck," Hudson groans, and the soft whirr of his hand on his cock ceases, replaced by the sound of heavy liquid spilling across the bed, repeatedly, shot after shot.

My eyes practically roll back into my head when I hear how much Hudson comes, and I'd sell my soul to Barbara Walters to be that towel right now, I swear I would.

But in good time, I will be his human towel. I have to keep faith that it's true.

An ambitious bit of cum lands on the floor behind me, off the bed, and my pulse skitters with excitement that my man can do that. I don't have experience, much less with a guy who ejaculates a ton or gets distance but, Jesus, that's hot. I realize he has little control over the speed of semen leaving his body but still, *fuck me,* I've never wanted him more.

A beat passes, my cunt pulsing madly in my panties as my hips still seek friction from the groan, and Hudson disappears into the adjoined bathroom. A moment later, he returns and then, after lifting the lid on the wicker hamper and dropping a towel in, he leaves. I stay on the ground until I hear his truck start, and then I dig out my phone.

Is he gone?

Yes

What did he do?

I reread her question.

I know that he's my future husband, and I also know that Hudson is a private man. I don't think he'd want me talking about his masturbation habits with my sisters, so in an effort to have less to apologize about later, I decide to tell Ivy a truth, without fully coming clean.

He forgot to do something

I hid under the bed

Phew

Cool

Almost done?

I slide out from under the bed and get to my feet, going straight for the hamper. Lifting the lid, I retrieve the towel and place it on the bed, carefully unfolding it.

And there is it, pearly, thick streaks of Hudson's cum. Some soaked in, some still sitting atop the terry, all of it absolutely perfect.

Three more minutes.

Cool

I stare at the ivory for less than three seconds before I gather my hair in one hand, and lean down. With my nose just barely above, I inhale, filling my lungs completely with the mouth-watering scent of his cum. My lips tingle and my tongue presses against my teeth, dying to jut out for a taste.

But this is not how I'm going to taste my future husband's cum the first time. No way.

I can't help myself, though—I need to feel it. With my nipples poking through my top like a goddamn offering, I take one last smell, committing it to memory.

My favorite smell.

While my entire body tingles and pulses at the scent of his cum heavy in the air, the thrill of his urgent need to return home and unload his burdens into a towel—I am vibrating with excitement and happiness. I move my finger through a particularly thick ribbon along the towel, then bring my fingers together, loving the slick glide of his seed.

I have to replace the towel in the hamper and immediately wash my hands in an effort not to lick them. After taking the new toothbrush out of the packaging, I do my usual swap, sliding his into my mouth before retracing my steps and closing the back door behind me.

Ivy is on the porch clutching her stomach as I approach, eyes wide. "Fuck me sideways," she breathes. "That was close."

I take the porch steps and peer down at her sketch pad. Today's sketch is a viper, highly detailed, each scale bearing so much complexity I wonder how long she's been working on it.

And why does this viper look... *familiar?*

"Damn, Ivy, that's hot... Why do I feel like I know that viper?" I tip my head to the side, trying to place it. A million things flash through my mind and I try to imagine it, but I come up short. "Not a billboard, not a business logo... why does that look so familiar?"

Her lips remain in the flattest of lines as her hand, smudged with graphite, comes to her collarbone. "It's... a tattoo," she says, her fingertips exploring her neck as she stares at her creation.

A tattoo— "Trace has that on his throat," I announce, earning me an eye roll from Ivy.

"It's Trace's tattoo, isn't it?" I nudge her.

She shoves her pencil behind her ear, collecting her things from the porch. "You worry about not getting caught, stalker."

I wear my smirk inside, where I change my panties and clothes, put some loose curls in my hair, and meet up with Ivy and Juniper by the truck an hour later.

Two hours later, there are three garment bags hanging in the living room from the mantle. Hudson's truck is back, and I've seen Everly in the house. She smiled and waved to me while grabbing the mail when I was heading into my barn earlier.

And now I work on the final piece of the project because something in my gut tells me this gift will be of use very soon. After placing the final swatch on the hidden project, I remove the dummy wall, folding it up and sliding it out of the way. With the project still covered by drop cloths and old sheets, I rinse my brushes, put my supplies away and lock the barn.

Bear and I have worked tirelessly on this for a year and though Bear was unaware he was helping me with a project this large, I'm so glad we did it together. I smile as I think of him doing the last swatch last week, and how he was so excited to show his daddy. It will be a surprise for him, too, in a way. And I'm glad to be able to give them that.

I stop by Hudson's house while he's out, giving Everly a three inch by two inch piece of linen paper that I'd painted a small skyscape on. The linen came from a destroyed canvas of mine—one that used to have Henry Cavill on it. The skyscape used to belong in Cannes, but with a little phthalo blue, the sky becomes Bluebell. And I tell her it's old, borrowed and blue.

We hug, and I tell her how excited I am to watch her marry Deuce tomorrow. And I mean it. Because Everly is wonderful, sweet, and charming, and I cannot wait until our kids play together, and we have holidays together, and all of this time is far behind us.

When I get into bed, I think about the wedding tomorrow. It is Everly and Deuce's day; I won't make it about me and Hudson. But now that he knows I looked into Tiffani, it's time to make the last move.

To come clean.

twenty-two

BECAUSE I LOVE YOU.

Hudson

"I don't know, man... I don't know what's going on. I don't know why my head's a mess. And today of all days," I breathe, knowing that Deuce should be the one spewing fears and stresses on the morning of his wedding, not me.

But he's calm, cool, collected and ecstatic as ever to marry my little sister. The fact that he's not even rattled about walking down the aisle only makes me more grateful that Ev has him.

He doesn't question his love for her, her love for him, their truth together, their loyalty for one another—he doesn't question any of it. He trusts in it. He trusts in them and what they've built. And that trust has allowed him emotional freedom and safety. Every day he's happy, carefree, he doesn't stress or overanalyze and while that could just be him, I believe a lot of that is… being in love.

I want that, I do. I've always wanted that comfort and trust, and when I learned that Tessa does actually swallow —just not for me—that's when I discovered just how bad I want a good marriage.

I've got my boy, I've got the land, and now I just need the love, trust, and *forever* with someone to share it with.

"So she punctured Tiffani's tire," Deuce says, tossing my tie over my shoulder as he gets to work on tying. "She's also twenty. She's still got that fuckin' spark," he says as I lift my chin, giving him access to my throat.

"That's part of the problem. I mean… hell, I think that's *the* problem." Deuce finishes the knot, adjusting it before giving it a final pat of approval. Adjusting my cuff links, he puts his on. "She's too young for me."

Deuce freezes, his face twisting up with folly. "Uh… what?"

I lower my voice, since Bear's audiobook is likely coming to an end. Keeping a little boy in a suit nice, unstained, unwrinkled and dry for an hour is a feat.

"She's too young."

Deuce puts the cuff link on the kitchen table and turns to face me, holding my eyes with serious sincerity that makes my gut clench. Again, shouldn't I be the guy doing the deep talks on his wedding day? I'm a shitty best man.

"Does it go beyond physical attraction?" he asks, taking a different tactic. I don't have to think about my answer at all, which is the answer in a way.

"Yes," I admit easily. "I mean, hell, she's sweet and smart, she's so fucking good with Bear, she loves the ranch and Bluebell, and God, man, she's funny. She says some off-the-cuff shit that has me smiling for days."

"Okay, so you like her and you want to fuck her—"

"Ho—" I halt him with a hand. "First, Bear. Second, that's…"

"Not your style, I know," Deuce supplies, returning to his cuff links. "All I'm pointing to here is that you like her and you're attracted to her. And you're freaking out because you're thinking about her."

I nod, because when laid out that way, I sound dramatic. "Yeah."

"You thought about Tessa when you two first met, right?" he asks, finishing with one wrist, moving to the other. On his wedding day, Deuce went with a cleanly styled, neat bun, and paired with the suit, it's a great combination.

"Right," I say, plucking my hat from the table, carefully lowering it over my styled hair.

"Then this is no different." He pauses, "Except she kinda stalked Tiffani and then slashed her tire… which, honestly, man, I think is kinda badass."

Bear comes out with his headphones on, talking loudly over his audiobook. "How much longer, Daddy? I'm hungry."

"Five minutes," I say, pulling the headphones off long enough to relay the message. I turn back to Deuce. "Badass?"

He shrugs, spritzing cologne on his throat and wrists, then pulling his pants from his body, spraying it there, too. I cast him a disgusted glance.

"Pretend you didn't see that," he says with a shrug,

returning to the topic at hand. Dolly. "And yeah, you know, a woman who slashes tires and is holed away in her room googling shit? That's.... passion. That's fuckin' loyalty, man." He shakes his head, smoothing his hands along the sides of his hair to tuck back flyaways.

I squint at him, discomfort wrapping my throat as I choke out, "Did Ev slash tires for you because, I don't think—"

He stops me with a raised palm and a dark smirk. "*I* was the passionate one. When I met your sister," he says, smiling a little as he relives what I'd be willing to bet was the best day of his life and in an hour will become the second best day of his life. "She had this stupid dude hanging around and... God, he wasn't worth it in hindsight but the way I fucked with that guy," he breathes, chuckling as Bear takes off his headphones, sliding them and his tablet onto the table.

"How sharp are we looking?" Deuce says to Bear, taking his hand to guide him to the mirror in the foyer. They do their best modeling poses, and I dig out my phone to snap a photo. Bear asks to see it, and my breath catches as I swipe past the photo of Dolly with the milk on her lip.

Guilt makes my cheeks warm as I hold the photo out for Deuce and Bear to analyze. Yesterday all I could think about was how Dolly came to stand behind me when Tiffani came over. The way she then stepped in front of me. How she's never missed a call, and never turned down an opportunity to spend time with Bear. She's loyal, and what Deuce is saying... makes sense. That passion and loyalty is what I want to give someone, too.

I thought about her so much yesterday that I had to

come home and jerk off because running errands with a hard-on the size of a forearm is painful.

I came in less than a minute thinking of that thick strip of milk on her upper lip.

I haven't been like this—a horny mess who can't stop thinking about sex— in years. *If ever.*

I loved Tessa, but I didn't have to touch myself because I'd thought about how caring she is too much. I didn't know that was a thing until now.

The doorbell rings, and a moment later Deuce is directing the diner's owner, Tom Goode, on where to set things up. Everly's maid of honor, Deuce's sister who lives up in Oakcreek, comes to the door, asking for Bear.

"We gotta train him on the rings and flower petals," she says, smiling down at Bear who looks adorable in a tiny-ass tux.

The walk down the porch steps is toward Dolly's barn, the place the Ellington sisters so graciously allowed us to wait for the ceremony music to begin. Closing the door, I turn to find Deuce extending a shot of whiskey to me.

I take it, we clink, and before he drinks, he holds my eyes and says, "I promise you, man to man, I will love and honor your sister for my entire life. And even when I come back as a ghost."

He tosses it back and I do the same. Wincing, I say, "I know." We hug but when we step apart, the mush is gone and the devil has returned to Deuce's eyes.

"Don't be freaked out that she's super into you. You gotta embrace that shit and... get happy, man."

I arch a brow, slipping into my dress shoes. "You think so?"

He nods. "I'm super good at love and shit. Look, I'm getting married," he says, widening his arms to put his tuxedoed body on display.

I chuckle, but the truth? He's right.

And as much as the logical part of my brain wants to hit pause and dig into the fine print, the rest of me—most of me—says go. Go and talk to that woman who loves your son and is fiercely loyal.

And after Ev's wedding, I think I just might do that.

The way my land has shaped up to be the host site of a beautiful wedding is absolutely tremendous. Everly has been working on this for months, and this morning, in sweats and a t-shirt, she and women from town set everything up.

White chairs where the canopies usually are, an iron garden arbor wrapped in ivy and white silk centering all of it, twinkle lights hanging off the oak in the distance, the cool fall air the final touch on a perfect scene. People are filtering into their chairs, and when I peer back up at the road, cars are bumper to bumper.

Bluebell loves Everly and Deuce, and most of the town is here. It's an honor I don't take lightly. With my chest already tight, I take another sip of whiskey, which Deuce handed to me a minute ago.

"It looks fantastic," I tell Deuce as we watch people slide into seats and make small talk, the soft breeze lifting the tulle bows tied around the chairs.

Deuce lifts his brows.

"What?"

Quietly he says, "Excuse me for a moment."

Someone takes my elbow, and I turn to find Dolly.

My chest constricts at the beautiful sight. Her blonde hair is wavy around her face, with a clip holding some off of her face. She's wearing a shiny gown, maybe satin or silk, I'm not sure, but it wraps her like a hug. Her nipples are hard, pressing into the slinky fabric as she blinks up at me, her full lips painted all rosy. She's gorgeous, and my cock thickens when I look down and see her feet are bare.

"Wow," she breathes, stepping back in the dust to take me in. "You look mighty handsome, Hudson Gray."

Hudson Gray. *Fuck me.* Why does Dolly saying my full name make me smile? I don't know, but I'm smiling. "You look beautiful tonight, Dolly. Truly, gorgeous."

Pink floods her face and neck. "Thank you." Then she clears her throat, and though I don't move, my insides jump to her attention. "I was hoping to get a dance with you tonight." She shrugs, rocking to her bare toes to pluck lint from my shoulder. "If you can fit me in. I know I can't be the only woman who wants to dance with the handsome Hudson Gray."

There it is again. My full name on her plump lips is unraveling my already worn and loose ends. I want Dolly, I do. But I gotta know what she isn't telling me. There's something. I'm not stupid. And her puncturing Tiffani's tire only proves there is something more.

"I'd love to have a dance with you, Dahlia," I say, trying her first name on for size. It sizzles on my tongue, infusing her face with heat.

"I thought you were gonna ignore me," she admits quietly, looking down at her pink toenails. "I thought because you asked me to go last week, you were gonna ignore me."

Just then, Everly walks up, wearing a white robe to hide her dress, and loops her arm through Dolly's. "Bear wants you to show him one more time," my sister says to her, guiding her away with only an over-the-shoulder wave for me.

Something twists up my insides at Dolly's soft-spoken admission. She thought I was gonna ignore her, and the fact that I'm feeling some type of way because of that? I lift my hat from my head and stroke a hand over my hair, thinking about those words. A woman comes over, rushing us into our respective places and within a few minutes, I'm standing adjacent to an archway, behind Deuce, waiting for my boy to come down the aisle.

Everyone coos and ahhs when Bear appears, his little tux still in perfect condition. He tosses all of the rose petals in the first few feet, then decides on a gracious beauty queen wave the rest of the way to the altar, eliciting laughter from the guests. I wear a smile the entire time, making sure I keep my focus on my sister and Deuce. It's their day, but I can't deny, my eyes itch to roam to Dolly, to take in the sight of her wearing that dress from another angle.

It isn't until the rings have been exchanged and the big

kiss is over that I'm able to look her way, and that's because Bear runs to her when he's done. He sails into her open, waiting arms, and she tucks her face into his neck, patting his back. The words on her lips are clear as day to read. *You did so good. I'm so proud of you.*

The blood in my brain starts moving south at the sight.

And she never once looks to see if I'm watching, or even glances my way. She slides him off her lap, waffles their fingers together, and leads him to the reception area. It renders me motionless amidst the celebrations and cheers around me.

I want Dolly.

I know it now.

But my trust issues have me stuck in cement boots, scared to go for what I want. Dolly's got secrets, and I don't know how deep they run, but I can't do secrets again. I can't have a relationship with someone who isn't my best friend. My wife will be my world, and I want to be hers. Call me selfish, but that's what I want. That's what I want Bear to experience for his role models, too.

All thoughts on my love life are put on pause as I begin greeting guests, showing them to the reception area, and accepting a slew of congratulations on Deuce's behalf. I don't see much of Dolly at dinner, but glance her way a few times as Bear chose to sit with her and her sisters. He alternates from her lap to his own chair, and they share a piece of cake, and the entire night, I can't stop watching her.

She's so beautiful and charming. There isn't a person here that didn't walk away from a conversation with her without wearing a smile. She knows how to talk Bear down from his fits, and she's content being with her friends and family under the stars on a cool Saturday evening. She thrives in Bluebell, and her bare feet and gentle waves have me dreaming of quiet Sunday mornings with the paper, her body nestled into mine, the kids playing quietly by the fire.

Kids.

I pull my hat from my head and lay it on my chair, getting to my feet. It's the end of the night, I'm three whiskeys and two glasses of champagne deep, but there is no buzz in my veins, no ringing in my senses, no dips in reality or fuzzy, foolish happiness. I feel sober as ever as I tread through the dwindling sea of wedding guests, toward Dolly, who appears to be tipsy as she dances with Deuce. Everly and Bear are sharing a dance, and I did promise Dolly a dance.

Deuce peers at me over his shoulder, and grins in a way that makes my blood pump a little quicker. "Dol, might I pass you off?" he says, his mouth close to her ear. So close that her blonde hair sticks to his scruffy chin, and this man just married my sister, but still, a bout of jealousy surges through me.

He spins her, and her glassy, red-rimmed eyes meet mine. The way her entire face and body softens at the sight of me has my cock hard and my chest tight.

"Dolly," I greet, taking Deuce's place.

"I wanted to dance with you all night," she breathes, her eyes fluttering closed as she closes the inches between us, sinking into my chest. "Put your arm around me, tight. Hold me close like we're really slow dancing." Her words are so light, they're almost a sigh, and the way her hands cling to my back have me following her commands, wrapping her up so tight I feel her hard nipples through my dress shirt.

"Did you have a nice time tonight?" I ask her, lowering my head to reach her ear. She's tiny in my arms, and the urge to protect her and keep her safe has overwhelmed me since the day she broke the vase. Seeing her bloody and upset made me realize how much I love seeing her happy. With her tiny body pressed to mine, the stars casting an ethereal glow over the scene, the desire to keep her safe for her entire life engulfs me, powerfully. I tighten my arms around her, and a tiny sigh slips free from her plump lips.

"That's nice," she sighs. "And yes, I had a nice time tonight. Did you?"

I see Dolly in my mind, her bare feet tucked into the dirt, that dress clinging to her hips and ass. "Great time, yeah."

She hiccups. "I drank alcohol tonight."

I peer down at her, hating the way my cock loves the subtext. Dolly doesn't usually drink alcohol, except once she told me she drank a bottle of champagne. She's never given me a reason why she doesn't usually, but I've always known she doesn't drink. I like that about her. But tonight, she drank. And I like that she's admitting it quietly, like being a bad girl is just for me.

"How was it?" I ask, hoping she doesn't shift in my arms and brush against my erection.

"Bitter. But... I like feeling swimmy," she says, her voice growing more and more distant. I glance down at her, surprised by the way I feel. I love how she looks tucked against me, and erection aside, I love how it feels, too. How *she* feels.

"How many drinks did you have?" I ask, realizing now that she's not just buzzed but drunk. I slow our dancing and take her chin in my hand, tipping her face to mine in the moonlight. "You have any water, Dahlia?"

Her tongue darts out, swiping her lips, stealing some of my finger, too. "Hmmm," she hums, eyes fluttering closed, sinking her face into my hand.

"I think I should get you home," I tell her, looking over her head, searching for Juniper or Ivy. But I recall them saying goodbye, so they're likely home.

"I think your sisters are home, so I'm gonna take you there and tell them to get you into bed." I push blonde hair from her face, stifling a groan at how good she smells.

"Juniper sleeps with earphones on," Dolly tells me as I link my arm through hers, nodding to Deuce in the distance. "And Ivy didn't go home. She went out."

"All right," I tell her, "I'll get you inside and to your room."

Dolly's bedroom. The thought of being in her space has my skin hot. Nothing is happening tonight because she's drunk and we need to talk but... still, I will be spending time with that farmers market photo tonight.

The front door is unlocked, which I don't really like. I make a plan to lock it with a key on the way out, and return the key to Juniper tomorrow, along with a healthy lecture. Dolly's legs go a little wobbly in the entryway of her dark, quiet house, so I scoop her up, keeping her safe against my chest.

"Which way, baby?" I quietly croak, stopping in my tracks. The way baby rolled so easily off my tongue is... alarming, but also... fuck, it felt good. It feels good to have a place to put my love and care, in a way that a man wants to care for a woman. I love my son, but caring for Dolly fulfills things inside me that only this kind of relationship can.

"Last one on the right," she sighs, nuzzling her nose into my throat, my pulse hammering. "You look so handsome tonight."

"And you look gorgeous," I remind her, heat prickling up my neck, my jaw burning as the words I've felt forever finally tear free. "You're so beautiful, Dahlia."

"I hope I remember you said that," she says as we arrive at the end of the hallway. I bend slightly, not letting go of Dolly as I reach for the doorknob. I nudge open the door, and her hand, full of my dress shirt, flies to my cheek. "Leave the light off," she says, a moment of clarity peeking through her champagne haze.

I nod. "Okay."

I step inside, giving my eyes a minute to adjust to the stark darkness. When the shape of the bed materializes, I take a few steps, carefully laying her in the center before taking a seat on the edge.

"I'd ask to take your heels off, but you aren't wearing any," I tell her quietly. I'm not ready to leave her, but I know staying makes no sense.

"I love my naked feet in the dirt," she says. "I love Bluebell."

"I love that you love Bluebell," I admit, feeling a bit guilty to take advantage of her ephemeral memory. Sorting out how I feel about Dolly has been complicated the last few weeks, but as I watch her breathing level out, sounds of love and happiness being celebrated in the near distance, things become a lot more clear.

I want Dolly.

I just need to know why.

"Dolly, when you're sober, I want to talk to you."

Her eyes open, and though she doesn't move her head, her gaze finds mine in the low light of her private room. "You want to know why I looked up Tiffani," she says quietly, still sounding a bit fuzzy and muffled. I swallow hard, because I do want to know why, and the carrot she's dangling to find out is tempting. But a serious talk while one person is sober and the other isn't is just wrong.

"Tomorrow," I tell her, "come over. Let's talk."

"I looked her up because I had a gut feeling about her. I knew she wasn't right for you," she says like it's an admission.

"How?" I knew Tiffani wasn't right for me either, but I'd love to know how Dolly knew. Because she was right. Tiffani wasn't for me, and she isn't for my little family, and she doesn't make much sense in Bluebell either.

"Because I know you, and I know what makes you tick, and I know what you need, and I know what hurts you, Hudson Gray." Her eyes close and I think she's going to doze, so I selfishly inch my fingers into her hip.

"Why are you so good to me, Dahlia? Hmm? Why are you so loyal?" Something warm swells inside me, making my pulse skip and my balls tighten.

Headlights shine directly into her bedroom window, piercing through the linen curtains, briefly illuminating the space.

Laughter sounds off, paired with muffled conversation and a running engine. The headlights keep the room dimly lit as the person getting into the truck is clearly saying their final goodbyes.

Their goodbyes are giving me a look at Dolly's room.

I grip her hip more tightly, blinking at the space around me, my breath catching.

The walls are lined with photos.

Some are actual photos taken from this very room, some taken from other places around her property or mine.

One of me with a rope looped over my shoulder, hat soaked with sweat, face turned up to the sun. Bumps spread down my arms beneath my dress shirt as my focus moves from photo to photo.

One of me in jeans with my shirt off, a bale of hay balanced on my shoulder, Bear thirty paces ahead of me, in nothing but boots and a diaper. That photo is at least two years old; he was potty trained right around two and a half.

The photo next to it, held to the wall with a blue push pin, is me sitting in my pickup truck, a tumbler of coffee at my lips. I had no idea Dolly even owned a camera.

Held by a strip of tape, next to it is another photo, this one of Deuce and myself, Bear between us. This one is a professional photo from Deuce and Ev's engagement shoot. They'd invited us to knock out family photos in the same pass. I've never even seen this photo. I lean in, and some of the other images catch my eye.

Torn from magazines, photos of families, women baking in the kitchen with happy children around them, family portraits with barns in the background... then one of a black pickup truck, the image aged by sun, taped right by her bed.

That's the same truck I drive.

Getting to my feet, I turn, but before I can take anything else in, the truck outside finally veers off, leaving me in darkness.

I glance at where Dolly lies motionless in bed, her chest rising and falling softly as she finds rest.

My mind spins out of control. There are photos of me everywhere. But also... photos of a life Dolly clearly wants.

"It's because I love you," she murmurs from the bed, causing my focus to snap from the dark room to where she is on the bed. "I'm loyal to you because I love you," she says simply before slipping into a boozy slumber.

I close Dolly's door behind me, loosening my tie as I quietly make my way to her front door. I take Juniper's keys off one of the hooks by the door, and lock up on my way out, assuming Ivy's got a way back in.

Another hour later, I'm finally getting Bear in his pajamas and into bed. With my tux still on, I fall across my bed, waiting for that terrible feeling to sink in. Waiting for the realization to hit me.

But it doesn't come.

Because as wrong as it may be, the idea that Dolly has been pining after me? Looking at my photos and dreaming of being my girl?

I know I shouldn't.

But goddamn it, *I love that.*

twenty-three

HE GOES. AND I FOLLOW.

Dolly

"You ready?" Ivy asks. I know she isn't yelling, or even talking loud. But still, I bring my hands to my temples and grab my head. "Here," she says, lowering her voice as she slides me a mug of coffee. "This will help."

"It tastes like shit," I groan, bringing the mug to my lips. I may complain, but if she says it will help, I'll do it. I take a sip. "Gross."

"Oh, so it's fine when it's cold and filled with Hudson's backwash, but when it's freshly ground Colombian in a mug it's gross?" She smirks.

I nod. "Exactly."

Shaking her head, she continues sliding work into her leather portfolio, zipping it when she's done. This morning we're heading to Ink Time to set up Ivy's station, and when I agreed to this, I definitely didn't think I'd be hungover.

"Doesn't the fact that Hudson brought you home and tucked you in at least make you feel a little better?" Juniper asks as she loads jars of mulberry jam into a corrugated box.

I sit up straight, causing pain to jolt up my neck, spearing through my brain. "What?" Shock echoes through my core, leaving me trembling on the barstool, my hands immediately clammy. "He *what?*"

Juniper stops, a jar of jam in her hand as her eyes come to mine. "Yeah," she replies, "he brought you in and put you to bed. I saw it on the security feed this morning."

My lips tremble. "Did... did he turn the lights on?"

Ivy's and Juniper's attention snaps to me, as they realize exactly why I'm freaking out at the exact same moment.

"Oh shit," Ivy breathes.

"Oh no," Juniper comments.

"Maybe he didn't turn on the light because it was so late," I say, hoping to God he didn't see. I don't care that he knows me, that he sees where my heart and mind have been for years. But I need to tell him first. I need to prime him. Else... it's shocking.

"Oh god," I breathe, letting my forehead fall into my hands. "I was so close. I could feel him coming to me," I tell them.

"Don't freak out yet, okay? Let's just... see how he is this morning," Juniper says, adding the last jar to the box. The outside of the box is labeled BLUEBELL POLICE DEPARTMENT. Amidst my chaos, the label grabs my attention.

"You're taking jam to the police department?" I ask. I've

been so self-involved lately, I didn't realize Juniper had been filling large orders.

"Hmm," she agrees. "I am. They work so hard. They deserve something sweet."

Ivy slings her bag over her shoulder. "Okay, let's go. I cannot arrive after that asshat or I'll never hear the end of it."

"Deuce is not—" Juniper defends, but Ivy stops her.

"Trace, not Deuce. That guy is a sexist, misogynist pig."

Headache or not, I laugh at that truth because everything I've witnessed of Trace Calhoun, well, she's not wrong. "It's the slight fame. A talented man with a touch of fame becomes an ugly, untamable beast. He doesn't just become his own god, but he *thinks* he's our god, too."

I mime vomiting, and Ivy laughs. "Nailed it."

A few minutes later, we're in the truck, riding into town. Deuce is leaving for his honeymoon next week because this week he's putting the final touches on Ink Time. Helping him put the final touches on? Hudson.

Juniper carries the case of jam in her arms, tipping her head down the street toward the police station. "I'll meet up with you guys." She smiles.

I nod in her direction as I pass Ivy her portfolio from the back seat. "You sure you don't want us to walk you down first?"

Ivy adds, "It's fine. I'm still really early."

Juni wrinkles her nose. "No, no, that's okay. I'm all good." She takes a few steps back. "I'll meet up with you guys."

With a shrug, we finish gathering everything Ivy has

loaded up to make her space her own. Aside from her portfolio, we carry in a box of assorted succulents, a Metallica poster, her *Game of Thrones* Funko Pop collection, and a bag of Laffy Taffy.

Ivy sweeps while I use a cleaner to make her glass-topped table pop, and when we have a good handle on things, Deuce appears.

"Congratulations again," I greet him as we hug hello. He knocks knuckles with Ivy, who isn't a hugger.

"Thanks. And welcome to Ink Time, officially," he says, peering around Ivy's space. "I dig the Funkos," he says, lifting the Robb Stark figure, touching the tiny sword.

"It's a 'look, don't touch' type of collection," Ivy adds, making Deuce smirk. I'm glad he likes her salty persona, and something tells me it's just what a male-run tattoo parlor needs— a strong woman who takes no shit.

"Trace will be here soon," Deuce announces, eyeing my sister. "I'd like to formally introduce you two, since you'll be his apprentice."

"I thought I was, like, the shop's apprentice. Learning from everyone and stuff," Ivy says, a spike of nerves in her tone. Deuce doesn't hear it, or if he does, he doesn't let on.

"You will be our collective brain to fill, yes," he says, "but when it comes to line work and detail, you'll be shadowing Trace." Deuce rocks on his boots, his long hair down today after being up last night. There's a kink from his hair tie, but it looks good, and that's just not fair.

"He's the most requested line artist in the country, Ivy. He's supremely talented, and the fans love him."

"Fans?" Ivy chokes on the word, and I hold back a chuckle.

"The reality TV show fans. And tattoo fans, too. They adore him."

"They must not really know him then," Ivy deadpans.

"And do you?" Deuce folds his arms across his chest.

"I know enough."

"You're about to learn a lot more, little girl, so I'd put a smile on and be appreciative that the best artist in the country is training you," Deuce says, his tone even keel. It's not a reprimand as much as it is a reminder.

The bell on the door jingles, and our gazes shift to the visitor.

"Speak of the devil." Deuce laughs as Trace saunters in, large sunglasses covering his face, a tiny cap on his head. Sometimes I think when men have super high opinions of themselves, they think they'll look good no matter what. But the tiny penis cap isn't working for me, and neither is the "I just rolled out of bed with pussy dried on my face" look, either.

Deuce and Trace clap hands then bump chests, but I keep my hungover head in mind when I want to roll my eyes. Deuce pulls Ivy aside after he and Trace are done greeting one another, leaving the world's greatest artist and myself alone.

He eyes me as he flips his shades to the top of his head, having pulled off the tiny hat as soon as he entered. "It's you," he says.

I blink at him. "And it's you." I shake my head in confusion.

"No, I mean, you're that crazy chick," he draws out, moving his eyes over my leggings, then my off-the-shoulder lavender-colored t-shirt. He nods to my sandals. "Birkenstocks. Oh yeah, you're crazy. I've taken one of those upside the head more times than I can count."

I brace my hands on my hips. "Why do you keep calling me crazy?" I hate that word. Hate. It.

"I saw you, that day at Deuce's brother-in-law's house," he says, peering over the half wall to inspect Ivy's space. "Beating that other woman to a pulp." He mimes choking himself, smiling, and says, "Strangling her, too."

I narrow my eyes. "You don't know the specifics. I'm not crazy," I tell him.

"Hey," he says, raising his hands in an innocent act of contrition. "You don't gotta lie to me. I love crazy chicks. They are the freakiest in bed."

My head tips to the side on its own, I swear. "Bragging about sexual conquests is super slimy, just so you're aware."

"Aware," he retorts, reaching for one of Ivy's sketches of a butter knife being sharpened by a black-haired vixen wearing a corset. "Don't care." He smiles, his shaggy blond hair making this morning's coffee climb up my throat, along with stomach acid.

"You're so full of yourself," I say, knowing I should wear the filter since this is Ivy's mentor now but god, I do not know how women can stand men like this. Men that think because they're talented they can treat women however they please, and can get out of their awful behavior because they have a penis and a sexy smile. Barf.

Before Trace can hit me with a retort to further make me gag, the shop door dings, gathering my focus. Trace looks to the door, too.

Hudson emerges from the stream of sunlight as the door swings shut, bringing the darkness back to the space.

"My legal brother-in-law." He smiles, closing the distance as he shakes Deuce's hand, pulling him into a hug. Over Deuce's shoulder, Hudson's dark eyes come to mine. Heat simmers in my belly, melting into my groin, flooding my panties with warmth and wetness. The way I get instantly wet for him is one of the many signs pointing to him being my soulmate. But in the light of day, after what happened last night, I can't take pleasure in the rush of heat between my thighs.

I'm too worried about what he's thinking.

Deuce and Hudson take a few steps away from Ivy's station, Deuce's arm draped along Hudson's mountainous shoulders. He's wearing his black jeans this morning, and a Gray Farms long-sleeved button-up, the same color as his jeans. I could bottle him up and drink him down, but right now, all I want to do, surprisingly, is talk to him.

When he returns to where Ivy and I are lingering, his focus lands on me, making my skin hot. "Dolly, would you like to take a walk?"

I nod, and follow when he turns toward the door, pulling and holding it open for me. Ivy winks, and I know I'll catch up with her later, so I trail behind Hudson until we're in the middle of the sidewalk out front, sunlight warm on my nose, the winter air nipping at my cheeks.

"Dolly," he starts, his eyes holding mine in a way they never have, simmering with intensity. "Did you make your bank card PIN my birthday by choice?"

Oh fuck. It's happening. I lick my lips, my nostrils flaring as I trap a breath in my chest, willing to exhale it normally. *Stay calm, Dolly.* Now is the time to make sure he understands you're not crazy, all the things you've done aren't because you need a mental healthcare professional.

You did those things because he's your *soulmate*, I remind myself, as I tuck hair behind my ears and clear my throat. With a straight spine and my chin held high, I meet his gaze.

"Yes. I wanted it to be a combination of numbers I'll never forget."

His nostrils flare, and his broad chest rises as he holds his breath.

"Your birthday is perfect for that."

He studies me, as if my answer doesn't provide the clarity he's looking for. But I want him to find that clarity, and know that I am transparent for him.

"I'm an open book, Hudson. When it comes to you, I'll tell you everything you want to know," I say bravely, my confidence faltering for a terrifying moment.

What if he doesn't find my passion endearing? What if...

No. Stay true, Dolly. Stay the course. He's yours. He will understand the depths of your love and welcome it with open arms, as long as you tell him the truth.

"I took you home last night, do you remember that?" he asks, stepping closer to me, his shadow engulfing me.

"Juniper told me," I admit. "I unfortunately don't remember." My nerves get the better of me, and I shift my weight on my feet, blinking up at him. "Would you like to sit down for the rest of this conversation?"

He nods, still focused intently on my face. "That'd be good."

I want to slip my hand into his and link them, swinging

them as we walk to the bench that will forever, after today, be our bench. The place where he realized I'm his girl.

But I walk next to him and we sit at the same time, leaving a foot between us so we can easily angle our bodies to talk. His hair is shiny today, and he's not wearing his cowboy hat, which I love. I love him that way, too, though.

"Dolly, I'm having trouble talking around this, so I'm just going to spit it out." He sits tall and holds my gaze. "Do you remember what you told me last night?"

My heart slams into my ribs. What did I say? I shake my head. "No."

He chuckles uncomfortably as his eyes study the tops of his boots, and I can tell he's questioning if I was honest in my drunken admission, whatever it is. That what I said to him shook him so deep that now, in the light of day, he's gaslighting himself not to believe it. "You told me... that you're in love with me."

Finally, his eyes come to mine. "And I saw your room," he admits, his voice so quiet and low that if a breeze had ruffled the trees around us, I would've missed it.

I nod as all of my nerve endings stir to awareness along the surface of my skin. I've been waiting to come clean this way for years. "I didn't want you to find out this way, truly. But... I'm glad you know. Because I *am* in love with you, Hudson. I have been in love with you since I was fifteen years old and I know that it probably makes you uncomfortable to find out this way, but here it is. I love you and I believe *you* are my soulmate. I believe my horizon is filled with you and Bear, and Bluebell and Deuce and Ev. I believe you were meant to come here with Tessa, and have your son and start the farmers market and launch Gray Farms, all so you and I could find one another." My heart has never beat so hard. He just blinks at me.

"Say something," I whisper. Now that the veil has been torn away and my secrets have been exposed, some of my assured *certainty* grows wobbly.

"Please say something," I beg.

"I have trust issues," he announces, still holding my eyes. It's not what I thought he was going to say but it's better because he's clearly thinking. Had he said *"I need to process"* or something alike, that would've meant he got weirded out. But he's still sitting here, and in fact, he hasn't moved a muscle. And what he's saying is that he needs to know all of my secrets. He needs to know the ins and outs because Tessa left him a distrusting, brokenhearted mess.

"I have a speech, you know," I tell him, sliding closer on the bench. He looks at the gap between our bodies, a growl sounding off in his chest. My skin prickles with heat. "Something I planned for this moment. When I finally get to tell you how I feel. I have a speech that covers all of the things I've done in order to learn more about you or feel closer to you over the years."

"Feel closer to me," he repeats, his tone husky but quiet.

I nod. "I knew a respectable man like you would never be with a girl, so I learned as much about you as possible, stole as much of you for myself as I could, and then when I became a legal adult, I'd start trying to get your attention."

He shakes his head, widening his knees as he gets comfortable on the bench. "I don't—" He pauses, then tries again. "You're twenty."

"Almost twenty-one." That feels important to say.

"You've been trying to.. Get *my* attention for two years?"

I nod. "It's been hard. The fence damage and repairs, the storms, Ev's wedding. It's been difficult but yes. I've been begging for you to see me for so long, it's why I'm a little smiley right now... finally, you see me."

His face grows serious. "I've always seen you, Dolly."

I shake my head, and move my tongue along my bottom lip. "Not in the way I want you to see me."

"Jesus Christ," he growls, tugging at the knees of his jeans to adjust his pants. My belly flares with heat. His eyes come back to mine. "And Tiffani?"

"Was in my way."

He blinks. "And after the creek, when you attacked her..." he trails off, and though my first reaction is anger, I don't. I take a breath and sort out what Hudson's after. He doesn't truly think I'm a killer, but he has to know that what I did that day was in defense of Bear, not because of him. He has to see that my passion is rooted in a place of love.

"I attacked her because she was negligent with a child. A child whom I love very much. I won't say that I wouldn't have killed her had Deuce and Trace not been there. I don't know if I would have. I couldn't see or think straight, Hud." I swallow hard around the emotion that appears in my throat at the mention of that scary day. I scoot closer to him, and my knee hits him mid-thigh. I slide my hand over his leg, sinking my fingers into his thigh, smiling despite the rush of arousal that hits my panties at freely touching him in broad daylight. "I love you, Hudson, and I love Bear too. And I'd do anything for either of you. Even if that meant giving my life."

I thought I'd feel like a Band-Aid was ripped off, but as

he blinks at me, saying nothing, I'm overwhelmed with the worst thing: *doubt.*

He stands, and my hand falls from his thigh to the metal bench below. "Bear and Ev are waiting," he says, stroking his big hand through his soft hair.

I stand too. I knew this was a possibility. I knew that it may seem like too much. But knowing something and planning on it are two different things. My heart drops. I really thought he'd understand me.

Don't do that, Dolly, he does understand you.

He just needs time.

He hasn't been loved hard in a long time.

He isn't used to what true love feels like.

"Hudson," I say, putting his name between us as if it will stop him from going.

But it doesn't stop him. He goes.

And I follow.

twenty-four

ALL RED FLAGS.

Hudson

Last night, I don't know who was in charge. But today, the logical father in me is at the forefront of my consciousness, driving the ship.

The walls of Dolly's room flash behind my eyes, hundreds of photos scattered about, all with me in them. The flat tire. The way the words *I love you* so easily fell from her lips. The bank card PIN.

Fuck.

Those are all red flags. *I know it.*

I. Know. It.

The confusing part is that I still want her. Hell, if I'm being honest, part of me wants her fucking more. It's sick and twisted, I know, but the thought that sweet Dolly is sitting in her room dreaming of a life with me and my son? Fuck.

She's pining away, playing the long game, obsessing over me.

Find me a man who doesn't want that.

But I have a son. And yes, Dolly loves him, but as she trails behind me on my way to my pickup truck, I think only of him.

Red flags breed instability. I need stability for my boy.

Linking my hand through the door handle, I turn to face her. "Dolly, it means a lot to me that you care so much," I begin, unsure of what to say because every word that leaves my mouth feels wrong. Still, I want stability for Bear. He deserves that.

"Please don't get scared," she begs softly, making my cock thrum.

"I think it's just... too much," I say, scrubbing a hand down my face. "You're young and... maybe confused. And... I don't know, Dolly." I take a breath. *"I need to process."*

She steps back as if I've mortally wounded her, one of her hands coming to her stomach. "Okay," she nods, eyes filling with tears, tears that physically hurt my chest as they fall. I don't want to see her hurt... but I don't know.

I shake my head and reach for her, because it feels right, though it directly conflicts with my words. "Dolly, I don't want you to feel bad or..." I trail off, navigating the unstable terrain poorly. But a woman stalking me? It seems like I'd be a fool to invite a stalker into my son's life, no matter how sweet or beautiful.

No matter how wrong it feels to turn her away.

"Fine," she sniffles, her brow cinching up, casting lines

of strain across her forehead and near the corners of her eyes. I hate seeing her pained, and then I think about Tiffani by her car that day. She was hurt. She was pained. She was upset. And despite what happened with Bear, her pain did not affect me whatsoever. "Will you do one thing for me?" she asks, her rocky voice tearing through my heart.

Stay strong for Bear.

I nod. "Okay."

"Come to my barn when you get home." She wipes a tear from her cheek using the hem of her t-shirt. The wind picks up pieces of her golden hair, tossing it over her lips and nose. She tugs it back, pushing it behind her ear. "I'll leave you alone forever, Hudson, but I need you to come to my barn, okay? Promise?"

I nod, willing to promise nearly anything to get her tears to stop falling. She nods, and walks away, and watching her leave feels all wrong. All the things that are keeping me rooted to the concrete with my hand on my truck door are the same things that have my heart racing, my blood pumping, my dick hard.

The passion and obsession that makes me feel loved and special, that drives me toward her, that has me wanting to fall to my knees and worship her in equal measure, those are the things that, as a father, tell me to step back.

Confused, I get into my truck and wait for Deuce, who is saying goodbye to Trace in the doorway of Ink Time. He slides into the cab, grabbing the roof handle. "All right. Ev and Bear are done returning the linens. We gotta swing by the rental place to pick 'em up." He points down the road like I don't know where I'm going, and usually, that'd spark a salty banter.

But I don't have it in me today.

When I don't put the truck into drive, Deuce flips up his sunglasses, itching the spot on his neck where a mermaid with a sugar skull head is etched. "Why aren't we going?" He twists in the cab to peer at me.

"Last night I took Dolly home," I tell him, my mind swimming.

"I know," he draws out. "And?"

I swallow, staring at a piece of asphalt that jumps up in the road as a car passes by. "Her bedroom walls are covered in photos of me."

Deuce just stares at me, and I stare back, adding, "You're in some. So is Ev, and Bear. They're mostly me, but yeah... the entire room is..."

"A shrine," Deuce supplies, falling back, letting the truck chair absorb his shock.

I scrub my hands down my face. "Yeah. And... she told me she's in love with me."

"Whoa," Deuce says, blowing out a long breath. His knee starts bouncing as he stares at me. "And her PIN code is your birthday."

I nod. "I asked her about that. I asked if that was a coincidence."

He snorts. "If she's got a shrine—"

"I know, I know. But... here's where I'm all fucked up," I admit, letting my head fall against the side window, staring at Deuce. "If I were watching a movie, and there was this gorgeous young woman stalking some man, and she was all obsessed and shit. I mean, slashing tires and all that, I'd be like, that man is a fool to stay with her."

Deuce's lips curl.

"Stop."

He smiles even harder and I let out the world's heaviest sigh.

"You're into it, aren't you?" he questions, socking me in the thigh.

I squeeze my eyes shut. "I know I shouldn't but... I don't know, man," I say, reopening my eyes, sifting a hand through my hair. "I've always liked Dolly. And after what happened with Bear and the creek... I don't know. I've been looking at her so differently. Seeing her not as the fifteen-year-old she was when I moved in but... as the woman she is now."

Deuce shrugs. "So what's the problem?"

"I don't know, man..." I sigh. "It feels like if anything ever goes wrong, I'd look back and hate myself for seeing the signs but blowing past them anyway."

We sit in silence a few minutes before I start the truck, but Deuce reaches over and kills it, twisting the key back.

"Listen, normally, I'd agree with you, okay? I've met a lot of unhinged women working in my industry. When I was working at the Ink Time in Calabasas, it was wild. Some of those women worshiped Trace. Waited by his car. Called his parents' house. Friend-requested his real friends on social media. Snuck into barber shops to steal his hair and shit." He shakes his head. "That ain't Dolly. I mean, she may want your hair clippings and dirty underwear, I don't know, but she's not the same as them, so she can't be graded on those standards. Okay? She loves Bear. She's got substance, and she loves all of us, too. That's not fake, and that ain't about getting to you. That's real."

"I know," I say easily. "She said she'd give her life for him, or for me," I admit.

"I believe her," Deuce replies. "Look, you've got trust issues. I get it. But guess what? Trusting someone comes with the territory. You wanna be with someone who loves you inside and out? Who loves your kid and your entire life? You're going to have to risk getting hurt no matter who you risk it for."

I nod, starting up the truck so I don't piss off my sister and add to my day's complexities. "She invited me to her barn when I get back. She was crying. She's... upset."

"How'd you leave things?" he asks as I pull into a parking spot not far from where we were, Bear and Ev emerging from the shop as soon as I put the truck into park.

"I told her I need to process. I told her it was all too much," I admit, hating the words more the second time than the first. "She cried," I tell him, which causes him to audibly wince in reaction.

Everly climbs into the back seat, squeezing Deuce's shoulders over the top. "Hello, husband," she enunciates.

"Hello, Daddy," Bear emulates, squeezing my shoulders, too.

We drive home chatting about the wedding, and how beautiful everything looked, how well it went, and how happy Everly was with it. Deuce shoots me glances across the cab the whole drive, and when we get home, the door to Dolly's barn is cracked.

"Ev, can you take Bear inside for a few minutes?" I ask. She clutches my seat and Deuce's, her head moving between us.

"Sure. C'mon, hon," she says to Deuce, who attempts to climb out. I grab his forearm and look at my sister.

"Can I borrow him for another minute?"

She smiles. "He's the best, isn't he?"

"Quit," I deadpan, "or it'll make me like him less."

She laughs, taking Bear by the hand as they filter inside. I look at Deuce, who is rolling his knuckles against his palm, popping them.

"Am I crazy for wanting to see her?" I ask, scratching the side of my jaw.

He pats my shoulder. "You're not crazy. You guys already have a good thing. I think now it's time to explore more." He levels his gaze on me, serious and prodding. "Stop worrying, okay? You're a good dad, but you deserve more. She wants to give you more. And, Hudson, I've known you a long time. You and I both know, *you want more. With Dolly.*"

He gets out of the truck, and I do, too, except I veer off to the barn. I don't give Deuce a second glance as my eyes catch on the sparkling lights shining from the split door.

My stomach clenches as I pull the door open. My breath catches and my mouth falls open, speechless at the sight.

twenty-five

IVY'S RIGHT.

Dolly

Ivy hands me her gloves, and Juniper does the same, wiping sweat from her forehead with the back of her wrist. "Need anything else?" she asks, catching her breath.

I step back, my arms full of tangled sheets and tarps. I don't look at her and Ivy, I only stare at my masterpiece, my eyes hot. It's so fucking beautiful. It turned out better than I could have ever imagined, and seeing all of Bear's artistry and hard work has me choking on a proud sob.

"No," I manage to squeak. "Thank you."

Ivy kisses my cheek as Juni pulls her fingers through my hair. "Good luck," she whispers. Tears slide down my cheeks but I ignore them as Ivy pulls me into a surprising hug. Hugging is usually a Juniper trait, but Ivy sinks her chin into the top of my shoulder, our hearts beating in sync for a quiet moment.

"If he doesn't see that everything you've done is out of love, you're too good for him, remember that, okay?" she says softly, preparing me for what she believes is the end.

Deep inside, I question everything as I watch my sisters leave the barn. The last five years, I was so certain. So sure. Every Google search, every time I tailed his truck, hid in the alley and watched him get his hair trimmed at the barber, read all the books on his shelves to understand what he likes, kept track of what foods he ate most to know his favorites, made a list of places he avoided and even kept track of what jeans and boots he wore and when to understand his laundry cycle. Everything I've done has been to learn every detail about the man I love so that when he sees me, I'm ready for him.

I believed bone-deep I was putting in the time so that when he came around, we'd be ready to take off and start our life together, skipping past months of getting to know one another.

I know Hudson Elijah Gray as well as I know myself. I'm ready for him.

I've never wondered if I was wrong. I've always held tight to my passionate faith. I've shrugged off the devil on the shoulder moments that popped up here and there over the years, asking me if I'm in love or if I'm crazy.

I told him I loved him at the park. I came clean about loving him for so long.

And he walked away.

It's not a good sign, I'll admit.

But I refuse to acknowledge the sliver of doubt because

letting in negativity will only breed more negativity. And the only thing I want bred is me.

I plug in the twinkle lights that I've nailed up around the barn, positioning the strands to accentuate the large piece of art. Broken into three floor-to-ceiling canvases, all of Bear's watercolor swatches have come together perfectly to create a beautiful mosaic image of Gray Farms, complete with Hudson and Bear standing hand in hand under the oak tree, the backdrop a sherbet sunset. I did Bear and Hudson, but Bear did the rest, following my directions on which color should be on each swatch.

I had the vision, and it came to fruition, and I choose to see this piece of art as a metaphor for what is going on between Hudson and I.

Wiping my palms down my thighs, my sundress clinging to me from the nervous sweat, I stand in front of the massive creation and wait.

It's funny, I don't hear his truck when he gets home but I do hear his boots as he enters, clumps and dried hay and gravel crunching and popping as enters.

Staring at the creation, the accomplishment, the beauty of what Bear and I have created, I don't turn to face him. I can't take my eyes off of it.

Whatever happens in this barn tonight, I will always be proud of what I have with Bear, our relationship and the bond we have.

Ivy's right.

If Hudson can't see how much I've given to him over the years, if he can't see that I've given and am willing to give all my love and more, then maybe I was wrong.

"Dolly," he breathes, his husky voice sending a torrent of

heat down my core. His voice has always been one of my favorite things, so masculine and deep.

I feel him in my periphery as he comes to stand at my side. Finally, with another look at our creation, I turn and face him, still loving the way I have to tip my head up to find his eyes. His overwhelming size drives me wild, even now with the uncertainty between us, my belly quivers at his nearness.

"Bear painted every single swatch, with the exception of the silhouette of you two. I did that one. But we've been working on this for a year. Every time he came over, we'd do a swatch. I'd tell him it was for our secret project for Daddy, and I'd mix his paint and let him at it. He never questioned the process," I say, staring into the eyes of the man who created that little boy I love so much.

He twists his head, like everything that I've told him makes him want to look at the art installment again, but he can't take his eyes off me.

"We did this for you." I swallow, finding another truth. "I did this to show you how special Gray Farms is to Bluebell, and how much you and Bear mean to *me*."

Finally, Hudson looks at the massive art wall again. I study his profile while he takes it in, bringing a hand to his chest to stroke the length of his sternum. The twinkle lights glitter against his eyes. I drop my voice and speak from my heart.

"I'm sorry if my love is overwhelming. I'm sorry if my unknown devotion to you is jarring. My intention was never to weird you out, which seems... stupid, I know. But... I love you, Hudson Gray. And I love Bear, too, but I think you know that. And if you give me the chance, I will show you that you can trust me. I will tell you every single thing I've done to learn about you, to get closer to you, to feel connected to you while I waited for you to come to me. And then there will be nothing between us but the love I have for you, and the hope I have for you to love me back."

He doesn't move or speak. I slide my hand into his and give it a squeeze then turn and leave the barn, my cheeks stinging from the cool air nipping at my tears.

The uneasiness of rejection begins to worm through me, so I kick off my sneakers and sink my feet into the ground beneath the oak tree, centering myself for a moment.

"Dolly."

Tears streak my cheeks. I can't bear to be let down easily by the man whose existence has kept me going for so long. I can't face him.

But I don't have to.

Because he grabs my wrist, spinning me around, yanking me toward him. His arms capture me as he holds me tight to his chest and *finally, finally, finally* crushes his mouth against mine.

twenty-six

I WANT MORE...

Hudson

"I want to hear every last detail, Dahlia Ellington, and you will not leave a single moment out," I demand, our lips grazing, her face held securely between my hands.

I'd decided *before* I stepped foot in that barn, but after seeing what she created with my boy, *whatever doubt was inside me is gone*. She nods and I use the pad of my thumb to wipe the tears on her cheeks. "No more of that," I tell her, because her pain brings me pain. That's a revelation. I feel that for Ev, Deuce, and, of course, Bear the most. But now...

"Come home with me," I whisper before crushing my lips to hers again, suddenly starving for more, needing everything she can give me. She's so sweet and soft, her hungry little moans radiate through my cock, now full of blood.

"Okay," she nods.

"You gotta tell your sisters?" I ask.

She shakes her head. "They'll figure it out."

I lift her from the ground and cradle her to my chest, my heart dashing when she laughs softly. I love that sound. Marching through my back door, I set her on the counter, causing Everly and Bear, who are at the table working on a puzzle, to freeze.

"Ev, can I talk to you?" I question, a bit out of breath from my racing thoughts. Pressing a kiss to Bear's head, I greet him hello. "Heya, buddy, I missed you."

Dolly takes Ev's seat, slipping into the activity with my son so easily that I've never been more eager to get my kid out of the house than now.

I step to her, out of earshot of Bear. "I'll owe you forever. Can you take him tonight?"

She looks over at Dolly, then to me. A slow smile spreads her lips. "I think the shrine is sweet."

I tip my head. "Fucking Deuce. Doesn't he know *the brother code*?"

Everly pats my chest. "We're married now, stupid. Wife code beats brother code." She leans in. "You deserve this kind of love."

I blink down at her, not expecting her candid response. I open my mouth but struggle to reply to something so kind. I don't feel like I deserve that compliment, and as I've been thinking about it, I don't know that I *have* earned Dolly's adoration and love.

But I will.

"I'll take Bear. Have fun." She smiles, adding, "I love Dolly. For what it's worth."

A few minutes later Bear and Everly are gone. I lock the front door and press my back to it, staring at Dolly across the living room. She uncrosses her legs and grabs the hem of her sundress with both hands, pulling it up to her thighs.

"We're gonna play a game," I tell her, using one hand to free the collar at my throat. Working the column of buttons, I peel off my long-sleeved shirt and kick off my boots. "You're gonna tell me everything. And while you do, you're gonna show me how I make you feel," I tell her, breathing hard, my cock pressing into my fly.

She nods and her soft lips fall apart slightly, and I quickly vision spearing my cock past those plump little lips. I lick my lips and drop my gaze. Her nipples pebble beneath the soft linen before my eyes. Being able to freely look feels nice. I've been *not looking* for so long.

I ogle her perfect tits, and the little hum of approval that slips out of her has me getting harder by the second.

Unclasping my belt, I tear it free, letting it drop to the floor with an echoing thunk. Holding her intense gaze, I ask, "Have you ever entered my home when I was not there, *without* me knowing?

She nods her head yes, but the way she bites her bottom lip as if there's a contingency to that question has me groaning. A flood of precum surges from my aching cock as I take one more step toward her.

"Tell me."

She swallows. "I set an alarm every Friday morning. I get up and watch you leave for your errands in town, Ivy sits watch on the porch as a lookout." Her tongue swipes over her bottom lip as she pushes one strap of her dress down, leaving her shoulder bare. "I go inside your house and I take your coffee mug out of the sink and I drink what's left. Then I lick the edge where your mouth touched."

I groan as a brave drop of precum bubbles up, further wetting my boxer briefs as I reach for my fly. My zipper goes down and Dolly's eyes roll back into her head a minute.

"More," I urge, taking another step.

"I go into your closet and I try on your shirts and soak up your smell. I spray your cologne on my panties sometimes, so I can smell you in bed at night."

Fuuuck. I unclasp the button of my jeans, and my cock forces them open as it juts out. Her eyes fall to it, the size and shape partially visible but still all clothed. She whimpers, writhing a little in her seat. Her knuckles go white as she grips the edge of the chair. Her throat bobs and sweat beads above her upper lip as she hones in on my cock with amateur precision, so beautiful and raw.

"Hudson..." she breathes, swallowing so hard that my balls rise to my body, hot and full, pounding for her.

"More," I urge, taking one more step.

"I have a drawer at home. Full of red toothbrushes," she breathes, her nostrils flaring as she slides toward the edge of the chair.

"Stay put," I command, "and tell me more." I love the obedience I get in return as she quickly sinks back against the chair, nodding.

"I take a new one with me on Friday. I swap yours for the new one," she admits, chin sinking to her chest as her eyes topple down my t-shirt, back to my cock. She moans as she presses a hand to her belly, like the sight of my sheathed dick alone is driving her mad.

I can't deny — *I like that.*

"Why?" I take one more step toward her.

"To taste your mouth," she admits, quickly and easily. Her hazy eyes drift toward mine, fogged over with desire, lids heavy with lust. "I want to taste every part of you, Hudson."

Another step, another question. "Have you taken anything else?"

She nods. "Pictures."

My chest fills with pride. I know she's taken pictures, I saw them in her room. She is doing what she promised—coming clean. And that makes my cock that much harder. "How many?"

"One hundred and twenty-seven."

I shove my jeans down so they're banded at my thighs. She sucks in a breath, sitting up straight, watching as I sink a hand down my boxers.

"Please," she whimpers, her bottom lip trembling a little. "Let me see you. I *need* to see you, Hudson," she says, her voice growing louder, her body beginning to tremble slightly.

I pump my cock and she folds in half, dropping to her knees on the floor, slithering toward me on her hands and knees. "I can't wait any longer, Hud. I need you. *I've earned you.*"

My heart pumps so goddamn hard that my ears ring and my mouth goes dry. Goddamn it, this is the sexiest thing I've ever seen. Beautiful, sexy Dahlia, crawling to me while shaking with need...for my cock.

For my body.

For me.

"Not 'til I say, baby," I warn. She stops beneath me, resting on her knees, feet tucked beneath her ass. With her palms on her thighs, she blinks up at me through her thick, dark lashes.

"Feed me, just a little. Please?" She opens her mouth, letting her wide pink tongue jut out like a sinful invitation.

A reactive raw moan rattles through my chest as I pull my cock free from my boxers. Her eyes go wide before a heaviness takes over her lids, making them droop. She plucks at one of her nipples over her dress before pushing down the other strap. I want to see her tits, I want them in my mouth and hands, and I want to devour *every inch* of heaven between her thighs.

But as she studies the vein throbbing up the length of my shaft, I notice she's fully trembling, a glaze of sweat shining on her chest. "*Please*, let me suck on you," she whines, a tear sliding down her cheek, coaxing precum to my slit. Her eyes flash to mine, panicked and wide. "Let me have it, *please*," she whimpers.

I reach out, sifting my fingers through her soft hair, gently tugging her head back. "I need to suckle you badly," she pleads, and I can't hold back.

I plunge into her mouth and the low hum that wraps my cock has my head falling back, a feral noise erupting from me. It's been so long since I've had a warm mouth take me. But having *her* mouth on me feels like divine intervention.

Her tongue envelops my shaft as she gently suckles, so softly it's almost imperceptible. My cock expands, and when

I look down at myself disappearing past her lips, her big eyes blinking at me, tightness runs through my chest.

All I've wanted is love and loyalty, and a woman to worship me, who I can worship right back. "You've been so loyal to me, Dolly," I rasp, still holding her by the top of her head. "You're *my* good girl."

She whines around my cock in her throat, so I pull back, going mad at the sight of spit threading between her lips and my dick. "Now, you want more? *You give me more.*"

She wastes no time. "I hid in the hall outside the restrooms at Goode's Diner before you went in," she whispers, guilt and shame flooding her cheeks. "I wanted to hear you pee."

"Why?" I ask, heat spiking in my groin. I never thought I was into anything off the beaten path, but as I blink down at Dolly, I know I'd go anywhere she wanted, because watching her have what she wants is the hottest thing in the goddamn world.

"If you had a big stream," she comments shyly, "then I could better fantasize about what it might be like when you *come.*"

Jesus Christ. That *is* strange...but unexpectedly hot. I stroke my knuckles down her cheek and grip my shaft right below the head. "*Open.*"

She does, and drool dribbles off her bottom lip, down the front of her sundress, making the fabric transparent. I tease her by brushing my red, tender cockhead along her tongue, then steal myself away.

"*Hud,*" she whines, her whole body tremors starting up.

"Did you like it?" I ask, tracing her lips with the slippery tip of my cock. "Listening to me?"

She nods, lunging forward with her mouth open wide. But I jerk back, my hand on her head preventing her from moving too much. *"I'll feed you when I'm ready."*

"*Uhh,*" she moans, her thighs slamming together, toes curling into her ass. "I'm making a mess. *I need you so bad.*"

A mess? Bending at the waist, I hook a finger in the bunched hem of her sundress and lift, exposing Dolly's bare pussy. No panties. Goddamn it. My grip on my cock tightens immensely as I stave off the urge to paint her puffy little lips with my cum.

On the floor, beneath her hot little box, is *a puddle.* I drop her dress and get back to standing.

"I get so messy when I think about you," she says, swallowing hard as a bead of sweat traverses her arm.

"So you did like it," I reply, sliding my cock back into her mouth with a groan. Her lips seal tightly around me, letting me rest in her mouth as she blinks up happily. I take my cock away and she pounds her little fists against the ground.

I have myself a little brat, and judging by the way my cock bobs angrily between us, *I think I like it.*

"More," I command, loving these secrets she's sharing. Not only because it means we have nothing hidden between us but imagining all the things she's saying is almost so far out there I can't believe it.

But it's true. And to know she wants me that much, that she cares for me that much—It's intoxicating, and I want nothing more than to make her feel equally cherished.

"Last Friday, before the wedding, you came home. You never come home during errands. Like, ever." Subtly she leans forward, and I allow her to wrap her hands around my cock. "Hud," she moans, swirling her tongue around my tip. "You're even bigger than I imagined."

I look down at the few inches she's suckling and licking, knowing that if she's ever going to take all of me, it's going to take time.

"Was that the only time you were in my house while I was and I didn't know it?" My pulse skips, because I strangely don't know which answer of hers I might like more.

"No," she breathes. "I was under the bed while you masturbated." Her cheeks flare with heat, when she quietly adds, "I took your bath towel from the hamper and touched your cum. I smelled it, too."

Holy. Shit.

That's an extreme invasion of my privacy, and far beyond licking dirty dishes. It's... fucking... I don't know. The C-word? I don't want to label it because... whatever it is, *I like it.* I want more of it. Hell, *I want her.*

"I didn't let myself taste it. I wanted the first time I ate your cum to be straight from the tap," she says, smiling. My dick jumps.

"More," I command. I think about Dolly dragging my cum towel from the hamper. The more I learn about the way she feels, the more I fall into a sick and twisted obsession with her right back.

Grown men have no business being obsessed. But this passion she has, this vibrance she carries–I never knew I wanted excitement and thrill until I had Dolly on her knees begging to suckle my cock.

"I stole the earrings you gave Tessa and I've been

wearing them for three years. Pretending you gave them to me."

My throat constricts and sweat curves down my spine. "More."

"I touch myself when I watch you sometimes."

"More." I drag my dripping cockhead over her lips, painting her in reward for her answers.

"Jade sent you a letter in the mail a month ago asking to come help with the farmers market. I put it under the faucet and washed the ink off, then tossed it."

"*More.*" Adrenaline soars through my veins as my chest inflates with a feeling I've quite literally never experienced. Raw, uncut desire. My senses sharpen, and my cock aches for her tight little pussy, my balls begging to unload, to bury my cum deep inside her supple cunt and make a baby. She's intoxicating. My chest can hardly contain the fragmented beats of my frantic heart. I *need* her.

"I said *more*," I growl, the words tearing through me as I dig deep for discipline and control.

"When I was younger, I would go through your garbage to see what your favorite foods were," she says, adding, "but now I watch you make dinner. My bedroom window has a perfect view of the front of your house and your kitchen." I give her a few inches as my core tightens painfully. I pull out, leaving her lips pink and swollen. "I changed rooms with Ivy so I could watch you while laying in bed. So I could touch myself."

"*Mmm*," I groan, wanting to know everything but also unsure how long I can play this game. "What do you like, Dolly? Hmm? What do you want from me?"

"Everything," she exhales, reaching up, gripping my

thighs as she drags her mouth closer to my bobbing hard-on. "I want to be yours forever, I want to belong to you, I want to take care of you, and I want to take care of Bear, too." I reach behind my head and yank my shirt off, and when our eyes meet again, Dolly's whole body is trembling.

"But right now," she murmurs, eyes hungrily traversing my bare chest. "I want to experience as much of you as I possibly can. I've waited years for you, Hudson Gray. So please, I'm begging you, *let me*," she breathes, bringing her hands together, steepled in prayer beneath her chin. Her blonde hair catches the dim overhead lights, illuminating her blue eyes, and I wonder, what will our children look like?

"Please, before I lose my mind, please, Hudson, let me have you."

I shove my jeans and boxers down, stepping out of them, along with my socks. "Are you on the pill?" I ask, my voice a bit wheezy. I grab my cock and pump, playing a dangerous game.

She shakes her head. "I'm not."

Gently, but with careful control, I grab her wrists, and bring her hands to my mouth. Dusting kisses over her palms, I quietly say, "Dolly, I wanna take you bare, I wanna feel your velvet soft pussy swallow my big, thick dick. But I don't think I should finish inside you just yet." I hate the way that sounds, but it feels like it's what I should say. She's so young. And I've never seen any men at the house for anyone other than Juni...

That means... "Are you a virgin?"

She smiles sweetly, looping a strand of hair around her

pointer finger over and over. "I don't have my hymen, but I am technically a virgin."

I narrow my eyes and kiss down her forearm, then along her inner bicep. "Explain."

"I fuck myself with things when I think of you, but I've never had a penis inside of me. Not a real one."

"Oh, Jesus Christ, Dahlia." The words sizzle in the air as I grapple with my composure. I'm going to own that devoted pussy, and leave her full and warm. But thinking of being the first man there is risking my ability to even get inside of her.

"I saved myself for you," she whispers as she feeds her fingers through my hair, guiding me to her breast. "Please, *Huddy*, suck on my nipples." My dick leaks, a streak of precum dribbling down my thigh. I scoop her up and take her to my bedroom, walking carefully with my dick spearing out in front of me.

"Show me your body," I say, lowering her to her feet. "Take off your dress."

Tears are filling her eyes and her body is still shaking gently as she pushes her sundress to the ground in a singular shove.

I don't look at her body just yet; I keep my eyes on hers. "Why are you trembling?" I ask, my voice thin. I don't want her to tremble and cry.

"I can't believe it's really happening," she whimpers, sitting back on my bed, propping her heels on the frame. Her pussy opens with her spread legs, leaving her sticky, swollen lips on full display. Her thighs are coated in it, too. "I need to see you go inside me, *please*. Please fuck me this way," she begs, her voice rising with her growing impatience. She shakes all over, and I finally look at her breasts.

Handfuls or maybe more, but plenty for her petite frame. Sexy as hell, with little pink tips, hardened by her arousal. I can't wait to suck those, to come on them, to *drink* from them.

"Dahlia, I don't want to see you shaking like that," I admit, my body magnetizing to the space between her spread legs. I hold my cock in my open palm, and we look down at it together.

"You're so big," she moans, a surge of sticky liquid rushing from her pussy. "God, Huddy, you'll see. I get so wet. I *gush* for you. I drench the bed thinking of *you* leaking out of *me*."

"Fuck," I hiss, "I need to get inside you." I lean over her and kiss her, seeking her consent one last time. "*Are you sure, Dolly?*"

She reaches up, wrapping her palm around my throat. "I love you," she says sternly as she lifts her hips off the mattress, her virgin pussy searching for what it needs.

My cock and cum.

It feels good to be needed so rabidly, yet so tenderly too. I love it.

"Okay," I tell her, our gazes falling to where I slowly fit my thick shaft into her tiny body. She squeezes and clenches as I give her an inch at a time, but she never wants a break. She only asks for more.

"In and out fast," she pleads as I ease into her, not wanting to shock her tight hole and hurt her. I would never hurt her.

She trembles beneath me, more wild, more frantic. "Oh

my god, Hudson, you feel so perfect," she moans, "it's so right," she cries. My cock swells inside her tight, creamy walls, then she bears down on me, *testing me,* making me groan.

"*Dolly*—" I warn sternly. I bring my lips to her throat and kiss down her neck, using my tongue to taste her along the way. "You let me fuck this pussy real good, you hear me?" I lift my head and stare down into her wide eyes. I reason with her in a language I think she'll speak. "I want to make you feel good, too, then and only then can *I* feel good, okay?"

I slide in and out and she gushes around me, making me clench my ass in desperation. She feels like heaven. I move my mouth down to her breast, and suck a nipple inside. My hips roll soft circles between her thighs, my groin grazing her blooming clit as I fuck her. She spasms around me as her back arches, I slip two fingers into my mouth, wetting them. "Huddy," she whines, driving me mad. Using my spit-slicked fingers, I curl them into her ass, and she clenches.

Fuck, she's coming.

"Mmm," I growl, "too fast. You're gonna have to give me another," I remind her as arousal gushes around me, causing me to curl my fingers into her ass deeper as I hold back my own orgasm.

She flails beneath me, and I use my size to keep her steady against the bed, keeping her safe and holding her tight. "Shh," I coax, my hips still rolling, still fucking her as she clenches and squirts. My legs are drenched and so are hers and it's the hottest thing I've ever felt. "I'm gonna get you through it, baby." I slide out of her and take a seat on the edge of the bed.

"Come here," I say, and I reward her with my cock for obeying. I take her by the hips and sink her onto my lap, burying my dick deep inside. Cupping her tits in my palms, I let the ends of her hair tickle my nose as she bounces on my cock, moaning and groaning.

"God, God, *God*," she pleads, "thank you, Hudson, oh yes, *yes, thank you*," she moans. My skin is slick with perspiration, and when my chest grazes her back, she writhes against me, howling my name as her pussy violently spasms. "Hudson! *I love you, I love you, I love you*," she chants, her spine quivering. The small cluster of beauty marks on her spine go blurry as my vision fogs over.

I tangle my fist in her hair and tug her head back to slow some of her shaking. My cock pulses inside of her, leaking. "See? You did it." I take a soft nip of the side of her throat, and groan at the sweet taste of her. "Mmm, you taste so sweet."

"*Oh, oh, oh*," she moans in warning, her hips grinding down against me, the shakes still moving through her. She's spasming and fucking and it's intense and hot as fuck. I almost can't believe it.

"Come on now, baby," I whisper, sinking comfortably into the role of the man who gives her orgasms and takes care of her. "*Give me another*, show me how bad you want me."

"No, Huddy," she groans, wiggling and writhing, her arms flailing. "I want your cum. You *have* to give me your cum. *Please*," she cries, and she's truly crying.

"Shh," I soothe, my voice thinning to ease her ache. I feel it, too. My balls are so full. I haven't pumped deep in years. And never with a woman I felt this crazy about. Ever.

She's my first truly passionate love.

"You can have my cum just as soon as you give me another orgasm," I say sternly before tugging her head back, my other arm wrapping around her hip, my hand working her clit. "Now ride my cock and unravel for me."

"Oh god, Hudson, that mouth," she moans, squirming in my lap as she rides toward another O. "I can't believe you talk so dirty. I love it. God, I love it so much, I need to come," She keens, grinding her pelvis deep against mine. The head of my cock presses into the deepest part of her, and I twist her head to capture the side of her mouth in a wild kiss. I'm taller than her still, even in this position.

"Give me another if you want my cum. Good girls get three in a row, that's the deal."

She nods vigorously, riding harder and faster, making me clench my core. "Yes, I'm your good girl, I'm your *only* girl," she hums, her shoulders sloping as the orgasm washes over. "Fuuck," she groans in the throatiest little voice.

"I need to come soon, Dolly. You have my balls so tight." I press my lips to hers and say, "And it's all for you. It's been all for you for a long, long time."

She shudders, and her walls begin constricting around my cock as she comes for the third time, liquid rushing from her pussy all around us. I tug her hair back and let my lips tickle her earlobe. She's still so pliable and eager, I think I can push for another. "If you give me a fourth, I'll let you suckle me after."

"Yes," she begs, "I want to taste us, and I want to swallow you. I want you warm in my belly when I go to sleep in your arms."

My dick pulses and I have to think about buying

groceries and upgrading my Netflix plan so I don't cream pie her right here and now. God I'd love to. But she wants to suck my cock after I've fucked her, then swallow my load.

Not missing that opportunity.

Her body racks up again, violently trembling. "I c-can't," she moans, her hips wiggling somehow out of sync with the rest of her body. She flails and moans, and I stretch my palm over her lower belly, applying pressure.

"Come on now, I know you want to come on my cock again," I whisper, "you can do it, I know that little pussy can do it, too."

She whines and comes, and I yank her off me, my hands under her arms. She's so easy to move around, it almost feels wrong. I put her on the ground. "Knees," I say, trying not to sound as urgent as it really is. My balls tighten, and heat creeps up my shaft.

I groan down at her on her knees with her face tipped up, mouth open, tongue out.

Choking down on my crown, I hold my cock out, watching as I paint her velvety skin in thick threads of pearly white. I groan at the sight of it dripping from her nipples, coating one eyelid completely, sliding down the valley between her handful of breasts. I stroke and pulse, painting Dolly with more and more, noticing as my orgasm comes to an end that her tongue is stealing swipes of my seed.

"Dolly," I groan, wanting to show her how much I appreciate this, how incredible it is, how incredible she makes me feel—but I don't know what to say, so I say her name again. "*Dolly*, baby," I groan, the last bit of my cum dripping onto her knee below.

"Take my picture," she whispers, trying not to move her lips.

I shake my head. "No. What if Bear–"

"He won't see it. It's just for you," she whispers, cum slipping off her lip. "*You deserve it.*" Fuck. That sends a shiver down my spine.

I get my phone and I take the picture, and as soon as I see her on my screen, covered in my cum, I blurt out, "I jerked off to the photo of you with the milk mustache. The one you sent me from the farmers market." *I guess I'm a little bad, too.*

She smirks. "My soulmate."

Her words warm my chest as I retrieve a towel from the bathroom, wetting it with warm water from the tap before returning to wipe her clean. But when I come back, damp terry cloth stretched between my hands, I find Dolly using her fingers to collect my cum before sucking it off eagerly, her tongue swiping up her thumb before sucking it fully into her mouth.

"Jesus Christ," I groan, some part of me wondering if I should be turned off by how intensely she desires all of me, but I'm not. "That's so hot."

"It's hot hearing you say it's hot," Dolly says, smirking. I use the towel to wipe her breasts and belly, and notice as I do that shudders ripple through her still, intermittent but present.

"You're still shaking," I comment, falling to a crouch at the edge of the bed where I lifted her up and sat her down. Eye level with her pussy, I run the tip of my finger between her lips and she reaches out, closing her hand around mine.

"I want more."

I can't help the smile that curls my lips as I study her little hole. "You sore? Did I hurt you?"

With her eyes still on my cock, she says, "I truly knew you'd be big. So I've been practicing with big things. So no, it didn't hurt. It felt incredible. Amazing. Better than every single other time I envisioned it."

"You want more?" I slide and curl two fingers inside of her, making her spine go wobbly. Never in my life have I been with a woman who wants to fuck all night, who wants more in this uncharted, carnal way.

"I want more... *of you*," she breathes. "I'm trying to process that I finally have you and... my body hasn't caught up." She spreads her legs as my thumb rests on her clit, my fingers hooking deep inside of her. "Until then, please Hudson, make me feel better?"

I move my hand but she squeezes it, stopping the motion. "More," she says, using my command against me.

"More... what?" I ask, lowering my mouth to her clit. "Like this?"

She shakes her head, sifting fingers through my sweaty hair. My hair hasn't been sweaty from sex in five-plus years.

"More fingers."

"What... like *three*?" I ask as I begin to work my ring finger in with the other two. Clenching all around me, she squeezes my hand and bites her bottom lip.

"Four?" I question hoarsely.

"Your entire fist."

twenty-seven

I'D CALL HIM GOD IF HE LET ME.

Dolly

"Baby," he cants, doubt thick in his voice. "My hand is the size of your head." His laughter pitches with unease. "That's... *excessive*."

I blink at him through the wetness that forms in my eyes. I can't stop the tremble in my lip when I hook my hands behind his neck, bringing our mouths together.

"Your babies are gonna come out of there, though, aren't they? As soon as you're ready to take the leap," I whisper, dragging the tip of my tongue along his lips, my cunt clenching around his fingers from the delicate arch of his Cupid's bow. "And when you give your cum to me, unstrained and deep, I'll make another baby for you. And she'll come out of my body, Hudson, she'll come out because you put her inside me. And if my body can do that because of how much I love you, I can handle your fist inside me." I seal my mouth to his, sucking his tongue into my mouth, earning me a sexy groan. I'm loving his noises. It's only been a few hours but already, I'm even more obsessed now that he's *all* mine.

"Dolly–" he starts, but I stop him with a finger forced onto his lips. Adrenaline and anger bubble inside me, but I keep calm for him, knowing he simply just doesn't understand yet. He doesn't realize how deeply I love him, but he'll learn. I take my finger from his lips.

"Do you want more babies?"

Hudson's eyes dart between mine, and his lips part, though he doesn't speak. His breath is sweet and warm against my lips when he finally utters, "Yes."

"Tell me. Tell me you want that, Huddy."

With his impenetrable gaze keeping me beneath him, he fucks me expertly, still stroking my clit as he gives me what I need. "I want to crawl over your young little body, spread your legs and watch those lips grip my cock and take every inch." Hudson's voice with those filthy promises threaten to do me in right then and there, but he continues as he strokes in and out, making me the happiest, craziest woman alive. "And when you're a squirming, wild mess, I'll calm you down by filling you full, then I'll take your hand and put it on your pussy and let your fingers feel what I gifted you." He kisses me, hot and messy, and in all the ways I imagined his mouth against mine, it was never like this. Reality is so much better. He's rougher than I imagined, but somehow softer, too, and god do I like everything that he is. I knew I would. Because the love I have for him is real. "Mark my words, I will put babies in you, Dahlia. I'll put them in you as fast as you give them to me, I promise you that."

His words set me on fire, leaving me frenzied and aching. "Hudson," I whine, bearing down on his hand, *"please."*

From my periphery his bicep flexes and his shoulder twists as his hand fucks me hard, his dark eyes pinning me to the spot. "Hudson Elijah Gray, I have waited five years for you. *Fist me before I lose my mind.*"

I reach out and grab his hard, bobbing cock, arousal dripping from my center as the slit on his head widens, a bead of cream slipping free. "Dolly," he warns, the intense talk of baby making and fisting clearly pushing him toward the edge.

See, we're soulmates. *He likes my intensity.*

"More," I command back to him.

He attempts to bring our mouths together, but I turn my head, pouting, thrusting my hips against his hand. He's so hard. When I steal a glance at my hand wrapped around him, and I see how my fingers don't connect around his massive dick, I start jacking him. "I've wanted you for so long," I murmur, my mind going a little fuzzy from the years of pressurized need mounting inside me. He gave me three orgasms, he turned me into his canvas, and if I don't get even more of him right now, I'm going to lose it.

"Please," I beg, my cheeks wet from fiery tears. "Hudson, please, don't be cruel," I plead.

"I... I don't have..." He takes his fingers out of me, leaving me in hollowed agony.

"No!" I scream, holding my hands tighter around his neck, my nails sinking into his sweaty skin. *"Hudson, put your hand inside me now!* Fuck me with your whole fist, please, *I deserve it,"* I cry, frantically pulling our faces together as I beg. "Please, don't say no, I need this, you're mine, that fist is *my* fist, so please *give it to me."*

His hand works fast to capture that monstrous cock of his, closing his fist around it. "Jesus, Dolly, I cannot believe some of the things you're thinking up there." Sweat slides down his temple and I want to lick it up, but first, the fist.

My trembling body twitches against him as more and more madness awakens inside me at the loss of his hand. "Shh," he coaxes, dropping his big palms on my shoulders, holding me holding him. "All I meant to say was, I don't have lube in here." He tips his head toward the adjoined bathroom. "I'm not doing it without lube." Carefully, he untangles us and gets to his feet, reaching for the sheet to wrap around his waist.

"Third drawer, inside the Ivory soap box, a quarter of the way full," I whisper, stopping him two steps into his short journey. The muscles in his neck twist as he slowly turns his head to peer down at me.

"You're gonna owe me three more for that," he drawls, leaving me with a wink as he slips into the bathroom.

While he's there, I create a comfortable nest with the pillows and position myself in the center of the mattress on my back. I take in all the familiar things around me. The painting of a dilapidated barn under a medusa sky. The stray children's book left on the floor near the closet. His socks rolled up next to a tin of boot polish on his nightstand. I take a deep breath in, tears stinging my eyes.

You did it, Dolly. You got your man. I curl my toes into his sheets, smoothing my hands along the soft cotton. The bathroom door opens and Hudson returns, the bottle of lube looking miniature against his vast palm.

He fills one hand, then brings them together, dark eyes set on me. "You will tell me to stop if it hurts, or if you change your mind," he commands, his stern daddy tone making my insides quiver.

"Yes, sir," I breathe, trying the title. I'd call him God if he let me.

"Mmm," he groans, "how do you do that?" he asks, using his sexy tone and intoxicating eyes to distract me from the soft press of him at my opening.

"Do what?" I question as he works two fingers inside, the lube and my arousal a torturous and teasing combination on my swollen, sensitive lips. My tummy clenches as I spread my legs wider. He lowers to his belly, pressing his lips into my inner thigh.

"Make everything incredibly sexy." He shakes his head, studying my pussy up close and personal as he adds a third finger. *Hudson Gray is between my thighs, traces of his seed still on my skin. Thank you, God, for listening.* "After you cut your foot, all I've been doing is convincing myself I don't want to bury myself inside you." He licks down my thigh before adding, "You're all I can think about, Dolly."

"More," I breathe, my lips unmoving as a controlled exhale flares my nostrils. He slips his pinkie in, all four of his digits splayed open deep inside me. My taint burns as my channel is stretched by the sexiest hand in the world. Flare after flare, he stretches me softly, almost delicately, as he showers me in priceless gifts.

"You are the sexiest woman I've ever laid eyes on, Dolly."

"You and this sexy little brain are all I think about, baby, do you know that?"

"Fuck, I love your filthy, twisted mind."

A few minutes of slow playing things and my spine begins to tingle. My thighs shake and pain circles my hard nipples, sweat bubbling up on my belly and neck. "Hudson," I hiss, breath shaky. "Do it now. Fucking do it, Hud, please, God, *do it!*" I scream, my throat straining with each command.

His eyes hold mine as applies pressure on my groin using the flat terrain of his opposing palm. Holding me steady as my body shakes, he drops his thumb below my clit and begins working it inside. The pure, unabashed need for him takes over my ability to function, and my eyes close as I sink my head into the pillows.

"Fu-fu-fuuuck," I groan, feeling my walls bear down, the urge to push him out overwhelming. The sensation reminds me of what childbirth looks like in movies, and my brain circles on what he said earlier. *That he wants to bury cum deep inside my womb and make babies with me forever.* I envision my belly nearly painfully round, my breasts large, nipples fuller. Hudson is between my thighs, his gold wedding ring glistening from his hand's position on my bump. He feasts on me until I'm screaming. The image is quickly replaced by a shirtless Hudson, gray peppering the sides of his hair as he holds a screaming, pink newborn to his chest, tears in his eyes.

"More," I howl, getting lost in fantasy, drunk on reality, high on my life. "Fist me now, Hudson, now! Fuck me! More, please!" I beg, rolling up onto my elbows to take in the largest part of his hand spearing into me.

My thighs attempt to clamp together, but Hudson's broad shoulders stop them. "*Ohmygod,*" I whine, sweat temporarily fogging my vision as I peer down at his wrist between my thighs. *His entire hand is inside me.* I bear down, wiggle my hips, grind and thrust. I'm so full, my walls tighten painfully and my belly aches, but God, it feels so good that my vision goes dark and my head gets swimmy.

"Come on now, baby," his voice finds me in the chaos. "*Show my fist what your little pussy does to my cock.*"

"Oh, Huddy," I moan, my orgasm washing over me violently, making my stomach clench and my body ratchet down. When I open my eyes, I see my cum dripping through the dark hair on his wrist, and I scream in reaction. "I'm coming, I'm coming, oh God," I breathe, my arms flailing, taking swipes at the pillows and bedsheets. I flounder on the bed in erratic waves of crippling pleasure until my limbs are weak and my pussy is sore. When I open my eyes, I find Hudson over me, in awe, watching his hand as he slowly pulls it free. When the largest part of him is out of me, I let out a sigh.

The bed between us is drenched, but my entire focus is his hard cock, the tip leaking into the cotton sheets as he takes my face in his hands.

"You took me so well," he praises softly, his gentle timbre rousing my senses from post-orgasmic bliss. Between my legs, there's a flare of heat reminding me that I am in the presence of Hudson Gray, the man I love– of course I'm ready for more. "I was so proud of how well you took me, you did so good," he says, scattering his lips over mine, kissing the corner of my mouth, above, below, everywhere.

Slowly, my body regains control and I raise my arm to capture his cheek in my palm, smoothing my thumb through the stubble growing there. "More," I tell him, my voice hoarse from screaming.

A smirk lifts the edge of his perfect lips, a piece of dark hair clinging to his sweaty forehead. I take in his broad, bare chest and the dark hair covering his muscles. His arms are huge, telling the story of a man who works the land more than twelve hours a day. My ovaries shudder at the memory of him out in the pasture, one of the herd dogs running alongside him, a bale of hay balanced on his shoulder. I love how hardworking he is, how good he is with his hands.

Before I know it, I'm flipping onto my belly and he's surging into me with a deep moan. "I don't know how long I can keep up with you," he warns, swatting his large palm over my ass. "Goddamn, your body is perfect." His compliment warms my skin. "Tell me something else. Tell me what else you did," he says, his breathing growing more and more uneven as he pumps hard and fast into me, my pussy sore and aching, but burning with pleasure, too.

"The diner," I moan, "the day I saw you on your date..." His hand slides up my spine, wrapping around the back of my neck. "Your fork..." I breathe, my eyes rolling back in my head as the wide head of his cock nudges my most sensitive spot, making my toes curl.

"I had to ask the waitress for another one," he recalls, his voice growing husky and distant as he clings to sanity with me.

"Juniper took it and gave it to me. And I sucked on it, I

sucked on it trying to taste you," I admit, the balled-up blankets beneath me rubbing against my clit. "I've licked your plates," I tell him as another orgasm stalks up my shaky legs.

"More."

"I would have killed Tiffani that day," I admit, breathy and quiet. His hips still their endless roving, and his cock expands inside me. "I would have gone to prison forever, for him."

A second passes and then my man is hammering into me from behind, pulling my hair and praising me all at once. "You're so good— take one more for me, please, Dolly," he rasps, rutting into me with reckless abandon. "You owe me one more and I need to watch you take it." More cock being shoved deep, more promises. "Take it, baby, take it and I'll let you suck the milk from my cock and fill your belly until it's time to drench your womb and breed you."

My walls shudder around his substantial size, a burning sensation tearing through my hips and belly. "*Oh god, Hud, yes,*" I moan as he makes me come yet again, my body seizing against the mattress as he fucks me into it. The bed wails loudly, and I twist my gaze to find our gauzy reflection in the window, his giant frame slamming into mine, owning me, making me his. "I'm coming, Hud, I'm coming, oh, God," I cry out, squeezing my eyes closed to soak in the feel of finally spasming around him and not some cucumber knockoff.

"Fuck," he grits, pulling me from my blissful stupor. "Get on your back," he commands sternly, and I'm on my back in the center of the mattress in a split second, obeying my man the way I always will. He knees his way over my torso, his heavy, dusky balls radiating warmth over my breasts. "Prop yourself on your elbows," he commands, his tone gravelly and raw as he squeezes his cock above my mouth. A lazy drop of arousal beads slowly out of his slit, rolling down the head, curving the crown, then slipping down his knuckles until I open my mouth, catching what's left of it.

"Seal," he barks. With my lips tightly around him, the first few inches secure in my throat, he holds my face with his massive palms. My cunt gushes from the tender way his thumbs stroke the corners of my mouth as his cock begins to rupture, pulsing out heated waves of cum that drip down my throat and coat my tongue.

I love the bob of his hefty cock as he drains himself into my mouth, groaning as he stares deep into my eyes. "Drink," he coos softly, a gentle smile praising me as he finally gives me my reward. "There you go, you're swallowing so well." The pad of his thumb strokes down the front of my throat and my clit blooms in reaction.

When I've drunk every drop he's fed me, we sink into the bed and he cradles me in his arms. The feel of his chest hair against my cheek is so surreal. The scent of his deodorant and aftershave, smelling his bedsheets because I'm really going to sleep in them—all of it is so surreal. I turn my head to meet his eyes in the quickly darkening room. "I love you so much, Hudson." I don't catch the tear that slips free, sinking into my hair and the pillow. "When I think about how much I love you and how now I have you, I almost can't stand it." I shake my head, feeling overwhelmed at the mention of it. "My feelings are so big and I am so small, it has nowhere to go, so it rattles me."

He links our hands together, brushing his full lips along our joined knuckles. "Your love is so fierce, I'm flattered and in awe of you, Dolly," he whispers slowly, making sure I take in and soak up every word. I press my tongue against the roof of my mouth, tasting his cum all over again. My mouth waters.

I want him so badly right now—even after *many* orgasms. But I have to stifle an impatient voice in my mind that begs to be loved. He'll tell you when he's ready. You don't want him to say it until he means it.

I curl into him, burying my face in this throat. "Thank you for a perfect first time."

His voice travels down my spine like a warm bath or a soft blanket. "I'm honored you let me be the first man inside you. You are exquisite, Dahlia, and I only hope I will earn what you've given me." He is perfect. I was so right.

"First and last," I remind him, then press my lips to his as he turns his head for me. I nuzzle into him, ready for sleep. But his big fingers pinch my side. I swat at his hand.

"I was inside you a lot tonight, Dolly. C'mon," he says, swatting my bottom. "Get up. You're going to use the bathroom and I'm gonna clean you up. No UTIs on my watch."

I sigh. "I like that you know that, but it makes me... murderously angry," I admit, weight lifting as I say things I've only ever told Ivy and Juni. I'm happy to tell him how deep my love goes. "Because I know you know that from being with someone else... long term." He opens his mouth but I stop him with a kiss, pulling back a moment later. "Don't say her name. Not tonight. Tonight is our night, not hers."

He gets me to my feet and, as promised, he carries me to the bathroom where he tends to my every need. We make it to the kitchen for toast with sunflower butter, because he's eaten it seven times in the last six months. He gets hard when I tell him that, but as it's getting late, we come back to bed.

Snuggled tightly next to him, I tell him I love him. And as I'm dozing off, I can't help but think... is there any possible way for me to have *more* of him?

twenty-eight

I'M GOING TO TAKE CARE OF DOLLY.

Hudson

I don't sleep soundly out of discomfort. In fact, it's damn near agonizing staying awake when I'm so comfortable. I bought my memory foam mattress four and a half years ago, when co-sleeping with an infant was my main concern. I've always found it comfortable, and nice.

With Dolly curled into me, my fingers stroking her naked back, I feel more relaxed than ever before. The mattress feels softer, and I feel lighter, the usual daily stresses no longer carrying the same weight.

I sink my lips into her hairline as she softly snoozes, trying to wrap my mind around all that's transpired.

The things I'd been feeling for Dolly in the last few months, everything I was fighting and gaslighting myself not to feel, I no longer have to hide that away. And Dolly doesn't just like me, she's in love with me. Inarguably obsessed with me, and she loves my boy—those two things are clearly separate, too.

I've come to see that all the times I asked Dolly to spend time with Bear was a little bit for me, too. I wanted to see her. Have a reason to bring her special things, under the guise of saying thank you. I never let myself believe a thirty-eight-year-old man whose refractory period is a bit slower, and whose hair is starting to pepper, who has a life of responsibility between Bear and the farm stretched endlessly before him would find passionate, all-consuming love.

Hell, I never thought I'd even trust again when Tessa left.

I trust Dolly with everything in me. I trust her with my heart, and more than that, I trust her with Bear. She wants me, she wants the life I want, and while I may have a lifetime of pacifying her intensity with my cock in her mouth—*is this real life?*—I want that. I want the ups and downs of a passionate woman, I want to be loved by a woman who stops at nothing to prove her loyalty. My healed heart needs that level of devotion.

In return, I'll give it back, tenfold.

I stroke her spine again, my cock twitching awake with morning wood at the little sigh that rushes past her lips as she adjusts. The thing that has me missing out on sleep is how much I want to have her here forever now.

And how jarring it is to want something so permanent so soon.

I have to slow it down a bit, *for Bear's sake*. I look down at the woman in my arms, the one who shakes and trembles until I feed her my cock, the one who licks my cum off her bare body and cries until I fist her because she needs to feel "more" of me. I'll have to explain to her why moving a little slowly is necessary.

I hate moving slow. Now that the seal is broken, I suddenly feel equally obsessed, fully aware of the blessing that is Dahlia Ellington's adoration.

But we have to show Bear we're not just friends anymore. That Dolly is more than the beautiful babysitter next door.

We'll have to start dating before she can come live here.

Jesus. My heart flips at the thought of Dolly moving into our house. Yesterday I didn't have a girlfriend, and today I'm thinking of how quickly I can make her my wife.

Maybe I'm crazy, too.

I lift the sheet and take a peek at her luscious little curves tucked into me, catching an eyeful of my erection. If I'm crazy, I'm fine with that. Because I'm crazy goddamn blessed to have such an emotional connection with an insanely hot physical one, too.

From the bedside table, my phone rings. Despite my best efforts to reach for it without waking her, she stirs as I bring it to my ear.

"Morning," I yawn, the clatter of dishes and patrons sounding off in the background.

"Good morning," Everly greets. "Deuce and I took Bear to the diner. How's an hour sound?" she asks, causing me to look down at a smiling Dolly, sleep heavy in her eyes as she tucks into me gently. God, that feels nice.

"Yeah, an hour's good. Thanks again, you know I appreciate it, Ev," I reply, glancing at the screen to check the time. It's half past eight, and I can't remember the last time I've laid in bed until this hour. Despite the lack of sleep this time, I know I could get used to spending my weekends so leisurely.

"See ya soon," she says, wrapping up the call, likely aware that her brother is naked in bed.

I slide my phone back onto the nightstand and return to Dolly positioning herself between my legs, yanking the sheet down. My cock spears the air, and part of me is overrun with the urge to cover myself. I'm not used to freely laying around with my cock and balls out, but as I reach for the sheet, she catches my hand.

"Gimme," she breathes, wrapping her hands around the base of my erection, pumping in unison so slowly that I lose my train of thought momentarily.

"Fu— God, Dolly," I keen, watching her work. "Ev's bringing Bear back soon."

"An hour," she repeats, "I heard."

"I gotta take a shower and..." I look around, but there is no evidence of the wild, unabashed sex we had here last night. "I guess that's it."

She smirks, her blonde hair wild and wavy from sleep. Taking the hem of the sheet, she parachutes it, trapping herself under the sealed bedding. I watch Dolly shift between my legs, beneath the fabric, and groan when she sucks my cock into her mouth.

"Dolly," I ground out, wanting to tell her we shouldn't, that there's not enough time, that... "Oh fuck," I breathe, losing sight of all of my protestations as she suckles on my length that's hardening in her throat.

She comes off it, but keeps herself sealed under the sheet with my cock. "Please," she begs, sliding her fingers through the hair on my thigh. Her hand trembles against mine. "I need you," she says before sucking me back into her mouth, holding me there, warm and safe.

Reaching beneath the blanket, I sift my fingers through her hair as she holds my cock steady on her tongue, softly moaning around me as my thumb dusts her cheekbone.

I don't know what she has in store, but for once, I let my head fall into the pillows, close my eyes and enjoy. The swipe of her tongue over my balls startles me, and when she sucks one into her mouth, I groan. With her palm wrapping my shaft, she strokes as she sucks, a familiar pressure moving through my thighs.

At thirty-eight years old, I assumed stamina would never be an issue for me. But that was before I fell for a twenty-year-old who adores me, for whatever reason.

"I want you to know, I wish I could unload inside you. I want nothing more than to hold myself deep inside your pretty little pussy and empty myself." I tug the sheet up and my chest constricts at the sight of her nestled between my legs, my cock in her hands as she sucks slowly on the first few inches.

Deep throat be damned—watching my big dick dwarf her hands and face has me thrusting toward her, craving more of her throat.

"I'm gonna come," I warn.

She gives it all she's got, taking another inch and a half. The curse and reality of a large cock is that it rarely all fits.

But I like it this way with her. I like watching myself slide past those perfect little lips. "Dol," I breathe, nostrils flaring as my tether on control snaps, leaving my core clenching and my cock pulsing. "I'm coming, fuck," I groan, arching off the mattress as I hold her mouth on me. I actually don't think I could pull her off of me if I tried.

I hold my gasps, instead listening to her soft swallows as she takes every single ribbon of release to her belly. I cannot wait until we're ready for me to finish inside of her.

I stayed up all night imagining asking her to date me, and now I'm thinking of ways to jump the line to get to marriage so I can breed her. Catching my breath, I realize... my mind is made up.

I'm as crazy as her, I guess, and I needed her to bring it out of me. But we are soulmates.

I want to slide a ring on her finger and put a baby in her belly. As soon as possible.

"Oh god," I breathe as she climbs up my body, pressing a salty kiss to my lips. She's on her feet, tight nipples and smooth belly on display as she stands at the side of the bed smiling.

"I'm going to go so Bear and Ev don't come home with me here," she says, gathering clothes from the floor. "But after he gets settled in, I want answers from you, Hudson."

My sticky dick stirs at the backbone in her tone. She's little but mighty, and the idea of being bossed around by her for a lifetime has me bricking up. "About what?" I muse, straight-faced, knowing all the while that after just one night with me, Dolly wants a title of some sort.

It's crazy but goddamn it, I want that, too. A little pressure comes down on my chest when I think about making Everly and Deuce understand and get on board. Bear loves

Dolly and holds no adult level knowledge or judgment on the matter.

That's one thing I have no worries about.

Dolly and Bear are the best of friends, and she's taken solid care of him for the last four years, more or less. And she saved his life. She risked her life twice for him, really, since she told me she'd have killed Tiffani.

She puts her hands on her hips, narrowing her eyes at me, waves falling over her shoulder. In the morning light, she looks her age in the best ways. With her dress held to her body, I take a peek of her pink pussy—the one where only I have been—before lifting my eyes to hers again.

"Don't you dare look at my pussy until you tell me that I am your girl." She snatches my shirt from the floor and throws it at me, giggling. "Now, get up and get ready for Bear to come back." She leans over the mattress, kissing me as she pats my chest. "I love you, and I'll talk to you soon."

She tugs on her dress as she leaves my room, casting a sexy little glance over her shoulder right before she's out of eye sight.

"Bye, baby," I call after her as I toss my legs out of bed, walking uncomfortably to the bathroom with a hard-on.

I smirk as I wait for the shower to heat, thinking of her demand to be made my girl. She's got no idea if she thinks I'm gonna reject that.

I'm gonna do more than that.

I only hope Ev and Deuce don't think I'm trying to overshadow them.

"How was it, buddy?" I ask Bear as I lift him off the ground, engulfing him in a hug. He pulls his head away, scowling at me. "What?"

"You smell like Dolly," he says. "You didn't hang out with Dolly without me, did you?" He worms his way down from my arms, putting his hands on his hips, and I can't help but smirk because... that looks familiar. "Daddy!" He stomps.

Ev eyes me as Deuce closes the truck door. The four of us walk into the house, and in the entryway, I crouch and have a word with Bear.

"I did see Dolly, but you know what? I think we can see her again, in a few hours. Would you want to see her again? We could go to the creek," I tell him, licking my thumb and swiping it over the traces of chocolate donut in the crease of his mouth.

He nods. "Yeah." He blinks at me.

"What?"

"I don't want Dolly to go in the creek." He looks down at his brown boots, the ones Ev got him that look just like mine. I hook a finger beneath his chin and lift his eyes to mine.

"Why not?'

He blinks a few times, trying to be brave in his fears. "I

don't want her to get stuck in the water like me." He swallows hard, and my heart expands beneath my ribs, in awe of the way my boy fiercely loves. "I don't want anything to happen to her."

I pull him into me, leaving my palm over his head as I assure him it will be okay. "Don't worry, Bear, Dolly's a real good swimmer, and nothing is going to happen to her, okay? I promise. She's going to be fine."

He pulls back, sniffling. "She was watching me... but who is watching her?" he asks, a tear dribbling through his lower lashes. I can't let him worry.

"Me," I whisper. "I'm going to take care of Dolly."

I glance over at Ev and Deuce, and motion for them to take a seat on the couch. I lift Bear into my arms and sink into the loveseat with him. It wasn't my plan to announce this in this way, but it feels right.

"I wanted to talk to you guys..." I start, drawing out my speech as I cautiously work the right words over in my mind. "I was going to have a grown-up talk with Aunt Ev and Uncle Deuce, but maybe we all talk through it now, hmm?"

Deuce's eyebrows come together in confusion but my sister is smiling, casually crossing her legs, smoothing her hand down her jeans.

"Bear, how would you feel if Daddy and Dolly were like Uncle Deuce and Aunt Ev? If we were a couple, not just friends." I press my hand to his chest and give him a little wiggle, watching his eyes closely. I know Bear loves Dolly but asking him to accept her into his life and home with permanence is different. I want him to have the choice, and to understand as best as he can for a four-year-old.

Bear slips out of my lap, his head moving between me and his aunt and uncle. "Yes, I want Dolly to be your girlfriend! Yes!" He claps. "She'll take me to the creek with you and she likes Bluey and she knows how to do the voices in the books, Daddy!"

He starts off down the hall but I stop him. "Wait, Bear, do you wanna talk about this?"

He shakes his head. "I'm gonna make her a card. With the invisible paint she got me!" Within a second he's gone, and I return my focus anxiously to my sister and Deuce.

"This is the first I'm hearing of this Dolly thing," Deuce starts, his voice husky.

I roll my eyes. "Shut up." I tip my head to my little sister. "She told me you told her."

Deuce gapes at Ev. "I told you not to tell."

She smiles. "I know. But that's marriage."

Deuce hooks a thumb toward her, blinking at me. "She's getting mileage out of that and it's day two."

I nod. "Anyway. I realize that this seems pretty... Well, quite frankly, it seems crazy. I know. I wasn't even dating her a day ago but..." Dolly trembling on my cock flashes behind my eyes, the bruise on her face after rescuing Bear comes to mind, too. "I love her passion and loyalty, I love her spirit and vivaciousness—"

"And you love that she worships you," Deuce starts. But I shake my head.

"No. I mean—yes, I'm sorry, Ev, plug your ears, but yes." I look up at Deuce and shrug. "It drives me fucking wild, I'm not going to lie about that."

He nods. "I get it." Everly smacks him.

"But," I continue, scratching my chest nervously as I find

a way to say this that doesn't make me look like a creep. "I've always had a thing for Dolly—" I look up, straight into my sister's eyes— "I never acted on anything or even so much as looked at her disrespectfully until this weekend," I say, feeling comfortable in omitting the hotel room incident in Vegas. I swallow around the nerves clogging my throat, and get the rest out. Like a Band-Aid, all in one go. "I'm gonna marry her. And if I know her, she's gonna be living here by the end of the month."

"Week," Everly corrects, smirking. Her easy response gives me hope there won't be warnings or arguments.

"You.. you don't think it's fucking insane?" I ask, because even I think it's a little insane. I just... don't care.

She nods. "Oh, it is but... I love Dolly. I always have. I love Ivy and Juniper, too. And Dolly has such a tight bond with Bear." Everly smiles, glancing at Deuce then back to me. "She worships the ground you walk on, and you've been through hell, losing Tessa with a newborn and having to figure it all out on your own. I'm proud of you for keeping Gray Farms going, for creating a thriving farmers market, for everything that you've done. She loves you, and that's all I want for you—to be truly loved."

We stand and hug, uncharacteristic but momentous and needed.

"That was a lot of nice things you just said," I tell her, blinking away the sting in my eyes. "Thank you. And thank you for not calling me crazy."

"It's a little crazy. But... I think you could stand to get a little crazy," Deuce says, getting to his feet.

"Are you really gonna get married within a month?" Everly asks, peering down the hall to check on Bear.

I shrug. "Truth? I don't see a point in waiting." I roll my lips together and scrub a hand down my face, heat flaring behind my ribs at the thought of her. "I gotta talk to Bear, though."

"Make him part of the asking process, so he feels like the two of you decided together," Everly says as she refolds a blanket from the back of the couch. I watch her ring sparkle as she does, and I realize, this is one of the last times she casually does something around my house.

She's married now and... Dolly's going to live here soon. My dick stirs at the thought. "That's a good idea."

Dolly's expecting me to ask her to be my girlfriend. She's got no idea what's coming. For once, I'll surprise her.

I call Bear from his room as Deuce and Ev head out, telling me they're on standby for five more days to celebrate until they leave for their official honeymoon.

With the house quiet and my nerves gone, I sit with Bear on the couch and have an open talk about our life, and things I want for us. He's four, so I keep it simple. Love and happiness, and lots of good times. I ask him if he would like Dolly to be a part of that, if he would like a brother or a sister one day, if he would like to spend more time with me and Dolly at the same time and finally, how he'd feel about Dolly marrying me and living here.

"As long as you don't hog her," he says. We hug, then I ask Bear the next most important question.

"Do you have any black paint?"

twenty-nine

WE NEED YOU.

Dolly

"And that he's had feelings for me he's been trying to ignore for a while," I tell my sisters, spilling the pertinent details the moment I step inside the door.

Juni, wearing a sweat- and jam-stained white tank top and cutoff jean shorts, paired with cowboy boots, wags a Merlot-stained wooden spoon at me. "I always thought he seemed… shamefully interested."

Ivy nods, her dark hair styled into a singular braid, thickly knotted down the center of her head. "Same."

I stomp my foot. "Seriously? You guys really thought at some point he started, like… actually liking me? Why didn't you say anything?"

Ivy clamps her hand down on my shoulder. "I was a

little busy being the lookout while you broke into his house."

"She didn't want to get your hopes up," Juni says instead, smiling as she wraps her arms around me. "I'm so happy for you. I'm glad you finally got him. You deserve it."

I snuggle against my older sister for a moment, soaking her in. Though I'll only live just over twenty three and a half feet away, still, knowing we won't live together anymore very soon... It's bittersweet.

"Thank you guys for believing in me and not calling me crazy," I tell them, holding the corrugated box out to Juniper as she slips her hand into a heat-resistant glove, ready to pluck jars from the heated pot on the stove. Ivy passes her tongs.

"You moving in right away?" she asks, slipping onto a barstool as she watches Juniper gather her last batch for the day. It smells... off, but I've smelled this scent before so maybe it's just the specific recipe. I don't comment, though, because everything Juniper's made that I've tasted has always been incredible.

"I hope so. I'm waiting for him to call or come by. He wanted to talk to Bear about us." I twist a lock of hair around my finger. "I don't think I can stay away for too long."

A silence settles between us as Juni hits the fan over the stove, circulating air to suck out some of the steam. Ivy works on a sketch, and I peer over her shoulder.

"Hey... is that..." I pinch my eyes on the sketch. A knife swinging above a man, like a pendulum waiting to decapitate him. The man drawn in graphite bears a snake tattoo on his throat, a nose ring, and tall black motorcycle boots.

"Is that Trace?" I ask, snickering a little when I realize it is.

"Yep. And I haven't even had my first day." She sighs, slipping her pencil through the spiral of the notebook. "He's such a womanizing pig."

I nod. "He seems like it."

She shakes her head. "I hate him."

I nod. "I bet."

She groans. "I can't stand him."

I smile. "Sure you can't."

Her eyes, rimmed with blue liner, slide to me. "I can't."

I lift my palms in mock defense. Ivy's never drawn a man who she hates. She's only ever drawn men she's... well, *drawn* to. "Okay." I chew the inside of my lip, glancing at Juni to gauge the situation. But she's engrossed in her final jar of jam, so I rise from the table, taking a few steps toward my room. "I'm gonna go take a nap," I tell them, sparing them the reasons why I'm so tired.

I slept great, but my body is exhausted. Wanting Hudson for years was tiring, but finally having him in the flesh? As soon as I lay eyes on him, I can't stop shaking until I taste or feel him in some private way. I swear, I'm more addicted to him than before.

As soon as my bedroom door is closed and I'm one step away from flopping down in my bed, hopefully for one of the last times, my phone rings.

The screen says *Future Husband* and I smile. "Hi, Hud," I answer sweetly, my body warming.

"Pick up the binoculars in the left-hand side of your windowsill, and find me," he whispers, his voice hoarse. He's whispering. Heat flashes across my skin, and I greedily snatch the binoculars up, pressing them into the window immediately.

First, I check his kitchen window, where he usually stands over the sink, washing dishes, listening to the news. He's not there. His breathing in the receiver sends a rush of heat to my pussy.

Next I look to the small window in Bear's bedroom, and smile when I see him there, waving. "I never looked in his room," I reply, feeling the need for him to know that.

"I believe you," he says quickly. "Look," he breathes. "Look down."

My eyes veer to the bottom of the window, where Bear's little hands are pressing a small painting into the glass. "When you're done watching us, you little perv," he whispers, his teasing voice smoky and low, "come over. We need you."

We need you.

Tears spring to my eyes and my heart races. "I've been waiting to hear you say that," I admit, slipping my feet into my sneakers, when Hudson says, "No."

I bring the binoculars to my eyes again, and find him in the window across from me. He's watching me with binoculars of his own, tiny little red ones that came with the explorer set I got Bear for Christmas last year. "I like it when you're barefoot."

"Hmm," I breathe, slipping my foot free from my sneaker. "Who's the perv now?"

He laughs. "Maybe both of us. But I wasn't lying. Get your ass over here, Dolly. We need you. Now."

"On my way," I say, hanging up and immediately storming through my house to get to his. I call goodbye to my sisters, but don't wait for their reply. I'm knocking on Hudson and Bear's front door in less than a minute.

He answers, his dark hair hidden by his hat. I look down to find him wearing his boots, too. "You going out to pasture? Need me to stay with Bear?" I ask, wondering why he's dressed for being outside. I look down at my feet but Bear appears in the doorway, grinning from ear to ear.

"Daddy says I can't say nothing till we go to your barn!" he says, taking off down the porch steps, doubling back behind the house toward my barn. I follow after him, loving the feel of the cool dirt against my bare feet as I chase Bear's laughter beneath the open California sky. It's the first moment of my new life that I'll remember forever. I know that for sure.

Out of breath, I push into the barn after Bear, who is standing right at the center canvas, his hands moving over the painting of him and Hudson.

"What are you doing, buddy? Are you adding something?" I ask, remembering that he had a piece of paper pressed to the window a second ago.

"There," he says proudly, shuffling back from the canvas to let me see.

I stare at the addition until I can't see it anymore, my eyes so full of warmth. "Is that me?" I ask about the small, black silhouette painted on paper, taped directly next to Bear, on the other side of Hud.

"Yup," he says proudly. "Daddy says you should be in it since it's gonna be your house, too." He claps his hands over his mouth, squeezing his eyes shut. "Oh no, I wasn't supposed to–"

"It's okay," Hudson's deep chuckle reverberates through

me as he steps inside, wrapping me in his arms. His lips come down to my ear as his belt buckle digs into my back from behind. "Live with us. I don't care how fast we're moving." He spins me in his arms and collects my face with his huge hands. "I love you, Dolly. Marry us."

My eyes veer to a bouncing Bear, who holds a tiny wooden box in his hands. "Here! Here! Here!" he squeals, pressing the box into my belly as I take it from him.

Carefully, I pop the top of it open, the faint scent of cedar hitting my nose. Inside the box is a scrap of paper rolled gently into a ring, secured with a piece of tape. "Bear painted it," he says, pinching it out. "But we'll get you whatever you want." He winks and my stomach incinerates. I love Bear, but I've never wanted to be alone with Hudson as much as I do now.

The slow tremble starts in my shoulders, and my knees grow weak. "Hud," I whisper. "I can't believe I'm really gonna be your wife."

One of his arms snakes around my waist and he yanks me toward him, lifting his hat from his head to provide a veil of safety from Bear for a moment. He drops his mouth to mine. "As soon as I *can* make you Dahlia Gray, I will. And as soon as you're ready to be a mama, you say the word." He presses his hot lips to mine, and my brain tingles from the delicious reality.

"You're mine, you know that?" I tell him as Bear runs up, tugging my arm.

"Yours and only yours," he says with a wink that causes a rush of arousal to soak my panties beneath my sundress.

"Let's skip stones! Please! Daddy, you said–"

"All right," Hudson smiles, scooping Bear up into his

arms. "We'll go, but first, I want to have a talk with you right here with Dolly about what we talked about earlier, okay?"

His little face twists into sadness, and I step toward my guys, taking his cheek in my hand. It's the happiest day of my life and still, my stomach twists at Bear's unhappiness.

"What's the matter, buddy?" I ask softly.

Hudson's eyes come to mine over Bear's head, which is tipped against his chest. Right there in my barn with a paper ring on my finger, Hudson and I have our first moment together as parents. I know I'm not Bear's mama, but I'll be as much of a mama to him as he'll allow. And right now, Hudson tells me whatever's about to come out of his mouth is serious to Bear.

"I don't want you to go into the creek anymore," he says, hiding his face against his daddy's shirt. My ovaries catch fire, I swear. Bear loves me. I knew he did, but this love he's expressing now... I feel important to him, and it makes today that much sweeter.

"He's afraid you'll get stuck like he did. And he doesn't want anything to happen to you." With the hand that isn't holding Bear, Hudson reaches out, taking care of both of us at once as he swipes my tears away. I shake the rumble from my throat, not wanting Bear to see how his love has made me feel.

"I love you, Bear," I say aloud for the first time ever. "And nothing's going to happen to me. Okay? I promise." I catch Hudson's intense gaze and my heart swells. "Your daddy won't let anything happen to me, I promise."

Finally, Bear shows his face, pink-cheeked and sweet. "That's what he said." He looks up at his daddy. "Promise?"

Hudson gives Bear his pinkie, and they promise forever to protect me.

I reach for Bear and take him in my arms, burning for my turn with the little boy whom I love so much. "Let's go to the creek and skip stones. All three of us."

Hud catches my hand as I let Bear to his feet, taking off out of the barn toward the creek. "I don't wanna rush you."

I arch a brow as we head after Bear together. "What do you mean?"

He clears his throat, sounding a little shy as he takes my hand in his. It's the first time we've held hands walking, and I'll never forget it. His calloused palm makes my nipples hard and my insides hot.

"I want more babies, Dolly, but I know you're young. And if you need time—if you have dreams to chase—"

"You're my dream. Bear is my dream. Living in Bluebell with you two *is* my dream. I want to paint in the barn and take care of the home and our babies and love you." I rock to my toes and kiss his lips, having to tug him down to me for access. "You are my dream."

We skip stones with Bear for two hours, laughing, falling down in the sand, soaking up the traces of sun that warm our skin. When the air gets chilly, we head back to their house, stopping by my place only to tell Ivy and Juniper that I won't be home until tomorrow.

Inside, Bear gets his pajamas on and picks a bedtime story while Hudson and I make dinner together, sneaking off to the laundry room three separate times so I can taste him, and just hold his cock in my mouth for a moment to get a fix.

And after the bedtime story is done and Bear's door is

closed, I step into the living room, standing in front of Hudson with the fire lit behind me.

"Fuck me bare, now, and give me your cum. I've waited all day," I tell him, the full tremble of need finally taking over. I drop to my knees. "I need your cock, Hud. Please. I'm going fucking crazy."

He rises from the couch, working open his jeans with one hand, sipping a glass of whiskey from the other. "I think you know the rules, baby. You gotta earn my cum."

I whimper. "Hudson… *I need you.*" I lift my dress to expose the translucent crotch of my cotton panties. "See?" I say, nodding down to my center where arousal has me drenched. My body quivers as the needful sweats begin, droplets moving down my spine.

"I haven't tasted that pussy of yours. See, I deflowered it and fucked it, but I haven't *eaten* it," he says, his filthy mouth causing my mind to literally go blank. I always hoped Hud would talk dirty, but what he's doing now is so filthy, I start to cry.

"Huddy," I plead, smacking the hardwood floor impatiently with my palms.

"I'm gonna wrap your little legs around my shoulders and hold you against my bedroom wall and suck on your clit until my chest is dripping with your cum," he says quietly, his face expressionless as he rubs his cock through his denim. Then he drops to his knees and holds his arms out.

"Hop on," he says, finally curling those sexy lips into a smile. Getting to my feet, I lift one leg, draping it over his shoulder as his large hand hooks around me, holding me tight by the small of my back.

"I don't wanna fall," I say before hooking my other leg over his shoulder.

He tips his head to the side. "You think I'd let you fall?" He gets to his feet without so much as a grunt, leaving me partially dangling as he holds me to his face. "I could hold you to my face for a week without breaking a sweat," he says, walking through the house as I cling to his hair. I hook my other leg around him, and when my back connects with his bedroom wall, I let out an aggressive, needy moan. He slips my panties off easily.

His rough mouth nuzzles me until my lips are spread and he's sucking my clit. My palms move from his hair to the wall, smoothing over the texture as I peer down at him. His lips seal around my throbbing clit, his hands up against the wall next to me as he casually holds me up with his mouth.

"You're mine," I breathe, watching him feast at the apex of my desire. "You're mine. You're mine," I chant, coming completely untethered with each pass of his tongue. "Oh god, Hudson," I manage to squeak out as my diaphragm constricts, my orgasm centering my core, moments away from eruption.

Taking a hand off the wall, he reaches down and drops the zipper of his fly, turning me full cavewoman. My eyes stay focused on the striations in his shoulder flexing and twisting as he strokes that monster of his, all while feasting on my needy pussy.

"Hud," I can hardly breathe when I whimper, "I'm gonna…"

He looks up, glistening lips and dark eyes. "If I'm yours," he growls, "mark me."

I nod against the wall, staring down at him. Not marking him would be impossible. My thighs tremble as he resumes his jacking and feasting, and a moment later my eyes roll back, my fists knocking the wall as I come in unabashed, unrestrained, chaotic waves, screaming and shaking as I do.

"Yes, yes, yes!" I howl, my head tipping forward as he continues to suck my clit, leaving my hole open and hungry. "God, Hud, fuck me, *please fuck me,*" I beg, waves of arousal rushing out of me in cadence with my orgasm. When I can finally breathe, I look down at the dark hair on his chest matted down with liquid, his lips swollen and pink.

With my breath sporadic and my vision fuzzy, I manage, "I need your cock."

His smirk is instant. "Not until I get two more."

Impatience and need slam together in my brain, and I smack his shoulders as I thrust my cunt toward his waiting mouth. "Give me your cock, Hudson!" I demand, fire surging through my veins. "I need it. I need it now," I tell him as he slowly lowers me to the ground. When he rises, he shucks off his jeans, leaving eight inches of veiny, hard cock on display for me to drool over.

"Here," he offers, "suck on my cock and calm down."

I drop to my knees, my body falling into a comfortable vibration as the salty taste of his precum floods my tongue. I press my hands to his groin, my pussy dripping from the rough feel of his pubic hair. I hold my mouth around him, moaning each time he flexes or thickens, when he spits a little more sweetness into my mouth, or when he strokes a hand lovingly through my hair.

"Now listen," he starts. "Bear's sleeping. I'm gonna give

you my cum just like you want but you gotta be good." He drags the tip of his finger down the bridge of my nose, and I sink down on another inch. One day I will deep throat him. That's a promise I'm making to myself.

I nod on his cock.

"You calming down some?"

I suckle him, and nod.

"Okay, now you owe me two more, baby, then I'll give you what you want." He strokes his shaft, and a puddle pools beneath me when I allow myself to consider how big he is. I'm holding him as deep as I can, yet he's easily stroking another few inches into my mouth.

My future husband is the hottest man alive, I swear.

I hear him telling me I'm going to get what I want, but I want it now. "Huddy, no. I need you now, please," I whimper, trying to keep my voice down but it's so hard. "You're mine, finally," I tell him as he lifts me from the ground and puts me on the bed with ease. "So let me have you."

He tips his head to the side. "Calm yourself down," he says, straddling my face as he fucks it, sliding his cock into my mouth. My body settles in the mattress, able to relax with him inside me.

"Now," he starts again, tracing my lips with his crown before plunging into my throat again. "Two more, and if you're really good, I'll bury my cum deep inside you."

I nod and before I know it, he's between my legs, three fingers curled into my soft spot as he fervently feasts. My knees pull up to my chest, and when he slips a finger into my ass, I cover my face with the pillow and let loose a needy howl. "Everywhere," I breathe, the familiar tremble of needing his cum setting in. "I want you everywhere. I want as much of you as I can take. Please, Hudson, I need you."

His appreciation echoes through my pussy as he drags his tongue up and around, bringing me to the brink yet again. He hooks his fingers inside me, leaving his lips over my clit as he says, "Are you ready for it? Are you ready for me to start unloading into you every day, multiple times a day, for the rest of your natural life? Because, Dolly, once I start filling you up, I won't be able to stop."

He brings his mouth to my center and sucks me in, nibbling my clit and flicking it with his tongue as my orgasm crests. "I'm crazy for you Dolly, and goddammit, I'm gonna spend my whole life showing you that I want you as much as you want me."

I nod, my core clenching, spine rolling as I come violently, squirting and slapping, drenching him and the bed. But I can't stop. I can't.

"Hud, please, put it in me," I whimper, my toes curling as another shudder rolls through my spine. "Please, please, please," I beg, dying to feel the hot explosion of his cum spearing through me.

He rocks to his knees, draping my legs over his shoulder as he notches his fat head at my tiny hole. He presses into me, feeding me the first few inches until I'm moaning.

"As soon as I feel number three, I'm gonna give you what you want," he tells me, dusting kisses down my throat and along my chest until he sucks my nipple into his mouth.

He uses his cock to tease my clit, then slides back inside, alternating this tortuous combination until I'm shaking so hard the bed frame is clipping the wall.

"Okay, okay," he soothes, feeding me a tiny bit more of

his dick as I reach for my ankles. "Show me how obedient you are, Dolly. Come for me. Right now, come on, you can do it," he coaxes, his mouth smearing along my flesh.

I nod, bearing down on him as I let go of control, free falling into oblivion as his thickness fills and stretches me. My womb thrums to be full, my belly aches to be round, and my mouth waters to taste him. I want all of him at once, in my cunt and in my mouth, even dripping from my ass into my panties.

I want more and I want it all, but that's impossible. All at once, at least.

Feral and mad, I hold a pillow over my face as I cum yet again, my body easily giving him more than it's ever given me. When I'm done clawing and moaning, I open my eyes and find him swaying above me.

"Are you ready, Dolly?" he asks, husky and low.

I nod. "Please," my voice trembles with unshed tears. "'I've been good."

"Mmm," he groans, sinking his mouth into mine. "You've been the best."

He pushes into me, holding his body up on one elbow above me, his other hand softly kneading my breast. When I realize we're making love, my eyes heat.

"I love how fiercely you love me, and Bear," he groans, his moving hips making the bed squeak gently. "I love how sweet you are, and how you're always willing to help." He fucks another inch into me, and though my taint burns and my belly feels full, still, I want more. I need more.

"I love that you tell me everything, and you're not embarrassed by anything. I love that you know what you need and go for it," he says, his eyes holding mine as he gifts me with yet another veiny inch. "I love you, Dolly, no matter how fast it seems compared to your five years of pining. I am in love with you, and it's important to me you know that I love you, and not because you love me."

My head is swimmy with all of his deep, beautiful admissions. I've never wanted a thick cream pie more than I do now. "Put your baby in me," I beg, lip trembling. "Give me your son, give me your daughter, please, give me your baby to grow and love."

"Mmm," he groans, dusting his lips against mine as his hands come to frame my face, holding me tight against the pillow. Our intense gazes idle and his breath warms my nose as he quietly prepares me. "Not much more now. Are you ready?"

I nod, sweat beading on my forehead. "I'm ready."

He kisses me, then stares deep into my eyes as he surges the remaining inches inside of me, making my walls sputter and clench. "Ready?" he asks again, and I nod my head, willing my body to stop trembling for a moment.

Hudson moves his hips a little, his monstrous frame melted over me as he comes to a stop again. "Feel that?" he asks before his cock pulses inside me, swelling in my channel before the first hot eruption spreads through me. My eyes threaten to flutter closed but I keep them open, and let him talk through his orgasm. "There," he growls, another pulse deep inside. Our eyes hold as his cock bobs and empties deep inside me. "I want to remember your face when I put a baby inside you," he whispers, and when the last ribbon of cum spears through me, he slowly resumes his pace, fucking his seed deeper into my cunt. I love it.

The lovemaking, the coming inside of me—all of it has

me reeling. I know I won't know if I'm pregnant for weeks, and until then, tonight in his bed, I need more.

He moves to pull out, presumably to clean us up. But I wrap my arms around his back and hold him against me as best I can. "Wait," I breathe. "I want more."

His chuckle is fast and easy. "I need... a few minutes."

I shake my head. "No." I know what I need and when I need it. Now.

His brow arches. "I'm not fisting y–"

I shake my head. "I want to know what it's like to be claimed by you in as many ways as possible." I run a palm over my flat belly and reach past my pussy. His eyes follow before jumping up to mine.

I love the way he gapes at me. "Dolly–" he starts.

I lick the side of his neck, swallowing his tangy sweat. "Take me to the bathroom."

After eyeing me with a smirk, he tosses my naked body over his shoulder with ease, and a moment later, we're in the bathroom, door closed.

"Bend me over the sink," I tell him, knowing that if he bends me over while I'm standing, his cum will leak out of me and slide deliciously down my thighs.

He pushes his hand into my lower back, and I curve willingly over the counter. Stepping away, a chill rolls through me from the cold tile. With Hudson breathing heavily behind me, I reach between my legs, moving my fingers between the counter and my body. Finding my clit, I start to rub, already swollen again from knowing what's to come.

Pun intended.

A rush of heat slips free and I reach down, drawing focus with my fingertips to the hot cum oozing out of me. "See?

That's what I want. I want to feel you leaking out of both of my holes at once, Huddy. Please."

"You want…" His voice is hoarse, and my insides flare with compulsive need. "You want anal sex?"

I twist my gaze, looking back at him over my naked, waiting body. "Yes, Huddy. I want you to claim and fill my ass so it's forever yours, just like my mouth and my pussy, and all of the rest of me."

His eyes go hooded, but I'm not done.

"I'm gonna use the cum you left in my pussy to get my ass ready for you," I tell him slowly, another orgasm already burning in my groin. "And you'll fill me full."

He grabs himself, eyeing me. "You really want it…" I love the care he takes. "You want it without lube?" he questions, hooking the tip of his finger past the tight ring of my ass.

I whimper in response. "I want it with *your* lube.."

Smiling sweetly, I reach through my legs and touch my pussy, coating my fingers in cum. "Stroke your cock along my fingers," I beg, urging him to add his orgasm as lubrication to better fuck me. Hud hollows my ass, driving his hard, hot length along my slick fingers, collecting our juices.

"I've dreamed of you for years. And now that you're mine, I want you to own every inch of me." I squeeze my ass. "Even there." I reach down and bring his purpling crown to my puckered hole, and move the slick head in circles, tracing me.

"Lube," he croaks, sinking inside. "You're sure you don't need–"

"I said your cum is enough," I breathe, loving the slick glide of his release spread across my holes. "Please, Huddy, please," I beg, the familiar feeling of uncontrollable obsessive need rippling through my shoulders. "Come in my ass. Show her who owns her," I beg, biting my bottom lip.

A groan moves through his chest as our eyes meet in the mirror. The reflection of him positioned naked behind me, bringing his cock to my ass as my cunt currently leaks his cum—"look how good you look about to own me," I whisper, my mouth going dry.

Pressure burns through my backside as he groans, the widest part of him sinking inside me.

"Fuck," he growls. "That's... tight." His eyes find mine again, hazy and lidded. "You feel so good," he tells me.

He groans, and our eyes fall to his cockhead nestling into me, while moving his fingers over my clit. Slowly, he pulls out then sinks in, groaning as his big hands stroke and knead my back.

"Dolly, you are so small and so tight," he groans. "*I'm close.*"

Another few strokes of heaven before Hudson holds his cock deep in my ass, making my belly ache, and a moment later, a heated stream sprays through me.

"Oh god, yes, it's so hot, it feels so good," I breathe, the sensation of being filled by him in both holes completely overwhelming. I finally peer up at him. His eyes are hazy, but focused on me.

"I can't believe you're real. But goddamn it, baby, you've made me the luckiest man alive," he says, leaning in to kiss me. When he's done, he presses a washcloth to my leaking places and lifts me up, placing me in the shower. "I love you," he says, stepping in to collect me in his arms under the warm spray of water. "But we gotta get clean and get to bed. No more tonight."

I curl my bottom lip in a pout. "Fine," I concede, already planning for him to wake inside my mouth in the morning.

Once we're out, he brushes out my hair and I lotion his callused hands. I make him a cup of tea as he changes the sheets, and when we're finally dozing off together, I wrap my hand around his fat, soft cock.

"Dol–" he starts to warn.

"I just wanna hold it," I whisper as my senses finally start to settle. "Please let me hold you all night."

He sighs, pressing a kiss into my hairline as I curl into him. "All right, baby."

"Good night," I breathe, softly stroking the vein of his shaft with my thumb as sleep creeps in.

"Good night," he says, kissing me again.

And we sleep soundly, but three times in the night I have to slip him into my mouth, just to prove to myself that we are real. That I finally got my man.

thirty

WE'RE BOTH JUNKIES FOR EACH OTHER.

Hudson

Six Months Later.

"You know," I muse, tossing the last bag of feed into the bed of the truck. "You could just have the party on the lawn, where we had Ev's reception."

From the sidewalk, where she's been watching me load the truck with hungry eyes, Dolly scoffs. "Hudson, no way! He wants to turn five near the creek, so the party will be near said creek!"

"I don't love the idea of you down there by the water in your state," I say, pulling off my gloves and tossing them in the bed of the truck. I step onto the sidewalk and pull my very pregnant wife into my arms.

As it would seem, Dolly is very fertile. The first time I came inside her, she got pregnant. And I still don't know how I feel about fate and signs and all that shit, but I do know this: my life finally feels like the life I wanted. And that's because of her. Bear started occasionally calling her Mama when we told him about the baby in her belly, and we don't push it. Though it's only been six months, I can hardly remember my life before her.

Truly.

We got married under the oak tree a week after we got together. Everly and Deuce stood with me, and her sisters stood with her. The only person to question our timeline, and the only guest at our wedding that I wasn't thrilled to have there, was Trace.

But because I don't let womanizing reality TV show stars weigh on my psyche, we brushed it aside. In fact, I'd hoped we could brush him aside, too, but now that Ink Time is open and thriving, Trace seems to hang around a ton.

I wipe sweat from my brow as I circle the pickup, opening her door. I take her hand and slip the other beneath her ass, helping her inside. "Then you can't say no to Deuce and Trace helping set up."

In the last six months, Gray Farms has had a surge. Nothing in my operation has changed, yet when Bluebell learned I took Dolly as my wife, well, things boomed. Everly claims it's because people are drawn to love, and I'm not thinking too hard about it. I'm enjoying the fact that I've been able to buy another whole herd of milking cows, repair Dolly's old barn, and build a new edition onto our place.

All that extra work means I'm a bit busier, so Deuce and Trace are helping with Bear's fifth birthday party setup while I repair the feeding ring on the east side of the property.

Now that Bear is in kindergarten, I find that I'm taking a few mid-morning breaks from working the land to come tend to my wife.

She calls my cell from the house, and I ride my horse back, finding her waiting barefoot on the porch, her blonde hair wild, her eyes full of need. As soon as the front door closes behind me, sweaty from work or not, she's on her knees, humming around my cock as she suckles. She needs a few minutes like this throughout the day, or else she gets frantic and shaky with how much she needs me.

I feel the same about her. I understand and share that unbridled passion she possesses. I called her last week when I was out in the coop, changing out the flooring. She didn't answer and by the time I raced back to the house to check on her, I realized I was hard and aching, throbbing to plunge inside of her.

I guess we're both junkies for each other, but I wouldn't have it any other way.

"Fine," she says, allowing me to tug the seat belt over her belly gently, clipping it at her hip. I join her in the truck, and love how she reaches for my hand across the middle seat. Before we knew she was pregnant, she loved sitting in the middle seat when Bear wasn't with us. She'd hold my cock and drag her nails over my denim-clad balls, and by the time we got home she'd be so worked up, the seat of the truck would be wet and I could hardly get her inside before she'd be tearing into me, rooting around for my cock.

"They can help but if Trace says a word about Ivy, I'll punch him," she says, speaking to the tumultuous and painful relationship between Ivy and her mentor. Trace is a handful, and I take Ivy's side because Dolly does, and we're a team.

When we get back to the house, Dolly asks me to rub her feet.

"Dol," I warn, knowing my wife very well.

"I'm pregnant." She pouts, sinking into the couch while wiggling her toes. "Please, Huddy."

I have no problem rubbing her feet. But I know my wife. It's never harmless. It's always packed full of sinful intentions. And while I'd love to come in her mouth right now, I know I've got just a few hours of daylight left.

"I gotta finish the coop today, baby," I tell her, sitting on the coffee table across from her, gathering her foot in my lap. "Just the foot rub," I warn, but already, her other foot is sliding over the ridge of my hard-on.

"If you only wanted to rub my feet, why are you hard?" She smiles as she asks this, tugging the straps on her tank top down to reveal her larger, darker areolas and her fuller breasts.

"Ahh," she breathes. "Freedom." As the pregnancy moves forward, she's getting more and more uncomfortable. Her nipples, she says, are so sensitive, she doesn't even want her clothes touching them if possible.

But having my beautiful young little bred wife walking around barefoot with her tits out? Groaning, I shake my head, reaching down to unzip my fly. I can't fight this, I can't fight her. I never can.

She smiles. "Thank you, Huddy," she says, fully aware than not more than thirty seconds after I told her no, I'm already taking my cock out.

I brace my hands on my knees, because I know my hands aren't doing any rubbing. I know why I'm here. With my hard cock sticking out of my jeans, I lean back, sinking my hands into the coffee table. A lot of good memories on this thing. This table has been drenched in her cum, I've had her on her knees and on her back. Hell, the last time I took her ass was over this table while she cried and shook for me.

She jumps up, returning a moment later with freshly washed feet, made warm by the water. She brings them to my cock, using her toes to tease my crown, moving them in unison along my shaft.

"I'm too pregnant," she breathes, her gaze locked on my cock. "Thrust," she begs. "Please, Huddy, please," she whimpers, begging me to fuck her feet.

This woman wants me to fuck every fucking part of her. She wants to feel the hot spray of my semen on her flesh in as many places as she humanly can—*her words, not mine.*

I thrust my hips and watch my fat cock slip between her petite feet, her pink toenails making me groan. I look at her bare tits, and the way she cups them, moving her tongue along her hard nipple.

She may be controlling me, but I know what she wants, and because I love her fiercely, I tease her with it.

"Tell me again, Dolly, about the red toothbrush," I groan, my cock thickening at the mention of my favorite thing.

She came clean to me about all of the things she did. And sometimes, when I'm feeling particularly greedy, I ask her to repeat those things to me. Knowing that she was sneaking around, licking my mugs and smelling my cum, sucking my toothbrush and wearing my clothes? Goddamn, that's sexy as fuck, no denying it. I love the toothbrush thing the most, and I don't care what that says about me.

"Huddy," she pouts as I slow my hips from thrusting off the table. "I need you to come, please. I need your cum." She nearly shakes as she says it.

"Tell me, mama," I command softly as I give her another inch, thrusting my cock between her velvety soft bare feet.

She swallows thickly, rubbing her breasts as her vision hones in on my cock. "I sucked them, and on the days where you'd casually touch me or say something nice, I'd come home and fuck myself with the handle, and rub the bristles along my clit, pretending it was you fingering and eating me out."

For that sexy admission, she is rewarded. "Sexy little mama," I praise, "what a good girl you were, loving me so patiently." I thrust through her feet, making her gasp, and she tightens her hold on my shaft, causing my orgasm to tear free.

My slit widens and the first rope flies up, dropping down along her bare feet and toenails. I groan at the sight, because my cum on her skin drives me mad, the same as it does for her. Again and again, I thrust and come, painting her calves and feet, the floor and the table, my jean-clad thighs even taking some of the load.

"Hmmm," she sighs contentedly. "Thank you."

I carefully move through the house into the laundry room, stripping out of my jeans. In high school, I got cum on everything when I discovered masturbation. But being married to Dolly, who is actually quite obsessed with my seed? I'm washing two loads of laundry a day.

I wouldn't have it any other way.

I return to her, wiping her feet as she slips into an afternoon nap. Later on, she picks up Bear from school and they spend time at the creek before painting in the barn and making spaghetti together.

And when we're snuggled into bed together, her bedtime ritual of sucking me all through, I stroke my fingers down her spine and tell her everything I want her to know on a daily basis.

"I love you. Thank you for being an incredible wife and mama."

She nuzzles into me. "Thank you, I love you, you are my everything."

I sleep better than I ever have with my wife in my arms, knowing the bond and loyalty between us is forever. That I don't have her temporarily, but forever. I have all of her, and she has all of me and all my love.

Forever.

No take-backs.

<h1 style="text-align:center">epilogue</h1>

AND WITH MY BOLO TIE ON, TOO.

Hudson

About a year and a half later.

"What's that, sweet thing?" I tap my earlobe, leaning in, her soft giggles curling against me.

Her cupped little hands collide with my face as she tips against me. "Ba-ba-da," she babbles, still giggling. My cheeks burn with my voracious smile as I loop my arm around her waist and drag her into my lap.

The back door kicks open, and Bear's thundering feet sound through the house until he's standing in front of us, chest heaving, a grin on his lips.

"Guess what, Honey Bunny?" he says to his sister. From behind his back, he produces a bunch of flowers picked from the hill near the creek. Not just any flowers—they're the wild honeysuckles that grow on the ridge where Dolly saved Bear nearly two years ago. "I got you flowers for your birthday."

Honey pushes off me, her sticky little fingers leaving dampness on my shirt as she topples into Bear's arms. He hugs her, keeping the flowers above her head so they don't get crushed. I take them, then sit back and watch Bear wish a happy first birthday to his little sister.

My gaze rises to the doorframe, where Dolly stands, feet bare, mud smeared up her calves. Her blonde hair is up, a few wild strands pulled out by the breeze, leaving her looking windswept and gorgeous. In her white sundress with a tiny shawl wrapped around her shoulders, she props one hip against the doorframe, bringing her hands together beneath her swollen belly.

In three months, we'll have another and it's Honey's first birthday today.

I can't keep my filthy hands off of her and her obsession with me? It's only grown.

And I return it tenfold.

"Happy birthday, Honeysuckle," she croons quietly from the door. She'd taken Bear out early to collect flowers for his sister while I got Honey dressed and up for the day.

When Honey hears her mama's voice, she pushes off Bear urgently, a little whine in her chest as she barrels full steam toward Dolly.

"Careful on Mama's belly," Bear warns his sister. I take his hand and pull him toward me.

"That was really nice of you to get your sister flowers," I

tell him, thumping a fingertip against his sternum. "You're a gentleman for that."

Just then, the back door opens, Everly, Deuce and Ace come through, a large cake in my sister's hands.

"Happy birthday, Ace!" Bear announces to his cousin, running to give my one-year-old nephew a hug. Somehow, our babies were born the exact same day. I'll admit, the idea of hosting joint birthday parties out here at Gray Farms for our kids forever? I love it.

"How you doing this morning, Dol?" my sister asks my wife, pulling her into a hug.

Deuce crosses through the kitchen, curving around the couch to drop a hand to my shoulder. "Ev and I want to take the kids to get pancakes for their birthday this morning. A special godparent birthday tradition we want to start," he says. "That cool?"

Ev and Deuce are godparents to both of the kids, as Dolly and I are for Ace. "That sounds good. Dolly's been out with Bear this morning—she'll need a few minutes to wash up—"

Deuce shakes his head. "Nope. Special godparents thing. No Mom and Dad."

I shrug. "Okay, that'll give us some time to finish setting up." I glance out the back window to where half of the farmers markets's canopies are set up outside, tables in every one of them. We invited every kid in Bluebell to come to a paint party for Honeysuckle's first birthday. We got most everything set up last night—just need to add some balloons.

Getting to my feet, I walk out with my family, helping

Deuce get all the kids strapped into the car seats. Honey holds Bear's hand, who sits between her and Ace, and I swear my heart melts every time I see them together.

Since the day Honey was born, Bear has only referred to Dolly as Mama. It finally stuck, and seeing how happy it made her to hear that word on his lips always? That's when my beginner's obsession with my wife turned into something else.

Worship.

Once we're back inside, she leads me to the shower where she tugs off her white dress, presenting her beautiful pregnant body to me. The only thing she's still wearing? A necklace. The same necklace I have on my neck.

Inside?

Blood.

I wear her blood, and she wears mine. At one point, I recognize I would have thought it insane to wear someone's blood on your neck.

But now? The way I feel about my wife? I touch that little vial on my chest at least once an hour and think about how much I love her, everything she's given me, and how much I want to give to her.

When Dolly went into labor, she begged me to deliver the baby. Begged me. Went hysterical over it. Said she wanted to watch me receive the best gift she could give me. She said she wanted to see my face when she pushed our baby into my arms.

I was scared as hell. We had an EMT outside.

But I did it.

Holding Honey against my chest as Dolly watched with

teary eyes, her legs open, chest heaving—it's a gift I'll never forget. And I'll spend my life repaying her for it.

That's when I came up with the idea of the necklaces.

Dolly came eleven times that night.

"Get Huddy 2 and get in here," she says softly, letting her waves crash down against her fair skin as she pulls the elastic free. Steam fogs the small space, but I keep my eyes on my beautiful wife. After undressing, I grab Huddy 2 from the drawer and step inside.

A month after we got married, Deuce needed me to travel across the state with him to pick up a new sign he'd had made for Ink Time. Though I'd only be gone two nights, Dolly insisted on using a cock-cloning mold from a sex toy company called Debauchery. Ever since then, she's been using my cock and a clone of my cock to get through her second trimester horniness.

"I saw you this morning," she whispers as I step inside, letting the hot water rain down my shoulders. "Thank you for drinking your coffee over the sink." She brings her hot little mouth to mine, kissing me with a moan. Reaching up, she hooks a hand around my neck and drags a thumb down my throat. "You know I love watching you swallow."

"Turn around and put your hands on the wall," I tell her, growing rock hard at the mention of her watching me this morning.

Since we've been married almost two years, Dolly still hasn't been able to give up watching me. In fact, at the same time she announced she needed a replica of my cock, she also got me a new bolo tie, one outfitted with the world's smallest camera. She told me, to be fair, that she wanted to see me all day, and that the only time I was allowed to turn it off was for the bathroom.

This morning, while Honey had her morning bottle, I drank my coffee over the sink so that my bolo tie would face the window and capture my reflection.

I knew she'd want to see.

I do a lot of things for her to see, knowing she's somewhere, touching her pretty pink pussy, moaning my name.

"When did you watch?" I ask, knowing she was out this morning.

"On my phone, on the walk back up to the house."

I should've known.

My cock lengthens as she smirks, obeying me as she turns to put her hands on the wall. She pushes her ass out and I press my groin into her, sweeping my palms around her full, round belly.

She moans when I rub her belly. She comes fast when I talk about how she got that belly.

Carefully, I grab the lube from next to the shampoo—when you fuck as much as we do, there's lube everywhere. I coat my hand, then the toy, then slip Huddy 2 into her open, waiting pussy, loving the way her lips grip him as I sink him as deep as he'll go.

"Yes, oh, yes," she moans, curling her fingers against the pale tile. "Huddy," she moans, her thighs and arms beginning their telltale tremble. She always shakes and writhes for me, and it makes me come so hard I nearly see stars.

Rubbing her belly, I use my thigh to keep pressure on the dildo, rubbing her belly the way she likes.

"You feel so good, Dolly," I tell her, watching her head tip forward as the shower rains over. Using lube, I coat her little hole, loving how she moans when I do. I keep a hand on her belly as I guide my swollen tip to her ass. Gently, I start working myself inside, loving her whimpers and moans.

My body keeps the dildo trapped deep in her pussy, allowing my hands to freely roam her full belly as I slowly make love to her ass. "My dirty little wife loves being full of my cock, doesn't she?" I start, knowing how she loves my filthy daddy mouth–her words.

"Both of my cocks inside you, my baby in your womb, my cum probably still in your belly from this morning—my perfect little slut, obsessed with her husband." She bounces back against me, lifting her head to let the shower pour over her face as she cries out in ecstasy.

"Oh my god, Huddy," she whines, her ass clenching.

This morning, I woke up with my cock in her throat, coming less than a minute later. We have a free use rule in our house—she's free to use my cock when she wants. I obviously accepted that when she proposed it on our honeymoon.

"You need your husband's cum, don't you, baby? Hmm?" With one hand still on her belly, I reach up, twisting my hand in her golden hair, tugging her head back.

Her spine lengthens and her ass bears down, telling me she's taking her first orgasm using my cock. I grind deeper into her, arching my body over hers to whisper more filth into her ear.

"There you go, my beautiful wife. Come on my cocks. Give it up for me, baby." *Happy wife, happy life,* after all.

"Huddy," she whimpers, and I know what's coming.

She's got a particular craving this pregnancy. Instead of sweet, she likes salty.

Jerking my hips back, I leave Huddy 2 inside her, and spin her around. "Knees," I command, watching her collapse to her knees instantly.

"How do I feel?" I ask of the replica cock still inside of her. She reaches down, her pink fingernails grazing her clit before feeling the place where the toy is tucked inside her.

"Perfect." She sticks her lip out in a pout, wiping water from her eyes as her chest heaves. Her nipples are hard, and she has never looked more beautiful than she does now, on her knees before me, my cock in her cunt, my baby in her womb.

"Open."

Her tongue juts out as I use the shower spray to wash my cock. I stroke my length over her lips, and she whines impatiently, touching the tip of my dick with her tongue. I pull back.

"You know I need two more."

I lift my shaft, presenting her my full, heavy balls. I know all the ways my wife likes to come, and this is one of them. "Come suck these," I command, a little thrill running up my spine at the way my wife loves the way I talk to her. Didn't think I'd like being dominant and a little demanding, but I'd be and love anything... as long as it's to please her.

She scoots on her knees, sucking my balls into her mouth one at a time. I groan, gripping her head as I stroke my cock, loving the way it feels with her sucking on me between my legs. When she starts bouncing on the cock and rubbing her clit, I know she's close.

"C'mon," I tell her, pressing her face deeper against my

sack as she tongues the underside. "Worship these big balls, they give you your babies," I growl down to her, knowing she loves when I talk about my reproductive system. Something about hearing that I make the thing that impregnates her always sends her over the edge.

Her body trembles on Huddy 2 as she shimmies her mouth against my sack, sucking my balls gently as she comes for the second time.

I could watch her come all goddamn day.

"Now," she whimpers, her orgasm still racking her shoulders. "Please, Huddy, I earned it. Please," she begs.

Two more tight strokes down my aching shaft and I'm painting my wife's face in pearly ropes of cum, abundant and thick.

I guess I couldn't make it to three this time.

Helping her to her feet, I watch as she licks her lips, and cleans herself up—not bothering to use the spray of the shower. She pushes every drop into her mouth, and I stand there watching like a fool in love.

After washing her hair and shaving her legs, we get out of the shower and get dressed, discussing the party.

"You think Honey will like the cake?" she asks, combing through her hair as she stands barefoot in front of her mirror.

I nod. "Of course." I wink. "Her favorite person made it."

Dolly's eyes come to mine in the mirror. "I love you, Hudson Gray," she says, the same way she makes a point to say every day. I love that she does.

"I love you, Dolly Gray."

"Just gotta brush my teeth and I'm ready," she says, replacing the hairbrush on the dresser. She slips into the bathroom, and from the edge of the bed, I watch her brush her teeth, getting hard at the sight of the red toothbrush that disappears past her perfect lips.

I know I'm going to sneak in here and put that toothbrush in my mouth later while I jerk off into the sink. I know because I do that often.

And with my bolo tie on, too.

And I can't wait.

acknowledgments

I couldn't have been a diligent little stalker girlie without my best friends...

TinEye: Reverse image search. Want to see if someone is reusing an image or where their stock image came from? Drop your image here, and it will tell you all the other places it can be found on the web.

    WaybackMachine: Timestamps of most major internet websites through time. Wanna what a website for a business looked like two years ago? Wayback has you.

    WhitePages: Great jumping off point for addresses, known aliases, family members, and current/former roommates.

I do not encourage, condone or support stalking.

if you liked this story...

Thoughtful, comprehensive reviews are the best way to help indie authors grow, both their skill and their business. Next to reading our books, reviews are the next best gift!

If you have time, I'd love to hear your opinion.

And thank you again for reading!

Sign up for my newsletter to keep up-to-date with my projects, deals on books, sneak peeks, and much more.

about the author

Daisy Jane is an indie author writing contemporary romance with kink. In her stories you'll find small towns, ordinary people and extraordinary sex lives.

Daisy enjoys reading, finding new ways to eat peanut butter, black coffee, funk music and cool cover bands, Yosemite, 90s movies, true crime, and so much more.

She lives in California with her husband of sixteen years, their two daughters and three cats.

facebook.com/DaisyJaneAuthor
instagram.com/authordaisyjane

also by daisy jane

Series:

Crave & Cure (3 Books)

Stuck With Tuck / male porn star / MF / Book 1

Cohen's Control / subtle femdom / MF / Book 2

Bound By Brielle / pet play workplace / MMF / Book 3

Wrench Kings (3 Books)

The Wild One / a reverse age gap romance / MF / Book 1

The Brazen One / a grumpy/sunshine romance / MF / Book 2

The Only One / a femdom romance / MF / Book 3

Men of Paradise (3 Books)

Where Violets Bloom / a stalker romance / MF / Book 1

Stray / a femdom romance / MF / Book 2

With Force / a CNC romance / MF / Book 3

Oakcreek

<u>I'll Do Anything</u> / a bully femdom romance / MF / Book1

<u>After the Storm</u> / an alpha MM romance / MM / Book 2

Standalones:

Undeniable / dual POV / MF / age gap / mom's ex

Raleigh Two / a taboo MFM romance / MFM

The Man I Know / a married couple romance / MF

<u>The Other Brother</u> / dual POV / MF

<u>The Corner House</u> / single POV / MFMM, MFM, MFM with an HEA

<u>Hot Girl Summer</u> / a taboo step sibling romance / MF

<u>Release</u> / a taboo MMF, MM, MF romance

Novellas:

Cherry Pie / very taboo why choose / MFMM

Sweet Clementine / why choose / MFMM

Peaches & Cream / step mom/sons why choose / MFMM

Candy Cane / why choose / MFMMM